ANNE MELVILLE

The Lorimer Line

GRAFTON BOOKS

A Division of the Collins Publishing Group

LONDON GLASGOW
TORONTO SYDNEY AUCKLAND

Grafton Books
A Division of the Collins Publishing Group
8 Grafton Street, London W1X 3LA

Published by Grafton Books 1986

First published in Great Britain by
William Heinemann Ltd 1977

ISBN 0-586-06606-3

Printed and bound in Great Britain by
Collins, Glasgow

Set in Baskerville

To
Jeremy,
Jocelyn,
and Jonathan

Contents

PROLOGUE

Ancestors

On a stormy day in 1677 a red-headed young captain named Brinsley Lorimer set sail from Bristol. He was bound for the Guinea Coast of Africa, to exchange his merchandise for a cargo of healthy slaves. Not all his purchases would survive the Atlantic crossing, but when he had sold all those who arrived in Jamaica alive, he would return to Bristol with a load of sugar, rum and indigo. If his fortune held, there would be a profit at every port. Not for nothing had this route been christened the Golden Triangle.

Brinsley Lorimer was a merchant adventurer in the true sense, although not by charter. He owned the ship he sailed, and his daring challenged more than the elements. He was braving the anger of the London merchants, who claimed a monopoly of the Slave Coast trade and backed their claim with a royal patent. He was leaving behind a great burden of debt, but that caused him no anxiety, for he had no dependants who could be called on to make repayment. If his ship, the *Star of Bristow*, foundered, the captain's debts would sink to the bottom with him.

But the *Star of Bristow* did not founder, and so with the profits of his voyage Brinsley Lorimer paid off his patrons and bought another ship. Before he sailed again he chose a wife, begat a son, and commissioned the building of a Guineaman that was to be longer and taller than any ship which had yet sailed out of the great port of Bristol. From Brinsley's enterprise was to grow a great shipping company and a wealthy merchant family. The foundations of the Lorimer line, in both senses, had been laid.

Two hundred years later, the head of the family was

9

John Junius Lorimer. During the two intervening centuries daughters as well as sons had been born to the Lorimer family, but they had never been regarded – even by themselves – as of much significance. The line descended steadily from eldest son to eldest son, and a pattern became established over the generations. The Lorimer fathers were autocratic, natural commanders of ships or offices: the Lorimer sons sought their own fortunes while waiting for their inheritances.

Brinsley's son, William Lorimer, did not go to sea like his father, but he did continue to trade, becoming prosperous and re-investing his profits in the building of more and more ships. While still in his twenties, William's son John equipped a privateer at his own expense and with patriotic zeal captured a Spanish ship worth thirty thousand pounds. Even before his father's death, a sugar refinery built near the Bristol docks with John's prize money was bringing more wealth into the Lorimer family with every smooth white sugar loaf it produced.

None of these early Lorimers spent much money on his own comfort. Whether tossing in a cramped ship's cabin or calculating figures for long hours in an ill-lit office, they were too busy building a fortune to enjoy it. But in 1785 John's elder son, Samuel, used part of his substantial inheritance to buy himself a choice piece of land on the outskirts of Bristol – high above the Avon Gorge in the fashionable district of Clifton. There he built a mansion which he named Brinsley House, after his great-grandfather. Although Samuel's wife was rarely without a small black boy in handsome livery to run her errands and amuse her with his antics, the word 'slave' was never mentioned in the magnificent drawing room of the mansion.

While Samuel Lorimer worked at the task of becoming respectable, his younger brother Matthew – who had inherited the dare-devil blood of his ancestors, and the red hair which went with it – took the one ship which was his share of his father's estate and became her captain. In the *Rose of Redcliff* he roamed the seven seas, looking for adventure and profit in new ports and cargoes. While Samuel saw his fortune increasing in the careful records he kept of his ships commissioned and built, and of his trading profits, the gold coins which Matthew accumulated on his sailing exploits grew to a value almost as prodigious as rumour reported it to be.

The route of the Golden Triangle was of little interest to Matthew because it came into his brother's sphere, and he was middle-aged before he first saw Jamaica. Its balmy climate and unconventional society immediately delighted him, and he welcomed the chance to remove himself for good from Samuel's sanctimonious respectability. In the lush foothills of Jamaica he bought a cheap estate of uncultivated land and enough slaves to clear and plant it, and he designed for himself a great house to rival the mansion in Clifton. Then, as the work of construction began, he loaded the *Rose of Redcliff* with tobacco and sailed back to Bristol to take his profit and collect his savings. When he left his home port again, only part of his cargo was for sale: most of it consisted of the furnishings necessary for a gentleman's residence. Matthew ensured that his cupboards would be well stocked with linen and his pantry with silver, but he neglected to provide himself with a wife. Nevertheless, his life in Jamaica did not prove to be a lonely one, and he never returned to England.

Meanwhile, in Bristol, Samuel Lorimer worried himself into an early grave, so that his son Alexander – Brinsley Lorimer's great-great-grandson – inherited the family responsibilities while he was still young. Under the influence of a pious mother Alexander abandoned the slave trade before it became illegal at the beginning of the nineteenth century. He continued the direct West Indies trade, but at the same time developed new routes – to Australia and Canada and round the Horn to the west coast of America. The risks of the long voyages were great, but the profits were even greater.

When Matthew Lorimer died in Jamaica his descendants were all of a colour which made them ineligible under island law to own property. Alexander therefore inherited his uncle's sugar plantation and the workers on whom it depended: he also inherited a deathbed request from his uncle that three women and the ten children they had borne him should be provided for during their lifetimes. Alexander's high moral sense forbade him to comply with this suggestion, but for some years he enjoyed the income from his inheritance. After the slaves were emancipated he allowed the plantation which he had never visited to run quietly to seed under an agent, whose reports on its unprofitability arrived at increasingly long intervals and were not missed when they stopped altogether.

The compensation which was paid for the slaves in 1833 enabled Alexander to found a bank – a bank which proudly bore the family name. From its headquarters he chose a prime site in Corn Street, the commercial centre of Bristol. There, immediately facing the Exchange, he erected a palace of marble and mahogany. Its facade, in bright yellow stone, had friezes, pediments and pillars that put the Parthenon to shame.

While Alexander reigned in this financial palace, his son, John Junius – Brinsley Lorimer's great-great-great-grandson – waited to prove himself a worthy successor to the Lorimer reputation for profitable adventure and accountancy. Like every Lorimer eldest son before him he looked for a way in which he might occupy his energy until the time came for him to inherit.

It was an age when coal turned everything it touched to gold, and so John Junius dedicated himself to the cause of industrial progress. He persuaded his father to order new sailing ships made of iron for the run to Australia, he encouraged the coming of the railway to Bristol and the

12

building of the *Great Western* in its shipyards. An engineering genius like Brunel could do almost anything with iron and steel. Young John Junius regarded it as a duty to see that such a man was liberally supplied with funds on advantageous terms – advantageous to John Junius as well as to Brunel.

The direction of his interests led him, when his father died in 1840, to attach more value to the family bank, Lorimer's, than to the shipping line. Bristol's triumph in constructing the earliest steamships was marred by the discovery that once the ships left port they never returned to Bristol: their captains refused to venture the new vessels along the seven miles of tortuously winding tidal river which led from the Bristol Channel to the harbour within the city limits. This was a lock-controlled basin with deep water for all the ships which reached it, but too many fell victims to the muddy banks of the river at low water as they made their way towards the docks. It was obvious to all except those who profited from the high duties charged by the Bristol Docks that deep-water berths must be built at the mouth of the River Avon. Only then would a shipping company such as the Lorimer Line be justified in buying the steamships which John Junius already regarded as the craft of the future.

With the wealth and reputation of Lorimer's Bank at his disposal, John Junius invested widely. He looked for short-term gains in the construction of factories and engineering works, and he used the profits for long-term advantage by supporting one of the new dock schemes. In the middle years of his life John Junius displayed the same flair for recognizing promising openings that had distinguished all his ancestors, and his faith in his city's future was rewarded by a generous share in its increasing prosperity.

From its earliest days, Bristol had been a city of adventurous seafarers and honest merchants. They earned their rewards by courage or application and were not extravagant in spending them, despising the soft luxuries of London society. As the two strands in the city's life mixed and married, great fortunes were built and proud names established. It was a city without respect for the aristocracy of land. There were no dukes to dominate society, no duchesses to impose their whims on fashion. But the city was, in its own way, as conscious of status as any court. In every walk of life there was a family recognized as supreme; a dynasty whose members, in each generation, were not ashamed that their wealth came from trade.

Certainly John Junius had never been ashamed: not of that and not of anything else in his life. At the age of seventy-seven, two centuries after the *Star of Bristow* had embarked on its first voyage in the Lorimer interest, he was the head of such a line, perhaps the greatest of all the Bristol dynasties. His fortune was huge, he had an income of a comfortable fifteen thousand pounds a year, and his reputation was untarnished.

Nothing but death could humble the chairman of Lorimer's Bank. Or so it seemed in the spring of 1877.

BOOK ONE
The Chairman

1

On the morning of Whit Monday in 1877 Margaret
Lorimer hurried down the marble staircase of Brinsley
House. Punctuality was more important than dignity –
most particularly when her father, John Junius Lorimer,
was the one who would be kept waiting. It was time for the
day to start with family prayers – if a day could be said to
start when already the servants had been hard at work for
more than two hours. Ranges had been stoked and blacked,
water heated and carried, horses groomed, carriages polished, lamps trimmed, gravel paths raked, flowers cut and
arranged. The footmen had little to do at this hour except
look handsome. To the housemaids and parlourmaids and
kitchen maids who had crept down from their dark attics
so much earlier in the day, however, the assembly afforded
a welcome rest from their scrubbing and polishing.

Although the occasion was called family prayers, few of
the family were expected to attend. The younger son of the
house, Ralph, had already left for school. A day boy at
Clifton College, which his father had helped to found
sixteen years before as a select school for the sons of the
rich Bristol merchants, he was required to attend morning
prayers in chapel with the boarders. His elder brother,
William, had married six years earlier and was established
in his own home. Their mother, Georgiana, did not nowadays leave her boudoir before noon, although Dr Scott
had never been able to find a name for the illness of which
she complained. Margaret, slipping quickly into her place

in the great dining room, was the only member of the family to await the arrival of the head of the household.

As was his custom, John Junius Lorimer arrived in the room while the grandfather clock in the hall outside was striking the hour. In his old age – for he was now in his seventy-eighth year – he had become heavy and moved slowly. But his white hair was thick and plentiful, curling on to his collar, and his square-cut beard and sideburns framed a pink and healthy face. His bushy eyebrows had not turned white but remained the rich chestnut red of his youth. From beneath them his greenish-blue eyes, missing nothing, took a quick roll call of the room.

The force of his personality dominated the room at once. When John Junius expressed a wish in the boardroom of Lorimer's Bank, of which he had been chairman since his father's death, that wish passed swiftly downwards as an order not to be questioned. At this hour of the day his requests were addressed upwards in the hierarchy towards the Almighty, in the form of prayers, but this did not prevent them from emerging as instructions. With equal clarity he read a passage from the Bible. Margaret, who knew it by heart, allowed her attention to wander.

The great dining room was used only for entertaining guests and for family prayers. It was furnished on a grand scale, with Venetian chandeliers suspended over the huge mahogany dining table. Round the walls hung a set of family portraits, and from her earliest childhood Margaret had enjoyed studying them and wondering what the men depicted there were really like. Samuel Lorimer had at first commissioned paintings of himself and his youthful son, Alexander, from life. Then – mindful of the social respectability bestowed by the possession of ancestral portraits – he had ordered a complete set of forefathers from the same artist – who consequently found it easy to indicate a family likeness. Even that light-hearted Stuart adventurer, Brinsley, had been awarded a resolute Hanoverian jowl.

18

With surprise Margaret noticed that since yesterday there had been an addition to the black-framed line – the portrait for which her father had been sitting earlier in the year. She scrutinized it with interest. The artist had succeeded in catching the subtleties of his subject's expression. The long nose and downward turn of his mouth gave John Junius a forbidding look: yet his cheeks curved with benevolence. It was an accurate picture of a man who tyrannized both his family and the bank which bore his name but who was at the same time capable of large generosities and small kindnesses, a man who judged every business venture by its profitability but who would buy a new piece of carved jade with no motive except to delight his own eyes with its beauty. There were few amongst his business associates, or even within his family, who wholly understood John Junius Lorimer. The artist, Margaret decided, had well earned his handsome fee by suggesting the inconsistencies of character without attempting to resolve them.

Guiltily she realized that the reading was over, and that while she was staring at the portrait, its subject was staring at her. In the same grave voice with which he had intoned the final prayers, he requested his daughter to follow him to the tower.

This was an order which on many occasions in the childhood of his three children had filled them with terror. Every morning after prayers John Junius turned his attention to whatever domestic problems had arisen the previous day, so that by the time he left the house his mind would be free to concentrate on the affairs of the bank. All too often these domestic problems had been solved by harsh discipline. Today, however, Margaret could reasonably hope that he wished only to discuss the arrangements for the afternoon. She climbed the stairs without apprehension.

The situation of Brinsley House was a dramatic one. All its best rooms afforded a spectacular view of the tree-clad cliff on the further side of the gorge. From the lowest terrace of the steeply tiered garden it was possible to look straight down at the water of the Avon itself as it curved towards the estuary and the open sea. But the panorama from the tower dwarfed both these spectacles. Through the windows around its highest room John Junius Lorimer was able to look down on the city or over to the hills. From here he could admire the miracle of the new suspension bridge, which owed its existence to his efforts, or catch the first glimpse of a pennant which meant that a ship of the Lorimer Line was returning safely to port. He could watch with pride as the tall ships passed almost directly underneath, pulled by the little steam tugs which made it no longer necessary for them to wait at the mouth of the Avon until a high enough tide could bear them in. He could observe the bustle of the docks as one cargo was unloaded and another loaded, as sail-makers and carpenters repaired the ravages of a voyage round the Horn. And with pride again he could watch the slow and graceful start of a new voyage which would take the ship and all its crew away from their home port perhaps for as long as three years.

The ships, it was true, belonged to William now. John Junius had made that part of his empire over to his elder son six years earlier – not because at the age of seventy-one he felt himself any less competent to run the line, but in order that William should taste responsibility whilst his father was still in a position to advise him. Soon there would be no more masts, no more of those breath-catching moments when the unfurled sails filled with the wind, seeming almost to lift the craft out of the water and fly with it through the air. But even William's enthusiasm could not transform the whole fleet to steam overnight. The sailing ships still came gliding up the river, and every member of the family took a personal pride in their brave adventures. With the Lorimers 'all ship-shape and Bristol fashion' was no idle boast.

John Junius was standing in his favourite place by the window as his daughter came into the tower room.

'Good morning, Papa.'

'Good morning, Margaret.' He accepted her kiss without warmth. He had never been a demonstrative father, and since the incident of the Crankshaw alliance eleven months earlier he had deliberately withheld even the pretence of affection. Grudgingly permitted to have her own way, she could not expect to be quickly forgiven for it. 'I wished only to remind you that today is the Bank Holiday.'

He spoke the last two words with distaste, as though he had been asked to sample a new dish prepared from suspicious ingredients. Still as active physically as he had been ten years earlier, he had nevertheless lost the ability – and indeed the wish – to take kindly to new ideas. It was the business of Government, in his opinion, to see that the affairs of the country were run for the maximum of profit and prestige, but with the minimum of interference with the private affairs of its citizens. To impose the obligation of leisure on a conscientious staff and to compel Lorimer's Bank to close its doors on a day not determined by its chairman was an impertinence. However, the imposition was a law and must therefore be obeyed.

As a sign of his acceptance he had last year for the first time invited the entire staff and board of directors of Lorimer's, together with their families, to take tea in the gardens of Brinsley House on the afternoon of one of the unwanted holidays. On that first occasion it had been an innovation involving the anxious organization of food and entertainment and an apprehension of awkward social encounters. This year it would be merely a repetition, the development of a new tradition which would one day become an old tradition. Although John Junius had been grumbling about it for the past three weeks, he was in fact reconciled to the prospect.

In theory, of course, his wife was in charge of the domestic arrangements for the afternoon. She could be expected to appear as the guests arrived, since the occasion was one which justified expenditure on new silks and ribbons, but it was realistic of John Junius to go over the arrangements in advance with his daughter. However much he might deplore Margaret's stubbornness, he was bound to recognize that she was efficient as an organizer.

Margaret was able to assure him that everything would be to his satisfaction. The only choice still to be made was whether the trestles should be set out in the house or the garden, and she had promised to give a decision not later than noon.

'In the garden,' said John Junius definitely. He could lock up his collection of jade animals in their glass cases, but the Indian and Persian screens which he also collected might be jostled or even fingered by a class of person not accustomed to such beautiful objects or aware of their value.

'The ladies will be wearing their best bonnets,' Margaret reminded him. 'If there should be rain – '

'It will be a fine day,' her father told her. 'Surely you heard me mention the matter in prayers this morning? I have had occasion before to remark on your lack of concentration.'

Margaret was tempted to defend herself by saying that she had heard the request, but without recognizing it to be a guarantee. However, she had been accused of pertness too often already, and there was a matter which troubled her more than the weather.

'Will Mr Crankshaw be present this afternoon, with his family?' she asked.

'Naturally. All the directors have been invited. You can hardly expect Mr Crankshaw to absent himself in order

22

that a foolish young woman shall be spared a moment of embarrassment which, I am bound to say, she richly deserves.'

'Of course not, Papa.' It was not the director of the bank whom she was reluctant to meet but his son, Walter. A year ago the two fathers had proposed a business arrangement which would have linked their wealthy families by marriage to the benefit of both. The Crankshaws owned the site of the new docks which were under construction at Portishead and which the Lorimer Line would need to use as its new ships, with their larger tonnage, found it impossible to come up the river to the Bristol docks. The details of the settlements to be made on the young people had already been agreed before Margaret was informed of the plan. She felt no responsibility for the feelings of Mr Crankshaw, but it must have been humiliating for Walter – who had agreed to the proposal with apparent enthusiasm – to be told that she had rejected it. She had not seen him since then.

Both Margaret and her father had another matter which they wished to raise during this daily conference, but neither was anxious to appear too eager. It was John Junius, accustomed to taking the initiative, who spoke first.

'That young woman who used to give you music lessons,' he said. 'Italian.' He paused to allow Margaret to remind him of the name.

'Luisa,' she obliged. Her teacher was only five years older than herself and they had become friends. 'Signorina Reni.'

'Of course. My carriage happened to take me past her in the city on Friday. I had remembered her as a handsome young woman who dressed with some style, considering her circumstances. I was shocked to see that she had become shabby. And too thin. In fact, as though at any moment she might faint from lack of food.'

23

'I am sorry to hear it, Papa. She left Bristol a year ago to nurse her sister. I was not aware that she had returned.'

'Could you not send a message to her and suggest that she might come here this afternoon and accompany you in a few songs? Perhaps even join you in a duet. I remember that her voice was pleasing. It would give us the opportunity to make her a small present.'

'At such short notice it would hardly be possible, Papa. If she has no suitable dress, she would not like to appear before company. Besides, we have not practised together. And I think it would not be proper for me to sing this afternoon.'

'You have a beautiful voice,' John Junius declared. Margaret flushed with pleasure at the compliment, not only because her father paid her so few, but because he himself in his younger days had possessed a fine voice and still retained his musical sensibility.

Margaret knew well enough that nothing else about herself was beautiful. She was too small and her expression was too determined, even fierce. Her step was firm and bustling: she had never found it possible to languish in an elegant manner. Her complexion was freckled, and she had inherited the curly red hair which had made her father a striking figure when he was young. On a young man it was no doubt acceptable, but she felt it to be unseemly on herself. She plaited her hair as tightly as she could and coiled it round her ears; but its tight waves eluded her control and she could never give the proper impression of calm tidiness. She knew that her father, who loved beautiful things, who would sit for an hour staring at a detail painted on one of his screens or caressing some tiny jade animal within his cupped hands, had never been able to find in his own daughter anything for his eyes to admire. But it was true that her voice, although not strong, was clear and true.

Nevertheless she felt bound to press her objection.

24

'Most of the bank staff are strangers to me, Papa,' she said. 'We have hired musicians to entertain them after tea. If I were to join that entertainment, it would be to make myself a public performer.'

'If you have nothing prepared, that's the end of it,' said her father. His displeasure was clear in his voice. Margaret had a favour to beg and could see the need to change his mood before she introduced the new subject.

'I shall invite Luisa to luncheon tomorrow,' she said. 'At least she may enjoy a good meal to start with, while I discover what the trouble is. And then I shall ask her to practise with me. When we are ready, we will sing together for you and Mama and your friends one evening after dinner. You know that I am always ready to do that. The opportunity to make her a present can easily be arranged.'

Her father nodded his approval.

'The thought does you credit,' he said, as though he had forgotten that the thought was in the first place his own. He nodded at his daughter to dismiss her. But Margaret's own request was as urgent as his.

'I would like your permission, Papa, to engage a lady's maid for myself.'

'What's wrong with Marie-Claire?'

'She is Mama's maid. She thinks it wrong that she should be expected to wait on more than one mistress.'

'Lazy good-for-nothing,' growled John Junius, but Margaret persisted as tactfully as she could.

'Mama's state of health makes it necessary for a great deal to be done for her. I think that Marie-Claire's time is in fact fully occupied.'

'I recall that we have discussed this subject before, in a contrary direction. Your mother said that she could not spare Marie-Claire for you any longer, and you were most definite that you did not require a personal maid.'

'I realize now that I was wrong,' said Margaret, knowing

that the admission would please her father. He grunted a sort of approval.

'No more Frenchies, though. I absolutely forbid it. Two in one house, jabbering together all day long, idle themselves and setting a bad example to the other servants, definitely not!' John Junius had been a boy in the years when Napoleon Bonaparte was the Bogeyman whose name was used to frighten children into sleep or obedience. The war had been over for sixty years, but Margaret knew that her father had never learned to like the French.

'I quite agree, Papa,' she said tactfully. 'What I suggest is that I should employ a young girl to be trained to my own taste. Marie-Claire could be asked to instruct her at first in such matters as sewing and ironing. She would not expect, of course, to be paid the salary of a lady's maid until she had acquired the necessary skills.'

Margaret was never sure whether a consideration of this kind was more likely to persuade her father or irritate him. John Junius Lorimer was probably the richest of Bristol's rich citizens. He kept not one carriage but two and lived in the grandest mansion in the whole of Clifton. Whenever a subscription list was raised for a purpose which he thought worthy, it was a point of pride that the name of Lorimer should be at its head. His collection of Eastern art was rumoured to be priceless. It had already been promised to the city on his death, with money enough to build a public gallery in which the precious objects could be displayed and admired by the public without charge. And yet Margaret was forced almost every day to listen to her mother's complaints that she was unable to take her proper place in Bristol society because of her husband's meanness in such matters as dress and jewellery. Without taking sides in parental disputes, Margaret was tempted on such an occasion as this to use the bait of economy for her own purpose.

'You talk as though you have the girl already.' John Junius spoke suspiciously.

'Naturally I have not engaged her, Papa. But it is true that I have a young girl in mind. I have known her since she was nine years old. Her family was one of those I used to visit in Peel Street.' It was necessary to hurry over this part of the story. Only with extreme difficulty had Margaret been able to persuade her father that the visiting of sick families in the slums of Bristol was neither dangerous nor unseemly. 'Her father died in the cholera epidemic. Her mother has been ill for some years. When the Froome flooded in November she lived with Betty for five weeks in a room whose floor was under two feet of water. Now she too has died. Betty has been taken to the workhouse.'

'Where she will be well looked after.'

'Where she will be neglected and corrupted,' said Margaret firmly.

Her father received this statement in silence. As a hardworking citizen he was bound to assert that the workhouse conferred more benefit than they deserved on those who were unable to support themselves. As a humane man he knew that what Margaret said was true.

'If you wish merely to find a better home for the child, I can nominate her for the orphanage at Ashley Down,' he said. 'Mr Wright has reason enough to know of my interest in his work there.'

Margaret shook her head.

'Thank you, Papa, but her twelfth birthday is approaching and she is ready to work. I have been told of the situation proposed for her, and I am horrified by its conditions. She is an intelligent girl, cheerful and clean, and she deserves better.'

'She is fortunate to have employment offered to her by those who have her interests at heart.'

'She would be more fortunate to have it offered to her by myself,' said Margaret.

She had judged her time well. John Junius had had enough of domestic matters.

'The engagement of servants is a matter for your mother, not for me,' he said. 'Do whatever she thinks is best.' They both knew that, though there were still formalities to be observed, the matter was now settled.

Margaret went straight to her mother's boudoir. A fire was burning there as usual, although it was May. Georgiana complained incessantly of the dampness of the Bristol climate and exposed herself to it as little as possible. She was almost thirty years younger than her husband, but ever since the stillbirth of her last baby, eight years earlier, she had retreated from her marriage – as from every other form of exertion – into the shelter of this one stifling room.

As well as being over-heated, the boudoir was over-furnished. It was impossible to move anywhere without brushing against some small side-table laden with ornaments or silver-framed family photographs. The day-bed and the chairs were covered in plush and protected by tasselled antimacassars, and the heavy curtains were never fully drawn back. The smell of Georgiana's pug dog and of her latest meal or hot drink always lingered to make the room stuffy. Margaret could hardly bear to remain in it for long. She had been brought up in a house which had been built and furnished in a classical style a hundred years earlier and little changed since then, and liked its uncluttered spaciousness. She did not begrudge her mother this private island of clutter, of course, but she spent as little time in it as possible.

The doctor was just leaving the boudoir as Margaret arrived. Dr Scott had brought all Georgiana's three surviving children into the world, as well as the four who had failed to reach their first birthday, and since then his weekly visits had brought him near to being a friend of the family. Through his wife he was well-connected, and had recently inherited from his father-in-law a legacy which

28

John Junius's interest had helped him to invest to advantage in Lorimer's Bank. His new prosperity had enabled him to move to the growing suburb of Clifton, in which so many of his wealthiest patients lived. His only regret at this time of his life was that his son, Charles, on qualifying as a doctor, had taken a permanent appointment on the staff of a London hospital instead of returning to join his father's practice.

However, Dr Scott had no intention of retiring for a good many years, so there was time enough for the situation to change. He was in a cheerful mood as he greeted Margaret and asked for her co-operation in ensuring that in the afternoon Mrs Lorimer did not go straight from her overheated room to the garden.

Georgiana too was in good spirits, less petulant than usual. Although the afternoon's party was to be of such a humble kind, it would provide her with the chance to show herself as a hostess. She agreed without argument that Betty Hurst should be engaged and trained as a lady's maid, and then spent half an hour quizzing Margaret about which costume she intended to wear for the afternoon. It would be too cool for lace, Georgiana said; safer to wear the brown dress which had a velvet jacket. Margaret listened politely to her mother's opinions without allowing them to change her own plans. She was shown Georgiana's new buckles of cut steel and admired them dutifully, although in her heart she considered such small details of costume to be worth no more time than was needed to buy them. When the arrival of the chairs which had been hired to set around the garden was announced, she took the opportunity to escape.

Supervising the arrangements could have occupied her for the whole morning. But the household servants were well trained. Margaret had already explained the day's requirements, and they would work with more responsibility if she did not oversee them directly. It was as much

29

to remove herself from the temptation to interfere as to implement her father's wishes without delay that she asked for the victoria to be ready for her at eleven.

First she went to her music teacher's old lodgings and was there able to discover Luisa's new address. This was in a respectable area, although not a prosperous one. Margaret was admitted at once and shown to a small room on its upper floor. Like her father, she was shocked by Luisa's emaciated appearance, but concealed her horror by a close embrace.

'You should have told me you were returned,' she said when Luisa had recovered from her surprise at the visit. 'I am here only to insist that you come to Brinsley House tomorrow for luncheon. I shall expect to hear all your news then. And news of your sister.'

'My sister?'

'Have you not been nursing her?' asked Margaret.

'Oh yes. That was my reason for leaving Bristol. She recovered quickly, but afterwards I was myself ill.'

Luisa's cheeks flushed briefly as she spoke, but at once returned to the unhealthy pallor which Margaret had observed when she first arrived. The skin had tightened over her high cheekbones and her eyes seemed to have sunk into sockets darkened by tiredness. It was difficult to remember how vivacious she had been at their last meeting, and how strikingly good-looking.

Once Margaret had obtained Luisa's agreement to come the next day, she turned to leave, feeling that she ought not to prolong an unexpected visit. But her attention was caught by the sound of a cough coming from a dark corner of the room – a sound so small and faint that perhaps only a woman who loved babies as much as Margaret did would have noticed it. She stopped and turned back.

For a moment the two young women stared at each other. Luisa met Margaret's gaze steadily. Then she stepped aside, allowing her visitor to go further into the room.

Looking down into the wooden cradle which stood against the wall, Margaret was amazed. The sleeping baby was very young, but her peaceful face was in an extraordinary way mature. It was impossible to doubt that she was a girl, and one of exceptional beauty. Already all the features of her oval face were perfectly formed.

'She's lovely,' whispered Margaret. 'Luisa, you should have told me of your marriage.'

Luisa did not reply and Margaret, startled, looked again into her steady eyes.

'You mean – ?' But the question was unnecessary. It was Margaret's turn now to flush, for it was difficult for her not to feel shocked. 'It would perhaps be as well,' she said doubtfully, 'if we did not mention the baby to Mama.'

Luisa continued to keep silent, forcing Margaret to make up her own mind. Postponing a decision, she looked again at the baby.

'What is her name?'

'She is christened Alexandra. But the name is so long for someone so small. I call her Alexa.'

'Goodbye, Alexa.' Margaret stroked the baby's downy golden hair softly with a finger. Then she kissed Luisa goodbye. It was time to return to the arrangements for the afternoon.

They had proceeded smoothly in her absence and by two o'clock it was obvious that John Junius's instructions about the weather had been obeyed. The sun shone from a perfect May sky. Even the wind which at almost every season rushed up the gorge to toss the heads of the chestnuts and acacias on the western boundary of the garden seemed today to be enjoying a Bank Holiday rest. Margaret could think of nothing likely to spoil the occasion except her meeting with Walter Crankshaw.

What made the situation more difficult was that she had

31

never liked to explain her objection to a young man whose reputation was a respectable one. Margaret visited her sick families under the auspices of the Gentlewomen's Aid to the Distressed, a charity sponsored by the most prominent ladies of the city. They subscribed generously to its purposes and by their names protected the reputations of the younger women who actually ventured into the less pleasant areas of Bristol. Margaret went into the slums without fear of scandal, but even she accepted that there was one part of the city which a young lady should never visit.

Just once, in an emergency caused by an accident to a child, she had broken this unwritten rule, protected by her father's coachman. It was on this occasion that she had seen Walter emerging from a house off Joy Hill. Unlike the dockside stews, the establishments in this district were outwardly respectable, but their costs were often defrayed by gentlemen who would not in public admit to knowing the females who occupied them. Margaret' upbringing had been strict, and she accepted the restrictions which were designed to protect her before her wedding day. But she was young enough to be an idealist, not accepting a double standard for men and women. If Walter behaved before marriage in a manner that she could not approve, might he not continue afterwards in the same way?

Margaret was well aware that she was not supposed to know why the Joy Hill area was forbidden to her. Georgiana would have been horrified to discover how her twenty-year-old daughter's mind had been corrupted by conversation with the sick and poor. Any admission of what she had seen, much less the deduction she had drawn from it, would result in an immediate prohibition on any further visiting.

But for Margaret these journeys were not merely a way of passing the time. They were the only part of her day's activities which she felt to be of any value, and she did not intend to put them at risk merely so that Walter could have an opportunity to explain his movements or, alternatively, that her own repugnance for the proposed association should be understood.

This was why she had given her father no reason for her rejection of Walter Crankshaw, which in turn made her fear an embarrassing encounter at the party. But when the afternoon came Walter bowed politely over her hand without speaking and his parents were fulsome in their compliments about the appearance of the garden.

With her small ordeal over, Margaret felt able to relax. The upper lawn and terraces, usually deserted, were crowded by now. Since everyone must have arrived, it would be in order for her to move away from her parents' side. But just as she began to turn away, a late guest made his appearance. He was a stranger to her – a good-looking young man, clean-shaven and bright-eyed, revealing dark curly hair as he raised his tall hat. She waited while the new arrival exchanged a few words with her parents. Then Mr Lynch, the manager of Lorimer's, brought him across to be introduced to her.

'Miss Lorimer, you will not have met our new company accountant. He is only recently arrived from Scotland to take up the post. May I beg leave to present Mr David Gregson?'

2

When an employer extends a social invitation to the members of his staff, acceptance is taken for granted. The fortunate minions need only consider how best to express their gratitude, and take pains to be punctual in arriving and leaving.

David Gregson had been in grave danger of offending against this unwritten rule as the time approached for the

33

start of the garden party at Brinsley House. To spend his free time in the company of fellow-workers offered little prospect of pleasure, and he had been put to an expense he could ill afford in order to dress in the check trousers and cutaway coat prescribed by Mr Lynch as suitable for his position. Nevertheless, he had recognized that it would be unthinkable to refuse his chairman's invitation and was prepared to utter all the polite insincerities which the occasion would demand.

As a comparative newcomer to the city, however, he had not realized in time how much the residents of Clifton valued the exclusive character of their suburb. Only when he was leaving his lodgings did his landlady warn him that the tramway company had never been allowed to lay a line there in case the general public should be tempted to intrude. He would have to walk the whole distance. As he strode up the steep hill from the city centre his thoughts were solely on the undesirability of being late. He had no premonition that the next hour would change the course of his life.

A footman with a fine pair of calves, wearing the family's green and gold livery, showed him to the lawn at the rear of the house where the chairman of Lorimer's was waiting to greet his guests. Mr Lynch was hovering near at hand in order that the lowlier members of the staff could be introduced by name. David had met Mr Lorimer at the time of his appointment and had not been forgotten yet, but Mrs Lorimer was a stranger. Plump and pale, she gave him a gracious smile but had nothing to say. Mr Lynch led him the few steps necessary to present him to the daughter of the house.

David had seen Margaret Lorimer on two or three occasions in her father's carriage, but they had never spoken. As they exchanged politenesses he could tell that the occasion was a strain for her, but one on which she was determined to do her duty more conscientiously than her mother. Even so, he did not expect to be allotted very much of her time. The Lorimers had invited the staff of the bank, but they would prefer to converse with the directors. He had exchanged only a few words with her when he became conscious of Mr Crankshaw approaching with his wife and son. Taking this as his cue to bow and withdraw, he noticed just in time that the chairman's daughter was deliberately turning away from the Crankshaws.

'May I show you our gardens, Mr Gregson?' She began to move across the grass even as she spoke, as though unaware that anyone else might be seeking her attention. The flush on her freckled face revealed, however, that this was not the case.

He wondered for a moment, as he thanked her for the privilege and offered his arm, whether there was any significance in the small incident. Lorimers might possibly be able to quarrel with Crankshaws, but Crankshaws could in no circumstances afford to quarrel with Lorimers. David's responsibilities at the bank covered the checking not only of the ordinary deposit accounts, but also of the far larger amounts which Lorimer's lent to a variety of local undertakings. He knew, for example, that besides being a director and a large shareholder in the bank, Mr Crankshaw was heavily indebted to it. The money which he had borrowed was being well used to develop new dock facilities at Portishead, near the mouth of the river. One day these would certainly prove to have been a good investment, but that day was still in the future: in the meantime the security which he had given for the first loan, nine years earlier, no longer came near to covering the further borrowings which had become necessary as the scale of the development enlarged. If Lorimer's was to call in the loan, Crankshaw's yard would go bankrupt.

Since in those circumstances Lorimer's would lose all chance of repayment, this was a situation unlikely to arise; but as an accountant David could not help being conscious of the size of the unsecured part of the loan. As a relatively junior member of the staff, however, he could do no more than bring the situation to the attention of the manager at the end of his preliminary study of the bank's financial affairs, and this he had done.

All this, of course, was a confidential matter, not to be thought of outside business hours, and most certainly not to be mentioned to Margaret Lorimer, who would know nothing of her father's affairs. Instead, he stooped a little to listen as she told him the names of unfamiliar ferns and flowers. He had no taste for botany, but her voice interested him.

David Gregson was an ambitious young man. It was ambition which had carried him out of his first apprenticeship to the study of accountancy: it was ambition which had brought him south out of Scotland. Only twenty-seven, he had moved a long way already from the poor home into which he was born, and he intended to move further. So he was sensitive to the manners and the accents of the rich: studying and copying them had become a habit.

The country customers of Lorimer's Bank spoke a Somerset dialect, and the accent of the town was lazy as well, although in a different way, softening the consonants which fell in the middle of words until they could hardly be distinguished at all. None of this slovenliness could be heard in the Lorimer voice. The chairman spoke with a sharp gruffness; it could not be copied without producing an immediately recognizable imitation which would give offence. But his daughter was a different matter. Her voice was clear and precise, the vowels pure and the consonants sharp. She had had lessons in elocution, perhaps, but long enough ago for her not to be self-conscious about the effect. Her sentences were phrased in a formal way, very different from the shouted exchanges of the women who lived near

36

his lodgings. She had been taught to be polite rather than spontaneous.

David was not, at this first moment of meeting, greatly interested in pursuing his acquaintance with her, since he was unlikely to meet her again until the next Bank Holiday. But he listened with care to the construction of her sentences and made a mental resolution that from now on he would always say 'you' instead of 'ye.'

Perhaps the fact that he was listening to the sound rather than the content of her words made his hostess become aware that he had no great interest in plants. She changed the subject as they came to the steps which led down from the upper terrace, and enquired where he had found lodgings.

It was an unfortunate topic. Knowing nothing about Bristol when he arrived, he had taken rooms in a quarter which, although conveniently near to Corn Street, he now knew to be lower in status than his new employment made proper. But the young foreign woman who was the only other tenant in the house and who supported herself by giving piano lessons was very often, he knew, behind with her rent, and the widow who cleaned and cooked for him had come to depend on his more regular payments. He mentioned the district reluctantly, without giving exact details of his address. At least he could feel that a young lady like Margaret Lorimer was unlikely to be familiar with it.

He was wrong. Explaining why she often passed through that part of Bristol, Margaret told him also about her visits to sick families in the depressed area to the east of it. Her voice lost the polite formality with which she had greeted him: her face, which until now had expressed only conventional politeness, became animated. It was enough to make her appearance immediately attractive, although there was nothing, he felt, that could be called pretty about her. At first David was amused by the vigour with which she expressed her feelings. Then he found himself becoming both flattered by her confidences and impressed to the point of admiration by her sincerity.

'Your work must give you a deal of satisfaction, Miss Lorimer,' he said.

'What I do is second-best.' She was firmly scornful of her own efforts. 'The houses round the Froome flood in every rainy winter. To take a warm blanket to a woman whose room is perpetually wet is almost useless. The funds that are raised would be better spent in providing a building with a healthy atmosphere in which such a woman could recover, or by controlling the river so that the cause of the illness is removed.'

'And can such things not be arranged?'

'I have no authority even to suggest them,' she said. 'And althought the gifts of money we receive are generous, they are not sufficient for more than the day-to-day needs of the families I visit.'

'Your interest in the sick is unusual,' he suggested. It was common enough, he knew, for young ladies with time on their hands to make charitable expeditions, descending from a carriage with a bowl of broth prepared by a servant. But Margaret Lorimer's descriptions of her arguments with landlords and disinfectings of rooms indicated a more practical approach.

'It is a very particular interest,' she told him. 'I wish to see women give birth to healthy babies, and to watch those babies grow up to be healthy children. Do you know how many of our city children die before their first birthday, Mr Gregson? It is a number that shames us all.'

'We need more doctors, I suppose,' he said. It was a casual conversational remark, but its effect startled him.

'Yes,' she said with a sudden emphasis, stronger than any she had used before. When she repeated the word it was in a quieter manner, almost as though she were talking to herself. 'Yes. We need more doctors. I wish very much that I could become a doctor.'

Now she had surprised him indeed. For the first time since his arrival he looked directly into her eyes. There was an earnestness in her expression which bore a family relationship to the determination to be seen in her father's eyes at all times. But John Junius was a man who not only expected instant obedience to his orders: he was confident of obtaining it. His daughter's opinions might be equally strong, but it seemed that she had accepted defeat so far as putting them into practice was concerned.

'And is this not possible?' he asked cautiously. It was true that he was not acquainted with any women doctors, but he had assumed that this was because girls found the profession too unpleasant or too intellectually demanding for them to attempt entry into it. Even before he asked the question he guessed that he was wrong.

'There are obstacles on every side, so grave that any one by itself would be enough to make such a wish impossible of fulfilment. Here in Bristol, for example, a new College of Science is due to open in October. For the first time women will be admitted to the classes – in every subject except one. The exception is medicine.'

'You must go to London. There is a School of Medicine for Women, is there not?'

'Yes,' she agreed; and she must have been pleased that he had troubled to remember the fact when he heard it, for her sudden smile was charming. 'I suppose it is a great advance. Women are allowed to follow the same courses off study there as male students. But when the first women to enrol finish their studies, they will find that no university in England is prepared to examine them. Without a degree they cannot be admitted to the medical register. Without such registration they cannot practise.'

'Surely some women doctors do exist.'

'A handful, yes, but each of them has had to qualify in

39

France or Switzerland or the United States. How can I ask my father to pay the expenses of a course which may prove to be entirely wasted, or else to allow me to live alone in a foreign country? Since he would disapprove even of the ambition, the means needed to achieve it would seem quite insupportable. And even if all these problems were to melt away – ' He saw her lips tighten in disapproval. 'Three years ago a female physician was appointed to the staff of the Children's Hospital in Bristol. Immediately the appointment was known, every other member of the staff resigned.'

'And so what happened?'

'Do you really need to ask, Mr Gregson?'

Of course he did not. They were both silent for a moment, turning back from the parapet of the lower terrace without even pausing to admire the splendour of the view. David was sorry that he had allowed the subject to be discussed to a point which obviously caused his companion distress. He could tell that it was still on her mind, for she gave a sigh of hopelessness.

'It might be possible to oppose one's family with the backing of society, I suppose,' she said. 'Or to oppose society with the backing of one's family. But when both unite to regard a woman as ...' She stopped abruptly, and the flush which he had noticed at the approach of the Crankshaw family rose again to her neck. 'I am speaking too freely, Mr Gregson. It is most improper of me. I must rely on you not to reveal my indiscretion.'

The appeal in her eyes had an effect on David as disturbing as it was unexpected. Her hand was still resting lightly on his arm. He had a sudden overwhelming desire to take it in his own, to press it to his lips, to promise its owner anything in the world that her heart could wish.

This is absurd, he told himself. He had heard often enough of young men who were swept off their feet by the first glimpse of a beautiful girl. But Margaret Lorimer was

40

not beautiful, and he had survived the first glimpse of her without the smallest increase in the tempo of his heartbeat. Nothing of significance had occurred in the past few minutes. As a man who had already pulled himself a little way up in the world he had been drawn into an immediate sympathy for someone whose ambitions might be just as strong as his own, but who found wealth more difficult to escape from than poverty. But their conversation should, if anything, have diminished his interest. His companion's thoughts were clearly concentrated on a subject which left no room to spare for young men. It was ridiculous to expect that she had formed any opinion about him at all. It was still more ridiculous to feel sorry for a sheltered young woman who would probably never in her life know a moment's anxiety about anything of real importance. It was overwhelmingly ridiculous – he put it bluntly to himself – for a young accountant, even one earning a salary of more than a hundred pounds a year, to fall in love with the daughter of his employer. It was all so ridiculous that it could not possibly have occurred.

What happened next was unpremeditated. At no point did he tell himself that the simplest way to destroy his own wishes before they became important to him lay in discourtesy, but only some feeling of this kind could have prompted his next remark. They had by now climbed the steps from the lower terraces to the garden which lay on the same level as the house. The appearance of the mansion on this side was not so grandiose as the approach from the carriage drive, where the new arrival was greeted by eight Italianate pillars supporting a row of marble figures in ancient Roman dress. But even from the garden the grandeur of the property was apparent. The pinkish local stone with which both the house and the orangery were built had been stuccoed over in grey. The long windows which overlooked the lawns gave the property a peaceful look, and the wisteria and evergreen magnolias which rose to

41

the height of the roof witnessed to many years of calm and prosperous living.

'A fine house,' said David. 'The reward, I suppose, for a century of slaving.'

As soon as he had spoken he was appalled by his own words. He stood still, expecting the daughter of the house, the slavers' descendant, at the very least to stalk away affronted. Instead she seemed too startled to move.

'You are very direct, Mr Gregson.'

He dared to look at her, and found that she was staring steadily into his eyes. There was no reason, after all, why she should be ashamed.

'We Scots have an unfortunate habit, I fear, of calling things by their names.' Now he wanted to beg her forgiveness, to explain what he had meant and not meant. No woman in his life before had ever reduced him to such a state of confusion.

He was saved from argument when her elder brother emerged with his family from a small marquee in which ices were being served. Margaret ran forward with a cry of pleasure to pick up her three-year-old nephew Matthew, and cuddle him for a moment before setting him down again on the ground in order that his new sailor suit might be admired – this was, he proudly informed everyone within earshot, his first day out of skirts. It was David's chance to move away, although he was held in conversation for a moment or two by William. Such was the shipowner's indignation with Mr Plimsoll, whose unwarranted interference in the business of shipping had so impertinently been given force by Parliament, that he felt obliged to express it to every new audience.

David naturally knew a good deal about William Lorimer's affairs. He knew, for example, that the Lorimer Line was more deeply indebted to the bank than even Mr Crankshaw's business, and with less security. Besides being

42

the son of the chairman of Lorimer's, and a large shareholder in his own right, William was presumably destined to be chairman himself one day. Sometimes he behaved as though he regarded the bank's funds as his own, and it was difficult for anyone but his father to oppose him. The purchase of steamships was an expensive business and their running costs were high. David could not help suspecting that, in the rivalry with Liverpool, pride sometimes counted for more than economic considerations.

Although he knew something of William's financial affairs, David was less well acquainted with him as a man. John Junius had married late in life, so his elder son was still under thirty. Lacking the authority of his father's age and position, William made no attempt to emulate his domineering manner. Instead, he had a reputation for being devious, for arranging what he wanted with one person at a time in such a way that each believed he was being asked to accept a plan to which everyone else had already agreed.

David had heard that Sophie, William's wife, was a beauty, but at this first meeting he did not feel disposed to agree. Perhaps it was only that her pale face, sleek black hair and languid manner gave a colourless impression when compared with the repressed energy of her smaller sister-in-law. Or perhaps her placidity had been imposed by her present condition. Although the slim lines and fluid fabrics of the latest fashion had not yet spread out from London, even the provinces had some time ago abandoned the crinoline. This season's slimmer hoops afforded no disguise to the later stages of pregnancy. Sophie held out a limp hand to David as William presented him, but showed no interest in conversation. With the feeling that he was intruding on a family occasion, David withdrew as soon as it was polite to do so.

For a time he explored the gardens. Eight ladies were

playing a game of croquet on one lawn, while their husbands drank sherry and seltzerwater and made teasing remarks. There was a good deal of laughter and a certain amount of cheating – David could see more clearly than the players themselves the way in which a long skirt concealed both a ball and the foot which rearranged its position. The tennis lawn, on the other hand, was not in use. Even if the members of the bank staff had known how to play the new game, they were not correctly dressed for it. David stood for a moment at the edge of one of the two terraces above the gorge, leaning back against its stone balustrade and staring at the mansion.

He was not envious. In his feelings at this moment there was no resentment that the Lorimers should live in such style whilst he must be content with two dark rooms in an insalubrious neighbourhood. The same ambition which prompted him to copy the accents and manners of his betters allowed him to admire their possessions without rancour. One day he intended to be a wealthy man himself. A fortune on the scale of the Lorimers' was not to be acquired in a single lifetime, but it represented a goal at which to aim. As long as such rewards existed at the top of the ladder, the struggle at the bottom was worth while. Even if David himself should never live in a palace like Brinsley House, it was necessary to his ambitions that homes such as this should stand ready to welcome the son he hoped to have one day.

From the upper lawns he heard the sound of tea cups: it was time to be sociable again. As soon as he appeared he found himself encumbered with Mrs Lynch. She had been ordered by her husband to be affable to his subordinates, but was not prepared to lower herself too far down the hierarchy. It was a relief when the military band began to play and made conversation superfluous.

Just as it seemed that the afternoon's entertainment

must be drawing to a close, he was surprised to be approached by Margaret Lorimer.

'It was impolite of me to leave you so abruptly before tea, Mr Gregson,' she said. 'I take such pleasure in the company of children that it leads me to forget my manners. I hope you will forgive me.'

Had she forgotten his own earlier rudeness or was this her way of assuring him that it was to be ignored? David was too flustered to think of a proper response, and this in turn seemed to make her feel that she had indeed offended him. Her next suggestion was an undisguised olive branch.

'I wonder whether you would care to see my father's collection of Eastern art?' she said. 'I believe it to be highly esteemed.'

David bowed his appreciation and followed her across the lawn. A double stone staircase led from the garden to the centre of the house, but the door at the head of it was closed to discourage intrusion. He was taken instead to a side entrance. It opened into a conservatory in which a fountain splashed to provide a humid atmosphere for palms and aspidistras. David himself had been born into a house where a single room served as kitchen and dining room and living room. But here – because there were no corridors on this floor, and each room led into the next – he found himself walking through a morning room, a grand drawing room and dining room and then a smaller version of each, presumably for the family's use when they had no guests. Finally they arrived at the central hall. Its marble floor stretched from the front of the house to the back. On its further side one door of polished red mahogany was closed, whilst another stood open to show a large billiards table, covered with a white cloth, and a small smoking room beyond it. But the central hall was their destination.

David looked dutifully around. Art had little interest for him, but he would have liked to study the row of portraits hanging in the upper gallery. He recognized the chairman at once and guessed that all the subjects were members of the family. But to mention them might bring back the forbidden subject of slavery.

Clocks, however, held a greater fascination. On either side of the front door stood a matching grandfather and grandmother, and a hanging timepiece on the wall was almost certainly a Tompion. But he had no time to examine it, for his guide was already showing him the Eastern collection. He did his best to make appreciative comments about the dozen or so folding screens in which scenes of love and war were painted in the miniature mogul style against a golden background, but was relieved that Margaret Lorimer herself showed little interest in these. Instead, after putting up her hand to find a key in some concealed place, she unlocked one of the showcases and took out a piece of carved jade.

'I love all the animals, but the squirrel is my favourite,' she said. For a moment she cupped it in her hands, seeming to warm it. Then she handed it to David.

He took it cautiously, afraid of dropping an object which might be worth a fortune. The surface quality of the stone he found unpleasant to the touch. As soon as was polite he handed it back and with much more enthusiasm pointed to an object which had caught his eye at once: a golden cage containing a tiny jewelled bird. Margaret agreed with his admiration.

'Unfortunately, my father has never been able to find a jeweller to repair it,' she said. 'It should turn and sing. A gift for an emperor, I believe.'

'May I touch it?'

Margaret smiled and gestured towards the cage to show that she herself was too small to reach it. David lifted it carefully off its high shelf, but kept it above his head so that he could study the bottom without tilting it.

His attention was distracted for a moment by the sound of shouting in one of the rooms which led from the main

46

hall. The sound of John Junius's voice raised in anger was a familiar one to all the staff of Lorimer's, but David was surprised to hear it on a social occasion. As he looked towards the door a young man flung it open. He was only about seventeen, but tall for his age and already sporting a fine pair of side whiskers to match his golden hair. He wore a white blazer braided with dark blue and held himself well, a handsome, athletic figure. John Junius's voice followed him and he flushed with anger as he realized that a stranger was within earshot. He closed the door and strode without speaking across the hall.

'My poor brother,' said Margaret, laughing affectionately. 'It is a difficult time for him. At school Ralph is a hero, almost a god, to the younger boys. Outside their classes the masters leave the boys very much to themselves, and the captain of cricket has only to call once and there will be a score of fags ready to do his errands. Unfortunately, his Greek marks are not as high as his cricket scores, and in his own home he is treated with less respect.'

'He might be happier as a boarder,' suggested David.

'Undoubtedly he would. But my father was one of the men who founded the school. It was very soon after Ralph was born. One of the objects was to provide the sons of the Clifton community with a good Christian education without removing them from their homes. You touch that like an expert, Mr Gregson. Have you seen such an object before?'

For the past few moments David had forgotten that he was still holding the cage, but during that time his fingers had caressed it with the special touch which his father had taught him. He wondered for a moment whether his hostess had any real interest in the answer to her question. But she had asked it, so he replied.

'My father was blinded in the Crimean War,' he said. 'He was a locksmith before he went for a soldier, and when he returned he found he could still practise his old skills. Where delicate mechanisms were concerned he had the ability to see with his fingers and ears. Something of that I've inherited. I've never rationally understood it, any more than he did. It's like the gift of healing, but applied in this case to cog-wheels.'

He had thought she might laugh, but instead she watched with fascination as without looking down at the cage he opened it and began to stroke the tiny bird upwards with his finger tips.

'And he allowed you to waste these gifts on accountancy?' she asked.

'I was apprenticed to a watchmaker as a lad,' David admitted. 'But most of my master's business was in the importing and resale of clocks, and he soon found me more useful at keeping the books.'

He had sent David at his own expense, in fact, to study book-keeping, and for two years the young apprentice had been able to earn a small but useful income in his free time, assisting several local tradesmen who were clumsy with figures to keep their accounts in order. This had brought him into frequent contact with the manager of the local bank, who recognized the young man's ability first by offering employment on his own staff and later by recommending him for promotion to the head office in Edinburgh. It was the experience he had gained in the Scottish capital which had encouraged David to apply for his present responsible position at Lorimer's. However, he could not expect his hostess to be interested in all that. He concentrated in silence on the jewelled birdcage.

Under one of the bird's feathers he found a tiny lever and moved it in a dog-leg pattern. Jerkily the bird began to turn and a high-pitched squeaking came from the base of the cage. The mechanism had been fully wound, so the sound continued for a considerable time. John Junius Lorimer appeared in the hall with his mouth open to

48

protest in fury. But when he saw the cause of the noise his annoyance was replaced by surprise.

'Miss Lorimer allowed me . . .' began David when at last the bird was still, but his chairman waved the explanation aside.

'Yes, yes. But why couldn't that fool Parker discover what was wrong, if you could do it so easily.'

'There seems to be little wrong with the mechanism, sir,' said David. 'It needs cleaning, of course: it'll be a good many years since it was last used. What your jeweller failed to find was the secret catch. If I may show you, sir . . .' But it was obvious that the thickened joints of John Junius's fingers would never allow him to reach the lever. The chairman's daughter must have seen this as quickly as David himself. Slipping off her glove she asked that she should be given the demonstration instead.

David showed her first of all the shape of the track through which the lever moved. Then he took her hand and turned it so that her finger could slide beneath the jewelled feather.

Her hand had been firm, he remembered, as he took it earlier that afternoon, but her fingers were soft and cool. For a second time that day David found himself disturbed by her nearness. He licked his lips nervously and edged quickly away when, having moved the lever once, she checked her knowledge by sliding it back again.

John Junius was not a man given to thanks so far as the affairs of Lorimer's Bank were concerned, but his private collection was a different matter. He was brusque, as was his habit, when he expressed his appreciation, but David was aware all the same that he had done himself some good. Perhaps one day some question of promotion might arise, and his name would be remembered with favour.

In the meantime he prepared to take his leave. He would see John Junius from time to time at the bank, of course, but Margaret Lorimer he had no expectation of meeting again, unless the Bank Holiday invitation were to be repeated next year. As he bowed low over her hand before going in search of her mother, he told himself that it was perhaps just as well.

It happened, however, that a meeting came sooner than he expected. The approach to it was a curious one. It was not part of David's duties at Lorimer's to prepare or revise the valuations of properties which had been accepted as security for bank loans: he was merely required to incorporate the agreed figures into the annual statements of accounts. But as he studied the amounts, noticing the changes in valuation which had taken place annually on the same property, he became too disturbed to remain silent. Etiquette forced him to use Mr Lynch as his channel of communication, but he addressed his written conclusions directly to the chairman.

They were as straightforward as they were critical. For a good many years now the trade and prosperity of Bristol – and indeed of the whole country – had increased steadily with each year that passed. But within the past eighteen months the tide had turned. The cotton industry had suffered earlier from the effects of the American Civil War and agriculture from an influx of cheap food. Now, abruptly, a lack of confidence in every sphere, increased by the costs and uncertainties of wars and unrest abroad, showed itself in a general depression of trade. Income tax had already been raised by a penny and a further increase was thought to be imminent. Values were falling now, not rising. It seemed to David that Lorimer's directors were proving slow to adjust their business to this new situation.

Such an opinion, strongly expressed, might well be regarded as an impertinence. David waited in some anxiety for the chairman's response. It came in a form he could not have anticipated. He was summoned to John Junius's

50

office, although not invited to sit down. At no time in the interview was his statement mentioned.

'My daughter,' said the chairman without preamble, 'interests herself in the sick of the city.'

Bewildered, David bowed his head to acknowledge that he was already aware of this.

'The charity she supports is generously maintained. But until now, only on the basis of annual subscription. Miss Lorimer has persuaded me of the advantage of opening a capital fund. She is peculiarly specific about her wishes. She appears to have convinced herself that there would be great benefit in acquiring a building on a high and healthy part of the Downs, in which mothers with wasting diseases might recover their health while their children are cared for away from the risk of infection. It is thought that the women would not be so ill as to prevent them taking some domestic responsibilities during their stay, so that running costs would not be too high. All that is required is to meet the cost of purchasing a suitable building.'

He paused, but David had nothing to say.

'I propose to head the appeal for such a fund. It seems to me to be a suitable charity, and Lorimer's Bank will make a generous contribution. A very generous contribution.'

There were two comments which David would have liked to make at this point. One was that Miss Margaret Lorimer must be a very persuasive and determined young lady indeed. The other was that Lorimer's was not at this moment in any state to make very generous contributions to anything, however worthy. The first matter was none of his business. On the second he felt unable to keep silent.

'Our present state of liquidity,' he began, and was at once interrupted.

'I am fully aware of the present state of our available assets. I am aware that a run on the bank in this unrepresentative period could be a cause of some anxiety. I am

51

also aware, as no doubt you are, Mr Gregson, that there have in the past few months been unfortunate rumours about other banks: rumours which were unjustified when they began but succeeded finally in bringing about precisely the disaster they foretold. I do not intend to allow such a situation to arise here. Lorimer's ability to contribute so generously to this charity will be sufficient proof that there is no anxiety of any kind in its chairman's mind. I did not call you here to ask for your opinion on this point, Mr Gregson, but to request you to keep the accounts for the new fund: more specifically, to act as its treasurer. Until now the ladies supporting the charity have paid money in and drawn it out as they needed it; with good intentions but very little control. It will be necessary now, with larger sums involved, to be more businesslike. Naturally you will receive a fee for the extra work. Since my daughter is to get her way in the larger question of the building, she might as well supervise the small details of expenditure also. I have authorized her to call on you within banking hours whenever she has any matters which need discussion. That is all, Mr Gregson, thank you.'

David accepted his dismissal without further protest. After all, he thought to himself as he left the rich mahogany panelling of the chairman's room for his own austere cubicle, the old man is no fool. The new fund would inevitably use Lorimer's as its bank, so that the first generous contribution would, to start with, represent only a paper transfer. If the appeal were successful, more funds would come into the bank and might not all be spent at once. It was not surprising that John Junius had made sure that the new treasurer should be one of his own employees. The choice of David in particular, and the offer of a fee – to come, presumably, out of the charity's funds – might represent the chairman's indirect thanks for the matter of the golden bird-cage, but at no point had good business sense been sacrificed to sentiment.

David did not find it so easy, as he went back to his desk, to separate the principles of accountancy from the yearnings of his heart. Throughout the rest of that day an unbusinesslike thought interfered with the concentration which all employees of the bank owed to their work. It seemed that he could after all hope to see Miss Margaret Lorimer again.

3

A young lady who wishes to impress a young gentleman with her business ability must naturally take pains to consider her appearance. Margaret Lorimer looked critically at herself in the glass as Betty crouched at her feet to fasten up her neat kid boots with a last twist of the button hook. Mr Gregson had been appointed by her father to supervise the financial affairs of the fund which would soon be at her disposal, and it was essential that at their first discussion he should recognize her as someone who knew exactly what she wanted. She had particularly chosen the most severely cut jacket she possessed, and it was a coincidence that it happened to fit most tightly round her tiny waist. The plainest bonnet in her wardrobe went with it: it was another accident that it happened to suit her better than any of those whose brims were frilled or pleated.

The need to look businesslike was created by the fact that she had no idea of business whatsoever. Even when she shopped for herself, she carried no money. Every tradesman in the city knew the Lorimers and sought the privilege of opening an account for them. Margaret could select whatever she wanted and walk out of any shop, leaving her purchases to be carried to the coachman or brought up to Brinsley House later. When she needed a new gown she chose the stuff and described the style and allowed herself to be measured. No price was ever asked or mentioned. She assumed that her choices were reasonable only because when the accounts were eventually presented to her father he made no comment, reserving his disapproval for her mother's extravagances. Since she did not even know the price of a yard of ribbon, she could foresee the difficulty of persuading Mr Gregson that the property she wished to purchase was good value.

Half an hour later she dismounted from her father's carriage in front of Lorimer's head office in Corn Street. Mr Lynch, as obsequious to any member of the family as he was overbearing to the staff, showed her to the cubicle in which the accountant was at work. He was not expecting her, and tugged his paper cuffs off in embarrassment as he jumped to his feet. It was some consolation for her own blushes, Margaret felt, that he appeared to be flushed as well.

'I'm afraid I disturb your work, Mr Gregson.'

'I wish every day would bring such a disturbance, Miss Lorimer.' He hesitated for a moment, but proved to be waiting only for the arrival of a more comfortable chair, sent on the instructions of Mr Lynch, so that he could invite her to sit. His working space was not private, being partitioned off on three sides only, but there was no movement past the open part.

'My father told you, I imagine, that I would come?'

He nodded his head. 'I have to congratulate you, Miss Lorimer. Your powers of persuasion must be strong.'

'My feelings are strong,' Margaret corrected him. 'To tell the truth, it was a surprise to myself when I learned that they were to be indulged.' She had expressed them as a wish only, a vision of something too ideal to be likely. It had taken her by surprise to be told a few days later that she had permission to produce a detailed plan. Her father was unlikely to be interested in the scheme for its own sake. She had taken his brusque approval as a sign that he

54

wanted to please her, a gesture signifying reconciliation after the coolness caused by her rejection of Walter Crankshaw. It was not John Junius's way to express in so many words his forgiveness for what he saw as her stupidity, but perhaps he had realized that some excuse was needed for her to display again her real affection for him, and for him to accept it. He had seemed pleased when she kissed him in thanks for his unexpected announcement.

Once his support for the plan had been won, Margaret did not wish to weary her father with the discussion of details. Or, to put it more realistically, she knew that if she were to ask his opinion on any matter, he would give not advice but a decision, and one which might not always please her. It would be disloyal to express this attitude to a member of his staff, so she had taken care before she arrived to prepare an alternative explanation of her visit.

'I have two errands, Mr Gregson,' she said. 'My mother has promised to give an evening reception to launch the new fund. She will invite those of our acquaintances who may perhaps be persuaded to support it, and also the ladies who have already agreed to serve on its management committee. I hope that you will be able to attend, to make the acquaintance of the committee before its first business meeting is held.'

She delivered the invitation as though it were the most natural thing in the world. Mr Gregson must not be allowed to guess her mother's preliminary horror at the suggestion that a mere accountant should mix socially in her drawing room with the most respected families of Bristol. Nor must he be able to divine the inexplicable confusion she felt at the thought that if he came he would hear her play and sing, for on this occasion she had promised her father that she and Luisa would entertain the guests. Her secret pleasure at the thought that she would be able to display her only talent in his presence must certainly be unladylike; if it could not be suppressed, it must at least be concealed.

He accepted the invitation before even enquiring its date, and with more difficulty she approached her second request.

'All decisions regarding the fund must necessarily be made by its committee,' she said. 'But my experience is that when committees of ladies meet a great deal of talking takes place, not always to the point, and at the end the matter discussed may be left as indefinite as in the beginning. The most important decision naturally relates to the building required: its size and position and whether it should be purchased or built to order. My own views on what is needed are very clear, and I think a great deal of time could be saved if I were able to put a specific proposal to the committee instead of inviting a discussion of possibilities. Are you laughing at me, Mr Gregson?'

She had tried to speak in an efficient manner, so that it was disconcerting to realize how difficult he was finding it not to smile. Her question allowed him to abandon the attempt at concealment.

'Indeed I am not, Miss Lorimer. I admire your discovery of a principle which many gentlemen in the world of business are never able to comprehend. If I smiled, it was at the thought that you are a true daughter of your father.'

Margaret knew what he meant, and joined a little guiltily in his laughter. But she was pleased to see that this did not divert him from a businesslike attitude.

'So you have found a suitable property, Miss Lorimer?'

'I have found one which could be made suitable,' she replied. 'Its position is ideal, and it possesses the separate outbuildings which would be necessary if children are to be kept out of contact with their mothers. But some alteration would be essential, of course. I am unable to estimate even approximately what this would cost. Nor do I know whether the price being asked for the estate is a fair

56

one. I have in the past had no occasion ever to consider such prices. But the bank, I believe, often lends money to its customers for the purchase of their houses. I have come to ask you whether you would be willing to visit the estate in my company and give your opinion on the price: whether it is reasonable, and whether our fund could expect to raise the necessary amount.'

She saw him hesitate and took pains to conceal her disappointment.

'This is a matter for a professional valuation,' he said. 'And you would need an estimate from a builder with regard to the alterations.'

Margaret had known all that. This was the moment when she had to recognize what she had not admitted earlier, even to herself – that she had used the property as an excuse to visit a young man whom she had found interesting. It seemed he was not willing to make use of the same excuse.

'Yes, of course,' she said. 'And you have so little free time. I could hardly expect . . .'

He was quick to interrupt her.

'I was meaning that my opinion would be of no great value, Miss Lorimer,' he said. 'But since, as your treasurer, I may one day have to pay the bill for your purchase, I would certainly be glad of the opportunity to inspect it with you.'

She had accused him at their first meeting of being too direct. Now he was expressing himself in the formal politenesses appropriate to a conversation between two people who were still almost strangers. But his eyes were as straight-forward at this moment as his words had been earlier and showed clearly the sincerity of his pleasure at the invitation. He was smiling at her as though they were friends. Margaret tried to keep the triumph out of her own smile, but she must have been unsuccessful, for his dark eyes sparkled with amusement as he accepted the arrangments for the expedition.

'Do you always get what you want, Miss Lorimer?'

'Until now I have never had what I want,' she said. 'I hope that perhaps my fortune is about to change.'

She said goodbye and returned to her carriage, hardly able to believe her own boldness. The next stage was to obtain her mother's permission for the visit, and this proved simpler than she might have expected. Georgiana had been shocked by the necessity of inviting Mr Gregson to her house, but did not object to her daughter being accompanied by one of the bank staff for business reasons when she went on her tour of inspection. They both knew that Margaret ought to be chaperoned by a married woman on such an occasion, but Sophie was confined to her house after the birth of her second baby and Georgiana was too lazy to make the effort herself. She merely gave strict instructions that Betty should go in the carriage with her mistress.

The estate which had attracted Margaret was a large one on the far side of the river, bordered by Leigh Woods. After its buildings had been inspected she and David took advantage of the September sunshine to walk in its woods and gardens, while Betty remained behind to improve her acquaintance with the coachman. Margaret felt a kind of happiness which she had never known before as they talked together, abandoning all pretence of further interest in the charity's affairs, and comparing their own childhoods. The end of the visit came all too soon for her.

'I have promised to take tea at my brother's house,' she said. 'I have a new niece waiting to be inspected, and my sister-in-law to congratulate. Before we part, will you give me your opinion of what we have seen?'

'Your judgement of the house, as a house, could not be criticized,' he said. 'And its position in the sun and wind is undoubtedly healthy. But the park is larger than would be needed. And I cannot help wondering whether the situation might not prove inconvenient. To bring the mothers and children so far from their homes would be an expense, and the lack of public transport would deter their visitors.'

'So what do you advise?'

'My own suggestion – it is no more than that – is that we should study the tramway routes and look for a property which can be reached from their highest points: in the Redland area for instance.'

It should have been a disappointment that he did not approve her choice, but Margaret was not disappointed at all. There would be other expeditions, other walks and conversations. She was in a good humour as she arrived at William's house and told the coachman to take Mr Gregson on to whatever address he gave.

Although not as palatial as Brinsley House, William's home, The Ivies, was a sufficiently substantial affair. John Junius had given it to his elder son as a wedding present. It was a solid, five-storied house with six bays of windows, built in the local red stone but almost entirely covered by the ivy which had given it its name. Unlike Brinsley House, which was surrounded by its own extensive grounds, The Ivies stood in a street of equally prosperous houses. It was also in Clifton, but to the north of the suspension bridge, near the Zoological Gardens. William came out to greet his sister at the sound of the carriage, and looked surprised when it drove away. Margaret did not explain where she had been, nor in whose company, for she felt instinctively that William would disapprove.

If she had not known her brother in the schoolroom, she would have thought that he had been born at the age of forty. Although still only twenty-seven, he had none of a young man's enthusiasms and never seemed to unbend. In person he was quite unlike his father. Everything about John Junius was on a large scale, but William's frame, like Margaret's, was slight. He did not share his sister's expression of determination, however: his features were sharp and his temperament withdrawn. He gave the impression of being always absorbed in his own complicated plans. It was even hard to tell today whether he was pleased with the birth of his daughter, who was to be called Beatrice after the Queen's youngest child.

Out of politeness Margaret sat with Sophie for a while after her first glimpse of her niece, but was glad when the young mother said that she was tired. Margaret had never been on intimate terms with her sister-in-law, but she had the ability to establish an instant relationship of warmth with any child, however young. She indulged herself with the baby until the nurse ordered that Beatrice should be put back to rest. Then she went in search of her nephew, Matthew.

To her surprise she found that Ralph was there before her, although he was normally intolerant of children and not at all disposed to seek their company. On this occasion, she supposed that he had come out of family feeling to congratulate William and Sophie.

'Uncle Ralph's playing with me while Claudine fetches my tea,' said Matthew, rocking vigorously on his wooden horse. 'I'm four now.'

It was an announcement which he had made at each of their last three meetings, as ten days had already passed since his birthday, but Margaret accepted the news with proper congratulations. Even her pleasure in playing with him did not prevent her, though, from noticing that Ralph looked pale and worried. It seemed unlikely that he was working too hard at school – at least, this was not a danger to which he had ever exposed himself before, and the new term had only just begun. It was more probable that the headmaster's sermon that morning had in some way upset him. Mr Percival's eloquence had more than once reduced Ralph to despair at the sinfulness of his thoughts, although the strict timetable of his life made it unlikely, she imagined, that he had ever committed any greater crime than that of borrowing from another boy without permission.

The nursery governess arrived with a tray before Margaret had time to enquire into her brother's anxiety. Claudine had arrived from France two months earlier, ready to take charge of Matthew when the new baby monopolized the attention of the nurse. Soon after her arrival she had been dispatched by Sophie to Brinsley House for a brief stay, together with her young charge. No reason had been given to Margaret, although perhaps her parents were better informed. But the visit had coincided with Sophie's departure to stay with her own mother for two weeks. It had been Margaret's amused deduction that William was not to be allowed to keep Claudine under his roof during his wife's absence.

Privately, Margaret did not consider that William was ever likely to allow any young woman to divert him from the task of making money, but she could sympathize with Sophie's attitude. There was an expansive and undeferential warmth about Claudine's behaviour, warmth of a kind not usually found amongst domestic staff. She was a country girl, not qualified to be a governess in any way that Margaret could see, except that of having French as her native language. But she was healthy and good-natured and her experience in caring for her own five younger brothers and sisters had enabled her to win Matthew's heart at once. The schoolroom to which he was now promoted was a far happier place than the nursery over which Nurse Grant had always tyrannized.

Claudine greeted Margaret politely and spoke to Ralph in a way which made it clear that they had conversed earlier in the afternoon. To Margaret's still greater surpise, Ralph answered the question in halting French. She asked him about this later, when the carriage had returned to fetch her and they were both on their way back to Brinsley House.

61

'Claudine is to teach Matthew French,' said Ralph. 'They are to speak it together all the time when they are alone. I asked her to help me with the language as well.'

'But surely you don't attend the French classes at Clifton?' said Margaret. Even as she asked the question she guessed the answer. French was taught only to those boys who lacked the ability to be successful in Latin and Greek. If Ralph had been moved from the Classical to the Modern Side, he would have reason enough to look anxious. John Junius had no great regard for the virtues of dead languages, but he expected that in any selection which took place within the school his son should always be chosen for the upper part, whether it related to work or sport.

Her suspicions were right. Ralph was silent for a moment and then burst into a sulky tirade.

'They told me in May that I must spend less time playing cricket and more on Greek verse,' he said. 'But suppose the Cheltenham match had been lost because I was out of practice. The masters would have been the first to complain that I wasn't showing the proper school spirit. And it was unfair to make me change so late. Now I'm behind everyone who started French earlier, so I shall do badly on the Modern Side as well.'

'Never mind,' said Margaret soothingly. 'This is your last year at school. It was a marvellous century you scored against Cheltenham and Oxford surely would rather have a first-class cricketer than a mediocre scholar.'

'I may not be allowed to go to Oxford. William wasn't.'

'Papa wished William to go into his business as early as possible. Your talents are different. He will be proud to see you captain the university at cricket one day.'

'You think I'm to be a gentleman, do you?' Still resentful, Ralph tried to laugh. 'Well, I see I'm fit for nothing else. So I must chatter to servants and hope that a boy of four doesn't prove more apt to learn than myself.'

It was not easy for Margaret to sympathize with him. She had for some years been well taught in the schoolroom of Brinsley House. Because William was ten years older than his younger brother, a time had come when he was ready for school but Ralph was still too young for serious study. John Junius, recognizing a good tutor when he had one, had retained Mr Pennydale's services until Ralph should be ready for him.

But in the Lorimer household value was always expected for money. With Mr Pennydale on the premises and a daughter whose time must somehow be occupied, it had seemed the most natural thing in the world that Margaret should be given almost the same education as her brothers. Some of the effects were unusual. Most girls were taught to paint delicate water colours. Mr Pennydale, finding himself expected to demonstrate an art for which he had no talent, had chosen instead to equip Margaret with a knowledge of anatomy so that she could attempt figure drawing in a scientific manner. She had rebelled against Greek, but worked hard at Latin – and enjoyed her lessons.

By the time she was sixteen, Ralph was ready to begin his career at Clifton College and Mr Pennydale's services were no longer required. She had pleaded with her father to allow her to join her closest friend, Lydia, as a boarder at the Ladies' College in Cheltenham. This request was refused, and from that time onwards Margaret's life had been the conventional one of the daughter of a wealthy family. It was not surprising that she sometimes felt jealous of her brother's greater opportunities, realizing that she would have made better use of them if she had been in Ralph's position.

The unfairness of the situation was often on her mind. Just because she was a girl, so many doors were closed to her. The conventions of her society allowed her only a single choice. She could marry, or she could remain single, living in her parents' home. There was no other decision to be made, and she was not free to make even that one herself.

Sometimes, when her wish to be a doctor overwhelmed her, she raged silently against the restrictions of her life. But there were more frequent periods when she was able to accept her situation with contentment. There was just one door which would open to her and never to her brothers. She could give birth to a baby, as they could not. One day, she promised herself, she would have children of her own.

4

Before any bowl of soup can reach the lips of the poor, a good deal of champagne necessarily makes its way down the throats of the rich. When the need is for something as substantial as a building, the fertile soil of a wealthy community must be cultivated with both energy and style. Margaret gave a good deal of attention to the details of her mother's evening reception, but naturally her own direct contribution to it exercised her most. Almost every day she sent the carriage for Luisa, using the need to practise together as an excuse to provide her friend with a good meal.

On these occasions the baby, Alexa, remained behind. Luisa's relations with her landlady had been strained for a time because she had difficulty in paying the rent promptly every week. But recently there had been no mention of the arrears, and Mrs Lambert had even volunteered to look after the baby occasionally. Luisa considered that this new reasonableness was caused by the regular appearance of the grandest carriage in the city outside Mrs Lambert's front door, but it was Margaret's opinion that Alexa herself was irresistible to any woman.

After their practice the two young women walked

together on the Downs. Good food and fresh air had already worked a small miracle on Luisa's appearance. Her long black hair had regained its glossiness and her skin, although still pale, had lost its strained appearance. She had somehow managed to acquire a new gown which, although plain, showed off her slender figure to advantage.

A little to Margaret's surprise, Luisa's wardrobe had also been the object of John Junius's interest. When he heard from his daughter of the occasion on which she proposed to sing with her former teacher, he made it clear at once that Luisa must be dressed in a manner suitable for the company. Margaret and she must go together, he commanded, to order gowns of equal elegance to be made up and charged to his account.

Margaret suspected that the result might not be quite as he intended. Luisa had spent the months of her absence from Bristol in London. She had visited a new store called Liberty's in the first week of its opening and was overwhelmed by the new aesthetic style of dress which she saw there – so different from the tightly fitted gowns which had been fashionable until then, with their bustles and trains and the necessity for stiff-backed corseting. At that time she could not afford to indulge herself in the new fashion, but John Junius's offer gave her an opportunity now which she could not resist.

While Margaret watched doubtfully, Luisa chose a shimmering Indian silk for her gown and sketched the soft and fluid line in which it should be made up. Because of her tallness and the grace of her movements she would look striking even in a style so unfamiliar to the ladies of Bristol society. But Margaret, lacking her presence and confidence, was not prepared to stray so far from what was expected. She ordered her own gown to be made from a stiff blue silk which rustled so loudly with every movement that Luisa laughingly declared it would be a miracle if any of the singing were heard at all.

When the evening of the reception came, it was natural that Margaret should feel responsible for putting David Gregson at his ease. He would know none of the wealthy citizens who had been invited, and they might behave coldly to someone who was present only as a servant of the charity's committee. Margaret faced this prospect on David's behalf before the guests arrived. Her duty as a hostess, she recognized happily, would force her to make sure that he was never left alone.

The reality was a little different. She had a more important duty this evening – that of persuading her mother's richer guests to subscribe to the charitable fund. There was a good deal to say about the insanitary conditions in which so many sick women lived, and the urgency of the need to remove both the women themselves and their children. It had all to be said again and again, to one person at a time, so that everyone would believe her own contribution to be vital. Margaret promised herself that when the time came for the company to remove into the great dining room, where the refreshments had been laid out, she would find the opportunity to apologize to David for treating him so discourteously.

The moment came. The butler bowed in the doorway, the footmen with their trays of glasses stepped back out of the way, and Georgiana graciously indicated that a small supper was prepared for her guests. Looking round for David, Margaret discovered that after all he was not alone. He was offering his arm to Luisa.

Margaret stifled her disappointment as best she could. David's behaviour was perfectly proper. He was recognizing that the daughter of his hostess must necessarily concern herself with guests more important than himself. It had been clever of him to identify the one person present whose status was as low as his own.

By the time the company returned to the big drawing room, which was used only on occasions such as this, its sofas and chairs had been rearranged to face the piano. David, at the back of the room, remained standing, looking at the two musicians over the seated ladies. Margaret's throat went dry with nervousness. But she was to start the concert with a piano piece which she had practised to perfection. There was no reason to be apprehensive, she told herself.

Taking her seat at the piano, she caught the attention of the whispering audience with the dramatic opening chords of *The Maiden's Prayer* before showing off her agile fingers with the rippling arpeggios and trill-like bird songs which one hand provided as accompaniment for the melody played by the other. The piece was bound to be well known to all the ladies in the audience who had daughters of their own. Perhaps it was for that very reason, because they had heard it more stumblingly practised in their own drawing rooms, that they were generous in their applause.

The two girls then changed places so that Luisa could play the accompaniments to their songs. Margaret stood stiffly, half facing her, with one gloved hand resting on the piano. Her first solo was an old favourite: *I dreamt that I dwelt in marble halls*. Luisa played the introduction and Margaret began to sing.

Throughout their little concert David's eyes were fixed on the performers. An hour earlier Margaret would have taken it for granted that he was watching her. But now her pleasure was spoilt by Luisa's presence. When they began their duets, Luisa sang the alto part and, although she took care to adjust her voice to Margaret's sweet but less powerful soprano, the richness of her tone left no doubt that hers was the superior talent.

Margaret, recognizing that Luisa had few advantages in life to compare with those of her own birth, had never before experienced any jealousy. Now, for the first time, she found herself resenting not only her musical inferiority but also the fact that her friend, unlike herself, was so poised and stately. Elegance was a gift which Margaret had always affected to despise, since she knew that she could never possess it, but at this moment she was brought near to tears by the knowledge of her own lack of style.

The reason for her jealousy was not hard to find when she looked at it honestly. As she ruefully castigated herself for not allowing poor Luisa her superiority in these areas, she realized the explanation with a shock so sudden and intense that for a moment her head swam. What she felt was not just pique. She had fallen in love.

She did her best to conquer the surge of emotion. David had appealed to her at first sight for no better reason than the look of his curly hair and handsome face and slim figure. Later in their first meeting she had approved of his honest outspokenness and was grateful for the sympathy he showed towards her ambition. He was ambitious himself – she was sure of that, and in turn sympathized with him. Although conscious of being in this one respect held back by the wealth and position of her family, she could understand how much more severely David was handicapped by the poverty into which he had been born. From their conversation in Leigh Woods she knew that he had been an only child and that his parents were already dead. He was alone in the world in a way which she could hardly imagine. All these different impressions had combined to make her aware of a peculiar interest in him, but only now did she realize how much her feelings had deepened.

After the music was over, the sight of David coming towards the piano made her steel herself to hear his compliments directed elsewhere. Yet it was after all her own hand over which he bowed. She told herself that this was merely social politeness, but his admiration appeared to be sincere. A little at a time she allowed relief to creep over her and dared to feel pleasure in the conversation with an intensity heightened by her earlier apprehension. It even seemed safe at last to turn towards Luisa.

'I believe you are already acquainted with Mr Gregson,' she said.

'It's a strange coincidence,' David replied. 'Miss Reni and I lodge in the same house. We keep different hours, so that even on the staircase we have never met until tonight. I have often heard her practising the very songs which you have just performed, but without knowing that I should have the privilege of attending their performance. Mrs Lambert, my landlady, knowing my employment, mentioned to me on one occasion the arrival of the Lorimer carriage to call for Miss Reni, and still it did not occur to me that I might meet her here tonight.'

There was no hint of confusion in his voice, so that the thought which flashed through Margaret's mind was unprovoked. Could it be that David was the father of Luisa's child?

She dismissed the idea as soon as it occurred to her. David had come to Lorimer's only in January, and at that time Luisa was in London and already pregnant. Margaret flushed with shame at the wickedness of her own thoughts. She began to turn away from David, feeling that she was unfit to converse with him. But he took the opportunity to raise another subject with her.

'I learned yesterday of another property which might be worth inspection, Miss Lorimer,' he said. 'I wondered if we – if you would allow me . . .'

He had apparently not enough courage to come to the point, but Margaret was eager to rescue him.

'Oh yes, Mr Gregson, let us by all means make another expedition. Perhaps on this occasion we shall be more fortunate.'

They appointed a time. The evening, which until a few moments earlier had seemed in ruins, was suddenly a triumph. Margaret's happiness must have shown in her face, for even her father commented on it as he came across now to compliment the singers.

69

'You are looking very well tonight, Margaret. Extremely well. And you sang, I thought, with great expression. He turned to Luisa. 'I must thank you on behalf of our family, Signorina Reni, for devoting your talents to this cause. I hope it may not be too long before you sing for us again. It was most beautiful. My carriage will of course take you home whenever you wish to leave, but I hope that we may enjoy your company a little longer yet.'

'Papa,' said Margaret, and then hesitated. But her father seemed to be in a more affable mood than usual. 'Papa, Mr Gregson lodges, it appears, in the same residence as Luisa.'

'Indeed!' said John Junius. His bushy eyebrows lowered in a disapproving frown, as though it were not correct for an unmarried lady and gentleman to share a landlady. But almost at once he gave David a cool nod of recognition.

'We must leave Signorina Reni, I think, to decide whether she wishes to be escorted on her return journey. All the seats in the carriage are entirely at her disposal.'

After he left, Luisa laughed gaily at David.

'Well, I hope, Mr Gregson, that you will accept a seat. Your journey will be unpleasant otherwise, for I can hear that the rain is heavy.'

'I hardly need the threat of rain and mud to drive me into such charming company, Miss Reni.'

An hour ago the exchange would have made Margaret even more jealous than before, and the thought of David closeted in the carriage with Luisa would have been insupportable. But by now she was beginning to recognize the humour with which he paid the compliments expected by society, laughing at himself even as he did so. And a woman with a baby was no sort of rival. She was even able to raise a smile as she saw them leave together.

She was still smiling as Betty unpinned her hair later that evening and warmed her nightdress before the fire. But later still, as she lay in bed, the smile faded, replaced by anxious consideration. It was not enough to acknowledge her own feelings. It was not enough even to hope that her father's accountant found her of some interest. If the relationship were to develop further, it would be necessary for some initiative to be taken. She had the wish to act: had she the courage?

5

When a search has provided the excuse for companionship between a young lady and gentleman, its successful conclusion is not always greeted with the satisfaction it might seem to deserve. It was with dismay that David realized, on a bleak and snow-swept day in January, that his expeditions in Margaret Lorimer's company had come to an end. Croft House – the fifth property they had inspected together – was precisely suitable.

The house was old and spacious. It had been the centre of a manorial farm before the city swelled to engulf it, allowing an astute owner to grow houses rather than corn on his fields. He had kept enough land to provide a pleasure garden, however, so that the surroundings were verdant. The barns and stables which clustered round the old farmyard had not been used for many years, but were still dry. It would be a simple matter to convert them into dormitory accommodation for children.

Best of all, there was a separate dower house, Lower Croft. More modern than Croft House, it had been designed in the gothic style, with two turrets and a wealth of lead in the windows. Some of its rooms were small and dark, reached only by narrow and twisting staircases; but the drawing room, in which David and Margaret paused to discuss their conclusions, was high and spacious.

'If you are to appoint a resident supervisor, the offer of a house would make the position a very attractive one,' David pointed out. 'You could take such a benefit into account when determining the salary.'

'So you think this is a purchase which could safely be recommended to the committee?' asked Margaret.

'If the price is right, yes.'

David felt little doubt that the price would be right. All through the city – and indeed, all over the country – money was becoming tight. His earlier efforts to persuade John Junius that the debts owing to Lorimer's Bank should be reduced had met with little success. But although these old debts were still outstanding, the directors had decided to restrict new loans to a minimum. Other banks were acting in the same way. It was a time when those who needed funds would have to sell property, while those who might wish to buy would find it hard to borrow the purchase price. With the fruits of its appeal waiting accessibly at Lorimer's, the Gentlewomen's Aid Fund could reasonably hope to be the only bidder for Croft House.

'Then you should sound more cheerful, Mr Gregson. This is an exciting moment, if our search is over at last.'

'I've no doubt it's exciting for you, Miss Lorimer,' David said. 'But it means that our afternoons together have come to an end.'

He had been surprised at the free and easy manner in which her mother had allowed Margaret to accept him as an escort. The simplest enquiry would have elicited the fact that Betty did not keep her mistress company while the houses were inspected. He could hardly expect such a providential state of affairs to arise again.

'The committee will need to discuss the conversion and equipment of the premises,' said Margaret. 'There will be frequent meetings. We shall see each other often again.'

'Only in company.' A kind of desolation swept over him at the thought that she would never know what he wanted to tell her. Dare he declare his feelings to a young woman so far above him in fortune, a woman to whom he could offer nothing? If he let this last opportunity of privacy slip away, he knew that he would never forgive himself.

He might have hesitated still, but Margaret was pulling up the fur-trimmed hood of her cape. It was a sign that she was ready to venture out into the snow again. Desperation drove him to speech, though even now he found himself unable to broach the subject directly, but came at it sideways.

'I imagine that before too long you may be looking for a property of a different kind,' he said. Margaret's expression of surprise made it clear that she did not understand what he meant. 'I mean . . .' he found himself almost stammering in the effort not to put into words what he meant, but nevertheless to have it understood. 'I mean that ye'll soon be wishing to set up an establishment of your own. A young lady of your character and prospects – your father must be pursued with proposals for your hand in marriage.'

'My father has never consented to regard himself as a quarry to be pursued,' said Margaret. Laughing at the idea, she allowed her hand to slacken on her hood so that its fur framed her face loosely and seemed about to slip back again. Whether or not she knew the direction in which David wanted to steer the conversation, it appeared that she was not rejecting the subject as impertinent. 'You may be sure, Mr Gregson, that in any arrangement, *he* is the one to make the first proposal.'

'And has he made any such proposal to you yet?'

The laughter faded from Margaret's face.

'Yes, Mr Gregson. Almost two years ago he planned an alliance which would have been convenient to the business of the Lorimer Line. In case my person should not by itself have been sufficient to allure the other party, a very generous portion would have been allotted to me.'

'But the arrangement was not concluded?'

'No. I don't see myself as a princess to be ceded in a

treaty. My brother William, as you may imagine, was not pleased with me. The benefit of the marriage would have been mainly to his ships. We have not been such good friends since that time.'

'You are telling me that you refused?'

'I accept your astonishment as a compliment. Yes, I refused.'

'I've never heard anyone say No to Mr Lorimer.'

'Had you been within a mile of Brinsley House, you would have heard what happens when anyone does. My father believes that he knows what is best for everyone. It is a sincere belief, and I truly think a well-meaning one. He was not pleased with me. But even he was not prepared to turn the princess into a slave.'

'He'll no doubt make other suggestions of a similar nature.'

'I think not, Mr Gregson. He will not lightly expose himself to another refusal on my part, nor will he bend to ask my opinion in advance. It was made plain to me at the time that if I refused the arrangement he had made, I could not expect him to repeat his generosity. I would of course be permitted to remain at home as a companion to my mother.'

'And does that prospect satisfy you?'

'Indeed it does not. Any position of dependence is abhorrent to me. I see no means of escaping it, but I would rather be dependent on a husband than on a father. And I have a very strong wish for children of my own.' She checked herself anxiously. 'I am being very free with my secrets, Mr Gregson. I hope I may rely on your discretion.'

'Would it be impertinent for me to ask, Miss Lorimer, what your present situation is?'

There was a long silence. If it had been torture for David to begin the conversation, it now seemed that they had reached a point at which it was as painful for Margaret to continue it. He was asking too much, expecting too much, he realized. She had given him no encouragement to speak, unless smiles and a frankness in conversation were to be counted as encouragement, but his forwardness had not been snubbed. No doubt she had been brought up to believe that it must always be the gentleman who first declared himself. If it had not occurred to her that the difference in their situations was sufficient to make this particular gentleman hesitate before pushing himself forward, that was to her credit. In the eyes of her father, David knew well that he would not be considered a gentleman at all.

'Forgive me for pressing so many questions on you,' he said. 'But my courage is unequal to asking the only one which comes close to my heart. I know that in your father's plans there could be no place for myself. And I have no right to hope . . .'

Once again he floundered to a halt, not daring to look at her. Had he made her angry or embarrassed? Would she turn on her heel and walk away from him for ever? To his astonishment he heard her laugh softly.

'At our first meeting you boasted of your Scottish directness, Mr Gregson. Has a year in our hypocritical English society robbed you of your talent, as it has of your accent? Or is the subject of slaving the only one which can arouse your passion?'

'I love you,' he said.

For a long moment they both seemed to be holding their breath. Then Margaret raised her head. Surely it was happiness he saw in her eyes. If so, it was of brief duration, succeeded by the determined expression which he had come to know so well. The hope that she would run into his arms was disappointed. It seemed, instead, that she intended to continue the conversation as though his declaration had not interrupted it.

'You asked what my situation was, Mr Gregson. Only a short time ago I discussed this question with my father. I

75

asked him what his attitude would be if I were to find a husband for myself. My father and I quarrel very often, but perhaps it is because – as you said once yourself – we are in some ways alike. We quarrelled on this occasion too, but my question was as steady as his anger. In the end, he respected it and gave me an answer.'

'Will you tell me what it was?'

'He reminded me that I had forfeited my claim to any marriage settlement of the kind which he had proposed two years ago. He said that in no circumstances would he renew the offer. He pointed out that I have no fortune of my own. He gave it as his opinion that no gentleman of wealth would wish to marry me under these conditions and that no one without wealth could afford to do so. Because I have been brought up in a houseful of servants he believes that I am incapable of living without them. He warned me that if I found someone whose attentions I wished to encourage I must first of all make it clear to him that I have no expectations of any kind. But if, having considered this fact, any suitor should still wish to approach my father, he would be interrogated only as to the respectability of his way of life, and not as to his fortune.'

'Am I to understand that you would be permitted to follow your own inclination?'

'Under the conditions I have described, yes.'

'Even if your suitor was as humble as myself?'

He foresaw the answer before she spoke, but needed the extra moment for his exhilaration to reach its peak. When he first fell in love with Margaret Lorimer he had puzzled over the reason, wondering what there was in her plain matter-of-factness to explain the strong attraction he felt. By now he had had time to learn the answer. It was the independence of her character which had reached out to engage his sympathies. While he stood there, awkward with admiration, Margaret was laughing.

'You know little of young ladies, Mr Gregson, if you

76

think that one of them would risk disputing with such a man as John Junius Lorimer for the sake of establishing anything as valueless as a general principle. My father was well aware of this, and pressed me for a name. In telling you of his conditions, I consider myself to be fulfilling them.' He noticed the merriment fade from her eyes, to be replaced with anxiety. 'My father told me roundly that my attitude was immodest. You may share his view.'

'I consider your attitude to be honest and brave and – oh, Miss Lorimer!' Despite the fact that her hand was gloved, he kissed it fervently. An ill-timed cough at the open door interrupted him. Betty Hurst stood there nervously, her fingers and nose red with the cold.

'Begging your pardon, Miss, but John said to tell you that the wind's blowing the snow into drifts against the hedges. He's feared of trouble with the carriage along the drive.'

'Our business is almost finished. We shall be with him directly. Go and tell him that.'

She spoke briskly and the girl left at a run. David turned back to Margaret, needing to reassure himself further.

'If you marry me, Miss Lorimer, there will be no coachman.'

'I am able to walk,' she said, and her smile was the sweetest he had ever seen. His own, in return, was full of wonder at his own good fortune.

'Do I understand, then, that your father will be expecting a visit from me?' he asked.

Still laughing, Margaret shook her head.

'By no means, Mr Gregson. In the first place, I was forced to confess to him that I had no reason to know what your feelings were, since you had been careful to conceal them from me. He felt this, I think, to be to your credit. I made it clear that I was approaching him solely because I wished to discover how you felt and could not in kindness

77

do so if it were likely to expose you afterwards to humiliation at his hands. In the second place, he is confident that without a marriage settlement I shall be of no more interest to you.'

'He does me wrong there. He may not expect me, but surely he will not be surprised if I ask for an interview?'

'He will be surprised, but even the chairman of a bank cannot expect everything in life to be predictable,' said Margaret. 'I imagine he will survive the shock.'

She pulled up her hood again, indicating that they should go, and they stepped outside into the cold. The bright sunshine of the afternoon had faded with the approach of evening, taking the sparkle from the snow and replacing it with a tinge of icy blue. The huge skeletons of trees on the skyline were frosted with white, and the lawns which separated the two houses of the estate were covered with a single smooth blanket of snow. The wind dropped for a moment, and David felt himself enveloped by the special silence of a snowscape, as though there were no one else in the world but himself and his future bride.

Alas, it was a silence which could not last. He heard from the farmyard nearby the cough of a horse, the stamp of a hoof, the flick of a whip as John stirred the dappled pair into action. But no more than that. The usual grating of the ironbound wheels was muffled and the carriage appeared and moved towards them almost as in a dream.

'There will never be another place in the world as beautiful as this for me,' David said. He felt Margaret's hand tighten on his arm.

'You do not think badly of me for my immodesty?' she asked, anxious to be reassured. 'I have pondered so often what might be best to do. My father commands us both equally. A woman and an employee. We have few weapons at our disposal.'

'I am ashamed that it should have been left to you to strike the first blow. From now on I shall speak for us both. You have been brave, not immodest, and we will be as bold to the world and as honest with each other for the rest of our lives as you have dared to be to your father and to me today.'

'It is not at all the custom.' He saw Margaret's lips curling with merriment and would have laughed aloud in the happiness of his situation had the carriage not by now come to a standstill in front of them. John dismounted to pull down the step and David handed Margaret in to her seat. In Betty's presence neither of them wished to talk. David allowed himself instead to dream.

How to convert the dream into reality was the next question. In the days which followed, it was necessary to plot and plan. Margaret had given him fair warning, and it was not a matter to be taken lightly that a gently reared young woman must somehow be made comfortable on an accountant's poor salary. Miss Reni had abandoned her apartments in his house shortly after the concert at which he had discovered her connection with the Lorimers, and no new tenant had yet been found. David inquired the price of the rooms if added to his own, but the accommodation, at the top of the house, was dark and damp, with sloping ceilings and small dormer windows. It would never do for someone like Margaret Lorimer. He began to see that what he had gladly accepted as a condition might in practice pose difficulties. John Junius Lorimer, of course, would have known this from the start.

When he had considered the situation as thoroughly as he could, David sent a message to the chairman requesting the favour of an interview on a private matter. He was kept waiting for three days and then summoned to the chairman's office. On this occasion he was invited to sit, but that seemed the limit of what the chairman was willing to concede.

The words David had prepared were frozen by the unyielding expression of the man who faced him across the

79

huge desk. The greenish-blue eyes were cold. It was never possible to deduce from them what John Junius was thinking, and today they were hooded more inscrutably than usual by the lowering of his bushy eyebrows. David licked dry lips and still found himself stammering as he formally asked to be accepted as a suitor for Miss Lorimer's hand in marriage.

The chairman did not answer at once, although the request could hardly have come as a surprise. Instead, he continued to stare steadily at this employee who had so sadly mistaken his place in society. The effect was perhaps not what he had intended. So far from intimidating him, the heavy period of silence gave David an opportunity to conquer his nervousness and determine that, like Margaret, he was not to be bullied. He sat up even straighter and set his jaw more firmly.

At last the chairman spoke.

'Miss Lorimer has acquainted you, I understand, with my intention to make no settlement on her in the event of her marriage.'

'She has, sir. It is this information which has encouraged me to approach you. In any other circumstances it would scarcely have been possible. You would have been bound to think me a fortune-hunter.'

There was no means of telling what effect this statement had on his hearer, but David's own eyes sparkled brazenly with the pleasure of turning the old man's weapon against himself. If there was to be a battle, he determined to prove himself a worthy opponent.

'Are you aware, Mr Gregson, that Miss Lorimer in a year spends as much on clothing and other personal needs as the total amount of your present salary?' John Junius paused briefly before answering his own question. 'No, of course you are not. Miss Lorimer herself is not. She knows neither what she spends nor what you earn. I do not expect in my daughter the ability to calculate expenses and incomes and to balance them to the last farthing. But you are an accountant. I expect it of you. You must know that what you propose is impossible.'

'I well understand, sir, that it will be necessary for some such account to be presented to Miss Lorimer so that she may fully comprehend the sacrifices which would be demanded of her,' said David. 'If I have not done that yet, it is because I have not felt myself free to speak of such matters until I have your permission to do so.'

He had won that round too. For the time being even Margaret was forgotten in the pleasure of pitting his wits against his employer, at whose frown half Bristol fell to trembling.

'Nevertheless, Mr Gregson, you have presumably considered the matter in your own mind. Do you, for example, expect my daughter to take up residence in your present apartments? I have been there to visit them. They are cramped and unhealthy. It would be out of the question.'

'I have given a good deal of thought to this matter, Mr Lorimer, and I believe that I have the ability to improve my situation. Certainly I have the ambition to do so. I recognize that it might cause Miss Lorimer distress to live in reduced circumstances in a city where she has previously graced the best society. It is possible that you yourself, sir, might not wish it to be directly observed that she had adopted the style of life of one of your own accountants. It would be my intention, if your permission is forthcoming and if Miss Lorimer accepts the situation when she has fully understood it, to apply for a position in some other place, and to ask only that the chairman of Lorimer's Bank should support my application with a recommendation which I trust my work here will have deserved.'

'You have in mind a post similar to your present one?'

David had hoped that this question would be asked, for he had already decided what answer he would give.

'To work as accountant in the head office of a bank such

81

as Lorimer's has been of great value to me,' he said. 'It is my opinion that I should now be capable of acting as a manager, perhaps at first of one of the minor branches of a metropolitan bank. In a small town this might afford Miss Lorimer a status of which she need not feel ashamed. Thenceforward I would rely on my own abilities to win promotion.'

Yet another silence settled over the chairman's large office, in which the air as well as the furniture seemed not to have been changed for fifty years. David judged that behind the frowning expression a decision was being made. Perhaps, he thought, it had been made even before the interview began, subject only to his own satisfactory performance. At any rate, the verdict flowed out without any hesitation.

'I have been over this matter with Miss Lorimer not once but twice,' said the chairman. 'On the first occasion at her request and again yesterday at my own. She is a stubborn young woman, and I should warn you that you may not always find that as much to your advantage as it is today. But I am not a duke or a marquis, insistent on pedigree with every marriage. My family has attained its present position by the exercise of its own talents. Never let it be said that a Lorimer undervalues skill and ambition. I have accordingly informed Miss Lorimer that she may receive you at Brinsley House.'

David bowed his head, ostensibly in thanks but actually in relief and pleasure and surprise. He was allowed no time to speak.

'I do not intend to change my mind on the question of a settlement,' the chairman said severely, as though repenting of his weakness; but then went on in a more encouraging manner. 'However, although her behaviour in the past may have been foolish, Miss Lorimer remains my daughter, and I shall make her a small personal allowance. As for yourself, you are correct in believing that the status of my son-in-law cannot be a matter of indifference to me. I shall recommend to the Board of Directors your appointment as manager of Lorimer's Bank with effect from May.'

This time it was all David could do not to gasp with amazement. What he had said earlier had certainly been intended to win the chairman's support for his advancement, but he had not anticipated any height as dizzy as this. Whatever the chairman recommended, the directors would accept. This could be no spur-of-the-minute decision. It had all been thought out in advance, no doubt from the moment when David requested the interview.

'Mr Lynch will be taking his departure then?' he queried.

'He will. He is not yet, however, aware of the fact, and he will not learn it from you.' Suddenly the great eyebrows lifted and the whole force of the chairman's stare was directed at David. John Junius Lorimer knew as well as Jehovah himself how to make clear the orders which were not to be disobeyed. 'You will leave for London at the end of this week with a recommendation to a friend of mine at Gurney's Bank. He will instruct you in those areas of management which are not ruled solely by accountancy. When you leave Bristol, you will give no indication to any of your acquaintances, and particularly not to any member of the staff here, that there is any possibility of your ever returning.'

'Not even to Miss Lorimer?'

'I have already told Miss Lorimer that I require her to accept a separation of three months in order that her feelings for you, and yours for her, may be tested. The stubbornness to which I have already referred has caused her to accept my statement as a challenge. She takes it at its face value. She certainly will hope for your reappearance in May. But she must know nothing of my intentions as far as the bank is concerned.'

This time the silence was a final one. All he intended to say had been said.

83

David stood up.

'I hope you will allow me to express my appreciation of your attitude sir,' he said. 'What you have offered is much more than I deserve or could have presumed to hope for. I would like to say, if I may, that my admiration for yourself is exceeded only by my affection for Miss Lorimer.'

John Junius Lorimer's head bowed in a nod which was so slight as to be almost imperceptible. It was a gesture which accepted the sentiments and dismissed the speaker. David bowed in farewell and withdrew.

Back at his desk he sat without moving, almost unable to believe his luck. What would his mother have said, he wondered with amusement, if she could have heard that fulsome compliment he had paid the old man? She would have sighed to discover how quickly her straight-speaking Scottish son had been corrupted into mouthing the insincerities of Southerners. It was even likely, David realized, that the chairman himself had little use for such flattery. But he would accept it as an indication that his future son-in-law had good manners and respect for the way of the world. The whole interview had been satisfactory beyond all expectations.

Mr Lynch, passing in front of David's desk at that moment, paused to stare pointedly at the ledger which lay closed on its surface. David dipped his quill in the ink as a sign that he was resuming work. His gesture of apology was a mock one, but he acted it well. He knew what Mr Lynch could not guess, but he must wait a little while for his triumph.

6

The secret impulses of the heart may drive a young woman down unexpected paths in the maze of social observances. When she was heart-free, with no attachment – either formal or unofficial – to bind her, Margaret Lorimer had spent little time enjoying the more frivolous diversions of her contemporaries. She loved to dance, for example, but disliked the prickly hedges of etiquette which gave significance to the smallest gesture. Dances were too often organized as though they had been invented by the old for the purpose of marrying off the young.

During the months of David's absence, she was surprised to realize that her attitude had changed. Naturally she missed him, but the security which she felt in his love made the parting bearable. Her happiness at being wanted relaxed her normally firm expression, and her new gaiety was quickly observed. It was ironic that while her heart yearned for one man only she should find herself pursued in an unaccustomed way by so many male partners, but she was easier in their company than before because she knew – although they did not – that they could never be of more than passing interest to her. She accepted invitations to evening concerts or subscription balls or private routs as though her promise to John Junius demanded it. Her father had required only silence, but she was impelled to go further, justifying each venture into mixed society as a deliberate means of concealing her true situation.

Her father encouraged this increased social activity, and pressed new gowns upon her with a generosity which caused Margaret to wonder whether they represented a disguised contribution to her future life. John Junius's willingness to accept David as her suitor had revived all the warm affection which she had felt for her father but was not encouraged to express. Was it reciprocated? That was more difficult to tell, but perhaps he had concealed his feelings for so long that he could not now bring himself to put them into words, expressing them instead in generosities.

Yet though Margaret's family life at this time was unusually warm and her social life unusually crowded, the days passed slowly. Spring in that year of 1878 seemed very long in coming. Bristol lay snugly protected beneath the heights of Clifton, but even in the heart of the city, to which the westerly winds usually brought warm Atlantic rain, the snow showed no sign of melting. For almost ten days in March, when the sharp heads of daffodils were pushing upwards into the frosty air, the most sheltered basins of the dock were frozen. This enabled skating parties to be added to the list of pleasures on offer, but made the month of May seem still as distant as when David had departed for London.

The need for a new distraction combined with the strain of secrecy to make Margaret seek an interview with her father one evening. She found him working at his papers in the library which he used as a study when the tower room was too cold. Georgiana rarely sat long in the drawing room, unless there were guests and the possibility of making up a table at cards. When she retired to her boudoir it was usual for John Junius to retreat to the library in order that he should be free from interruption. She could tell on this occasion that he was irritated by her intrusion and unwilling to be distracted. Sheets of figures were spread over his desk and had caused the frown-lines of displeasure to deepen between his eyes.

'Yes?'

Margaret recognized that her intrusion was badly timed. But to retreat without speaking would be to annoy him all the more, and so would any elaborate apology. She hurried to put her request into the briefest form.

'I would like, Papa, to invite Lydia to stay for a short visit.'

She watched him gradually pulling his mind away from whatever was worrying him and making the effort to recall which one of her friends she meant.

'Miss Morton? Naturally you are welcome to entertain her here whenever you like. There is no necessity to inquire of me, if the date is convenient to your mother.'

Margaret had known that, of course, but needed a way of leading to her real request.

'She has recently become engaged, Papa. She can talk of nothing but her handsome lieutenant. He has been posted to Quetta, which is why I have suggested the visit. It is to console her, for she is sure that her heart will break. You told me that I should not mention Mr Gregson's name, nor my feelings for him, to any of my friends, and I have done as you asked. But it is very hard to have no confidante at all. And it will be doubly hard when my guest is so much burdened by her own separation.'

John Junius sighed. Reluctantly he was preparing to give his full concentration to the matter.

'If your understanding with Mr Gregson breaks down for any reason, Margaret, and if in the meantime you have allowed it to become known, your situation will be a humiliating one.'

'I am sure that will not happen,' she said firmly. 'In any case, my friend will be discreet if I ask her. Doubly so if told she is entrusted with a secret known to no one else.'

'No doubt,' her father replied dryly. 'But I am aware that girls like to chatter. Although I sympathize with your wish to make your situation public, we cannot be sure that Miss Morton may not succumb to the same wish. There is only one way to keep a secret, Margaret. I must ask you to observe the wishes I have previously expressed on the subject.'

Margaret had long ago realized the wisdom of defying her father only on matters of extreme importance. It was necessary to make small surrenders if she were ever to win any battles at all, and to tell the truth her hopes of success in this particular campaign had never been high. She sighed more loudly than was necessary, but already her father had returned his frowning concentration to the figures in front of him.

As she closed the library door she saw her younger brother standing in the shadow nearby. It was clear from his troubled expression that he too sought an interview with John Junius and needed time to collect his courage before facing it. He came forward as Margaret moved away.

'I could hear that there was someone in the library,' he said. 'Although not the words. Were you asking for something? And did you have any luck?'

Margaret shook her head.

'Take my advice, Ralph. Postpone your interview. Papa is not in his most amenable mood and I have already irritated him by interrupting his work. If you go in now, you will have to bear my share of his annoyance as well as your own.'

'Thank you for the warning.'

They moved away together. Margaret's thoughts were on the forthcoming visit from her friend, so she made no attempt to hold Ralph in conversation. After they had parted, she felt guilty, for it was clear enough that he had a problem to discuss. What could it be? If it was important, he would have mentioned it to her, she assured herself, and gave the matter no more thought as she went to give instructions that one of the guest rooms should be prepared.

Anticipation of the visit made time pass more quickly, and she was happy and excited by the time her friend arrived at Brinsley House the next Sunday. In spite of the fact that Lydia was younger than Margaret, the two girls had been friends since their earliest childhood; although they saw less of each other now that the Morton family had bought themselves a country estate near Bath. Lydia was so far from being good-looking that William had once, with the taunting typical of an elder brother, accused Margaret of seeking out as a friend the only girl in England who could make her seem beautiful by comparison. But Lydia contrived that her ugliness should not be noticed by keeping her face so much moved by animation that no one had the opportunity to study it in repose. She teased everyone she met – even, to Margaret's astonishment, her own parents – and her merriment and perpetual good nature made her a most welcome companion. The two young women embraced each other with enthusiasm, and there was a great deal of laughter and chattering as Betty unpacked Lydia's valise and trunk.

When the visitor was ready, they went together to Georgiana's boudoir. At this time of year the weather outside justified the fire which roared in the big stone fireplace, making the room cosy rather than oppressive. Georgiana, too, was less petulant than usual as she welcomed her daughter's friend. She had always liked Lydia, whose conversation was devoted to such interesting subjects as fashions and scandals and who – unlike Margaret – did not expect her to concern herself with topics like the insanitary housing conditions of the poor or the deficiencies of the city's water supply. Bath society, unlike that of Bristol, was kept in touch with metropolitan tastes by those who still came in the season to take the cure – although Lydia was careful to point out that nowadays these visitors tended to be elderly and could not safely be assumed to be leaders of fashion.

'But you are to have your own excitement, greater than

anything Bath can offer!' Lydia remembered. 'The Prince of Wales!'

Margaret and Georgiana looked at each other and found that neither was enlightened.

'Surely you have heard! The Prince of Wales is to visit Bristol in July. It is only for some dull exhibition, but the city will surely not allow the occasion to pass without celebration. There is certain to be a ball.'

'No doubt.' Georgiana's eyes had sparkled with unusual interest at the mention of the Prince, but she was quick to shade them again with sulkiness. 'However, if there is I shall not attend it.'

'A ball graced by a royal personage – Mama, I defy you to resist!' exclaimed Margaret, laughing.

'I have nothing to wear.'

'Papa would be the first to recognize that on such an occasion a new ball gown would be a necessity. He has been most generous to me in these past weeks, and for events of lesser importance.'

'There are times when silks and satins are not enough,' said Georgiana. 'Look in my jewel box and tell me what you see. Garnets and glass! It is ridiculous. I have told your father over and over again that his wife might as well appear naked as display trifles so unworthy of his dignity.'

This time it was Lydia and Margaret who caught each other's eye and decided that it was time for the guest's arrival to be formally notified also to her host. They walked down the main staircase and through the central hall in which John Junius's Eastern art was displayed.

'Show me your pet squirrel,' demanded Lydia, pausing on the way to the study door. When they were little girls together they had not, of course, been allowed to touch the jade animals. It had been one of the indications of accepted maturity when first of all Margaret and then her friends had been allowed to handle the treasures.

Margaret smiled and turned back towards the case in

which the squirrel was kept. Then her smile changed to a frown.

'Papa must have rearranged them,' she said. She walked round the hall, looking quickly at each case. Then she made a second circuit and this time studied the collection more intently. Lydia waited to be told what the matter was.

'All my favourites have gone,' said Margaret. 'And also all those which Papa told me were the best pieces, though I might not admire them myself. There are some new animals here. I am no very good judge, but to me they look much inferior to the old.' She unlocked the nearest case and took out a coiled snake. Still frowning, she stroked it slowly. But it felt wrong to the touch, and the carving was crude compared to the missing pieces. Her mind was still on the small mystery as she led Lydia into her father's library.

On Sundays John Junius did not work. But after the rituals of morning service and midday Sunday dinner had been observed he allowed himself to read any journals which had arrived during the week; and even for this relaxation he preferred the high-backed leather chair behind his desk to the elegant but uncomfortable sofas of the drawing room.

Margaret could tell as soon as she went in that her father was in an affable mood. She despised herself for the feeling of anxiety which afflicted her on each approach to his presence, but it had its reward in the relief when the atmosphere proved to be serene. John Junius welcomed Lydia politely. He remembered to congratulate her on her engagement and even listened with no visible boredom to her description of her lieutenant's charms. His general good temper emboldened Lydia to repeat to him the conversation she had recently had with his wife.

'I fear I have done you a grave disservice, Mr Lorimer,' she said, after the coming of the Prince of Wales had been described. 'Mrs Lorimer may at this moment be designing for herself the hugest and most expensive bodice ornament that Bristol society will ever have seen. Nothing less than diamonds, I fear, will satisfy her.'

It seemed to Margaret, who knew her father better, a dangerous joke; and indeed there was a pause which, although short, was curiously intense. Then, without speaking at once, John Junius unlocked a drawer and took out a small casket which he set on the desk.

'Do you think Mrs Lorimer might be persuaded to forgo her diamonds for these?' he asked. He took the lid off the casket and tipped its contents out.

Margaret and Lydia held their breath together as the pile of red stones grew. They were of different sizes, but carefully matched as to colour. They had already been cut and polished, and even in the cold winter light they glowed with warmth.

'Rubies?' asked Margaret.

John Junius gave the short nod which meant that a question was not worth his answer.

'Pick them up,' he said. 'This is how a precious stone should be enjoyed. Set it in a necklace and it becomes lifeless in imprisonment. But let a dozen run through your fingers and you will understand why so many crimes are committed for what are only piles of stones.'

Margaret did as he said, allowing the rubies to dribble between her fingers back on to the desk. Without speaking, Lydia followed her example. Taking a sign from her father as an instruction, Margaret spared his stiffer fingers the task of returning the stones to the casket.

'I had intended to surprise Mrs Lorimer with the finished piece,' John Junius said. 'I have the design ready, and have already instructed the jeweller to collect small diamonds in which these larger stones may be set. But it seems I must reveal my intentions at once, before either disappointment or the desire for some other stone bites too deeply.'

'You knew already then, Papa, about the Prince's visit?'

'I had been informed, yes. Miss Morton is correct in assuming that there will be a ball on the eve of the exhibition. Will you tell Mrs Lorimer that I will wait on her in five minutes' time. And I hope, Miss Morton, that your stay with us will be a pleasant one.'

The excitement of seeing the rubies had driven the matter of the jade out of Margaret's mind, but she remembered it just as she reached the door, and turned back to enquire.

'The squirrel in which I take such pleasure is missing from its case, Papa,' she said. 'I hope there has been no accident.'

For the second time within a few minutes her father appeared to be taken aback; but again he recovered himself quickly.

'You are very quick in observation, Margaret,' he said. 'The squirrel, and some other of the more valuable pieces, were removed only yesterday. On Friday there was a meeting of the Board of Directors at Lorimer's. In the moment of social conversation which preceded it, Mr Eddison mentioned that his house had received the attention of robbers on the previous evening; and this prompted Mr Crankshaw to remark that his closest neighbours had suffered in the same way within the week. My collection and its value is so well known in the city that I began to fear its presence here might invite a similar attention. I have therefore arranged for the most precious pieces to be stored in Lorimer's strong room until law and order can be preserved more efficiently. I have also ensured that a paragraph mentioning the transfer will appear tomorrow in the *Bristol Times and Mirror*. So we may hope that Brinsley House will no longer appear too tempting a target.'

'You seem to assume that all robbers can read, Mr Lorimer,' said Lydia, who had waited with her friend in the doorway. 'But we are assured, are we not, that all the products of the board schools are honest and industrious members of society. So must we not think that those who break into other people's houses have already shown their ingenuity by evading the fetters of education?'

It was amazing to Margaret that Lydia should dare to tease a man like her father, and even more astonishing that the lightness of her tone should arouse no disapproval. John Junius never laughed, but he nodded his head now in what was the equivalent of a smile.

'The rubies must also be of great value though, Papa,' said Margaret. 'And easier both to steal and to sell than carvings which could be recognized if they were to appear in any other collection.'

'The presence of the rubies in the house is not known to anyone outside it,' said John Junius. 'And they will leave it tomorrow, to be handed over to Parker so that the setting may be made. I think you may sleep easily enough in your beds tonight. And now, you were about to convey my message to your mother.'

They returned to Georgiana's room at once to do so. Marie-Claire, wearing her afternoon cap and lace apron, had just served a dish of hot chocolate to her mistress, with an extra saucer so that the pug might share it. On hearing the warning of John Junius's visit she made a show of tidying the room in preparation, although she was not prepared as a rule to save the housemaid a journey for even as small a chore as the plumping of a cushion. Inspired by her friend's light-heartedness, Margaret could not resist a tease.

'I advise you not to go too far from my mother, Marie-Claire,' she said. 'In six minutes' time she may well have need of her salts.'

The advice was unnecessary – the whole household knew that any word spoken in Mrs Lorimer's boudoir would be overheard by her lady's maid. Nevertheless, it enabled Margaret and her friend to laugh as helplessly as schoolgirls as they emerged from the overheated room.

94

'Wait for me just a moment in your own room, Lydia,' asked Margaret. 'I have one more message of my own to carry.'

She hurried to Ralph's room and found him sitting at his books, although his startled jump when she opened his door suggested that his mind had not been on his work.

'I gave you warning before of Papa's black mood,' she said. 'Have you had with him yet the interview you sought at that time?'

Ralph shook his head and his handsome face looked alarmed, as though she had guessed the subject he needed to discuss.

'Then I am come to tell you that I have not for many months seen Papa so generously disposed as he is at this moment. I ask only that if your request is likely to cloud the sunshine again for the rest of us, you should postpone it to the end of the day.'

If she had not already observed that her brother was under some strain, she could have discovered it now. He jumped up at her first words to go straight to their father's study, and then seized with relief on the excuse for a further postponement. Margaret did not wait to see what he would decide. She was anxious not to leave her friend alone for too long.

There was a great deal of news to be exchanged. Naturally the most important item came first. A locket containing the likeness of Lieutenant Gerald Chapman was produced and his virtues expounded in detail. His seat on a horse, his grace at a dance, the elegant curl of his moustaches, all were the finest that had been seen in Bath that season. He was handsome and brave. Now that the system of obtaining promotion by purchasing commissions had been abolished, he would be able to rise on his own merits to become a general in no time at all.

'Is it, then, your ambition to become a general's lady, Lydia?' laughed Margaret.

Until that moment Lydia had allowed Margaret to tease her and had joined in the laughter at her own expense, recognizing the over-exuberance of her enthusiasm. But the laughter faded from her face as she looked down at the locket cradled in her hand.

'My ambition has never been more than to find someone who would love me,' she said. 'I shall never have any fortune, because my father's estate is entailed; and I know well enough that I am not to be admired for my beauty. I have spent many hours weeping over the length of my nose and the sallowness of my complexion. But Mr Chapman thinks these things of no importance. For all I care, he may remain a lieutenant all his life, with nothing but his pay to live on, and I shall never cease to love him for loving me.'

The sincerity of her voice affected Margaret more than she dared admit. She knew and shared Lydia's feeling, and the temptation to reveal her secret was very strong. The two girls sat in silence. Margaret was yearning for David, and it was certain that Lydia was in the grip of a similar emotion.

Their thoughts were distracted in the end by the sound of a carriage pulling to a standstill outside the house. Margaret looked from the window and saw that it was drawn by William's chestnuts, not their own piebalds. She frowned to herself in surprise as she saw Sophie waiting to be handed down. Even within the family, this was a curious time for a call of which no warning had been given. As the coachman hurried to ring the doorbell, Margaret could see that her sister-in-law was in a fury. What could have happened at The Ivies to cause Sophie's usually placid face to frown so angrily and her foot to tap with such impatience?

7

More powerful than any magnet is the possibility of discovering a scandal in one's own family. Margaret made her voice sound casual as she proposed to Lydia that they should move downstairs, but it was curiosity which drew her. They passed Nathaniel, one of the footmen, as they reached the gallery. He had just discovered that his master was not in the library and was now on his way to the boudoir to announce Sophie's arrival.

She had brought the nursery governess with her. Claudine was standing in a corner of the hall, shivering with cold because she wore no coat.

'Is Matthew here?' Margaret hoped for a chance to show her young nephew off to Lydia. Claudine shook her head, as though she could not decide which language to use and would therefore attempt neither.

Sophie herself, standing in the family drawing room, was equally uncommunicative. She had something to say to her father-in-law, she told Margaret with a brevity which was a deliberate snub. Margaret heard her father's heavy steps coming down the stairs – she had noticed that he was moving more slowly in the past few months. He glanced into the drawing room, but went first into the library, no doubt because he wished to dispose of the casket of jewels he carried before receiving a visitor.

Sophie heard the sound of the closing door.

'My conversation is private,' she told Margaret rudely, and swept into the library. Margaret waited to hear an explosion of wrath. But it seemed that the intrusion of a daughter-in-law, even without proper announcement, could be tolerated for just long enough for her to explain her business. No sound, in fact, penetrated the heavy door for almost ten minutes. When the explosion did come, it was not directed against Sophie.

John Junius flung open the library door and strode into the hall. His face was purple with anger.

'Ralph!' he roared. He caught sight of Ransome, the butler. 'Inform Master Ralph that he is to attend on me in the study at the instant. And hurry.'

It was beneath Ransome's dignity to hurry, or even to run his own errands. But beneath his master's furious eye he went up the stairs with an appearance of bustle. The library door slammed as John Junius disappeared inside again.

Ralph's face was white with fear as he came running down the stairs, but the sight of Claudine standing in the corner provided a final shock. He checked his run so abruptly on the bottom step that he was forced to put out a hand to steady himself. Claudine took a step towards him. She spoke to him in French, pronouncing the words clearly and slowly so that they could be understood by a boy whose aptitude for the language was not great. This enabled Margaret also to understand her, even at a greater distance.

'I am sorry,' Claudine said. 'Madame's suspicions were of her own husband. It was necessary to tell the truth.'

Ralph's answer was also in French, but his face was turned away from the drawing room and he mumbled the words, so that Margaret was unable to hear what he said. She noticed only that Claudine's face, which had been unhappy at first and then compassionate at the sight of Ralph, brightened briefly.

Margaret looked steadily at Claudine. She had always been a sturdy girl, and very often had Matthew clasped in her arms, so it was perhaps not surprising that an occasional visitor should not have become aware of her condition until this moment.

Margaret was tempted to remain as an audience, watching at least the comings and goings of the protagonists in the drama, but she could see that it should be kept private even from her best friend. She closed the drawing-room doors and proposed a game of backgammon.

Later that evening Margaret was summoned to the library. Ralph had not appeared for supper, but his mother – who had clearly not yet been informed of the day's later events – was in such high good humour on the subject of balls and rubies that she not only took her meal in her husband's company but after it showed herself delighted to chat with Lydia. Margaret could see that her own absence would make it possible for the virtues of Mr Chapman to be rehearsed yet again to a new audience, so she did not feel that she was being inhospitable in abandoning her guest.

John Junius, having ordered her presence, appeared not to know what to say. He turned his hand in the direction of a chair and she sat down. The silence extended itself for some time.

'Did you wish to speak to me about the events of this afternoon, Papa?' Margaret ventured at last. It had occurred to her that he might be wondering whether an unmarried girl could be expected to understand the situation; and this thought might not have struck him until after he had sent for her. 'I could hardly help observing something of what was happening. I believe I understand what the position may be.'

'Are you trying to tell me that you knew what was going on and said nothing?' he thundered, revealing that his anger still lay near the surface. Margaret hastened to reassure him.

'Not at all, Papa. I knew nothing until today. If I had discovered anything, I would have told you, for Ralph's own sake. It is merely that I had the opportunity to observe Claudine. The rest is all a guess.'

99

It seemed to come as a relief to him that he could share the secret without needing to put it into words. But he was still angry. There were mutterings about French hussies, which made Margaret wonder whether Claudine's nationality was in his eyes her most grievous sin. Slowly he came to what appeared to be the focus of his wrath.

'I refused to promise you a settlement on the occasion of your marriage,' he said abruptly. 'Yet although in the past you may have been headstrong and disobedient, you have at least done nothing to shame your family. And now I have to give money to this slut. You have been honest, even when your wishes have not matched mine. But this money has been forced from me by deceit and depravity. I pay it only in order that my family shall not be disgraced and that my grandchild may not starve. A French grandchild!' He considered the prospect as though it were the unkindest cut of all. 'At least I shall never see it. The girl will return to France tomorrow. It is a condition of what I give her that she shall never return to England or make contact with any member of the family.'

There was another long silence.

'I cannot give less to my daughter than I have given to a stranger,' he continued at last. 'I happened recently to discuss with Mr Trinder the affairs of your fund.' Mr Trinder was the new accountant at Lorimer's, who had taken over David Gregson's role as the charity's treasurer in addition to his bank duties. 'He showed me the particulars of the property you have just acquired.'

'Yes, Papa.' Margaret found it difficult to follow the connection between the subjects they were discussing.

'There is a dower house on the estate, I understand.'

'Lower Croft. Yes. It is small, but conveniently arranged. Mr Gregson and I considered . . .'

'Would you like it?' interrupted her father.

'I?'

'It appears to me that the other buildings on the estate

100

are quite sufficient for the women and children you wish to help. They may profit from the good air of the parkland without requiring to exercise themselves in more than a small portion of it. It occurred to me that you might care to live in the dower house. I assume that there will be a housekeeper or other responsible person in Croft House to take responsibility for the care of the inmates. But I have had the opportunity to observe that your interest in the project is a serious one. Although you are very young, I think it likely that you could prove yourself as competent to oversee the general running of the establishment as any paid supervisor. If this proposal is of interest to you, I will buy Lower Croft from the fund, with some acres around to preserve its privacy.'

'Papa!' At first it was astonishment which robbed Margaret of speech. Afterward, it was the need to control the tears which ridiculously threatened to flood her eyes.

'You've had presents before without crying over them,' said her father gruffly.

Margaret gave an unladylike sniff.

'It's not only the gift, Papa, though indeed I am grateful for that. It's just that – oh, Papa, I thought that no one would ever understand!'

Even as she flung herself into his arms it occurred to her that such a confused statement was not itself much help to understanding. But that was of no importance for the moment. What mattered more was that for the first time for years her father was allowing her to embrace him, accepting the affection which she had never been encouraged to show. The moment was a brief one, and she was careful not to prolong her gesture past his tolerance of it. Returning to her own chair, she dabbed at her eyes.

'I understand that you are my daughter,' said John Junius. 'And a worthier representative of the Lorimer Line than your younger brother. I understand also that you see yourself as a member of a family which has received many

101

privileges from society. It is natural that you should wish to give something in return to those less privileged. In the past I have found some of your proposals unsuitable for a woman. But though I may have refused your requests, I am able to appreciate your motives.'

It was the end of a softness not normal to his voice. When he spoke again, it was in a more businesslike manner.

'When I have purchased Lower Croft I shall make it over to you directly, as a gift for your twenty-first birthday,' he said. 'There is nothing to be gained by putting it into a settlement, for Mr Gregson has nothing with which he can match it. If you marry Mr Gregson, he will have the advantage of it. If you do not marry him, it will still be yours.'

Not since the moment when they declared their love had Margaret considered the possibility that she would not marry David Gregson. She looked up at her father in sudden alarm. He seemed to read her anxiety.

'I am not bribing you to withdraw from your understanding with Mr Gregson,' he said. 'Nor am I insinuating any suspicion that he may wish to do so. Indeed, I am sure he will continue to see the marriage as greatly to his advantage.' His eyelids hooded his eyes briefly, in a movement which Margaret had learned to recognize as signifying the end of an interview. 'I shall retire directly to bed now. Give my apologies to Miss Morton.'

'Good night, Papa. And thank you.'

John Junius nodded. On this occasion he accepted her kiss in his usual manner, without any hint of the emotion which he had briefly allowed to show.

Later that evening, after she had assured herself that Lydia was provided with everything she could want for the night, Margaret went along the corridor to her brother's room. Her relationship with Ralph had been a loving one ever since he had been placed, as a baby, in her three-year-old arms. William had quarrelled incessantly with his sister, but she had always felt a protective affection for her younger brother and could guess the misery he was enduring now. She found him on his knees beside his bed. From the stiffness with which he rose to his feet as she entered, she realized that he had been in this position for a considerable time.

'I know what has happened,' she told him. 'And I know that Papa is deeply grieved. But his anger will not last for ever, Ralph. I have angered him myself many times, but he has shown himself generous in forgiveness.'

'I am unworthy of forgiveness,' said Ralph. 'Father is right to be angry. I have been wicked, and I deserve more punishment than he can give me.'

'You ought not to blame yourself entirely. I hardly imagine that you pressed your attention on Claudine by force.' Margaret offered this consolation out of kindness, for she knew in her heart that even when there was no physical compulsion it was difficult for a servant to evade the attentions of the son or master of the household. Claudine's situation was not a unique one. Most of the well-brought-up young ladies of Bristol society could have produced a memory of some young maid who had left their family's service in a hurry.

'Oh, no!' Ralph was horrified at the suggestion. 'It was an accident. You remember that Sophie sent Claudine here with Matthew, just before Beatrice was born. I had started French lessons at school, and found them difficult. I asked Claudine to help me. I meant only help with the French language, but she misunderstood me. She said she would give me a lesson after Matthew was asleep, and when I went . . .'

Margaret put a hand on his arm to interrupt him. Her sympathy did not extend to a wish for details.

'It sounds as though you are very little to blame. Papa will understand that later. It's natural that he should be shocked at first. You should not reproach yourself too much.'

'I have sinned in the eyes of God and the world,' said Ralph. He flung himself back on to his knees again and buried his head in his hands. Margaret could hear him muttering the words of contrition. And perhaps, she thought, it was right that he should not forgive himself too soon. She went quietly back to her own bedroom.

Early the next morning she was awakened by the sound of a door closing and of footsteps hurrying along the corridor. Her first thought was of the thieves whose presence in the city her father had mentioned the previous day. She sat up in bed with her heart beating loudly enough, it seemed, to be heard by any intruder. There was a moment in which she felt too frightened to move, but something must be done. The servants slept on a higher floor, and her father's room was in the other wing of the house, on the far side of the staircase. Ralph was her nearest protector. She covered herself with a wrap and went to rouse him.

To her surprise, his room was empty. But the sheets of his bed were still warm, and when she put her finger to the glass of his lamp she was forced to jerk it quickly away to avoid a burn. It was clear that he had only just left, and that almost certainly his were the footsteps she had heard.

Margaret frowned to herself as she went back to her bedroom. Had Ralph's guilty conscience driven him to run away from home? She could think of nowhere he could go. Both his parents had been only children, so there were no aunts or cousins to offer refuge, and Sophie would take pleasure in turning him away. He was not fitted to earn his own living in any way. But even as she assured herself of this, Margaret stiffened with fear. Any able-bodied man could find employment on the sailing ships of the Lorimer Line – and even some who did not seek it had been known to find themselves waking to the sound of a creaking mast on the morning after a heavy evening's drinking. There were few who willingly undertook the rigours of a voyage round the Horn.

Margaret gave the thought her serious consideration. No ship could leave the Bristol docks until the tide from the estuary filled the river. From the last occasion when she had noticed high water she calculated that Ralph could not escape in that particular manner before eleven o'clock. No other decision on his part would be irreversible in quite the same manner, for her brother would surely not seek to escape from the guilt of one sin by the far greater one of taking his own life. She told herself that even her earlier thought was perhaps too drastic. Ralph had suffered a sleepless night, no doubt, and was refreshing an aching head with an early walk on the Clifton Downs.

Her conclusion seemed to be confirmed by the later discovery that Ralph had returned to the house. She met him, in fact, just as he was leaving for school: his face was as pale as usual, but his expression was calmer than on the previous day and he gave no indication that he had already been awake for several hours. Margaret respected his silence and was glad to abandon her own fears.

Dr Scott arrived for his regular visit to Mrs Lorimer just as Ralph was leaving, and Margaret accompanied him up the stairs. It gave her the chance to voice a second anxiety which had invaded her mind after Ralph's departure had woken her.

'How do you find my father's health?' she asked in what she hoped was a casual tone of voice.

Dr Scott gave the jovial laugh which was his chief contribution to the health of his patients.

'How should I know anything about your father's health?' he asked. 'It is so good that I am never allowed to approach him. A man of most remarkable constitution. Even age seems unable to attack him.'

'I thought yesterday he appeared a little tired,' said

Margaret hesitantly. Dr Scott gave her a quick look, but did not change the tone of his voice.

'Not letting all those rumours upset him, I hope,' he said. 'Nothing in them, I'm sure. Difficult times, though; difficult times.'

'What rumours?' asked Margaret.

'Nothing for you to worry your pretty little head about.'

If he had intended to annoy her, he could have thought of no better phrase. Margaret left him at the door of her mother's room without pressing the conversation further. She forgot the mention of the rumours at once, because she had not in fact been telling the truth when she claimed that John Junius looked tired. Her questions had been prompted by the suspicion that her father's sudden generosity to both her mother and herself might mean that something had prompted in him the thought that he would not live for ever. For a second time in a few hours she was able to dismiss a problem which had never existed outside her own imagination. It was a good start to the day and the morning sparkled with sunshine. It seemed that Spring at last was on the way.

8

The promises of princes are often warped by expediency, but the word of a banker must be his bond, for reputation is the tool of his trade. The proposals made by John Junius Lorimer to David Gregson in the January of 1878 had been unequivocal. If David – lonely in London during those three cold months – sometimes asked himself whether there was any means whereby those promises could without dishonour be left unfulfilled, it was more out of astonishment at his own prospects of good fortune and respect for the known subtlety of his employer's mind, than because he had any good reason to fear disappointment. Margaret's constancy he trusted absolutely, and all the rest depended on that.

The thought sustained him through the dullness of his social life. The gentleman to whom John Junius had sent him for training invited him once for dinner, to eat plain food with his plain wife and two plain daughters. Apart from that one evening, his helpfulness was confined to business hours. Within the walls of the banking house David found it easy to grasp the practical advice he was given, but less easy to become intimate with the members of the staff, for his status was too uncertain. He was no longer an accountant, but not yet a manager, and no one seemed prepared to invest time in developing a friendship with a stranger whose stay would be so brief. He ate alone in chop-houses, entertained himself occasionally with visits to music halls, but spent most of his evenings studying the notes he had made during the day or writing to Margaret and reading her replies, which told him that he had not been forgotten.

Constantly he assured himself that there was no reason why John Junius should change his mind, yet the letter which summoned him back to Bristol came almost as a surprise as well as a relief. He was to take up his new duties as general manager of Lorimer's on May 1st, wrote John Junius. Mrs Lorimer would be pleased to receive him at Brinsley House on April 30th. It seemed that all his dreams were going to come true.

When the time came for his visit to Brinsley House, only a man too much in love to notice anyone other than his beloved could have deluded himself into thinking that Mrs Lorimer felt any pleasure at all in receiving him. Georgiana's off-hand sulkiness was that of a woman to whom an intolerable arrangement had been presented as a *fait accompli* and who was required actively to endorse it. But David still took at face value Georgiana's claim to invalid status and assumed her petulance to be caused by ill-health. All that mattered to him was the radiance on Margaret's face as she greeted him. While he had been away he had told himself over and over again that she loved him, but he had forgotten how it felt to be so obviously adored.

The only way in which Georgiana could express her ill-temper was by ensuring that David and Margaret would never be left alone together. A maid or a coachman had been sufficient company when she had been able to believe that the meetings of her daughter with the bank's account-ant were on matters of business only, but if the two young people were considering marriage, the rules of chaperonage must be invoked. Ralph and Sophie were allotted this responsibility between them and resented it equally.

'I have a surprise for you next Sunday,' Margaret whispered when they had exchanged all the news of their separation.

'Tell me now.'

'It has to be shown, not told. Keep the afternoon free. Ralph has promised to come with us.'

David wondered what it was, but his mind was too fully occupied in the days which followed to give the matter any thought. His return to Margaret had confirmed an existing relationship; but his return to the bank was the beginning of many new ones.

This was not an easy period. It was necessary for him to be less familiar with those members of the staff whom he had known before his promotion, and at the same time more at ease with the bank's customers, with whom he had previously had no direct contact. His time in London had been well spent, but nothing he had learned there could provide a short cut towards the assessment of each new proposition or request which was put to him. For this reason each day of his first week as manager left him tired and strained with the anxiety of taking no false steps. It was not until Friday, when the rest of the staff had gone home, that he felt able to spare the time to look back over the transactions which had taken place during his three-month absence.

What he found there appalled him. The bank's financial year had ended in early April. The annual accounts had been drawn up by John Trinder, his successor as accountant. They had been signed by Mr Lynch, and adopted by the board of directors as a true statement of the bank's situation. They bore no relationship at all to the state of affairs as David himself had left them.

It took him several hours of hard work to find out what had happened. By the time he went back to his lodgings that evening his eyes were swimming with strain and his head ached with anxiety. His first question the next morning concerned the previous manager. In as casual a way as possible he asked the chief clerk where Mr Lynch had gone. Even had he not been suspicious before, the answer would have raised doubts in his mind.

'Mr Lynch has left England for Boston. Mr Lorimer asked him to go, to open a new branch of Lorimer's. It was felt that many American gentlemen would find it a convenience to be able to use the same bank both in their own country and if they came to visit England.'

David made no comment on this. It was possible that it would indeed be a convenience for the American gentlemen, just as it was convenient for the chairman that the manager recently in charge of Lorimer's day-to-day running should be out of the country. It could hardly have been seen by Mr Lynch as a desirable promotion: he was fifty years old or more, and not a pioneering type of man. As soon as the chairman arrived in his office, David sent in a request to speak to him.

He was expected, of course. John Junius made no pretence of being surprised either by the visit or by the grim expression on David's face. Perhaps he had been amusing himself all week with speculations on how long it would take his new manager to appreciate the state of affairs.

'I would like to discuss the accounts for the financial year which has just ended,' said David. He set down on the wide mahogany desk the papers on which he had done his own calculations.

'Yes.' It was not a statement, not a question: merely a gesture of permission to proceed.

'I will start by raising one point which in any other year would seem to be of major importance, although in the context of these accounts it seems a small amount. I observe that thirty thousand pounds have been lent to further Mr Crankshaw's development of the new docks at Portishead. His company is already deeply indebted to us, and it appears that he was unable to offer any security for this new loan.'

'You have been away from Bristol and are no doubt out of touch with local events,' said the chairman. His voice was patient, as though accepting that the matter was a fair one to raise. 'You will recall that the new docks were due to open this summer. Unfortunately, in the middle of March there was a collapse of one of the main walls. The money to rebuild it must be raised from somewhere, and there are few individuals in the present state of society who could be approached for such a sum. Since Lorimer's would have more to lose than any other institution if the whole project were to be abandoned for the lack of a comparatively small sum, the directors felt it essential to increase the loan by this amount. Although no new security could be offered, the docks themselves, when they are completed, will be their own guarantee.'

'But the completion date has presumably been delayed.'

'Unfortunately, yes. However, the docks are expected to open in the Spring of next year.'

David did not press that point further. It was a trivial one compared to his main complaint.

'During my absence,' he said, choosing his words carefully, 'there appear to have been substantial changes in some of the major items in the balance sheet. I have been unable to find any justification for these. Perhaps there have been other developments of which I am not aware.'

'Perhaps,' said John Junius. 'If you will specify the points you have in mind, I shall no doubt be able to elucidate them.'

It was a complicated situation which David had discovered, in that part of the bank's dealings which concerned its loans to local companies. The securities – mainly property – which had been offered to guarantee the loans had been frequently revalued upwards in the years succeeding the original arrangements. This had no doubt been justifiable in the early days but, as David himself had pointed out almost a year before, the values had been falling again since 1875; and in addition some of the companies which had borrowed on them had been equally affected by the economic situation and were no longer stable.

David had advised earlier that the securities should be revalued in the balance sheet, and this had now been done to such good purpose that four million pounds had been cut from the statement of the bank's assets. In a sense this was a proper action, if somewhat abrupt, and one which he had attempted from his junior situation to recommend. But it should have revealed a deficit in the accounts. Instead of this the books were still balanced. He did his best to explain his uneasiness on this point.

'You do not deny that you yourself thought various properties to be over-valued,' said John Junius.

'I do not. But as well as writing down the inflated assets, you have written down the loans which were made on the strength of them. You have cut four million pounds off the

111

debit side to match the missing four million pounds of assets.'

'Any prudent business must write off a bad debt,' said John Junius.

'Any prudent shareholder may expect that by examining the accounts he may see that four million pounds have been written off,' David pointed out. 'In this case the loss has been concealed by balancing real loans against paper securities, values which never in truth existed. The shareholders will be reassured in a situation which should not be reassuring at all.'

'And what alternative do you suggest, Mr Gregson? The total money which we hold on behalf of our depositors – in other words, which we owe to them – is, as you have doubtless discovered in the course of your researches, in the region of five million pounds. If your prudent shareholder were to observe that the loans made by the bank are covered mainly by the amount held on deposit, your prudent depositor might be able to come to the same conclusion, especially as he is in many cases the same person. If he should seek to withdraw his deposit, and if his fellow-depositors should make the same decision at the same moment, the bank would be forced to call in its loans and overdrafts. You know as well as I do, Mr Gregson, that this would cause the ruin of several companies which are in fact likely to become highly profitable from the moment they complete their capital equipment and begin to earn with it. These are local companies and employ labour on a large scale. Their collapse would cause unemployment amongst the poorest members of the community. There would be no possibility then of full repayment of the loans, so at the same moment the collapse of the bank would cause suffering to the wealthier classes as well. We are talking about the ruin of a city, Mr Gregson.'

'We are talking, sir, about the fraudulent concealment of the true state of affairs in this bank.'

'I must remind you that we have had this conversation before, although then we discussed fewer details. The situation has not changed since then, except in one way. Because the unfortunate accident at Portishead is widely known, the need to maintain confidence has grown greater. It is only for a limited period of time that some subterfuge is needed. From the moment the Portishead docks open next Spring we may expect Crankshaws to pay off their debt from the profits of their berthing fees. I have already discussed with Mr Crankshaw a suggested timetable for this. His repayments will be on such a scale as to restore liquidity almost overnight. In addition to this, the new ship of the Lorimer Line is almost completed and will be ready for its sea trials in a few weeks. Mr William Lorimer has agreed that payment of interest on his loan, which was suspended during a difficult period, will be resumed from the moment the first voyage is completed. We are speaking of a period of a very few months only.'

'A crime is no less a crime for being brief in its operation.'

'A crime, Mr Gregson!' John Junius in anger was not an easy man to face. Only because David felt sure of himself could he stand his ground without trembling. 'If the small people of Bristol were to lose the five million pounds they have deposited with Lorimer's Bank, would that not be a crime? If the shareholders of the bank were to be asked to pay those five million pounds out of their own pockets, would that not be a crime? I have already referred to the possibilities of bankruptcies amongst our debtors. If you were to force this state of affairs on an innocent community for the sake of your own conscience it would be my opinion that you, Mr Gregson, would be the criminal.' He paused, perhaps feeling that he had gone too far. 'You may even consider, on reflection, that this is none of your business. You were not the accountant who prepared the annual accounts. You were not the manager who signed them. You were not a member of the board which adopted them.'

113

David had no answer to this. His first thought had been that he had been sent to London in order that he should not know what was going on. It was just possible, he supposed, that he had been kept out of the way in order that he should bear no responsibility for what he still regarded as a fraudulent manipulation of the figures. The chairman might have been acting in the best interests of his future son-in-law as far as this detail was concerned, just as he claimed to be acting in the interest of the whole community in the larger matter. But David's anxieties were not yet altogether allayed.

'If the future prospects of the bank are as good as you have told me, would it not have maintained public confidence sufficiently if the board had made a full statement of the facts?'

'The matter could certainly have been dealt with in that way. But there are always a few people who feel doubt for the first time when they hear that there is an answer to the questions they had not previously thought to ask. A far simpler way, although less direct, is to indicate the board's own confidence in the state of affairs by maintaining the dividend. The directors will be asked, in fact, to raise it to twelve per cent.'

'And you would expect my signature on that recommendation?'

'I hope that I have by now convinced you of the value of such a move,' said John Junius.

'I see.' David saw perfectly. By now he had discovered all he could hope to know about the situation. The chairman had stated a case and all that David himself could do was to decide whether or not to accept it. There was no possibility of persuading John Junius to change his mind by argument. 'I feel sure you will appreciate, Mr Lorimer, that I need a little time to consider my position.'

'Consider your position by all means, Mr Gregson. But if, having considered it, you find that you dislike it, I trust

114

you will have the good sense to remove yourself both from Lorimer's and from Bristol. The information you have acquired has been made available to you on a strictly confidential basis and in anticipation of your future status as a member of my family.' Unexpectedly he smiled. 'But if I did not trust your good sense and your financial ability, this situation would not have arisen in the first place. I feel sure that upon reflection you will consider that everything has been done for the best. I shall look forward to discussing the matter further with you on Monday.'

It was an ultimatum as well as a temporary dismissal, and not one to be taken lightly. David was thoughtful as he returned to his own desk.

But before Monday came, there was Sunday to be enjoyed. Margaret had promised to reveal her surprise on that day. She came down herself, accompanied by Ralph, to collect him in the carriage, and he noticed the excitement in her bearing at once. Perhaps her dress had a little to do with it, for instead of the demure bonnets or fur-trimmed hoods which she had worn on their previous outdoor expeditions she was wearing a jaunty hat perched on the top of her head with a cascade of feathers falling to the back. It did not precisely suit her, but it gave an impression of independence which aroused his curiosity about the purpose of their meeting.

When David found himself being driven up the long drive of the Croft House estate he assumed it was because the first beneficiaries of the Gentlewomen's Aid Fund were already in residence, and he prepared to express admiration of the speed with which the charity had acted. He was surprised, however, to be taken directly to Lower Croft, and even more startled by the style in which it had been redecorated since his last visit, and by the richness of its curtains and carpets; no other furniture had yet been installed.

'I feel it is just as well that I am no longer your

115

treasurer,' he said laughingly. 'I could hardly approve of such lavishness. Do you think that such good quality furnishings were strictly necessary?'

'If they were for yourself, would you approve them?' asked Margaret, laughing in her turn as she hung on his arm.

'Even for myself I would think them too luxurious,' David said. 'Although certainly I would covet them, for they are exactly to my taste.' He noticed that even Ralph, who had embarked on his duties as a chaperon with considerable sulkiness, was smiling. David looked from one Lorimer to the other for an explanation of the joke.

'Everything was chosen in the hope that it would be to your liking,' said Ralph. 'Margaret has been driving us all to distraction in these past weeks. "Do you think he will like that? Will he find this too bright, or too subdued?" As though we could guess if she could not.'

'Papa has given me the house,' said Margaret. 'It is to be our home.'

David looked round again, seeing the room this time through different eyes. They were standing at this moment in the smallest of Lower Croft's three reception rooms. It was panelled in oak and Margaret had provided it with a red Turkey carpet and curtains of red and cream brocade. The effect was warm and comfortable; it would make a most desirable study.

'Your father has acted very generously,' he said.

'You should not sound as though this surprised you,' said Margaret, teasing him a little.

'You have to remember that I know him only as a man of business, not as a father.'

'Yes, of course. I hope that soon you will come to know him and love him as I do. He is the kindest of men, and the most generous. You should see the jewels which he has given to my mother! And his purchase of Lower Croft is a kindness in more than one way, for our charity gains by the price. The house would not have been of direct use, but the money paid for it has helped us to furnish the larger premises completely. The first three women are already living in Croft House, and their seven children are in the old stable.'

David was less interested in the affairs of the charity than in the fact that Lower Croft was to be the home which he would share with Margaret. He asked to go all over the house again, so that he could look at it in this new light, and persuaded Ralph to explore the garden instead of accompanying them. This gave him his first opportunity to kiss Margaret since the engagement had been approved. It seemed right that this should happen in the place where he had first dared to declare his love. Lower Croft, it seemed, was destined to play a very happy part in his life.

Nevertheless, his contentment was invaded by doubt as he looked into one room after another. He found himself counting the fireplaces which would need to be supplied with coals, the stairs up which hot water would have to be carried. They would need to employ servants. Even a young maid would expect £10 a year: a cook would require £30. He found himself calculating what minimum would be required if Margaret were to live as the mistress of such a house should, and realized quickly that even on his new higher salary he could not support such an establishment himself.

John Junius would have come to that conclusion long ago. He had spoken of making a personal allowance to Margaret, and since he was the one responsible for the purchase of Lower Croft it seemed reasonable to wonder whether the allowance would be a more generous one than David had originally assumed. He frowned a little to himself. The picture of the loving and open-handed father which emerged more clearly with every day that passed did not, as Margaret had realized, square with his own impression of the chairman of Lorimer's. It was something

117

to be considered privately; but in the meantime Margaret had her own discovery to reveal.

'You did not tell me that you had succeeded Mr Lynch as the manager of Lorimer's.'

'I thought the news would come better from your father. To tell the truth, I hardly believed it could happen until I found myself sitting at Mr Lynch's desk.'

'My father must have an extremely high opinion of your abilities. I am pleased that he has come so quickly to share my own view.'

'I would like to think so,' said David. 'But I suspect that he has adopted your opinion out of affection for you. It's possible that if I had been completely incapable I should have been turned away both from you and from Lorimer's, but as it is I owe my promotion far more to you than to my merits as a manager.'

He was amused to see the uncertainty on Margaret's face.

'Is this right?' she asked. 'I see that it is convenient, but is it right?'

'Was it right that your brother William should be given charge of a great shipping line when he was barely out of school?' asked David in return. 'If you accept the right of a family to own a business, you must accept also its right to value the family as highly as the business in the running of it. No one would be foolish enough to destroy his own livelihood by entrusting it to someone, even a son, who was obviously incompetent. Whether or not it is right for a place in the banking profession to be filled by nepotism, I assure you that it is entirely usual. I am the manager of Lorimer's because the daughter of its chairman has agreed to marry me. The reason for my promotion does not worry me: my concern is to fill the post as though I had acquired it only on my own merits.'

'I am sure you will do so,' said Margaret.

'Already you are behaving like a loyal wife,' said David,

laughing, and kissed her again. They moved to a discussion of domestic details and were decorously considering the cost of installing gas lighting – for the house was thirty years old and had not been modernized – when Ralph returned to join them.

It was the need, a little later, to choose a place for Margaret's piano which reminded David of Luisa.

'Are you still seeing Miss Reni so frequently?' he asked Margaret.

She shook her head.

'She has left her lodgings, as I believe you already know. I received a note from her to say that she had obtained a residential situation in which the baby would be better cared for. She did not come to say goodbye; nor did she give me her address. I was disappointed that she should break off our friendship in such a way.'

'Well, I have another question to which I hope you can give me a happier answer,' said David. 'Is your father ready, do you think, to appoint a day for our marriage?'

As he had hoped, Margaret's face brightened at once.

'On July 13th the Prince of Wales is to come to Bristol,' she said. 'There will be a grand ball on the previous evening, and my parents will be giving one of the dinner parties before it. You are to be invited, and our engagement will be officially announced then.'

July seemed a long time to wait, and the wedding itself would not presumably be until several weeks later than that. But the choice of occasion suggested that the Lorimer family intended to put a good face on the situation instead of avoiding publicity for an unworthy alliance.

It was odd, David thought to himself when he was alone again in his lodgings that night, it was very odd how difficult he found it to take John Junius's actions at their face value. From the moment when Margaret had first mentioned her attachment, everything that the old man had said and done indicated that he accepted the situation not merely in a neutral way but with positive generosity. It was presumably only his reputation as a hard man of business which tempted David to examine every gift as though beneath the sugar coating might be concealed a dose of poison.

Such suspicions could not be allowed to continue. Now was the moment when once and for all David must decide whether John Junius Lorimer, both as chairman of the bank and as a future father-in-law, deserved to have his gifts taken at face value. David would have had no doubts as far as domestic generosities were concerned if he had not become so perturbed by the state of affairs at the bank. Had he been appointed manager as a mark of favour on being admitted to a family relationship? Or had the relationship been allowed to develop in order that the bank might have an excuse for appointing a manager who could be relied on to be complaisant, not asking too many questions? And now that the questions had been asked, could the answers be believed? He must make up his mind on this point, so that it need never trouble him again. It was all a matter of trust. The whole business of banking was a matter of trust. If David was to rise in the profession he must learn when to doubt and when to be convinced.

It all depended, as he realized after anxious consideration that evening, on whether the chairman's arguments could be believed. John Junius Lorimer was by far the largest shareholder in the bank. If it were to crash, he would find himself personally responsible for a high proportion of its debts. Lorimer's had been founded long before the limited liability acts had been passed by Parliament to protect shareholders, and had not changed its structure to take advantage of them. Rich though he was, a demand for three million pounds would certainly bankrupt him, and would leave his daughter destitute.

So it was true that the chairman was speaking out of self-interest, but his interests ran with those of all the other shareholders. If he succeeded in maintaining the necessary confidence in the bank's affairs until the end of the year, everyone else concerned would benefit as much as himself; he was not trying to preserve his own fortune at the expense of others. Indeed, the affair could be considered from an opposite aspect. As the man who knew most about the bank's dangerous situation, John Junius could quietly both have withdrawn his deposits and reduced his shareholding. David decided to stake his trust on that one point.

As soon as he arrived at his office the next morning he sent for a considerable number of ledgers, in order that no one should suspect whose account he wished to check, nor at what date. The chairman's deposit account showed a normal pattern of payments and receipts, except for one much larger withdrawal. David followed the transaction through and found that it represented the purchase of Lower Croft from the Gentlewomen's Aid Fund.

He considered the entry, but not for very long. A twenty-first birthday present for a daughter could be thought of as normal expenditure, although non-recurring. There was nothing else to suggest that cash was being removed and stored elsewhere.

The same situation showed itself as far as the chairman's large shareholding was concerned. Over a year before, he had sold a small block of shares to his family doctor, Dr Scott. But David remembered this transaction, and knew that it had been arranged as a favour to the doctor, at a time when an interest in the bank was much sought-after and difficult to procure. There had been no change since that date.

The situation was clear enough. The chairman of the bank, although recognizing the dangers of the situation, was prepared to back with his own fortune his confidence that they could be averted. There was a risk involved, but David no longer felt justified in regarding it as a crime. He wondered briefly whether he had allowed his judgement to

121

be clouded by the memory of Margaret's face as she greeted him on his return from London, or as she showed him the home which they would share together. But he was able to assure himself that the figures spoke for themselves. For a second time he sought an interview with the chairman.

Inside the large office, he apologized for the sentiments he had expressed at their previous meeting – apologized more fulsomely than was strictly necessary, for he intended to use the occasion to take one small step in the direction of greater solvency.

'So I would like to assure you of my complete confidence in your handling of the situation,' he concluded. John Junius gave the brief nod that he had come to know well.

'I am very glad to hear it. My daughter will also be glad that your stay here is not to come to an untimely end.'

'There is, however, one point which I would like to press.'

'Yes?'

'I hope you will not think me impertinent if I refer to the case of your son, Mr William Lorimer. He owns a considerable personal shareholding in the bank, from which he receives a substantial income. Yet the Lorimer Line has paid no interest on its loan for the past four years. You spoke of a resumption of payments in the new year, but there is no provision for the arrears to be paid off. At the moment we are relying almost wholly on new deposits to preserve our liquidity. I would like to suggest . . .'

When it came to the point, he was not sure what he dared to suggest. But John Junius reacted with none of the coldness which he had expected.

'It would do my son no harm to be reminded of the principles on which a profitable business should be conducted. You have my permission to approach him directly with any proposals which you would suggest if he were not related to me. Subject to the proviso that he should not be pressed to take any steps damaging to the long-term interest

122

of the Lorimer Line. In the interests of family harmony, I would prefer you not to tell me what you suggest. I have no doubt I shall hear soon enough from him if your behaviour is thought to be intolerable.'

'Thank you, sir.'

'And that is all, Mr Gregson? Then I will express my hope that our association may be a long and successful one.'

To David's amazement, he found that he was being invited to shake hands. It was typical of the old man, that he should behave in almost every respect like a tyrant and yet be able by a brief relaxation of his intransigence to evoke something very near to affection. David could not have claimed that he understood Margaret's father, but he was beginning to like him.

9

Anti-climax is an inevitable ingredient of any supreme occasion. The eye of a great personage will rest for only a fraction of a second on some effect to which hours of preparation have been devoted. But once the prospect of a royal procession has set its own hysteria in motion, only the most cynical citizen is capable of announcing that he will treat the day as though it were as drab as any other. As the date approached on which the Prince of Wales was to visit Bristol, the city was transformed by pennons and streamers. Triumphal arches were erected over all the principal streets, some in Tudor style and some in Gothic. Venetian masts and flags sprang up in a forest of festivity and every tradesman competed with his neighbours in adorning his premises with flowers and flags.

Long before these decorations appeared, to the excitement of the general mass of the citizens, the fashionable society of Bristol was plunged into a whirl of activity. By the middle of June there was hardly a yard of silk or an inch of lace still to be found in the city. Glovemakers and bootmakers were forced to turn away the business of all but their most valued customers if their orders were to be completed in time, and dressmakers scoured the streets for young girls with fingers quick and clean enough to sew beads on to satins. Bosom friendships ended in tears when it was discovered that a dinner invitation had been refused in the hope that some grander offer might arrive, or that a cook had been enticed from one kitchen to another.

The Lorimers were not immune from the general flurry. John Junius himself was required to approve the list of guests for the dinner to be held at Brinsley House before the ball and to discuss the protocol of their seating. Georgiana, in her boudoir, received a stream of visitors. The cook came several times to discuss the menu and even the head gardener was summoned inside the house to confirm that he could provide all the flowers needed for the elaborate arrangements which his mistress had in mind. The corset-maker was received in private session, and as soon as her work was done it was followed by a series of fittings for a new gown.

Margaret was also required to be available for fittings, although not until a dispute between her mother and herself had been resolved. Georgiana considered that a young woman announcing her engagement should wear white. Margaret knew that the colour did not suit her freckled skin and argued that no convention existed to require it. Her determination won the day. She was allowed to choose a silk of emerald green shot with turquoise. The dress left her shoulders bare, with only a short cuffed sleeve at the top of her arm, and the embroidered neckline was cut straight and low. On the evening of the ball Betty dressed her long hair in a way which she had already practised under the guidance of Marie-Claire. Part of it was swept up to the top of Margaret's head and fastened in place by a pair of emerald-tipped pins lent by her mother: the rest was brushed to fall in a long wavy tail down the back of her neck. For the first time in her life, it seemed to Margaret as Betty held up the glass for her to see, she looked almost pretty. But perhaps it was only the happiness in her eyes which deceived her into thinking so.

Georgiana had not discussed her own gown with anyone. To set off the jewels which her husband had given her, she had chosen a creamy white fabric, decorated at the neck and all over the skirt with tiers of black silk tasselling. For a good many years she had been too plump to be beautiful, but her skin was good, and on the night of the ball she revealed it generously. Pale and smooth, it formed a perfect background for a necklace which caused even Margaret, who had seen the original stones, to gasp with wonder at its magnificence.

The craftsman had done his work with all the skill expected of Parker's of Bristol, jewellers to generations of merchant venturers. The centrepiece was a pendant in the form of a rose. A single large ruby was surrounded by others cut to the shape of petals, each set in silver and surrounded by tiny diamonds. Other rubies, similarly set, were joined to form the rest of the necklace; and the rose motif, on a smaller scale, was repeated in the rich drop ear-rings. Georgiana's hair was dressed high behind a matching tiara, and there in the centre glittered another rose fashioned from the deep red rubies. This rose was surrounded by leaves outlined in tiny diamonds and mounted on springs to form tremblers.

For her dinner party – although at this hour of a summer evening it was still light – Georgiana had ordered the lighting of hundreds of candles in the Venetian chandeliers used in the great dining room before John Junius had installed gas lighting in Brinsley House. Their flickering lights danced in Georgiana's hair and round her neck. As

125

they waited for their guests to arrive, Margaret kissed her mother in impulsive admiration and John Junius nodded his approval.

David came early, as he had been instructed. So did Sophie and William – both in a bad mood. William's bow to his future brother-in-law was abrupt and hardly civil.

'Take no notice of William's brusqueness,' whispered Margaret, drawing David a little to one side in the pause before the guests from outside the family arrived. 'He is worried because Sophie is unwell.' It would be indelicate, she felt, to go into more detail about her sister-in-law's condition. But all the family knew that Sophie had not wished to find herself pregnant again so soon after Beatrice's arrival, and particularly not on an occasion like this. She would have preferred to wear a more elegant gown and be able to dance until morning.

David shook his head.

'I fear I am responsible for your brother's black looks,' he said. 'He is not best pleased with me for my way of conducting the bank's business.'

'Why, what have you done?'

'I made a suggestion to him a few weeks ago. Instead of adopting it, he chose to dispose of his shareholding in the bank. I suspect that he acted in a fit of bad temper caused by what he saw as my impertinence, and now perhaps he regrets his action. I trust he will not allow his annoyance to spoil the evening.'

'William and I have never been close,' Margaret reassured him. 'If there is to be any dispute between my brother and my husband, you need not doubt where my support will lie.'

She squeezed his arm, but their conversation was interrupted by the approach of another carriage. Ransome moved across the hall to the front door and David stepped a little to one side, as befitted someone whose presence had yet to be explained. Margaret stood beside her parents to receive their guests.

John Junius had invited the most substantial of his friends to make up his table before the ball. They were all rich, and tonight their riches were on display. Not for many years had even the great dining room at Brinsley House sparkled so extravagantly with so many dazzling bodice and hair ornaments, so many pearl studs and diamond pins.

Georgiana outshone them all, and Margaret could tell that her parents had planned it and were proud of it. It was as though John Junius, for the first time in his daughter's memory, was making a deliberate public exhibition of his fortune. Never before had he behaved in such an ostentatious manner. On any other occasion Margaret might have paused to puzzle over something so uncharacteristic, but tonight she could think of little except David.

There was to be a late supper at the ball, so that the dinner could have been a simple one, but she noticed that the meal was unusually extravagant too. The first course was a clear turtle soup which she knew must have cost a guinea a quart. A dish of salmon was followed by an *entrée* of sweetbreads. Lamb had been chosen for the *relevé*; and then came *rôtis* of duckling and guinea fowl. Two savoury *entremets* followed, and three sweets. But the high point of the meal was undoubtedly reached when eight beautifully arranged dishes of fruit were carried in, for William had provided from a ship lately home from the West Indies, specimens of pineapple and papaya, melon and banana – so exotic that many of the guests had never tasted them before.

It was at the end of the meal that Margaret's great moment came. Her father arose to announce the engagement and propose a toast to the young couple. The secret had been well kept and Margaret could guess that her father's friends were startled. Back in their own homes they would no doubt speculate about the unknown young man, and perhaps express unkind surpise. But for the moment their host's own firm expression of pleasure was enough, at the end of such a good meal, to bring warmth to their congratulations. David, slim and handsome, was so very much the best-looking man there that Margaret could feel nothing but pride.

Since most of the guests were of the same age as their host and hostess, they were in no great hurry to move on to the ball. To be seen there at some point was all they wanted: they did not expect actually to dance. But for once John Junius seemed sensitive to the brightness of his daughter's eyes. This was to be Margaret's evening, and if she wished to dance, then dance she should. He cracked his fingers to hurry the servants, to such good effect that the Lorimer party arrived at the Assembly Rooms before the first quadrille was called.

They waited impatiently for the entrance of the Prince of Wales, who came at that moment, preceded by a fanfare of trumpets. He walked with dignity down a corridor formed by the other guests, an avenue of swaying ostrich plumes and dipping diamonds as the ladies in the front rank tried while curtseying both to drop their eyes demurely and to peep as the Prince passed them. He was reputed to be handsome, but Margaret found him already too stout for her taste. Her hand tightened on David's arm as they straightened themselves and watched as the mayoress, flushed with anxiety, allowed the city's royal guest to lead her on to the floor for the opening of the ball.

Margaret too found the excitement of the occasion almost too great to bear, but for a different reason. The ballroom, with its red velvet curtains and gilt pillars and chairs, was familiar to her, but never before had the air been so heavily scented with flowers. Never before, when the dancers had taken their places, had the bandsmen in their red jackets played with such sparkle and dash. It was not this,

128

however, which made her heart beat faster, but the ecstasy caused by the touch of her fiancé.

David danced extremely well. Now that she was openly acknowledged as his future wife, Margaret felt bold enough to express a teasing surprise.

'A month ago I would have disgraced you,' he confessed as they resumed their seats in one of the alcoves. 'But I chanced to encounter Miss Reni one day. Although her talent is for the piano, it occurred to me that she might be equally proficient in teaching the dance, or might at least recommend someone else who would do so.'

'And she taught you herself?'

'With great speed,' said David. 'It's not for me to claim that she was successful.'

'I thought that Luisa must have left Bristol, since I have heard nothing from her,' Margaret said. 'Where is she living now?'

David hesitated. For a second the jealousy which Margaret had first felt when she saw him with Luisa returned, but she quickly realized that the address was the cause of his embarrassment. It was a house in The Gazebo. Although situated in a good part of the city – in fact, not too far from Brinsley House itself – this was a terrace which suffered from the same reputation as the street from which she had once seen Walter Crankshaw emerge. As David mentioned the name, she could see that he was wondering whether she would guess its significance.

'With a baby to care for, I suppose it is necessary for her to have a protector,' she said. It was not a sentiment which her mother would have approved, and Margaret herself could not help being a little shocked, but she did her best to keep the doubt from her voice.

David seemed relieved at the quickness of her understanding that Luisa must have become a kept woman.

'I hope I don't need to assure you that the protector is not myself,' he said, smiling. 'And now, may I be allowed

129

to fill in my share of your programme? My lack of time for practice means that I have not yet mastered the Highland Reel. I must leave that to one of your other admirers.'

'On the contrary, you must sit it out with me, or I shall be jealous to think of you sitting out with someone else.'

They laughed together as he wrote his name in her programme. Then they looked up in surprise. John Junius Lorimer and his wife were making what could only be called a progress down one side of the assembly hall.

'I have rarely seen my father so expansive in public,' Margaret said. 'As a rule he has little use for social occasions. And to tell you the truth, since you are to be a member of the family, he has little use for my mother's company. Or perhaps it is she who shuns him. Certainly they are not often seen together.'

'It would be wrong of me to criticize my employer and future father-in-law,' said David. 'But my impression is that he keeps company not so much with Mrs Lorimer as with her jewels. They are certainly most striking. They must be one of the most precious heirlooms of your family.'

'You are mistaken,' she told him. 'They are new. A gift for tonight. I suppose every family heirloom must make a first appearance, though.'

'New?' queried David.

Margaret wondered why he seemed so thoughtful.

'My mother often complains that she is given few opportunities to show herself in public as a rich man's wife. Is it so strange that my father should yield at last?'

'Your father is not a man who yields in anything,' said David, 'except for some reason of his own.' The thought seemed to disturb him. 'I suspect that he has some reason for his indulgence.'

'At least it appears to be achieving its effect,' Margaret pointed out. The Prince had begun to move informally amongst the guests, stopping from time to time so that the mayor might present those citizens most worthy of notice.

130

John Junius and Georgiana Lorimer were at this moment receiving such a mark of favour.

'I must take an early opportunity to ask Mrs Lorimer to dance,' said David when the Prince moved on. 'And I see your brother is coming over to you.'

Margaret watched him approach her parents. It was proper that Georgiana, still flushed with her moment of social triumph, should give him the dance; but unexpected that she should actually take the floor with him, especially as the next number was to be a Galop. William, who had joined Margaret, noted the fact with disapproval.

'Mama exerts herself too much tonight,' he said. 'Already after dinner I thought her colour was high.'

'With excitement rather than effort, surely,' suggested Margaret. She saw David bow as the vigorous dance ended, leaving Georgiana fanning herself in a manner which bore out her son's opinion, and then retiring to the coolness of the terrace. When she turned back, William had disappeared as though to avoid David.

'The next dance is a valse,' David reminded her. 'I can allow no one other than myself to take advantage of its intimacies.'

'I hope I have not found myself an overbearing husband,' Margaret laughed as she took his arm again.

'By no means. The situation will simply be that my judgement will always be better than yours, and your own good sense will compel you to agree with me. That is the basis for a happy marriage.'

His teasing increased her fondness. She looked at him lovingly as they took the floor. The bay rum which had smoothed down his hair at dinner no longer held his dark curls in check and his brown eyes were at once merry and loving. Margaret blessed her good fortune. Never had she seen a man she liked better. That he should admire her too was a miracle she could hardly believe.

'I think I shall never be as happy in my whole life again

as I am at this moment,' she said softly as they began to dance and she felt David's arm tighten round her waist.

'I believe a time will come when we shall both be even happier,' he said. 'But I grant that this is enough for the present.'

Putting Luisa's lessons to good use, he swept her round the floor. Margaret was conscious of her father's eyes following her. She knew his opinion of the dance – he was old-fashioned enough still to regard it as immoral – but she could distinguish no sign of disapproval in his expression. It was as though he were determined to present himself to the world tonight as a contented as well as a generous man. This was without doubt the most perfect evening of her life.

But she had been right, all the same, when she recognized that such happiness could not last.

10

On the morning after a ball, jewels are locked away in the strong rooms of banks, dresses are returned to their closets, and ladies in middle life whose unaccustomed exercise has extended throughout the night take to their beds, giving orders that they should not be disturbed. All this is taken for granted; but it served on this occasion to disguise an unexpected and alarming consequence of the ball.

William's anxiety on his mother's behalf proved to have been well-founded. It was impossible to know whether what happened was the result of Georgiana cooling herself too abruptly on the terrace after the exertion of dancing, or whether the dangerous moment had come earlier in the evening, when she left the boudoir to whose warmth she was accustomed, wearing a dress very much lower in cut than usual. Whatever the cause, the effect was that within twenty-four hours of the ball she was complaining of a chill.

Later on, every member of the family was to feel guilty that Georgiana's first murmurs of complaint were not taken seriously. She had spent too many years suffering from illnesses which seemed to have no name for anyone to realize at once that this situation was different. She kept to her room – but that was her custom. She took to her bed – but it was assumed at first that this was no more than a reaction against the activity of the previous weeks, with their preparations for the dinner and ball.

William had of course returned to his own home with Sophie. Ralph had thrown himself into a frenzy of prayer and study ever since the day of Claudine's departure for France. John Junius was more than usually absorbed in the affairs of the bank, and spent his evenings in the tower room frowning over pages of figures. Margaret, in the days immediately following the ball, took it for granted that she should be the one to receive the courtesy calls of their dinner guests. There were calls of congratulation on her engagement too; and calls of her own to be made in return. Each time she went to her mother's door Marie-Claire greeted her with the news that Madame was resting, but there seemed no cause for alarm and she was too occupied with her own affairs to be worried. By ill fortune it happened that Dr Scott was spending a month in the country with his sister, and did not make his regular weekly call. Georgiana could, of course, have sent for his locum, but the selfish petulance with which she usually kept Dr Scott running to her call had been replaced by lethargy.

For all these reasons several days passed before Margaret, carrying in a silver bowl filled with roses from the garden, was horrified to see her mother, pale and lank-haired, fighting for breath as she lay propped up in bed by half a dozen pillows. A brief touch of hands was enough to tell Margaret, who had seen too many women lying ill in

133

damp basements, that the condition was dangerous. Wasting no time in bedside talk, she beckoned the maid to follow her out of the room. Once the door was closed, she intended to express her anger that Marie-Claire had allowed her mistress's condition to deteriorate in such a way, but for once the Frenchwoman was frightened rather than assertive.

'There has been no fever until today,' she said. 'This morning for the first time Madame would not allow me to do her hair. She said she was too tired. I did not like to leave her, but I have rung for a footman to call a doctor.'

Nathaniel arrived at that moment to prove the truth of what she said, and Margaret sent him off at once to fetch the nearest doctor.

It was Dr Scott's locum who came. After a long examination he applied a blister over the right lung. He sent for blankets and coals to sweat out the fever and prescribed doses of antimony mixed with syrup of poppies, promising to send round some laudanum so that his patient might have a restful night. Margaret watched with a feeling of helplessness, and was disturbed by the sickness which the antimony caused. As soon as her father returned that evening, Dr Scott was summoned from the country for a visit which for once was not a waste of his time. He did not actually criticize his own replacement, but withdrew the antimony and administered instead a medicine containing ammonia and ipecacuanha. A mustard poultice was placed over Georgiana's other lung: her weakness increased.

The days passed with no improvement in her condition. It seemed impossible that a woman who was only in middle life, with all the medical care that money could buy, should succumb to an illness which had so slight a cause and which seemed to develop so slowly. And yet, as days and weeks went by, Margaret noticed Dr Scott's face becoming more and more grim. He spoke to John Junius of a crisis, a low point to which his patient must now descend before any recovery could be hoped for. Margaret sat by the bedside every day and much of every night, but no miracle visited Brinsley House. Little by little the painful gasping of breath first quickened and then quietened. Before September ended, Georgiana Lorimer was dead.

She had never played any great part in her children's lives, leaving their upbringing to the care of nurses, governesses and tutors, but they mourned her sincerely now. She had hardly seen her grandchildren, for the shrill voices of small boys and the crying of babies gave her headaches, but Matthew wept at the news as though his heart would break. The servants had no reason to love their mistress, for she rarely spoke to them except to scold, and only Marie-Claire need fear to lose her place, but cook and kitchenmaid alike were to be seen with red eyes. She had long ago ceased to give John Junius the company of a wife, but even he seemed struck into silence by grief, or perhaps by the fact that such a change in his life should occur without his instructions and against his wishes. By marrying a wife so much younger than himself he must have thought himself safe from being a widower.

He shut himself away all day in either the tower room or else the library. When he appeared for a meal he had nothing to say to his children. As he sat in silence, finding no fault and giving no instructions, Margaret realized for the first time that her father was an old man. He signed an order to the undertaker, but it was Margaret who had to send out invitations and order seed cake and Madeira wine. Even a funeral was a social activity. Mourning rings and black kid gloves must be provided for the friends who would come. Black dresses and shawls and bonnets must be bought for the female servants, with armbands or hat ribbons for the men. For Margaret herself, who had been only a child when the death of the last baby occurred, a dressmaker had to be summoned from the Mourning Warehouse to supply what appeared to be a complete new wardrobe. It was bewildering to become involved in so much domestic activity at a time which should have been one of quiet grief.

As though one tragedy were not enough, another came hard on its heels. The funeral was to be on the Thursday after Georgiana's death. On the evening before it William had come over from The Ivies to sit with his father, brother and sister. They talked in low tones together. William had spent the day on board his newest steamship, which had been undergoing sea trials before her first voyage across the Atlantic. He told them about the ship and described his hopes for her future. She was to be called *Georgiana* for his mother. The decision was discussed and approved, and then the conversation lapsed. The four of them sat without occupation in the drawing room. It was an hour when Margaret normally worked at her *gros point*, but this seemed too frivolous a task at such a time. The dull blackness of their clothes made the atmosphere heavy, and there was an awkwardness in the silence as though each of them wished to break it but could think of no suitable subject to introduce.

The uneasiness was interrupted by the entry of Ransome. He murmured quietly to William that a messenger had come from the shipyard asking to speak with him. William frowned in surprise and then excused himself to his father and went out to the hall. When he returned, his face was pale.

'There has been an accident to the *Georgiana*,' he announced. 'An explosion in the engine room. You will forgive me, Father, if I go at once to the shipyard and see what has happened.'

'Is anyone hurt?' asked Margaret.

Her question was not answered, for her father asked one at the same time.

'Is there much damage?'

'The ship is on fire,' said William. 'It is too early to tell how much can be saved, but we must fear the worst.'

He turned to go, but his father called him back.

'William! There is more at stake here than a single ship. Can the fact of the accident be concealed?'

William shook his head.

'No. The man who brought the message was at home when he heard the explosion. The flames were visible while he was on his way. Many others will certainly have heard or seen what has happened.'

'Send me a message as soon as you arrive,' said John Junius. He spoke with an unusual urgency. 'And another when you have been able to assess the damage. Both must be completely confidential. Anyone who comes to the yard out of curiosity must be told that the accident is a minor one, of no importance.'

'I understand, Father.'

John Junius followed him to the hall and called Ransome to have his own carriage brought round.

'You are not going down to the yard yourself, Papa?' asked Margaret anxiously.

'No. Mr Gregson must be here when William's message arrives. I am sending to fetch him.'

Margaret could not understand why David should be concerned with an accident to a ship, but she was glad of anything which would bring him to the house. He came an hour later, and from the troubled look on his face Margaret could guess that her father had sent a note with the carriage to acquaint him of the trouble. His step hesitated as he saw her, but Ransome was waiting with instructions to take him straight to the tower room and he was forced to hurry away.

She left the door of the drawing room open and waited for David to reappear. A considerable time passed, and when he did come, it was in her father's company.

'I can close the door of Lorimer's for one day out of

137

respect for my wife on the day of her funeral,' John Junius was saying. 'Even those who disbelieve the excuse may not like to speak out. But one day is all we have. Pray God it may be enough.'

'I will do all I can, sir.' He looked longingly at Margaret as he spoke. John Junius intercepted the glance.

'You may see Mr Gregson to the carriage, Margaret, but you must not delay him. He has business of great urgency.'

Outside the door Margaret clung to David's arm and put the question which had been troubling her ever since the message came for William.

'I understand that my brother's affairs may now be in difficulty,' she said. 'But why is my father so perturbed? And why should you be expected to take action because of this?'

'Your brother's ships are built with Lorimer's money,' said David. 'This is known throughout Bristol. It is our gold which is burning down in the yard. And when our depositors hear of it, they will want to reassure themselves that their own money is safe. They will come as soon as the bank opens, to take it back.'

'But you have it there to give them.'

'No bank keeps all its deposits locked up in a strong room,' said David. 'The money must go out to earn its living, in order that business may be financed and that the shareholders may be paid. In calm times this principle is well understood by depositors. But an accident like this can cause a panic, and the panic itself can bring disaster. Your father is right to be perturbed. For your brother this is an unfortunate accident. For Lorimer's Bank it could be far worse than that. You will say nothing of this to anyone, of course.'

'Of course not.' She still did not understand why the bank was at such risk, but at least she could see the need to let David go. As she turned back into the house her

138

expression was troubled. The thought was mere super-stition, she told herself, but she could not rid herself of the idea that disasters came in threes.

11

The captains of slaving ships in the seventeenth and eighteenth centuries were not as a general rule renowned for their piety. Brinsley Lorimer was not seen inside a church building of any sort between the day of his wedding and that of his funeral. But his wife was a devout Baptist and because of her husband's long absences at sea was able both to continue her own Sunday observances and to ensure that her children were brought up in a Godfearing manner. Neither they nor her grandchildren could have been described as religious in their adult lives, but perhaps for this reason none of them felt strongly enough to desert the Baptist way of life. It was Samuel, his narrow-minded piety reinforced by a wish for social advancement, who moved the family out of the Baptist chapel and into the Anglican church. John Junius Lorimer, his grandson, had been christened into the Church of England and looked to it to provide any other ceremony of which he might be in need. The early Lorimers were buried in a humble position down by the river, but Georgiana's place was in the family tomb in the churchyard adjoining the Downs.

On the morning of the funeral John Junius conducted family prayers in the normal manner and took his usual place at the head of the breakfast table. William had arrived to join his brother and sister and support his father. Sophie, who was expecting her third child in seven weeks' time, was unwell and could not leave her bed.

At ten o'clock the friends of the family began to assemble at the house. It was Margaret's duty, as its mistress, to receive them and to apologize for her father, who did not appear in person to accept their condolences. She explained how deeply upset he was, although knowing that he was watching from an upstairs window for David's arrival.

Time passed, and it seemed that David would not come. Margaret excused herself and slipped outside. The undertaker was waiting to show her that everything was in order. Covered with its pall of black velvet, the heavy lead and oak coffin had already been unobtrusively carried out of the house and placed in the glass-sided hearse. The two mourning coaches stood in readiness behind, each with four black horses tossing the plumes on their heads as they waited. The coachmen were already sitting on their boxes. The pages and feathermen and attendants who would carry the coffin into the church waited in a line for the family to appear.

David arrived in a cab at that moment and hurried into the house without seeing Margaret as she stood behind the coaches. By the time he had been admitted to the hall, John Junius was there to greet him. The chairman began his questioning without taking any notice of the fact that Margaret had followed inside and could hear their conversation.

'Well?'

'I have been successful in the smaller matter. All the banks in Bristol have agreed that they will honour Lorimer's notes to a normal daily limit. I have arranged for this information to be spread amongst the managers of the principal shops, so that no anxiety should be caused by any refusal to accept our notes.'

'And on the larger affair? The gold?'

David sighed.

'There is goodwill towards us,' he said. 'All the banks are conscious of the danger to general credit if one of their number should fall. But none will act without the support of all the others. I have arranged a meeting of yourself and

140

five other chairmen at the Old Bank at three o'clock this afternoon. All of them have reserves which they would be able to transfer temporarily, but only on condition that the matter could be kept secret. Naturally, they will all expect security for the transfers.'

There was a silence which seemed to Margaret more ominous than any words which had been spoken. It was not often that her father could think of nothing to say.

He braced himself at last to be encouraging.

'We have been through all this before, Mr Gregson, and have survived,' he said. 'You would have been too young in 1866 to be aware of what happened when Gurney's discount house in London stopped payment on debts of ten million pounds. Six banks failed within a week entirely because of the panic amongst depositors. Most of those banks were in any normal circumstances perfectly solvent; in fact, two of them were later able to resume business. We in Bristol weathered that storm, Mr Gregson, because we stood together to hold confidence. The lesson will not yet have been forgotten. We shall find the support we need.'

It was David's turn to remain silent, as though he could not share this rosy view of the situation.

'One thought did occur to me as I was on my way here,' he said at last. 'I assume that the *Georgiana* was insured. If Mr William Lorimer, perhaps with your help or mine, could persuade the insurance company to make at least a provisional settlement at once, this would be of great value.'

'She was insured at Lloyd's,' said John Junius. 'But the news will scarcely have reached London yet. This class of business is so new that the insurers may well wish to send investigators to discover the cause of the damage. Undoubtedly they will meet their obligations in due course, but we can hardly expect them to consign a coffer of gold to the railway this evening.'

'I was thinking of the security required by the other

141

banks,' David said. 'A statement of intention to pay, if one could be obtained quickly, would assure its value in gold.'

'A policy with Lloyd's is sufficient security in itself,' said John Junius. Margaret could see that he was pleased to have been reminded of it. 'I will have a word with my son and bring the paper to the meeting.'

'And I will return at once to the bank to see what figures I can prepare,' said David; but John Junius shook his head.

'Now that your engagement to Margaret has been announced, your presence will be expected at the funeral. I am anxious that nothing should happen today which could seem worthy of remark. An hour will make little difference.'

David bowed his acquiescence and came to stand by Margaret's side.

'After the service I must hurry away,' he said to her. 'I shall be very busy for the next few days. If I fail to visit you, it will not be from my own choice. Will you give me your forgiveness in advance?'

'Of course. I know you will come as soon as you can.'

'There is one other thing,' said David. He hesitated, as though unsure whether he ought to say it. 'If any great trouble should strike your family, you will remember, will you not, that I am anxious to make a home for you as soon as you are ready. Perhaps a humbler home than Lower Croft. I should be happy in any place where you are the mistress. Your mother's illness prevented your father from naming a date for our wedding, as he had promised, and now I can see that her death must restrain you for a little while. But as soon as you are out of mourning and are ready to come, you will find me waiting.'

Too overcome by the emotion of the day to speak, Margaret held out her hand towards him. David pressed it between his own and raised it to his lips. Then he stepped away from her, as though anxious by standing alone to give the impression that he had had nothing of importance to say. Margaret was left to speculate on the nature of the trouble which he foresaw. She was already wearing her black veil, so that her own expression could not be discerned, but she could see well enough through it. Both David and her father – and William too, who came now to join them – had already ceased to grieve for Georgiana. Their melancholy expressions were caused by anxieties of a different sort. The realization that her mother could be so quickly forgotten increased Margaret's own grief, and she found it difficult not to weep as she took her seat in one of the mourning coaches.

The mutes stepped forward into their places and the undertaker's men in their tall black hats fell in behind. The other private carriages followed in a procession which represented much of the wealth of one of the wealthiest cities in England. Slowly the long line wound its way up the hill and over the Clifton Downs. There were a great many people in the streets. Margaret knew that the funeral cortège of a rich family could always be expected to attract sightseers from amongst those who had no better way to spend their time, and maids and tradesmen's boys were naturally glad of an excuse to dawdle. But today there was a different atmosphere, as though word of the event had spread through the city, attracting onlookers who had made a special journey to be present.

What seemed stranger was the reluctance of the crowd to pay its respects. Only at the last possible moment were hats doffed and heads bowed. Even then Margaret felt conscious that the occupants of the carriages were being closely observed, and that there was hostility in the stare. No one shouted out, and if there were mutterings they could not be heard inside the closed coach. Nevertheless, the uneasiness which had been born in Margaret on the previous evening and which had fed on the conversation between David and her father increased with every moment

143

that passed. She was glad when the yellow stone walls of Christ Church came into sight.

As she stepped out of the coach, Margaret gazed up at the huge building, which still looked as new as when it had been built some thirty years earlier. It was designed to the scale of a miniature cathedral, even to the grotesque heads carved above the door. Its tall spire soared towards the sky from almost the highest position in the city. Like the college and the suspension bridge, this was another of Clifton's buildings which owed much to the generosity of her family.

She remembered that again after she had made her slow progress down the centre aisle of the wide church to the family pew. As the lugubrious notes of the organ faded away, to be replaced by the equally mournful incantations of the rector, she considered the massive solidity of the structure in which she was sitting. It was built to last for ever. Just so secure had seemed her family life, broken now by Georgiana's death. And her father's financial empire, less vulnerable than either to the accidents of wind and weather or the certainty of mortality, had appeared the soundest institution of all. Could it be that this also was cracking? Surely it was not possible. If Lorimer's were to fall, then nothing in society could be regarded as safe.

Reluctantly she tugged her thoughts away from such worldly problems and gave all her attention to the service and to the memory of her mother. The funeral sermon was long and harrowing. Afterwards, in the churchyard, she looked round at the sombre group which had gathered round the vault, all dressed in deep mourning. Her feeling of unease returned, chilling her in spite of the warmth of an Indian summer and the heaviness of her dress. She could not reasonably have expected that life at Brinsley House would go on for ever unchanged. She herself had planned to leave it very soon. But that had been a change chosen with joy, not enforced in sorrow. Within a few days Ralph would begin his first term at Oxford. She might

144

have to wait longer now for her wedding day, but when it came her father would be alone in the enormous house: alone and growing old. Under the cover of her veil she wept for him, yet part of her disquiet was for herself. Were her plans safe, or might this new situation impose some obstacle?

It seemed to her as she looked at David, serious in expression as the last words were spoken over the coffin, that she could not bear to live without him. If anything should come between them ... But she shook the idea away. John Junius might be lonely, but he would never admit to being dependent. If he should ask her to remain at Brinsley House in order to take her mother's place in its management, he would put the demand as a favour to herself, by inviting her to make it her married home. As long as she and David were sure of each other, no outside force could separate them.

They returned towards the carriages. A messenger boy was waiting in the street, looking worried as though he had not known whether he would be more sharply criticized for delaying the delivery of the telegram he carried or for intruding on an occasion of family grief. Margaret was conscious of her father wishing to hasten his step but, like the boy, obeying the restraint of decorum. At last he was near enough to take the telegram. He turned away from the company while he opened and read it.

Margaret watched his face as he turned back. The other mourners, knowing John Junius less well than his daughter, might not have been able to recognize from the way in which his lips tightened that he was faced with some kind of emergency, but from the earliest days of her childhood Margaret had needed to know the signs which meant that her father had been thwarted beyond endurance in his affairs. She saw him catch David's eye and hand him the telegram. The younger man in turn read the brief message. He was less well practised than the chairman in the art of

145

concealing his emotions. He studied the words more than once. When he looked up again, his face was pale with despair.

12

When the sun of prosperity vanishes behind clouds, every community which has flourished in its warmth must expect to suffer from the storm which follows. It was unrealistic of David, when at last the chairman passed him the telegram, to regard the situation it described as a personal attack by the hand of fate. He ought not to have been surprised that the conditions of trade which had affected Bristol would have had the same effect on other mercantile cities. But in fact the news which he read was so unexpected, so overwhelming in the magnitude of the disaster, that the words swam before his eyes. He, as much as John Junius, needed time to compose himself.

What the telegram told them was that the City of Glasgow Bank had closed its doors, unable to meet obligations amounting to six million pounds. That was all, but it was enough for David – and he could tell that the implications were not lost on his chairman either. The community of Glasgow, the commercial heart of Scotland, would be ruined – had been ruined already, although its citizens might need a little longer to understand their fate. To Lorimer's the social effects were only of secondary importance. What mattered was that the fall of an institution so huge and so widely respected would shake public confidence all over the kingdom as soon as the news was known. Not even the most substantial financial institutions, the most cautious in their lendings, would be immune from its effects. No bank in Bristol, when it heard the news, would dare to deplete its reserves by a single sovereign at such a time, whatever difficulty the fall of a neighbour might cause in the city. The meeting arranged for the afternoon was doomed to failure before it began.

'Then we have lost the day,' he said, speaking quietly so that no one but John Junius could hear. The chairman did not show his feelings. His eyes were hooded in concentration.

'The information will not reach the general public until the arrival of the London newspapers tomorrow,' he said. 'They will come on the railway train which arrives just after nine o'clock. If the train should be delayed – or better still, if the consignment of newspapers should be misplaced at the London end . . .'

For a moment David wondered whether the old man's mind had been softened by the shock. It was one thing to look for a way to fight on while there was still ground beneath their feet, but it was no longer possible to return to the wild free-booting ways of the early Lorimers, advocating theft or an act of piracy when the only reward could be a few more hours of respite before the inevitable crash.

'The *Bristol Evening News* will have its own sources of information in London,' he pointed out. 'It will be on the streets within a few hours. And even if we could survive Friday, we would still have to face Saturday. If you will excuse me now, I will see if there is anything to be done.'

He paused only to kiss Margaret's hand again, looking into her eyes with a sympathy he had no time to explain.

'You will observe strict mourning tomorrow, of course,' he said, keeping his voice low. 'You will stay inside the house, pay no calls. Above all, you will not go down into the city.'

He could see that she was startled to find him giving orders in such a matter, but left before she had time to understand their significance. As he strode down the hill, not caring about the curious glances which followed him, he knew that there was no way in which Lorimer's could be saved. All he could do was to plan like a general for whatever form of surrender would cause the least harm to innocent victims.

And who, amongst the innocent, were the most deserving? It was a question which he was forced to put to himself when he opened the door of his office at six o'clock the next morning, long before any other members of the staff were expected to arrive. The ordinary depositors who had brought their money to the bank for safe keeping had a right to expect its return when they asked for it. The shareholders, the men who actually owned the bank, had a right to expect that the money they had invested had been secured, and even increased. And then there were the creditors – local firms representing almost every trade in Bristol, firms which had supplied raw materials or finished goods or services towards such enterprises as William Lorimer's new steamships, Edward Crankshaw's great complex of docks, John Grange's modern factory and a dozen other such businesses. Under the loan agreements which had been negotiated some years earlier they had been paid with bills drawn on the bank and had the right to assume that these would be honoured when they fell due. The staff, too, in all the bank's thirty branches, had worked conscientiously for the salaries which they would expect to receive that evening.

They could not all be paid at once. As David had explained earlier to Margaret, no bank could operate on the assumption that such a step would ever be necessary. It would be possible for David, if he chose, to meet the claims of the first few depositors who came to demand their money back; but by paying these in full he would be diminishing the reserve which would eventually have to be divided amongst the others. It was for this reason that he had come early to the bank. By the view from his window he might judge whether the prompt payment of the first few requests – payments made without any suggestion that

148

the outward flow of gold would at some point be halted – would be sufficient to send the less nervous depositors home again, happy to leave their savings in what appeared to be safe hands.

It was a hope which did not survive the first hour of his vigil. The bank normally opened its doors to customers at nine o'clock, the staff arriving an hour earlier. Already at seven the first anxious depositors were congregating in front of the building while other men, approaching from a distance, quickened their pace as they saw the numbers assembled before them.

There were even one or two women. David groaned to himself as he recognized Miss Langdon, who only three weeks earlier had deposited in her account the money inherited from her brother in India, with which she planned to buy a small house for herself. By the end of the day Miss Langdon would be weeping for the collapse of all her dreams, and she would be only one of many. By eight o'clock, as he estimated the wealth of those who were already waiting – with still an hour to go – he knew that Lorimer's could not open its doors again.

The realization was a bitter one. David had not been a citizen of Bristol for long, but it was long enough for him to have absorbed the city's pride in honest dealing. From the window of his office he looked across Corn Street to the Exchange, in which shiploads of commodities changed hands on the nod. Next to the Exchange was the merchants' cloister of All Saints' Church. The brass Nails which stood in it – waist-high pillars with round table tops – were used for the transaction of immediate business with an integrity which had made 'paying on the nail' part of common speech throughout the country.

In addition to this shame at defaulting, David could not help but feel another regret. He had been given responsibility young, and he had done his best; but no one in the future would remember that or make allowances for the force of circumstances. Circumstances were all that he considered to blame. In his mental listing of the innocent, it had not occurred to him to wonder whether anyone might be guilty.

The first of the bank's staff was approaching. David went down to the side entrance to make sure that the doorman was on duty and would admit no unauthorized person. He was just turning away when a visitor arrived: a sergeant of police.

'If I could have a word, Mr Gregson.'

'In my office, Sergeant.'

David knew the man well enough. All the Corn Street banks depended on him for protection if ever there was a need to move gold from one branch to another. Usually he was bluff and jolly, but today he was not smiling.

'I've been sent down, sir, to enquire whether you'd be doing normal business today.'

'Is that any affair of yours?'

'Come now, Mr Gregson. You've seen the crowd in the street already. If you were to open your door this minute, they'd be scratching each other's eyes out for the right to be first in. And if you don't open at nine, you may be glad of some help in getting yourself out of the building unharmed. I'm not here to give opinions, sir. If it's business as usual, I'll try to get these people into some sort of line. If it's not, I'll need to bring in more men to disperse the crowd. We have to take action if we think there's likely to be a breach of the peace.'

'I am awaiting instructions from Mr Lorimer,' said David. 'But it could do no harm, I suppose, to have a few more of your men in the neighbourhood.'

It was a sufficient answer. The sergeant's expression was clouded as he accepted it.

'You'll be on the bank premises all day, sir?' he checked.

'During normal hours, certainly.'

150

'And you've no plans for leaving Bristol in the near future?'

'What the devil are you getting at?' David burst out. The past few days, and particularly the last hour, had provided strain enough. To be questioned in such a way by a sergeant of police was an insupportable impertinence.

'No offence, I hope, sir,' said the sergeant. 'But we've been through affairs like this before. On a small scale, of course. People don't take kindly to losing their money. They'll be at headquarters to see what can be done about it. They'll lay complaints of theft or embezzlement. Not because they believe it, you understand sir, but because they know we can't interfere unless there's a crime been committed. And maybe even they *do* believe it. Ordinary people don't understand about money being theirs one minute and gone the next. Once there's a complaint, someone has to look into it. It's not a job for the likes of me, Mr Gregson, but you'll need to have your books ready. I'm sure I sympathize with you, sir. We've all heard about the accident down at the yard. A misfortune not of your making. An unfortunate affair altogether, sir, an unfortunate affair. The hand of God.'

He paused to sigh; then resumed more briskly.

'You'll be putting a notice up on the door, I take it, sir. If you could give me half an hour to get my men together, we'll do what we can to save your windows.'

The sounds of disturbance in the street below drew both men across the room to look out. John Junius Lorimer was coming to the bank as usual. His horses still wore their mourning ribbons, but nothing could camouflage the green and gold splendour of the carriage. The crowd outside recognized him at once as the man who would decide the fate of their deposits. Until they learned his decision there could be no demonstration of anything stronger than anxiety. They murmured and jostled amongst themselves, but John Junius would be safe, David reckoned, at this

151

moment of arrival. The evening departure might prove rather a different matter.

He hurried the sergeant out of the side door. Then he ordered the massive bolts of the studded wooden door at the front of the building to be drawn so that the chairman could enter with his usual dignity. Four members of the staff were at hand to make sure that no one was able to follow.

Half an hour later the notice which the depositors had feared was posted outside that same door. David, standing in his office, heard the groan of many voices, the rush of feet, the cries of anger and the furious beating of fists upon the door. Then he was forced to move away, feeling sick – not with fear, but with grief and helpless sympathy. It was the bitterest moment of his life.

The sergeant had given him two warnings, but so dark was his mood that at first he heeded only one of them. He looked to the protection of the windows and the safety of the staff and posted watchers to guard against any possibility of arson. Where the accounts were concerned, his own conscience was clear. There were so many other matters needing his attention that he did not immediately recall the doubts which he himself had felt and expressed when he took up his duties as manager.

Only later, when the street was empty again, was he able to consider his own position more carefully. The angry crowd, which during the morning had increased to fill the whole area outside Lorimer's, was by noon pressed back by half a dozen policemen, whirling their rattles as though they were weapons. At last, as evening approached, the depositors dispersed with curses and tears, enabling David to send for a hansom in which the chairman could be conveyed back to Brinsley House. John Junius did not argue. His recognition that the Lorimer livery would be stoned on sight was a mark of his acceptance of defeat.

David sat on in his office long after the heart of the city

152

had been deserted by all but the policemen left to guard his premises. He left the gas lamp unlit so that no light would attract attention from outside. Then at last he had time to remember the balances he had queried, the changes which had been made during his absence in London. He had accepted from John Junius an explanation which could only be excused by success. Now he realized that those figures would be scrutinized in the harsh light of failure.

There was no need to look again at the books: he knew well enough what they said. The sweat chilled on his forehead as he thought what use could be made of the figures by angry men looking for a culprit. Nothing could alter the fact that he had accepted them – his only defence could be that as manager he had been bound to obey his chairman's instructions. Could he rely on the chairman to agree that such instructions had been given?

At the beginning of the day David had been upset at the fate of the innocent victims of the collapse. As night came he felt the ground fall from beneath his own feet. But John Junius would surely not abandon the man whom his daughter loved. David told himself that such a possibility was inconceivable.

Later that evening, anonymous in a city which now reviled the name of Lorimer, he paced the streets and came to a halt at last on the bank of the floating harbour, the lock-controlled basin which ensured that once a ship had made her hazardous way up the tidal river there was enough water for her to remain in the Bristol Docks. A three-masted barque, with lanterns tied to each mast, was gliding to her mooring place after a voyage to West Africa and back. The wharf was crowded with men who hoped for the work of unloading her cargo and women waiting to greet the crew and relieve them of their wages. She was a twenty-year-old ship with long, low lines – more graceful than the high, wide hulls with which William Lorimer's new steamships faced the Atlantic waves. Within a week or two, no doubt, if she had suffered no damage on her voyage, she would be off again on some adventure. David allowed his imagination to sail with her.

But he was a city man, not an explorer, and he had no experience of trading. Such primitive parts of the world could offer him nothing but a refuge, and as yet he had not sunk as low as that. The interest with which he watched the barque reflected only an instinct which he had not yet consciously considered – that as soon as possible he must find himself fresh employment, and that he would have to look for it with no kind of recommendation and as far away as possible from Bristol.

The thought led him to consider Margaret. He had kept away from Brinsley House, feeling that it was the duty of her father rather than himself to explain to her the loss of everything which she had taken for granted all her life. It would be a sour moment for the old man, and not one which he would wish to share with someone who was still almost a stranger. He and his daughter would need to comfort each other, although it was difficult to see what comfort either of them could provide, except affection. But it was clear to David that he must call on Margaret as soon as she had absorbed the first shock. He had told her that she could rely on his constancy, and at the time she could not have understood what he meant. Now that she knew, she might forget the reassurance. It must be repeated.

Yet what had he to offer except affection again? A man without employment or prospects was hardly the most welcome knight to swear loyalty to a damsel in distress. He could tell her that he loved her, and it would be true, but how could he support her? Only a fool thought that two people could live on love alone. He could ask her to wait, but could she afford to wait? His head swam with the conflict. He could not bear the thought of losing her; nor could he think how to keep her. That night he lay awake in the lodgings which once he had thought too mean and which soon might be more than he could afford. He tried to look into the future and saw only blackness and despair.

13

Actions which betray an emergency speak more loudly than words of reassurance. On the day after Georgiana's funeral Margaret and Ralph were startled to their feet by a sound usually heard only before the family's annual holiday. The servants were bolting the shutters into position across the windows. John Junius must have given the instructions before he left for the bank. Hurrying to look from her bedroom window, Margaret saw that all the outside staff, although pretending to go about their business in the stables or gardens, were obviously on guard. The front door was chained as well as bolted and it was Ransome who, repeating David's earlier instructions that she must keep to the house, at last told her why.

When their father returned that evening they followed him into his study without being invited and stood in silence, waiting for him to speak. He sat at his desk and gave a great sigh of tiredness. Often in the past few months Margaret had thought he looked anxious. Tonight she saw that he was defeated.

'It was all for you, and for William,' said John Junius. 'I never wanted more than to give my children an even better life than I had myself. And now I shall see you with nothing. With the failure of the bank, my fortune is lost. Entirely lost.' He looked at each of them in turn. 'I'm sorry,' he said.

Never before in her whole life had Margaret heard her father apologize for anything. She hurried to embrace him, without giving herself time to consider the implications of what he said. But he was beyond comfort. He could only speak the words he had prepared.

'You are to go to your brother's house. I have sent a message that he should expect you. Until our affairs are settled, there may be ill-feeling towards myself. Take a few things and go at once. The carriage can return in an hour for your maid and whatever else of your possessions she has packed for you.'

'But you will come with us, Papa?'

'No,' said John Junius. Defeat had not diminished his ability to be definite. Margaret hesitated, but she was already sure that he could not be persuaded.

Half an hour later she and Ralph arrived at The Ivies. They were received by the butler. The master was down at Portishead, they were told, assessing the damage to the *Georgiana*, whilst the mistress had spent the day unwell in bed. It was a cold welcome for a visit for which no one was prepared. Margaret and Ralph did not speak as they were shown to musty rooms which were being hastily aired for them.

When she had changed her dress, Margaret found herself drawn to the door of Sophie's room, but reluctant to intrude. The sound of a groan decided her. She knocked on the door and went in without waiting for an answer.

It was obvious at once what was happening. Sophie's maid, a girl almost as young as Betty, was sitting beside the bed with a frightened expression, wiping her mistress's forehead with a cool cloth, while Sophie herself gasped and writhed with pain. Margaret hurried to the other side of the bed.

'Is it the baby?' she asked.

'It's too soon,' said Sophie. The pain passed and she collapsed back into the pillows again, gasping for breath. 'There are seven weeks before it is due.'

'But you must know if these are labour pains.'

'If the baby is born now it will die,' said Sophie. 'It

156

cannot be coming. A little indigestion, it can't be more than that. It was so hot yesterday. And the shock of hearing William's news about the *Georgiana*. And then this morning a message arrived to say that my father had been thrown from his horse and taken unconscious to hospital. I allowed myself to become upset. William told me that I should not cry, and I did not heed him. It will pass. Surely it will pass.'

Margaret turned to the maid.

'Has the doctor been sent for?'

The girl shook her head.

'Mistress wouldn't let me. She said it was nothing.'

Margaret tugged at the bell rope, then hurried downstairs without waiting for any of the servants to arrive. She found the butler in the hall and gave him quick instructions.

'Send the footman for Dr Scott. He must be found wherever he may be, and he is to come at once. The midwife as well. Do you know where she lives? Send the victoria for her. Ask Mr Ralph to go at once to find your master. Make it clear to them all that it is a matter of life or death.'

She ran back upstairs and then stood still for a moment inside the doorway of Sophie's room in order to steady her mind and banish any trace of panic from her voice.

'Tell the cook to have hot water ready,' she told the girl. 'Bring me clean linen. Find the cradle and scrub it clean, and prepare it for the baby. Where are Matthew and Beatrice?'

'Mistress sent them to stay with her mother this morning, when she began to feel unwell.'

'Off you go, then.' Margaret sat down beside Sophie again.

'If the baby is ready to be born, we cannot stop it,' she said. 'You will injure your own health if you try.'

'It's too soon,' moaned Sophie.

'You have two beautiful children. And you will have

many more. We will all do our best for this one. But the most important thing is to preserve your own health, to be a good mother to Matthew and Beatrice. The doctor is on his way. Lie back and calm yourself.'

It was easy to say, but the next three hours were by no means calm. William was the first to arrive, although he had had the greatest distance to travel. Margaret heard him talking agitatedly in the hall and went out to enquire what was the matter.

'The midwife was not due to come for five weeks yet,' William told her, passing on a message which had just been delivered to himself. 'She is in attendance at another confinement and cannot leave. She has given us other addresses. Ralph has promised to go out again at once.'

'And Dr Scott?'

'I don't understand why he's taking so long.'

He came at that moment, and the first words he spoke made Margaret look at him in astonishment and horror. He was drunk.

'Another little Lorimer,' he said in a voice that was thick and slurred. 'The Lorimers have need of a doctor. They snap their fingers and Dr Scott must come running. I snap my fingers back, sir. I say to myself, let the Lorimers show me the colour of their money. But the Lorimers have no money. And Dr Scott has no money either. His house will be sold over his head and his wife will starve and yet the Lorimers expect that he will run their errands and deliver their babies and be glad that there is one more Lorimer in the world to steal the bread out of the mouths of the poor. Well, I am come, sir, running to the snap of your fingers.'

'And you may run straight back to your own home,' said William, pale with anger. 'You have no right to enter my house in such a state. Certainly you are not fit to attend my wife.'

'Man has right to drink 's own brandy in 's own house, while he has it,' said the doctor, swaying on his feet and

158

waving his arms in an effort to keep his balance. 'Man isn't bound to spend every hour of the day waiting the pleasure of Lorimers. Message came. Doctor came. Colour of your money, Mr Lorimer, sir, colour of your money.'

'Get him back into his gig,' William ordered the footman. 'Then go to Dr Gregory's house. If you find him out, enquire – '

Margaret did not wait to listen as her brother's instructions continued. The messengers would no doubt do the best they could, but Sophie might not be able to wait. She went into her own room, where Betty was unpacking her trunk.

'Have you ever seen a baby born?' she asked.

'Not since I was eight years old, Miss.'

'The midwife may not come in time. Are you willing to help me?'

'If I can, Miss.' The workmanlike way in which she rolled up her sleeves gave Margaret confidence at once. 'And the baby comes by itself most times, Miss. It's the part afterwards that I don't know about. Perhaps the midwife will be here for that.'

'I pray so,' said Margaret. She led the way into Sophie's room and straightened herself to keep her courage up. She had never seen her sister-in-law except when she was dressed for company. To expose her naked limbs, to be forced to stare and to touch – would such an intrusion ever be forgiven? And yet if Dr Scott had been less obviously drunk, he would have been admitted to the bedroom to see and touch whatever parts of his patient's body he liked, and Sophie would not have protested.

Margaret realized that the objections were all in her own mind. No one, since she became a woman, had seen her own naked body: she had never even looked at it herself. But one day, if she married David, she would lie exposed to a doctor and midwife. Even before that David would have the right to share her bedroom. Margaret did

159

not know much more about marriage than most young women of her age, and her mother's warnings had served to frighten her. She knew that David would want to touch: she suspected that he might also want to look. Somehow she must make herself think of a body, whether Sophie's or her own, as an object which was sometimes in need of care or repair. It was not a cause for shame, she told herself firmly as she fought to control the deep flush which had suffused her face and neck at the thought of David in her bedroom. She forced herself to smile reassuringly as she walked across to Sophie and drew back the sheet.

Much later that night, in the unfamiliar bed, she lay awake for a long time in spite of her exhaustion. The baby was so tiny that the birth, for all Sophie's cries, had not been a difficult one, and a midwife had been found who arrived in time to slap the new arrival into protesting breath and to deal with the after-birth. So small a baby could not be thought of as having a secure place in the world, but for the moment the emergency was over. Margaret had discovered that she could see her own hands covered in blood without either faintness or disgust, and she had felt almost the same sense of achievement as the mother when she supported first the baby's head and then its whole slippery body in her hands.

The feeling which disturbed Margaret and kept her awake was a complicated one. She had been brought up to be useless. She had no training to do anything but live as a mistress of servants, and that life had now been snatched away from her. Although she lacked the skills, the events of the evening had persuaded her that she would not lack the ability to be useful if only she could be properly taught: she had always had the wish to undergo some kind of training. But then she had to remember that she had agreed to marry David, and no husband would allow his wife to be anything but a wife.

No sooner had this thought overthrown the previous one

than it in turn came under challenge. David had wanted to marry the daughter of a wealthy banker who was in a position to advance his career. He might be less enthusiastic about allying himself to a member of a ruined family, taking a bride who lacked a dowry as well as any domestic skills.

Such contradictory feelings fought in her mind to keep her tossing on the bed for half the night. Dawn was already breaking when at last she fell asleep, and it was noon before Betty came to wake her. The first sentence of greeting was enough to banish the doubts of the night.

'Mr Gregson called while you were asleep,' Betty said. 'They told him at Brinsley House that you were here. He asked most particular for you to be told that he'd hoped to see you and that he'll call again.'

Margaret hurried from the bed and called for her clothes as quickly as though he could be expected at that moment.

'And the baby?' she asked. 'Are he and his mother both well?'

'Mrs Lorimer is well enough. But not the baby. They found a wet nurse to come this morning, but he's not strong enough to suck. And now they say there's trouble with his breathing. He was christened an hour ago. They think he'll not last the day.'

The news increased Margaret's haste. She gave Betty no time to lace her more than perfunctorily, nor to do more to her hair than brush it and tie it back with a ribbon as though she were still a child in the schoolroom. She emerged from her room just in time to see Dr Scott leaving the house.

'How could you let that man come back?' she demanded as soon as she found her brother.

William shrugged his shoulders.

'He was sober this morning. Sober enough to apologize for last night. It was as he said – he had no reason then to expect a call.'

161

'But William, he hates us. If he had been sober he might not have spoken as he did, but those would still have been his thoughts.'

'It makes no difference,' said William. 'Sophie is well enough, and the nurse will care for her. As for the boy, there is nothing to be done for him. He will die, but that is no fault of the doctor. He was born too soon.'

'Was it the doctor who said he would die? And do you any longer believe what he tells you?'

'Look at the child for yourself, Margaret,' said William. He, like everyone else in the house, was tired and strained. With no energy left for argument, he turned away.

She did what he suggested and was shocked to tears by what she saw. When the baby was born his skin had been a beautiful reddish gold. Now all the blood seemed to have drained away, and his lips were blue. Margaret could tell that every breath was a struggle, and that he was too weak to fight for much longer.

'Doctor says there's some obstruction,' the nurse told her. 'And his lungs aren't strong enough to overcome it, poor mite.'

Margaret stared down at the tiny face, its eyes screwed up against the light. Then she made up her mind and knelt down beside the cradle, putting her lips to the baby's. When David called an hour later she was forced to send a message that she could not see him.

He came again during the evening of the next day. Margaret, who had been listening all afternoon for the ring of the doorbell, ran to fling herself into his arms as soon as he was shown into the drawing room. The household was too disturbed for anyone to reflect that a chaperone was required, and the events of the past hours had undermined all the formality of manner which had inhibited Margaret herself in the past.

'I'm so very glad to see you, and so sorry to have wasted your time yesterday. But William told you the reason?'

162

She became excited again as she described what had happened. She knew the importance of what she had done, for it seemed sure by now that baby Arthur had a good chance of life. The fortunes of her family, and the affairs of the bank, had been completely thrust out of her mind, even when she was describing Dr Scott's extraordinary drunken outburst.

'Then the next day, though he was sober, he said that the baby could not be saved. Yet as soon as I learned of the difficulty I could see what might at least be tried. Either he was ignorant or else he was lying, *wanting* the baby to die. I think his mind has become unbalanced. Why should such a thing happen so suddenly? And what have the Lorimers done to cause it?'

David took a deep breath and Margaret, suddenly sobered by the gravity of his expression, remembered that there were more things than a doctor's drunkenness to be explained.

'How much has your father told you of the affairs of the past few days?' he asked.

'He told me that the bank has failed, had closed its door. Nothing more. He was too upset to speak.'

'And what do you understand by the failure?'

'That all his money is lost. It was deposited, I suppose, in his own bank, and will not now be repaid. Although I hardly understand why, if it has been lent out, it should not be called back from those who borrowed it.'

'Some of the borrowers were businesses which have proved unsound,' David told her. 'Trading companies whose trade has fallen off in the past few years. They already face bankruptcy themselves. There are other firms, like the Lorimer Line and Crankshaw's dock development company, which will be able to repay their debts in the end, but only over a long period.'

'Is it true that Dr Scott will also have lost all his money?' asked Margaret. The doctor's outburst had for some reason made her more puzzled about his situation than about her father's or her own. 'Even if his deposits are gone, surely he still has his house. He can still practise as a doctor. His patients will continue to pay him for what he does now, even though he may have lost his savings from the past. Why should he say that his wife will starve?'

'It is not because Dr Scott deposited his money in the bank that he will find himself ruined,' said David. 'The depositors may be lucky enough to get some of their money back in the end. But Dr Scott was also a shareholder.'

'What difference does that make?'

'The bank is owned by its proprietors, the people who hold its shares,' David explained. 'When there are profits, the shareholders divide these profits between them. When there are losses, these also must be divided.'

'But Dr Scott is not a rich man. He cannot have invested any very large sum.'

'Unfortunately that makes no difference,' said David. 'His liability for the bank's debts is not limited to the amount of his shareholding. It is true that Parliament passed an Act a few years ago to ensure that the liability of shareholders *would* be limited to this amount in future. This was because so much distress was caused by bank failures in 1866. Newly-formed companies, including banks, were required to conform to the provisions of the Act. But existing companies could choose whether or not to change their articles.'

'And Lorimer's Bank?'

'Made no change,' said David. 'There are about fifteen hundred proprietors and they have provided the bank with a capital of half a million pounds. Its debts, represented by its bank notes, the bills drawn upon it, and its receipts to depositors, may amount to five million pounds. If Dr Scott has invested a thousand pounds, he will be called upon to pay ten thousand. And if he cannot pay, his house may indeed, as he fears, be sold to raise the money.'

Margaret had been sitting as close to David as she could on the sofa. Now she drew a little away, examining his expression in the hope that she would find he was exaggerating.

'But that is unjust!' she exclaimed, when his seriousness forced her to accept what she had heard.

David nodded his agreement.

'There is worse to come,' he said. 'Many of the proprietors are far from rich. The whole estate of a widow, or one that is on trust for a child, is often invested in an institution like a bank, because it seems so safe. Let us say that there is a shareholder with fewer assets even than Dr Scott. When he is called to pay ten pounds for every pound he invested, he cannot do it. He goes bankrupt. And then the money which was called unsuccessfully from him is added to the debt and divided amongst those shareholders who still have possessions: on them a second call will be made. Only the very richest men can survive such a system. For the others, bankruptcy is the only end. A man of Dr Scott's age can remember what happened in 1866. He knows what will happen now. He is right to be frightened – although wrong, of course, to vent his anger on an infant.'

Margaret was silent for a moment, but she understood David's explanation well enough to apply it at last to her own situation.

'And my father is a proprietor,' she said.

'The largest,' David told her. 'It is because he owns more than half the shares that he has been able to control the bank's affairs.'

'So his house too must be sold, and all his fortune taken away?'

'Unless he has assets about which I know nothing.'

'There is the jade,' said Margaret. 'But no, his wealth can hardly amount to five million pounds, and this is the amount which you say he might be called on to pay.'

Again she was silent, until her sympathy for her father desolated her. 'What can he do?' she asked herself aloud. 'He is almost eighty. He has been wealthy all his life, and accustomed to comfort and service. Oh, my poor father, what will he do? And I can do nothing for him, because I shall be destitute too.'

The realization came to her suddenly. She thought she had accepted the fact that she would be poor, but this was the first moment when she realized that she had nothing at all. She whispered, as though ashamed to be thinking of herself, 'What is to happen to me?'

'You will be my wife,' said David. He took both her hands and held them firmly. 'We shall be very poor at first, but I shall be all the less concerned about that for knowing that you have not had to leave a life of wealth in order to marry me. I am young and I shall work hard and we shall be together. We must make our own future, but it will be better in the end than living on someone else's past.'

'I have no right,' said Margaret. 'I can bring you nothing. I am no longer the woman you asked to marry you.'

'You are the woman I love, and nothing in you has changed.' He kissed her gently, and she clung to him for reassurance. Half an hour earlier, as she described the birth of the new baby, she had felt all the confidence of a grown woman; now, suddenly, she was young again, and insecure.

'There may be a few weeks' grace before the first call is made on your father's property,' David said. 'I will use the time to make some definite plans. Meanwhile, I am sure your brother values your presence here.'

He stood up to go, but he had reminded Margaret of another fear.

'You speak of my brother,' she said. 'Surely he too is a proprietor of the bank, I remember my father making over some of his own shareholding when William became twenty-one. Is his property also at risk?'

David gave an incredulous gasp and began to laugh, with bitterness rather than amusement. Margaret looked at him in perplexity, waiting for an explanation.

'William is safe, and I am the one who saved him,' he said. 'The situation is ironical. Only a short while ago I forced him to sell his shareholding in order to reduce the Lorimer Line's debt to the bank. The Line will be called upon to repay the rest of what it owes, but only in the normal course of business. Your brother has no personal liability for any of the bank's debts. Fifteen hundred citizens of Bristol may curse the name of Lorimer as they consider their ruin, but Mr William Lorimer will not be among them.' He stopped apologetically. 'I must learn to control my tongue. It was not your brother's own idea to relinquish his interest in the bank. He was angry, in fact, and would have resisted me if he could. He is not to be blamed for what in the circumstances is the greatest good fortune which could have befallen him. I hope he will remember that I, who so much angered him, was the one to do him so great a favour.'

The doorbell of the house rang as they used their last moment of privacy to say goodbye. By the time they arrived in the hall the front door had already been opened to show three men standing on the doorstep. One of them removed his hat and took a step inside. He took no notice of Margaret, but looked straight at David.

'Are you Mr David James Gregson?' he demanded.

'I am. What of it?'

'You may perhaps wish the young lady to withdraw, sir,' he suggested.

'No,' said Margaret. Suddenly frightened, she gripped David's arm more tightly than before. 'What is your business here?'

'I'm afraid we have to ask Mr Gregson to come with us, ma'am. I have a warrant here for his arrest.'

14

A man who knows his own guilt will evade arrest if he can, but one who believes himself innocent may feel a kind of relief when suspicion hardens to the point of accusation. David heard Margaret gasp with horror at his arrest, but his own feelings were more complicated. In one way he was as incredulous as she, and as sure that there must be some terrible mistake. Yet he had been expecting something of the sort ever since the police sergeant's visit to the bank. He could not be happy that the challenge had come, but it meant that there was now something more concrete to fight than his own apprehensions.

'On what charge?' he asked quietly.

The man who appeared to be the spokesman of the three pulled a paper from his pocket and read in a sing-song voice.

'You are charged with the felonious fabrication and falsification of the balance sheet of a joint-stock banking company trading under the name of Lorimer's Bank, with intent to defraud. And further with theft and embezzlement through the continued trading of the aforesaid company when known to be in a condition of insolvency.'

'Theft!' exclaimed David. 'I have never had a penny . . .' He stopped himself in mid-sentence. This man was merely a servant of the court, neither knowing nor caring about the details of the case. David forced himself to speak calmly.

'Am I the only one to be so accused?'

'No, sir. Mr John Junius Lorimer was arrested earlier this evening.'

This time Margaret cried out in distress. David turned quickly to support her in case she should faint, but her face showed only bewilderment.

'Send at once to William,' he told her. 'He must find a lawyer. Ask him also to arrange bail.'

Margaret nodded her understanding, but her hand continued to grip his arm so tightly that he could not move away until he released her hold.

'There must be an investigation, and this is the way to start it,' he told her, with more confidence than he felt. 'A formality, nothing more. But send for William.' He took his coat and hat and stepped out of the house.

Margaret obeyed him at once, and William worked fast. Early the next morning an application for bail was made at the preliminary hearing as soon as the charges and pleas had been heard. David knew that two of the magistrates were friends of John Junius Lorimer, men of his own generation, who were likely to regard it as unthinkable that a man who had led a respectable life for seventy-eight years should be forced to stay in jail while the lengthy preparations for a trial were made. Because he was too old and well-known to run away, there could be little point in refusing bail – and then David must have it too, or the magistrates would seem to be pronouncing in advance that one of the accused was less trustworthy than the other.

He was right. It was as a free man that he attended his first conference with the Lorimers' family lawyer. But it was as a worried man that he left it. He had hoped that the case could be defended in the same manner that the chairman had defended his actions to David himself, with a general argument about the benefits which would have accrued to everyone concerned if the bank could have maintained public confidence in its solvency for only a few months longer. But the solicitor, Mr Broadbent, dismissed the possibility from the start.

'I fear, Mr Gregson, that the law does not recognize an

end as justifying a means. You will be examined on your figures and required to explain them in the light of the bank's situation at that time. We shall be briefing counsel, of course, and he will need to know in advance detailed answers to the most detailed questions which the Crown can put. Let us take an example – one which may prove central to the whole charge. At the beginning of May you recommended to the directors that they should declare a dividend of twelve per cent. The effect of such a declaration was to attract an increased volume of deposits, and this was presumably its intention. We may take it that the prosecution will scrutinize with particular care the accounts by which this dividend was held to be justified.'

'The recommendation of such a high dividend was not mine,' said David.

'It bears your signature.'

'That was a formality. The decision was the chairman's.' He looked across the table at John Junius. The old man had not spoken since the meeting began; he did not speak now. David turned back to the lawyer. 'I must remind you, Mr Broadbent, that my responsibilities as manager took effect only from the first day of May this year.'

'And you accepted the situation as you found it on that day. Your promotion, I understand, Mr Gregson, was earned by your ability as an accountant. We may take it that you understood the figures which you were asked to approve?'

David looked for a second time at the chairman's massive figure. John Junius neither met his gaze nor turned his head away. He continued to stare straight ahead as though what was going on in the room was no concern of his. Was it the look of a man who might still be in a state of shock at the collapse of his empire and the attack on his own reputation? Or was it the defence of a man who had already decided on a way of escape from his predicament and was not prepared to jeopardize it by any show of sympathy. Search as he might, David was unable to decide which was the more likely judgement. He pushed back his chair and stood up.

'What I understand now is that my interests may not run with those of Mr Lorimer,' he said. 'It will be more satisfactory for all parties, I imagine, if I engage my own lawyer.'

He left the room with as much confidence and dignity as he could summon, but inwardly he was trembling. It seemed inconceivable that the man who had welcomed him as a son-in-law should be preparing to place the blame for the collapse of the bank on his shoulders, but it was difficult to interpret the chairman's silence in any other way. As David paced the streets, trying to unravel his thoughts and emotions, the realization came to him that he could state the position in an opposite way. Could it be that John Junius had accepted his relationship with Margaret precisely in order that he could be used as a scapegoat in a situation already recognized as almost hopeless?

Such a possibility was too villainous to be accepted at once, but David's anxiety increased as he considered its likelihood. Back in his room, he began to make notes of dates and conversations, trying to establish the order of events and to see through them to the motives behind. As he did so, he came near to panic. Everything that had happened had two possible explanations. Who would believe the version of a stranger to the city, who had lost nothing but his employment, if it was opposed by the word of a man who had always been respected and who was now old? When a rich man claimed that he had been duped by the young upstart to whom he had delegated business which in his declining years had become too much for him, the very men who today were cursing the name of Lorimer might even be persuaded to sympathize with his ruin.

David had said that he would engage his own lawyer,

but the defiance was a toothless one. He had no money to pay the bill for what was bound to be a complicated and costly case. Even if his defence proved successful, he would win back nothing but his good name. William had backed his application for bail, but would no longer support him once it became apparent that his interests directly opposed those of John Junius. Such was David's state of mind that he could not even bring himself to visit Margaret again. Days passed as he scribbled calculations which increasingly revealed to him the complexity of his involvement.

Of all the Lorimers, it was the least expected one who made the first friendly gesture. William appeared without warning in his lodgings one evening. He made no comment on the shabby furnishings or the empty grate which David could no longer afford to fill with coals, but kept his top coat on against the cold. David found it difficult to realize that he and his visitor were much of an age. William's small, precise body and tightly controlled emotions expressed themselves in a clipped voice which had the coldness of a far older man. But the offer he had come to make, though he couched it in businesslike terms, was not a cold one.

'You will appreciate, Mr Gregson, that at the time of my father's arrest, and your own, I had little knowledge of the true position at Lorimer's. I have never involved myself in the affairs of the bank. My father would not have taken kindly to such interference, and I have enough to do, looking after the Lorimer Line. What I have learned recently has come as a shock to me.'

He paused, allowing David to bow his head in acceptance of the fact, which did not seem of any great importance.

'It seems to me likely, Mr Gregson, that the prosecution case will be proved. I understand very well the motives from which my father and yourself acted . . .' he swept away David's attempt to interrupt – 'but I am afraid that a judge may hold them to be irrelevant. It is possible that all may go well. What I have come here to discuss is the other possibility.'

David waited. He had no liking for William, but at this crisis in his life he could not afford to be proud.

'If my father were to be the only defendant,' continued William, 'the verdict would still, in my reading of the situation, go against him. But it is possible that in such a case the sentence might be mitigated by sympathy. He may have been responsible for the bank's collapse, but he is quite clearly the one who has lost most by it. No one in his senses could impute an unworthy motive to such a man, even though his legal responsibility is admitted. It would be recognized that the failure is in itself almost a sufficient punishment. Although no doubt a token sentence of imprisonment might be imposed, we could hope that in view of his age it would be for a short period only. Do you agree with me so far?'

'Yes,' said David shortly. He had realized from the start that the chairman's best defence was the loss of his own fortune as a result of the bank's failure.

'But your own case is different. The facts and figures remain the same, but the motive for their manipulation will be represented differently, and the element of sympathy will be lacking. The case will be tried in Bristol, and you have no claim on the mercy of a city which already finds itself in great economic difficulty. A sentence in your case might be vindictive, longer even than the charge justifies. Yet British justice must be seen to be fair. If you and my father are judged to be equal in guilt, there will no doubt be some equality of sentence. If so, it seems to me more likely on balance, that my father's sentence might be increased to equal yours than that yours would be cut to match his.'

'You are making a good many assumptions, Mr Lorimer. I cannot follow you in all of them.'

'Then I will make the proposition which I came here to

173

offer, and leave you to consider it on its own merits. What I have been saying is only to explain why I believe it to be in the interest of my family. I have brought with me, Mr Gregson, a paper authorizing you to take passage on any ship of the Lorimer Line which leaves Bristol within the next fourteen days. You have only to present this to the captain; and you may use what name you choose. There will be no formalities.'

'The bail which you yourself have guaranteed would of course be forfeited in such a case.'

William shrugged his thin shoulders.

'There is a price to be paid for everything.' He hesitated briefly. 'I have told you, Mr Gregson, that I am anxious for my father's sake. But it is also true, as my sister has reminded me, that I am indirectly indebted to you for the fact that my own property is not at risk. One day I intend to be as wealthy and as highly respected in this city as any of my forefathers, so that this unhappy incident in our family history will be forgotten and the name of Lorimer will once again be recognized as a symbol of worth and prosperity. I should have achieved this ambition in any case, but I am ready to own that it will come more easily to the owner of a great shipping line whose future is widening before it than to a bankrupt. I trust that with this I shall pay off my debt to you.'

It was the most convincing argument he had used. David was prepared to believe that the offer was made by a man who did not care to be beholden to his inferiors.

'You mentioned your sister,' he said, not answering the proposal directly. 'Does she know of your plan?'

'No. It is a matter best not revealed to anyone. If it became known that you planned to depart, you would of course be re-arrested.'

'But I cannot leave England without speaking to her.' David looked down at the paper. 'You offer but a single passage.'

William showed signs of impatience.

'You could hardly expect my sister to accompany you to a destination where you have as yet no home and no means of support. Tell her by all means, if you wish, that you will send for her to join you when you are in a position to do so. I will gladly take a letter for you now if you wish. Margaret has not been brought up to face the rigours of colonial life. I can provide her with a comfortable home here until you are ready to replace it with another in Australia, or wherever else you choose to go. The debt I owe to her for my son's life is even larger than that to yourself. You will believe me, I am sure, when I tell you that I am determined to do everything possible to ensure her happiness. And she is not likely to be happy if you are in prison.'

For the second time a more personal argument made it easier for David to believe that William was sincerely trying to help him. The antagonism between them was one of temperament, but the fact that at bottom they disliked each other did not prevent their interests from running together. David allowed himself to be distracted for a moment by the memory of what had been happening during his last visits to The Ivies.

'Your wife and the baby are in good health, I hope?' he said.

'Both of them, by the grace of God,' said William. 'Arthur is still very small, but my sister has made herself responsible for his care. His strength increases daily.'

He stood up, his business at an end. David looked down at the paper which he was still holding.

'I need time to consider my predicament,' he said. 'May I keep this while I do so?' He looked up at his visitor and forced himself to speak the words which were owing, although they stuck in his throat. 'I am greatly obliged to you, Mr Lorimer.'

William nodded, using the same movement that David

had so often seen from his father. Each of them recognized that David would in fact use the passage he had been offered.

After his visitor had left, David tried to persuade himself that he still had a choice, but deep in his heart he knew that his position in Bristol was hopeless. He could not maintain his own innocence of fraud except by claiming that he had always acted on the direct instructions of the chairman. If the chairman chose to deny this, as clearly he intended, no jury would prefer David's word. Ever since the meeting with the lawyer he had been wondering how he could escape. Now the means had been put into his hands. There was nothing to stop him except the knowledge that his flight would be taken as a confession of guilt. Early next morning, knowing that every step brought him nearer to a decision, he walked down to the floating harbour.

Two of William's ships were moored in the basin, and another lay careened against the bank of the river. If a Lorimer steamship happened to be in England, it would be berthed at Portishead, in the estuary, for the Avon channel was not deep enough to take it. But until the new dock area was complete, the sailing ships still came into Bristol itself, as they had always done.

David did not need to enquire about the destination of any steamship, for it would have been built especially to challenge the Cunard interest in the Atlantic crossing to New England. But the three vessels in the harbour would go wherever the promise of a cargo sent them. Although it was still dark, the day's work had already begun. A squad of sailors was crawling over the hull of the careened ship, the *Rosa*, scraping it clear of barnacles. David found someone on the shore to tell him that she would be sailing for Australia in two weeks' time. Of the two ships afloat in the harbour, the *Diana* was bound for Jamaica, the *Flora* for California.

The *Flora* was being loaded at that moment. Standing

176

-

on the wharf, the supercargo checked off on his bill of lading the goods that were being carried out of a warehouse by the light of a lantern. David went to speak to him.

'What trade do you do?' he asked.

'We'll fill our holds on the West Coast with hides for leather, sir,' the man replied in a Somerset accent made even broader by his years at sea. 'That's to say, if we can keep the crew from the goldfields when they get there. This is one run that we've no need to shanghai for. A free passage to fortune, some of these scum seem to think it. We take none but married men, if we can find them, but even those will throw off a wife for the sake of an ounce of gold or silver, it seems.'

'I thought those days were over,' said David wonderingly.

'Ay, the days of scraping and washing are done. It's a mining job now, I'm told. But there's enough still there to make a millionaire of a man who starts with nought but muscle.'

'You haven't been tempted yourself?'

'There are other ways of making a fortune, sir.' The man gave a contented smile. 'The men who've made their millions come to live in the cities when they leave the mines. Rough types they are, some of them. But their wives, sir, that's summat else again. The ladies of San Francisco live in palaces you'd not believe. And they're not content with the furniture which their husband once made to fill a log cabin, I can tell you that. They want the best that Europe can send them. That's what we're loading now. Mr Lorimer's had his agents out buying for the past six months to fill these holds. Half of it's on special order, so there's not even any risk. There's a clock in the warehouse now, sir, come from Paris. If I were to tell you the price of it, you wouldn't believe me, just to tell the hour of day. But some rich lady's set her heart on it, and four days from now it'll be on its way.'

'You won't grow rich by supervising Mr Lorimer's business,' suggested David.

'He's a good master,' said the supercargo. 'Or maybe it's just that he's got his wits about him. I wouldn't like to say. He pays the lowest rate in Bristol for this run, and still he can make up a crew. Because every man may take one case of his own purchasings to sell at whatever profit he can. With a larger allowance for myself. Three crates of table silver I shall have stowed below there: thirty years old and the fanciest style I can find. My first voyage out, I borrowed more for my stock than I thought I'd ever be able to repay. But by now . . .' He broke off to admonish a group of men who were staggering with a heavy load towards the edge of the wharf. 'Go steady with that table, will you? That's best Italian marble you're carrying.'

'I mustn't hinder you,' said David. 'She sails in four days, you said?'

'On the morning tide, sir.'

David was thoughtful as he walked away. He turned his back on the ships and by the dawn light looked up at the terraces of the city which crossed the steep hills in tiers. He could disregard the slums which surrounded the harbour itself and appreciate the elegant houses of the elevated squares and crescents built in the previous century. This was a merchant city, grown rich by trading across the seven seas. The poorest member of William Lorimer's crew, filthy and illiterate though he well might be, was carrying on a tradition which was already centuries old. As a bank official David could never have achieved more than a respectable competence. To marry the daughter of a rich man had been one way, certainly, of putting himself in line for wealth, but it was a way now closed to him. If he was to raise himself in the world, he must be prepared to take a risk. William had offered him a passage as a means of escape. Its attraction to David was as the means of entry into a new life.

178

Of America he knew little. In his short period with Lorimer's he had done some business with New York, but not enough to give him any claim on that city's hospitality. What he did know was that the Americans themselves were going west, at first in a thin stream across the forbidding natural barriers of the continent and now in a flood carried by the railways. A city like San Francisco might well prove to be a place where a man could start again from the beginning, with not too many questions asked, and yet at the same time a place large and civilized enough for David to practise his urban skills. The empty acres of Australia held nothing to tempt him, but in a city of newly rich men he could surely find employment and the means of advancing himself.

The change of viewpoint excited him as he walked back to his lodgings. By now the decision which had been reached unconsciously on the previous evening was ready to be openly acknowledged in his mind. He would not think of himself as a fugitive, but as a pioneer.

The feeling of adventure raised his spirits from the depression which had leadened them for so long. It was necessary to remind himself that he had no capital which he could invest in even a sailor's modest case of goods. No one in Bristol would lend money to David Gregson, and even a whisper that he was seeking it would be enough to have him seized and returned to jail. He would begin a new life with no assets but his head for figures and the skills of his fingers.

They would be enough, he told himself, refusing to let his new excitement slip away. That expensive clock from Paris was not likely to take kindly to months of tossing through storms in a damp hold, and there would be others like it in need of attention. Light though his baggage might be, he would come to a new shore no worse equipped than many others before him. By the time he returned to his room, all doubt had vanished into the darkness. In four

179

days' time he would leave Bristol on the morning tide to make his fortune in America.

15

Few people can close the door on the past without some regret, however unhappy their memories of it may be. Back in his room after his decision had been made, David sat in front of the empty grate and thought about Margaret.

Nothing in his feelings for her had been changed by the fact that she was no longer a rich man's daughter. His body ached to hold her in his arms again: he longed to possess her wholly. He was confident that her nature was a loyal one. If he asked her to wait for him, she would wait. But was it a demand which he could honourably make? Although he had no liking for her brother, he recognized that one of William's talents was the ability to analyse a situation dispassionately and express his opinions with clarity. He had been right to point out that Margaret should not be expected to remain faithful to a man serving a prison sentence, and equally right that she could not be carried off into a strange country by someone who would hardly have the price of the first night's lodging in his pocket. Slowly David came to accept the fact that he would have to let her go. His disgrace and impending trial had brought him many hours of sleeplessness and anxiety and even fear, but only at the prospect of losing Margaret did he come close to weeping.

If he were to see her again, he was sure that he could never leave. Instead, he wrote to her on the day before the *Flora* was due to sail. It was the letter, he hoped, of a gentleman – releasing her from her engagement for her own sake, so that she could look for a happy future elsewhere. But even as he sealed it, the hope was in his mind that perhaps a small miracle would happen and that she would refuse the freedom he offered her.

Late that evening the miracle occurred. He heard a knocking on the door and the sound of his landlady expostulating. Margaret had come – and come unchaperoned. Although Mrs Lambert knew well enough who she was, the name of Lorimer was no longer one to command respect. David cut the protests short and hurried Margaret into his sitting room.

She had made the journey on foot, he realized, for her clothes were soaked, and the crape which trimmed her mourning mantle was ruined by the rain. This meant that she had not dared to tell William what her errand was. David stared at her, not daring to embrace or even touch her, in case the encouragement of hope should make a final parting even harder to bear. Margaret was also staring, but at the condition of a room which revealed so unmistakably that its occupant was packing for a final departure.

'You told me I was free to go, so I hoped I was also free to come. But you are leaving. Your letter did not tell me that.'

'I have no choice,' said David. 'Or rather, only the choice between a rapid disappearance and a prison cell.'

'Will you not take me with you?' she asked.

'Oh, if only I could! But what have I to offer? We could live on a very little, but I have nothing at all. Absolutely nothing.'

'I have something,' she said. 'I could sell Lower Croft.'

For a moment he stared at her in astonishment. In the strain of the past weeks he had completely forgotten the existence of the house which John Junius had given to his daughter. Margaret must have misunderstood the puzzled expression on his face.

'I had thought at first that Lower Croft must be sold together with Brinsley House and all my father's other possessions,' she said. 'Then William explained to me that the property was my own and that the officers of the court have no right to touch it. My second thought was that I ought to sell it in any case, and use the money to relieve some of the suffering which has been caused by the failure of Lorimer's. But your need of the money is just as great. I would be happiest of all to put it in your hands.'

He should have been grateful, both for the trust that she showed in him and, more practically, for the offer of money which could be invested in a new life for the two of them. Instead he was overcome by fury against the man who had done so much to wrong him.

'I ought to have understood it earlier,' he said. 'As soon as your father saw the crash coming he removed what he could beyond the reach of his creditors. He could not act in such a way without good excuse. What could be more plausible than the coming-of-age of his only daughter. Mr Lorimer will never allow you to sell Lower Croft. It is intended to provide him with a roof over his own head when everything else has gone.'

'I don't understand what you are saying,' she replied. 'My father could have had no knowledge in advance of what has happened.'

'He has known for months,' said David. 'That is why tomorrow I shall be a fugitive from a prison sentence.'

'Are you so sure that you will be found guilty?'

David had not intended to say anything to Margaret against her father, but anger at the mention of Lower Croft made him forget himself. It hurt his pride to think that after he had left, Margaret would hear nothing but ill of him, and there would be no one to speak in his defence.

'You know the mood in the city,' he said. 'Someone must be judged responsible for all the suffering that has been caused. Someone must be found guilty. Your father has decided that I, and not himself, should be the scapegoat.'

'You surely misjudge him. He would not do that when I love you and you are to be his son-in-law!'

'Did it not surprise you, Margaret, when he accepted me as your suitor? A man without either fortune or family to recommend him. When your father had already made it clear that he wished to use you to ally himself with one of the other wealthy families of the city.' His first use of her Christian name, though it was a sign that he was no longer prepared to bow to the conventions of her society, passed unnoticed by them both.

'I must confess to some surprise,' she said honestly. 'But I knew that his own marriage had been an alliance of this sort, and that it had not proved to be a happy one. I thought that this had determined him to allow me my own choice as a sign of affection for me. Besides, he knows as well as I do that I am not beautiful, and what it meant to me that I should have bestowed my affection on someone who seemed to return it.'

David leant a little towards her, longing to step forward and tell her that she was indeed beautiful in his eyes and that she had not been wrong in thinking her love returned. But instinct told him that this was a discussion which must be kept to the path of reason and not of emotion. He did not realize, even as he controlled his feelings of love, that he was already dominated by a deeper feeling of hatred.

'I think you may have been mistaken,' he said. 'In the same way I deluded myself when I believed that your father gave me promotion because he recognized my business ability. We both, I am afraid, allowed our hearts to overrule our heads. Your father is not a sentimental man. He had a purpose in arranging this engagement: he needed someone to take the blame.'

'The blame for what?' asked Margaret. 'For the slipping of a dock wall? For the burning of a ship? For the collapse of a bank in another city?'

David shook his head.

'The trouble was much more deep-seated than that,' he said. 'Those were only the windows which allowed the rottenness within to be seen. I'm not trying to say that your father was a wicked man where the affairs of the bank were concerned. But he made mistakes, and his pride forced him to cover them up.'

'How can you say that you are not accusing him of wickedness when you would have me believe that he intends to put all the blame on you?'

'I think that is the case,' said David. 'I think it was his intention from the start. That is why I am going. After I am gone he can say what he wants and there will be no one to contradict him. It will assist him greatly, I imagine, in the trial and when sentence is passed. But although the whole of Bristol will think of me as a villain or a fool, I trust that you . . .'

'You said that my father arranged this engagement,' interrupted Margaret. The colour was high in her cheeks for a reason that David failed to understand. 'He did not do so. He *permitted* it, certainly, but only at my most earnest insistence. Because I wanted it so very much and because I thought – I thought that you . . .'

The tears were in her eyes, ready to fall. David tried to keep his voice gentle as he answered.

'You were right to think that I loved you. I loved you then and I love you now. And it was necessary for your father's intentions that the wish should seem to come from you. But who was it who first threw us together, Margaret? Who made sure that we should see far more of each other than our stations in life would in the usual way have made possible? You are as well aware as I how little power of choice devolves on a daughter in the house of a wealthy man. You were allowed to choose only when your father had made sure that you would choose what he wished.'

'You speak of me as though I had no mind of my own!' cried Margaret, and David realized too late that the flush

184

he had observed was one of anger. 'As though I were a decoy, the bait placed in a trap to catch you by the foot. My father learned early enough that where marriage was concerned I claimed the right to determine my own fate. It was at my insistence that the alliance he planned with Walter Crankshaw was abandoned. And it was at my insistence again that you were accepted in Walter's place. It was not easy for me to face my father's displeasure, and I will not be told now that I was dancing all the time to his tune like an organ-grinder's monkey. I understand now that you were playing a tune of your own. You had a mind to marry the daughter of a rich man who would advance your career. But now the alliance is of no use to you, you give me back my freedom so that you may take your own, and you revile my father to ensure that I shall not try to hold you back.'

'Marry me, Margaret,' said David. It was only a few hours since he had written the letter which told her that they must part, but now he was overcome by a feeling of panic lest she should take him at his word. 'Marry me tomorrow and come with me to make a new life. If you made over Lower Croft to William he would advance you money for a passage and the price of a home.' He thought quickly. The *Flora*, on which he had planned to sail to San Francisco, would leave the city harbour in only eight hours – too short a time for Margaret to make the necessary arrangements. But that destination had been chosen at random. Any other would do as well. 'The *Diana* leaves for Jamaica in six days' time. Marry me, and we will sail on her together.'

He had chosen the worst possible time to renew his proposal. Margaret's eyes were still brimming with the tears which revealed how much she had been hurt by his accusations, and her voice as she answered was cold.

'So you are willing after all to use the money which you claim my father had no right to set aside.'

'I am willing to do anything which will make for your happiness.'

'And you think I could be happy with a man who believes that my father is wicked and myself weak? You must think again. You wrote this morning to offer me my freedom from my engagement to you. I accept the offer with gratitude, and pray that you may make good use of your own freedom in finding happiness in your new life. Goodnight, Mr Gregson.'

He put out a hand to hold her back, but she tugged her arm sharply away and swept out of the house as he called her name with one last cry of anguish. He heard her footsteps running down the wooden stairs and, a moment later, along the empty street outside. He could have run faster and caught her again, but it would have done no good. Nothing in his own situation had changed. He was still a man with nothing to offer. And about John Junius he had said only what he believed to be the truth. It would have been wiser and kinder not to have spoken the words, but he could not in honesty now withdraw them and make a hollow apology to heal the rift which had caused her anger.

Now the desolation which he had faced earlier and thought to have conquered returned again to drain away his courage. He stood for a long time with his head pressed against the door, knowing that he had lost her for ever. He tried to banish from his mind the picture of her appearance at this last meeting: a proud, indignant figure dressed in the unflattering deadness of black paramatta and crape. Instead he remembered the happy girl, her face framed in fur, who had looked so lovingly into his eyes in the snow-swept garden of Lower Croft, claiming his own heart with spirit and courage. He remembered too the radiant young woman, beautiful in her ball dress, with a long ringlet of red hair lying softly on her smooth white shoulders, who had danced with him at the ball for the Prince of Wales.

As his love ached in silent despair, so his anger grew against the man who had promised him this treasure but had never intended that the promise should be kept. With his lips tightened in a manner reminiscent of John Junius himself, David crossed over to the table and began to write.

He worked without stopping for three hours, using the notes which he had made earlier to refresh his memory of dates and figures. Dawn was already lightening the sky as he signed and sealed the statement. As soon as he heard his landlady stirring, he put it into her hands. She was to keep it, he told her, until the day before the trial of John Junius Lorimer began. Then she should take it to the police station. David had marked on the outside the instruction that it should be handed to the chief prosecuting counsel, but he could not expect Mrs Lambert herself to discover who that would be. He gave her a little money for her trouble, and settled the rent with the last of his savings. Then he whistled for a boy from the street to help him with his baggage.

Three hours later the *Flora* moved towards the estuary along the narrow and tortuous channel of the Avon. She was pulled by a steam tug and noisy with commands as the crew made her ready to catch the wind which would be waiting in the open water. David looked up from her deck towards the gardens of Brinsley House. The mansion itself, lying back from the gorge, could not be seen – except for the tower in which John Junius himself might at this moment be sitting. David stared for a moment, reflecting on the ruthlessness of the rich towards intruders in their midst. Then, as Brunel's miraculous bridge seemed to glide through the air far above, he averted his gaze from the tumbling woods and sheer cliffs and in a gesture of final rejection went down to his berth, turning his back on England and the Lorimers for ever.

16

Insolvency is infectious. In the weeks which followed the collapse of Lorimer's Bank the commercial life of Bristol came nearly to a standstill. The bank's larger shareholders were in many cases the owners of manufacturing or trading companies. As they came to be stripped of their assets they were forced to close their warehouses and factories and turn their workmen out into a community which had no new employment to offer. The depositors, although they might hope for the return of some of their money eventually, had for the time being no ready cash, so that tradesmen's bills went unpaid and new spending was restricted to the barest necessities of life. Drapers and tobacconists, milliners and dressmakers, horse-dealers and wine merchants, all found themselves with debts which might never be settled and stocks which could not be sold. They too reduced their staffs and this added to the poverty which every day settled more and more inexorably on the city. The ragged children whose profession it was to hire themselves out as the pitiable dependants of beggars joined the ranks of the unemployed, for there were enough truly destitute and starving families to absorb all available charity without the necessity to pretend despair.

The property market was as badly affected as any other form of trade. So many shops and houses were offered through forced sale at the same time – and so few buyers were to be found – that prices dropped almost to nothing, making removal impossible even for those who were not directly affected by the crisis but wished merely to escape from it. Stung by David's taunt, Margaret put Lower Croft on to the market. She was not prepared to believe that her father had made the gift deliberately in order that something might be salvaged from the wreck of his own estate, but her conscience told her that when so many people had been ruined through entrusting their money to the Lorimers, no member of the family should be immune from the penalties of failure. A charitable fund had been opened in the city for the relief of distress caused by the bank's collapse, and she intended to donate the proceeds of the sale to this. She was careful not to tell William of her plan, for she guessed that he would dismiss it as sentimental.

No buyer could be found. Quite apart from the general shortage of capital, the position of Lower Croft in the grounds of a hospital made it unattractive to anyone wanting a family home. After only a short time, the agents informed her that there was little chance of a sale, and advised her to let the property. Instead, she lent it rent free to a family whose own house had been taken from them by the bank's Receiver. On the first night of their stay, she cried herself to sleep. This was to have been her home as David Gregson's bride. In giving the key of the door to a stranger, she was acknowledging that they would never live there together.

The winter of 1878 was as bleak as the life of the city. Snow fell early, and the boys of the College, on the way from their houses to Big School, hurried past William's windows with blue fingers and shoulders hunched against the cold. November would normally have seen the opening of the social season, but this year there were no balls and no grand dinners. Even those who were still in a position to entertain could not be sure that their friends any longer kept a carriage in which to travel, or enough servants to make a return invitation possible. In the whole depressed city only the poor – those to whom debts had always come more naturally than savings – found their situation unchanged. The poor, and William Lorimer.

189

His sister, devoting her days to the care of baby Arthur and her nights to tears for her lost lover, did not appreciate how unusual William's position was. The requirements of mourning demanded that she should avoid all society after her mother's death, so she was exposed neither to the ostracism which might have faced her from unkind acquaintances nor to the facts and rumours of bankruptcies which she would have heard from her remaining friends. She noticed, naturally, that William was not as low in spirits as might have been expected. If she had been more knowledgeable about financial matters she might have connected this with a casual remark of his one day that Lloyd's had been creditably prompt in paying the insurance claim for the loss of the *Georgiana* and that this was no bad time to have a little liquid capital. What she did know was that he spent a good deal of his time with lawyers and accountants, and she was prepared to believe that he had inherited the financial acumen which had deserted John Junius only in the years of his old age. But she was too miserable on her own account to think very much about her brother's affairs. Every night as she went to bed she assured herself that she could never have been happy with a man who regarded her father as a criminal; and every night the hot tears cooled on her cheeks as she fell asleep knowing that she would never be happy with anyone else.

John Junius, all this time, remained alone at Brinsley House. Almost all the servants had been sent away, though a cook and a manservant remained to attend to him. The house became chill and damp, for only in the library was a fire ever lit. All the other rooms, except for his bedroom and the kitchens, were closed and shuttered, waiting for the furniture to be carried away and sold. He spent his time preparing explanations and justifications of the balance sheets which would be presented at his trial, and received no visitors except his solicitor and the members of his family.

190

The jade collection, and the Indian and Persian screens, were the first to go. Margaret and Ralph arrived at Brinsley House one morning to find a carter waiting outside, while a squad of men filled packing cases with the precious carvings. They were to be sent to London for auction, John Junius told them as he supervised the work. There was no money in Bristol to spare for such luxuries, and the Receiver who was handling the bank's affairs had arranged that they should be sold where the highest prices were likely to be obtained for the creditors. John Junius spoke in his usual brusque manner, as though the silent despair to which the death of his wife and the fall of his bank had reduced him was already a thing of the past, and the future something to be faced with confidence. He even turned on Ralph with an accusing air to demand why he was not at Oxford.

'There is surely no money to pay the fees,' answered Ralph in surprise.

'The money will be found. Your college will recognize that our difficulties are purely temporary.'

'But the fees are only a small part of the expense, Father. In such a place one must be able to live like a gentleman. I have accepted the fact that this way of life is no longer possible for me.'

'Then what, may I ask, do you propose to do with yourself?'

'I must look for employment.'

'With what qualifications? You are of no use to society in your present state.'

'That's hardly my fault, Father. Perhaps William will employ me as a clerk in his office.'

John Junius turned away, his fists clenched with anger. The door of the library slammed behind him. Margaret looked reproachfully at her younger brother.

'Oh Ralph, it is unkind of you to remind Papa that he is

191

no longer able to give you the kind of life he would wish for you.'

'He has always believed that he has some kind of claim on society, that he must always be well treated,' said Ralph. 'I make no such claim for myself. I have deserved nothing of anybody. And it seems to me that our family has lived for too long on the sufferings of others. If I am the one who must pay for this, it is a situation I accept.'

They began to walk together back to The Ivies.

'If William were to offer . . .' began Margaret; but Ralph shrugged his shoulders.

'He has not done so, though he knows my circumstances. I don't wish to sponge on him. Although he has not lost his capital, like so many of our friends, he hardly gives the impression of having more income than he needs.'

It was difficult for Margaret to make any comment. William had inherited from his father a dislike of any kind of ostentation. Although Sophie had brought him money, it might all have been invested in the shipping line for the sake of future profits. Margaret had no better idea than Ralph whether it would be easy for their brother to be generous.

'If you had the choice,' she said. 'If there were no problem of money, what would you do with your life?'

'That's something I've thought about over and over again. Before leaving school I discussed my feelings with Dr Percival and was told by him that if I prayed every night I would be guided to learn whether my wishes were in accordance with God's plan. So I have prayed, and now I am sure that it is my duty to atone for my own guilt and that of our family over the centuries. We have never deserved our wealth. It is not enough to do without it now. We should try to recompense in some way those we have wronged.'

Margaret looked at her eighteen-year-old brother with new eyes. After Claudine's announcement of her pregnancy and hurried departure for France, Ralph had changed with surprising speed from an idle schoolboy interested mainly in cricket to a serious young man dividing his time between his books and his devotions. The change had become most noticeable at the time of their mother's death and the unhappy events which followed, so she had not thought of it as needing any further explanation.

'Recompense them by earning a fortune and giving it away, do you mean? You are hardly likely to become rich as a clerk of the Lorimer Line.'

Ralph shook his head.

'You asked me what I would choose if I were free to do so. I would study to be ordained. And then, when I had taken Holy Orders, I would go as a missionary and minister to those poor wretches whose ancestors were transported by ours from their homes.' He shrugged his shoulders. 'But my choice is not free. Without money I cannot study. At least, not at once. So William is my best hope. If he will employ me for a little, no matter how humbly, I can perhaps work hard enough to earn promotion and begin to save. I shall ask him today.'

The conversation was a reminder to Margaret that she would need to consider her own future. But her thoughts were diverted from this by a letter which had arrived at The Ivies during her brief absence. She had written earlier to her friend Lydia to say where she was staying. Now she was alarmed to see that the letter sent in return was, like her own, sealed with black wax. She opened it hastily.

The news it contained made her cry out in sympathy. Lydia's news was as bad as could be imagined. Her fiancé had been killed in an ambush laid in the Khyber Pass by the Afghan leader, Sher Ali. This fact she stated baldly enough, but then her writing became a scrawl and her message distraught as she expressed desolation at the thought of the life of futility which lay ahead. 'For you know, my dear Margaret, how high I rated my good fortune in being chosen by so admirable a man when I had so little to recommend me.'

Margaret guessed what she meant. Even if her grief should abate sufficiently for her to take notice of any other man, Lydia herself knew well enough how lacking she was in outward grace and beauty. And although her parents lived comfortably enough in Bath, she had revealed to Margaret in past exchanges of confidence that her father's whole estate was entailed on his nephew. If she failed to establish a household of her own before her father died, she must look to a future life without independent means.

For a second time Margaret was reminded, even as she hurried to write her condolences, that this was also her own situation. She began to consider the possibilities seriously, but did not speak of them to anyone at first, preferring to wait until the family's affairs had reached a more settled state.

Ralph's position was more quickly improved. He burst into the nursery a few days later. Arthur was receiving his evening feed from the wet-nurse, so that Ralph ought to have retired from the scene at once, but he was still staring at the woman's bare breast when Margaret hurried him from the room. She intended to scold, but did not have the heart when she saw his excitement.

'I am to go to Oxford after all, Margaret. William has undertaken my support. I may repay him, he says, later in life when I have a stipend to bear the debt. He approves my plan of ordination and feels that it should not be prevented by an accident which comes at such an unfortunate time in my life. I should leave at once, he says, and work hard to make up the time lost.'

Margaret was pleased on his behalf, and called Betty at once to help with his packing. She wondered whether the generous offer came from William's own purse or whether by some miracle the jade collection had proved to be more valuable even than anyone had suspected, raising enough money at auction to pay off the whole of her father's debt. But William shook his head gloomily when she enquired after the success of the sale. The collection had raised a far smaller amount than expected. It was difficult to tell why. Perhaps the whole country was feeling some of the effects of the trading difficulties which afflicted Bristol and Glasgow with such particular severity. Or perhaps John Junius had exaggerated the value of his own pieces in order that the legacy he had intended to make to the city should seem more generous.

On the heels of the jade sale came the auction of Brinsley House. Margaret, of course, did not attend it, and it was once again from William that she learned how low the bids had been. There was no one in Bristol, he explained, who could afford at this moment to put down a large amount of capital for such a substantial property. The Receiver had been told in advance that this would certainly be the case, and that it would be necessary to place a low reserve on the house if it were to find a buyer at all, but he had refused to believe it. His reserve had been too high, and had not been reached. Now he would have to accept that its value today was only a fraction of what might have been asked for it a year or two earlier. He would have to sell it to anyone who was prepared to take it on, however low the price.

Margaret was disturbed by the news, but William tried to persuade her that it was not important.

'When all this is finished, Father will have nothing left in any case,' he said. 'You must make up your mind to that. Whatever the size of the total amount raised by the sale of all his possessions, the advantage can only be to the creditors of the bank. There has never been any possibility that the Receiver's calls could be met with any money to spare.'

It was what David had already told her, and this time she forced herself to believe it. She asked William more questions and learned that David's other prophecies were also coming true. The Receiver had made a first call on the shareholders for a sum equal to eight times the shareholding which each possessed. Even that would not have been enough to cover the debt, but still it was too much. So many had already been driven into bankruptcy, failing to meet the call in spite of the sale of their houses and businesses, that a second call had gone out to those who remained solvent.

'How is Dr Scott? Did he survive the first call?' asked Margaret, remembering how grateful he had been when allowed to invest in the bank, and how abusively he had reacted to its collapse.

William shook his head.

'His worst fears have already been realized. His house is up for sale, like so many others, but it is no longer his own property. The proceeds will go to the Receiver.'

'So what will he do?'

'He should be luckier than some, since his profession requires little capital. And he has a son, Charles, who is also a qualified doctor, working in London. He will presumably be able to find work in the capital if he goes to live with Charles. For the time being, I have come to an arrangement with him. If I pay his bills now, the money will go into his pool of assets on which the Receiver may call. I have promised instead to settle the whole account for his attendance on Sophie and Arthur after he has been formally declared bankrupt.'

Margaret had been so upset by the doctor's drunken behaviour on the night of Arthur's birth that she found it hard to be as sympathetic as she ought. Yet she could not help seeing that his provocation had been great – indeed, she was surprised that he was still willing to attend William's family.

Until a short time ago her life had been sheltered, allowing her no experience of the manner in which passion overcomes reason. By now she had learned the strength of love. What she had not yet experienced, and could not comprehend, was the power of hatred.

17

To a man of humbled pride, what generosity can exceed a gift made with such discretion that it is impossible to thank the giver? Not long after the auction at which Brinsley House had failed to find a buyer, Margaret was visiting her father when a letter was delivered for him. He read it through twice and then handed it across to her. It came from a firm of lawyers, not his own. They had the honour to inform Mr Lorimer that Brinsley House had recently been purchased by a client who wished for the time being to remain anonymous. Now that the price had been paid to the Receiver, their client wished to assure Mr Lorimer that he would be welcome to remain in the house for as long as he wished.

'Who can it be?' asked Margaret.

'I have never doubted that I still have friends,' said her father with some complacency. 'No doubt they have banded together to support me. Will you come back, Margaret, or do you intend staying with William?'

Margaret recognized the appeal which her father was too proud to put into words, and at once assured him that she would return. It proved a bleak homecoming. The contents of the house were to be auctioned *in situ* – notices of the sale had already appeared in the local newspapers. She arrived at the house with her luggage to find the auctioneer and his clerk busily naming and numbering each lot for the catalogue. They worked without sentiment, only pausing occasionally to debate whether a particular piece of furniture could be ascribed to a particular date or maker; whether the handsome leather-bound books whose gold tooling glinted behind the mesh which guarded the bookcases should be sold by the volume or by the shelf. Margaret watched as they inspected the portraits of her ancestors. They were unlabelled, because the family had always known who they were. 'Portrait of an unknown man in seventeenth-century costume,' dictated the auctioneer in a toneless voice, and Margaret turned away from the scene with a heavy heart.

One of the earliest pieces of property to be impounded by the Receiver had been the jewellery which John Junius gave to his wife on the occasion of the ball for the Prince of Wales. She had worn it only for that one event, the last social occasion of her life. The jewels had been sent to the bank for safe keeping on the day after the ball and were found there when the chairman's strong boxes were opened by court order. Like the jade, they were sent to London to be valued and sold. Their magnificence had so much impressed the fashionable society of Bristol that rumour increased their value with every day that passed. This made the news which finally arrived from London nothing short of a sensation. Every piece – necklace, ear rings and hair ornament – was made of paste! The imitation was of good quality and had been set with consummate skill, but as jewels the stones were worthless.

Margaret heard this news with bewilderment. The local newspaper, which printed it at length, filled even more of its space with an account of how imitation jewellery was made, describing in detail how much in such cases the colour owed to the foil which was used to back the paste. Margaret recognized that her opinion was uninformed, but she remembered the pile of stones which she had been allowed to slide through her fingers. Their colour and beauty even then, before they had been set, had taken her breath away. She had been certain that they were worth a fortune. Could she really have been deceived?

Others in the city shared her doubts. The affairs of the rubies took a prominent place in many subsequent issues of the *Bristol Mercury*. Mr Parker, the jeweller, was interviewed and made a statement. He had been given the larger stones by Mr John Junius Lorimer, who had asked him in addition to purchase a sufficient number of tiny diamonds and then to set the whole to a design which was supplied. The stones which he had set were the stones which he had been given. He believed them to be genuine. He had nothing more to say.

Mr Parker's situation was not a happy one. The correspondence columns of the *Mercury* were filled with theories from which he could not hope to escape with credit. Was he so unskilled as a jeweller that he could not distinguish between real and false stones? If he still maintained that he had been given real rubies, what had he done with them after replacing them with imitations? As he maintained his silence, other comments and accusations flooded in. There was someone who had been sure at the time and was prepared to swear now that Mrs Lorimer's jewels on the night of the ball, although showy, were worthless. There was someone else who had no doubt at all that on that occasion she had been wearing a small fortune round her neck, and that its subsequent disappearance must mean that her husband had abstracted it because of his advance knowledge of the collapse of Lorimer's Bank. Mr Parker, no doubt, had been asked by his client to prepare duplicates of all the pieces so that the real jewels could be hidden away in preparation for the time when the chairman emerged from that prison sentence which he appeared richly to deserve. Mr Parker should realize that although he had committed no criminal act in making an imitation at the request of his client – for it was well known that many wealthy women were content to wear replicas of the real jewels which they kept in the bank – his silence now constituted an act of fraud against those innocent creditors to whom all the Lorimer property rightfully belonged.

Mr Parker remained silent but consulted his lawyer. The Receiver took note of the correspondence and consulted the police. John Junius Lorimer asserted in a signed statement that he had commissioned the captain of one of the Lorimer Line's trading ships to buy rubies on his behalf, that the stones he had received from the captain were those which he had handed to the jeweller, and that the jewellery which his wife had worn to the ball was the jewellery which had been placed in his strong box the next morning and not removed by him at any time since then.

None of these statements did anything to quieten the public debate. It was as though a community which found the complicated financial dealings of the bank too difficult to understand had decided to base its estimate of the chairman's guilt or innocence on one comparatively small transaction, and was discovering that even this was far from simple. Into this atmosphere of surmise and suspicion another newspaper announcement fell like a bombshell: a *Mercury* reporter had visited Mr David Gregson's apartments and discovered that he had fled the country.

At once there was a swing in public opinion. Leading articles were written demanding to know why regular visits to the police had not been made a condition of his bail. In a new spate of correspondence it was pointed out that the manager of a bank must have more opportunity than anyone else for abstracting articles from his own strong room. The assumption that he had been responsible for fraudulent accounts was used to justify the accusation that he had somehow managed to steal and copy the jewellery; the assumption that he had in fact committed such a theft and had the replicas made was turned back on itself to prove that he was the sort of man who would have no compunction in defrauding his depositors.

As the accusations against David mounted, Margaret's

tears began to flow again. She thought that she had managed to control her emotions and reconcile herself to losing him. But if she had needed any proof that she still loved him, it was to be found in the distress she felt now. While unable to accept his criticisms of her father, she had recognized that they were sincerely felt; in fact, it was because he was sincere that he had so irremediably damaged their relationship. She still trusted her judgement of his sincerity; and if she was right, David himself could not be guilty of all the terrible things that were being said against him. She took her troubles to the library one afternoon when William had come to see her father. It was the day before the trial was at last due to begin, and all of them were feeling the strain of its imminence.

The lack of sympathy which greeted her suggestion that David could not possibly be such a villain as the newspapers were trying to suggest shocked her. William, in particular, gave the faint, contented smile which had irritated her ever since the days of their nursery quarrels.

'He should have faced it out like a man,' William said. 'If he was innocent, he would have been a fool to run. You must accept his flight, Margaret, as a confession of guilt. It will certainly be seen in that light tomorrow.'

Margaret turned to her father in the hope that he at least would provide reassurance. 'He only followed your instructions, Papa,' she said. 'You did everything for the best. So must he have done.'

'He was not equal to responsibility,' said John Junius dismissively. 'I am sorry, Margaret, that you should have had this disappointment. We were all mistaken in him, I fear. I blame myself for allowing you to become too greatly attached. I hope you will soon be able to forget him and to make a new life for yourself.'

Margaret stared at him for a moment. Then she ran from the room. For almost an hour she lay on her bed, sobbing with despair and helplessness that, in an affair whose truth she was incapable of judging, the views of the two men she loved most in the world should prove irreconcilable.

Her misery could not last. Whatever the rights and wrongs of the affair might be, David had gone out of her life for ever. She must be loyal to her father, because no one else was at hand to accept loyalty from her.

Taking a deep breath to bring her emotions under control, she put on her warmest cape and went to refresh her body with a walk in the gardens. The atmosphere of the neglected house was cold and damp, but she felt as much stifled by it as in the heaviest days of summer. Although she had by now emerged from the two-month period of mourning in which a bereaved daughter was expected to stay at home, the disaster which had struck the family had continued to confine her there, just as the need for economy prevented her from changing her dress from plain paramatta to the black silk which by now would have been allowed by convention. She felt the need of exercise and took no account of the cold as she walked briskly to the edge of the lower terrace and stood looking down over the river.

Down this channel, she supposed, David had sailed soon after their quarrel. Was it her fault that he had destroyed his reputation by leaving the country? She had offered to go with him at first, and later had allowed him to leave without her: at no time had she had the good sense to warn him that he would be criticized for going. If she had accepted his suggestion and gone to William to ask for the money for her own passage, her brother, with his greater worldly sense, would have pointed out the dangers of such a disappearance. Unsophisticated as she was, the conclusions which would be drawn from David's flight had not even occurred to her.

Again she reminded herself that it was too late for regrets. She made her way past the ice-house which would not be filled this year, and walked down through the wilderness which began where the formal part of the garden ended. The paths here were steep and rough, shaded with high banks of rhododendrons and accompanied by runnels of water which at this season became waterfalls, splashing their way down to the Avon. The climb back would be a hard one, although the paths zig-zagged to reduce the gradient, but she looked forward to the exertion.

She came to the point where the ground dropped sheer away in a cliff above the riverside road. The land still belonged to the Lorimers – or, rather, to the unknown gentleman who had bought it – but it was too steep here to be climbed. Instead she made her way to the side boundary of the garden.

Once upon a time, when she was a little girl, she had come this way often to play with Lydia. It was only about five years ago that the area adjoining this side of the garden, like the streets off Joy Hill, had acquired an undesirable reputation. Respectable families had moved out as unmarried but well-dressed females moved in. A half-crescent of bow-windowed houses came to an end here in a gazebo which afforded a view of the curving river, and which gave the whole street its name. Because of the steepness of the hill, and the erratic courses of the roads which climbed it, the entrance to The Gazebo was a considerable walking distance from the front door of Brinsley House. But for anyone whose legs were strong and who was not afraid of shadows, the path through the garden had made a good short cut. She had even persuaded her father to provide a small gate in the fence in order that she need not be tempted to climb it in a tomboyish manner.

The gate was still there, although several years had passed since Lydia and her family had moved to Bath from their home at the end of the street. Margaret pulled down her veil and stepped through, staring sentimentally through the window of the house which for a short time she had known almost as well as her own. As she did so, she was startled to recognize the occupant of the front room.

She ought not to have been surprised. David had mentioned – on the evening their engagement was announced – that Luisa had moved to live in The Gazebo. But the news had been pushed into the back of Margaret's mind first by the happiness of her few hours at the ball, and then by the disasters and tensions which immediately followed it. Reminded now of her friend's whereabouts, she was tempted to call, but was at once held back by doubts: the hour was late, and there was something about Luisa's quick movements which seemed furtive, as though she hoped not to have been observed. No one normally had any occasion to pass the house at night, since the street led to nothing beyond except the viewpoint.

While she hesitated, Luisa straightened herself, carrying a pile of clothes. She caught sight of Margaret through the window as she turned, and for a moment her expression was one of fear. It changed so rapidly that Margaret wondered whether she had imagined it. She stood still, waiting to see what was expected of her.

Luisa put down the bundle of clothes and a few seconds later appeared at the door of the house. This time there was no doubt about the furtiveness of her behaviour. She was making sure that no stranger was about to see her. Only then did she smile and invite Margaret to come in.

Once inside, Margaret looked curiously around the untidy bow-fronted drawing room. The little girl whom she had seen as a baby eighteen months earlier was standing in a corner of the room, sucking a finger and staring wide-eyed at the stranger. Luisa picked her daughter up and hugged her to her shoulder as if providing herself with a defence against Margaret's reproaches.

'How long have you lived here, Luisa?' Margaret asked.

'A year perhaps. No, less than that. I'm sorry.' She sounded as though she sincerely regretted the hurt which

Margaret was feeling. Almost as though it altered the situation she added, 'But tonight we leave.' She gave a short laugh. 'Doing a moonlight flit. This was one of the first English phrases I learned. Running away in the middle of the night, so that the landlord cannot claim my possessions.' She looked at Margaret with defiance in her eyes, daring her to criticize. 'There is two months' rent due, and I have hardly enough money for food. When times are hard the music teacher is the first to be turned away. This is no longer a good city in which to live. You know that better than most.'

Margaret nodded unhappily. Once before she had found Luisa in difficulties, and it had been the simplest thing in the world to make an excuse for providing her with food and a new gown and a present of money. One lesson which poverty was teaching her was that she could no longer afford the luxury of generosity. She could not offer even words that would be of any real comfort. After kissing Luisa and pretty little Alexa goodbye, Margaret climbed the steep path back to Brinsley House with a heavy heart. It seemed that the lives of all those who knew the Lorimers had been infected with ill-fortune.

18

The days which promise the most suffering are often the earliest to start. On the next morning, the morning of the trial, Margaret awoke at six o'clock after a night of uneasy sleep. As she looked from her window she saw the light of a lamp glowing in the tower room, and wondered whether her father had spent the whole night awake. Whatever the outcome of the trial might be, every day of its progress was bound to be an ordeal for a man who had never been accustomed to hearing his decisions questioned.

The proceedings were due to start at ten o'clock and he had been ordered to surrender to his bail at nine. Margaret was appalled to discover that as early as seven o'clock a crowd was beginning to gather outside the house. The gatekeeper had been dismissed with the rest of the staff, so that there was no one to prevent the intrusion. Although there was no demonstration of hostility, Margaret found the mere presence of the silent watchers frightening. She made no mention of them, however, when her father appeared for breakfast. Instead she studied him covertly as he sat motionless in his place.

His appearance was old-fashioned. Margaret was acquainted with the heads of the other banks in Bristol. They were all younger men than John Junius and were for the most part clean-shaven. To their business offices they wore high-buttoned coats of a light colour, with a loosely knotted tie or even a spotted cravat round their high wing collars. Sometimes they went hatless – certainly none of them wore on a normal working day the kind of tall black hat which the chairman of Lorimer's would wear to the courtroom. It was not only mourning which dictated that John Junius should be dressed today entirely in heavy black except for his white linen: he had never within Margaret's memory worn anything else. Whatever he had been in his youth he was a heavy man now, massively broad-shouldered, and his square-cut white beard and heavy eyebrows gave him an expression of authority even in this time of trouble. During the past year his shoulders had begun to stoop a little, but no one looking at him, Margaret felt, could fail to be impressed by his dignity.

Today there was something else: a determination to fight which revealed itself in the set of his lips. Only the fact that he would take no food at the breakfast table that morning testified to the strain of the occasion.

They were both startled by a ring at the door. Mr Broadbent came in with a flustered expression on his face, and John Junius looked surprised, for he had arranged to meet his lawyer outside the courtroom. Muttering something about a new development, Mr Broadbent began to pull papers from the case he carried, but John Junius stood up to stop him.

'We will go to the tower,' he said.

Margaret felt uneasy as she watched him stride out of the room. Everything about the day was disturbing – the tension in her father's mind, the watchers outside – even the numbers pasted on to each piece of furniture in preparation for the auction made her feel as though she were a trespasser. The house was no longer her home, the chair on which she sat did not belong to her, the portraits of her ancestors would soon hang in the house of some stranger who did not know who they were. Whatever the verdict, her father's life, as he had lived it until now, was finished. His business no longer belonged to him and he could not hope ever again to maintain the style or receive the respect due to a Lorimer. He would fight, she supposed, for his reputation; but even if he won the future could hold little for him.

Mr Broadbent returned alone.

'Your father was kind enough to offer me a little refreshment,' he said. 'I have left him some papers to study. We will travel down to the courtroom together in half an hour's time.'

Margaret was glad to offer him the breakfast which neither of them had touched, kept hot in the silver warming dishes which would soon disappear with the rest of their possessions.

'Are they new papers?' she asked, as she placed a plate of kidneys in front of him.

'Of a most disquieting kind, Miss Lorimer. They appear to have been prepared by Mr Gregson before he fled from the country. They will not have the force of a statement on oath, of course, and Mr Gregson will not be submitting himself to cross-examination. But they will undoubtedly suggest to the prosecuting counsel a number of awkward questions to be asked.'

'And my father will have answers to them?' Margaret inquired anxiously.

Mr Broadbent hesitated.

'Mr Gregson's statements do not entirely accord with the information in my instructions from Mr Lorimer. I have no doubt that your father will be able to substantiate his own version of affairs. But it appears that Mr Gregson was in the habit of making a note of any conversations he had with his chairman on matters of importance. Again, his notebook will have no legal force. But it will have been found amongst his papers in the manager's office when they were impounded immediately after the failure, and it is regrettable, to say the least, that I was not aware of its existence until today.'

'Mr Broadbent, you surely do not believe that my father was to blame for the collapse of Lorimer's?'

'Many factors were to blame, Miss Lorimer. Even the harshest judge will not attempt to lay all the weight on one man's shoulders. When our counsel stands up in court he will admit no fault at all. But since we are in private here, I should perhaps give you some warning of what may happen, so that you can prepare your thoughts. It is not an easy thing for a gentleman of your father's age and character to admit that he has made mistakes. But I fear that mistakes were made. Some of them many years ago, and none of them so grave that they deserved the penalty they have attracted. Your father will go on trial because he was too proud to say to the world, a year ago, "I have made misjudgements and now they must be paid for."'

'If you will excuse me, Mr Broadbent, I will go to him,' said Margaret abruptly. She ran towards the tower without knowing what she would say. She had nothing to offer except the assurance of her affection for him; and how

much would that weigh, she wondered, against the humiliations that today and the succeeding days would bring as
his judgement and even his honesty came under attack?
Her footsteps slowed as she climbed the spiral staircase,
and her heart chilled with the familiar apprehension which
had attacked her in this same place as a child on her way
to punishment.

She told herself to be brave, and began to run again, her
footsteps clattering noisily on the stone steps. As she flung
open the door without knocking she saw her father standing
by the casement windows which overlooked the gorge. One
of the windows was wide open, in spite of the cold winter
air outside, and he was pushing at the other of the pair as
though it had stuck. At the sound of the opening door he
turned to look at her. She did not at that moment understand the expression on his face, but she never afterwards
forgot it. For a few seconds father and daughter faced each
other across the room as though they had been petrified.
Then John Junius half turned and put the whole of his
weight behind the bulk of his shoulder as he flung it against
the jammed frame. There was a crash of breaking glass
and splintering wood. Then there was silence, for he uttered
no cry as he fell.

For a moment Margaret stood where she was by the
door, unable to move. Her eyes and her brain refused to
accept what she had seen. She wanted to scream, but was
unable even to breathe. Only when she felt herself beginning to fall did she clutch at the door for support and force
herself to steady her mind at the same time as her body.
Very carefully, with her breath panting outwards in little
cries, she crossed to the empty window frame and looked
down.

He was still alive. Even from this height it was possible
to see his head jerking backwards in agony. Margaret's first
hysterical scream had stifled itself, but now she screamed in
the deliberate knowledge that the sound would bring help

faster than any other cry. She was right, for both Mr Broadbent and her father's manservant came running quickly enough to be at the foot of the spiral staircase by the time she reached it herself. She had no breath to explain, but gestured that they should follow her into the garden.

Although later on she had time to ask herself whether a man who saw that his life was over would have thanked her if she had managed to save it, it did not occur to her in that moment of emergency that there was any choice. She left the two men bent over her father's broken body as they discussed in low voices whether he could be moved, and ran through the house to the steps which led down from the front door. The waiting crowd stirred and muttered as the door opened, and then prepared to settle back in disappointment when they saw who it was. But her voice made it clear enough that something dramatic had happened.

'A doctor!' she cried. 'Will one of you fetch – ' Her voice broke off in astonishment as she saw that one of the watchers was Dr Scott. At any other time she would have found it unbelievable that such a man should stoop to take pleasure in the humiliation of someone who had once been his generous patron, but now the doctor's presence seemed almost a miracle. She called him by name and he came, although reluctantly. The crowd murmured amongst itself, the volume of noise rising as their suspicions grew that at the last moment they had been cheated of their victim.

John Junius's eyes were closed when Margaret returned to his side with the doctor. He was groaning, as though he were trying to force words out of his mouth, but the sounds grew weaker at every moment.

'Have you something on which he could be carried?' demanded Dr Scott. 'If there is no stretcher, a door might serve. And more helpers will be needed to take the weight.'

Margaret nodded her understanding and hurried off

towards the house with Mr Broadbent and the servant, leaving Dr Scott kneeling on the ground with his head bent low over the jerking body as he strained to hear John Junius's gasping words. Suddenly there was a loud cry that stopped her in her tracks. She had never heard such a sound before, but had no doubt what it meant. At first she was unable to move. Then she forced herself to turn slowly back.

John Junius was dead. The limpness of his limbs and the impossible angle at which his head had twisted away from his body left no room for doubt. But for the first moment her grief was held back by incredulity. Dr Scott had raised his patient's shoulders from the ground and was shaking the body in fury, shouting as he did so in a kind of gibberish which Margaret could only just comprehend.

'Where is it?' he was yelling as she ran back, Mr Broadbent at her side. 'Tell me, damn you, what have you done with it?'

The lawyer was the first to reach Dr Scott. He pulled him away with a violence that sent him staggering off balance across the lawn. John Junius's body fell back on to the ground as it was released. Margaret knelt down beside her father, but for a second time the dignity of death was disturbed by Dr Scott's ravings.

'I'll find it,' he was shouting. 'He's buried his treasure, but I'll find it. No matter how deep, I'll find it.'

With each shouted sentence he tugged a plant from the flower bed and hurled it across the lawn. Then he flung himself on the ground and began to scrabble in the earth with his bare hands, flinging the soil in all directions as he continued to shout.

'He must be mad!' exclaimed Margaret, listening in horror as his ravings continued. 'I think his losses have unhinged him.'

She felt Mr Broadbent's hand touch her shoulder briefly. 'I will see that he is removed, Miss Lorimer. And I will

211

send at once for your brother. The court also must be informed. Is there someone I can call to keep you company here?'

Margaret shook her head.

'I will stay with my father until William comes.'

For a moment longer Mr Broadbent looked down at the dead man.

'It is God's will,' he said. Then he turned to help the manservant, who had already pulled Dr Scott to his feet and was struggling to control his wildly threshing arms.

After they had gone, the garden was very quiet. Heedless of the cold and damp, Margaret knelt beside her father's body. It was at this moment that she understood what an ill service she would have done him if her wish to save his life had been successful. She had always believed without question the definitions of good and evil which twice every Sunday thundered from the pulpit. To take one's own life was without question a sin; or so she had been brought up to accept. But the events of the past few weeks had made her less sure that it was as easy as the preacher claimed to judge between right and wrong, black and white. She knew that she ought to feel grief at losing her father, but instead she could not control a curious impulse of happiness on his behalf. He was a man who all his life had been accustomed to take decisions with certainty and courage. It would have been a poor ending to such an existence for him to hear the way he must spend the remainder of his days laid down by others. Mr Broadbent had said that his death was God's will. But it seemed to Margaret, as she kept a peaceful vigil by her father's side, that in death – as so often in life – it was the will of John Junius Lorimer which had prevailed.

BOOK TWO
The Children of the Chairman

PART I
Margaret and William

1

A dead man attracts more sympathy than the same man alive, even when there is no other change in his circumstances. John Junius Lorimer's final decisive act enabled the routines of disgrace to be replaced by those of death, to the great benefit of his reputation.

As soon as it was learned that both defendants were now beyond the jurisdiction of the court, the trial was adjourned *sine die*: it was unlikely to be resumed. The statement which David Gregson had left behind him when he fled from Bristol received no publicity and even the manner in which John Junius had died was concealed by a statement made by Mr Broadbent in the coroner's court. His client, he said, had been preparing to attend the court with a full defence of all the charges brought against him. But his health had been much affected by the strain of the previous weeks, and it was feared – there had been no witnesses – that a giddiness which had overcome him several times before had on this occasion occurred while he was leaning out of the window of the tower room in Brinsley House to watch the progress of a Lorimer ship below.

Almost as though it did not concern her, Margaret Lorimer listened to the lies. Her father had been right to believe that he still had friends. They united now to ensure that no stigma should attach itself to the name of a man who had deserved respect in his day. On the morning of the funeral they brought the city to a standstill. Even the Exchange was closed for three hours in tribute to the head of one of Bristol's great families.

His children had known their father only as an old man,

slow-moving in body and autocratic in temper. But he had been born into a world threatened by revolution and as a boy had shivered under rumours of invasion. If England had moved from those unsettled years to a state of security amounting almost to staidness, it was due to the efforts of men like these. If he became rich beyond the dreams of most men, at least he could claim that he had carried others with him to prosperity, and not all of them had shared his fall from it. There were still a few of his fellow-citizens old enough to remember a sturdy young man with bright red curly hair and a flair for recognizing the industries and inventions which would most successfully shape the new society. He was hailed as the last of the Bristol merchant adventurers, and even those who had so recently cursed his name were prepared, for this one day, to recognize his achievements.

Margaret had wept for the death of a mother she had never greatly loved, but she shed no tears for the father whose affection she had always craved. She came to terms very quickly with the fact of his death, regretting only that it could not have occurred a little earlier, to spare him the anxieties of his last months. With his death, she hoped that the period of nightmare had come to an end, but found that for herself it was only just beginning.

While John Junius lived it had been possible, although not always easy, to remain loyal to him, refusing to believe the attacks on his integrity. It had even been possible to let David Gregson go from her life because she believed then that their differences of opinion could never be reconciled. But from the moment before her father's death when Mr Broadbent first privately expressed his doubts about the chairman's case she had begun to realize that John Junius had not been entirely blameless. His motives might have been for the best, but it became increasingly clear as time passed that at least some of his actions had been illegal. Little by little Margaret was forced to admit to herself that David's view of the situation was probably correct. The chairman of Lorimer's must have hoped that confidence would be maintained for the short period in which the bank was at risk, so that no one would ever have any reason or right to investigate the methods used to achieve this; but he had taken steps to ensure that if such an investigation should in fact become necessary, there would be a scapegoat ready to carry the blame.

In this, posthumously, he was successful. Even before his death there had been many who were prepared to give the old man the benefit of a good many doubts because he could be seen to be suffering as much as the other shareholders. Now a more definite version of the affair found currency among the business community. It was the young manager who had defrauded the bank and hoodwinked its respected chairman, and who made off in the end with a tidy fortune from other people's money. The theory found favour with those – and they were many – who found it difficult to understand how gold could simply disappear. Many a ruined widow and bankrupted tradesman wept or swore at the thought of David Gregson setting himself up as a rich man under another name in some far-off part of the world where he would never be traced.

Because Margaret knew a little more than this, she was able to force the facts from a reluctant Mr Broadbent. It was not the sort of affair, he told her, which a young lady could be expected to understand; and Mr Lorimer, even dead, was a client whose confidences must be respected. But Margaret could be as determined as her father, and the growing suspicion that she had made a mistake made her persistent. She suspected that she was at least as intelligent as Ralph, who was considered fit to benefit from an Oxford education. If she had behaved stupidly in the past, it might be partly because she had been treated as though she were stupid. She had a right to be told the facts which had changed the future course of her life. If in the end she proved too unintelligent to understand them, that was another matter, and no concern of Mr Broadbent's.

He showed her the statement which David had left behind and she was convinced by its truth. That night her tears were of a different kind. Often enough since their last meeting she had been unhappy because it had been necessary for them to part. Now for the first time she knew it had not been necessary at all. It was David who had deserved her loyalty. Even if he had not been able to take her with him he should have sailed with the assurance that she would join him one day. Instead, she had dismissed him in anger, defending the undeserving and accusing where she should have been devoted. Because the fault was all her own, this was the unkindest cut of all.

Perhaps it was not too late. If it was possible to find out where he was she could send a letter of apology, a plea that he would after all allow her to join him. The next morning she went down to the floating harbour. David had mentioned Jamaica, so she asked particularly about this destination and soon learned that one of her brother's ships had sailed for Kingston only a few days after her quarrel with David. No one she spoke to, though, knew or was prepared to say whether the *Diana* had taken any passenger.

'How can I find out?' Margaret asked William when next she saw him. Since her father's death, she had returned to live at The Ivies.

'When the *Diana* returns to port, you can ask her captain, or I will do so for you. But you must consider that Gregson will probably have used a false name, and may well have offered bribes to make sure that no one would reveal his destination. After all, he was evading a criminal charge. He would not wish to be traced. You may be right in thinking that he has gone to Jamaica, although there are few prospects there for a man without capital. Australia is a possibility too. He could have travelled there on the *Rosa*. But I think it more likely that he would have taken the steamship to New York.'

'Or San Francisco? Might he have gone there?' Margaret's questions at the harbour had revealed that another of the Lorimer ships had sailed for that destination within the appropriate period.

'That is another possibility. But in that case your chances of finding him must be small. It will be two years or more before the *Flora* returns from San Francisco. Even if her captain confirms that a passenger disembarked there, you would have no reason to believe that he would have stayed in the city. The American continent is a large place.'

'A man cannot completely disappear!' cried Margaret.

'It is the easiest thing in the world. Few men wish to do so, because most hope to protect their rights in some property or other, even if it is only their reputation. But Gregson has lost his reputation already. He will take a new name and go where no questions will be asked. You would have little hope of finding him even if you knew his first destination.'

'I think you hope I will never see him again,' said Margaret.

'I never pretended to find the match a suitable one.'

'And what more suitable match am I likely to make now?' Margaret asked him, knowing that there was no answer. She still felt that Jamaica was David's most likely destination, and said so again. 'He was very short of money when he left. The cost of a passage to San Francisco would have been beyond his means, I think.'

'He had no need to pay. The letter I gave him would have carried him to any destination served by the Lorimer Line.'

'You gave him a letter? A passage?' Margaret stared at her brother, hardly believing what she had heard.

'I thought it the least I could offer. His troubles stemmed from his connection with our family. And you yourself passed on what I took to be a message from him, that I owed my own fortunate escape to his intervention.'

'But when you heard that he had left, you said that he was foolish, that it would seem to prove his guilt.'

William shrugged his shoulders.

'The offer of a gift does not force a man to accept it. Without my help he would have had no choice but to stay. I gave him the choice, no more.'

Margaret had controlled her temper only while she was taking care to understand the situation. Now it flared as she accused her brother of deliberately leading David into a false position, while William in turn expressed his anger at the damage which had been done by the statement which David left behind – a piece of spitefulness which had led directly to their father's death. This was not the first quarrel they had had, for their childhood relationship had often been stormy, but it was by far the bitterest. Margaret was still flushed with indignation when she left William's study and went up to the drawing room.

Sophie was sitting there alone. She did not look up from her needlework as her sister-in-law came into the room.

'I intend to visit my friend Lydia Morton in Bath for a few days,' Margaret announced without preamble. She had an open invitation to go there at any time and now, when she could hardly bear to remain under William's roof for another night, was the opportunity to make use of it.

'I am sure you will be a great comfort to her in her disappointment,' murmured Sophie. 'And I suppose that while you are there you may hear of a family where you could go as governess. You would not wish, I imagine, to take up such a situation in Bristol.'

It was the second shock of the day, and the unkinder. Margaret stared without speaking at her brother's wife. Sophie had by now completely recovered from the birth of her third child. Her tightly laced figure was almost as slim as before, her gown was elegant and her hair was dressed on top of her head as elaborately as though she planned an evening in society instead of being confined to the house by this second period of mourning. The unrelieved black which made Margaret seem colourless suited Sophie's complexion and emphasized her beauty.

But her voice was cold, making it clear that she was determined to forget the night when Margaret had untied her nightgown and seen her writhing naked on the bed. She had been glad of help then, but was now ashamed of her need. Perhaps she found it difficult to feel dignified even to herself while she feared that Margaret might remember how she had cared nothing then for dignity. Whatever the reason, the quietly made suggestion was bound to come like a slap in the face. William had told Margaret to treat his home as her own, but she could hardly do that if its mistress was not prepared to make her welcome.

There was nothing unusual in the suggestion Sophie had made, apart from its unfriendliness. Margaret knew well enough that, for a young woman of good family whose fortunes had come down in the world, the post of governess was traditionally the only one thought suitable. Poised uneasily in a stratum of social life between her employers and their servants, she would be a dependant in the family of a stranger instead of amongst her own kin – but given Sophie's hostility, the difference might not signify greatly. Margaret's liking for young children meant that such work would not be entirely uncongenial. Nevertheless, she had a different plan for her life, and this small coldness was enough to move it from the realm of day-dream into that of decision.

As soon as possible she travelled to Bath, where she discussed her idea with Lydia. Her friend was an essential part of Margaret's plan. To her relief, Lydia clapped her hands with pleasure at the proposal, smiling for the first time since the bad news had arrived from the Afghan frontier. Margaret insisted that she should take time for consideration, but Lydia could see no possible objection to the idea of going to London with Margaret and enrolling as a student.

Lydia was an only child, and clever. She had been sent as a boarder to the Ladies College at Cheltenham, ruled by the formidable Miss Beale. Even as a little girl she had been ugly, and the knowledge that marriage was unlikely had made her work hard. Unlike Margaret, she had studied a wide curriculum of subjects and had passed examinations at school. Moreover, although her financial position would be unenviable after her father's death – when her cousin would inherit the entailed estate – the family's income was good as long as he lived. If Lydia were to embark on a course of professional training, her educational qualifications were as good as those of any girl of her time, and her father could afford to support her. Fortunately, he was liberal in his attitude to women's education, and anxious enough about his daughter's future to support any plan which might make it possible for her to maintain herself. Even before Margaret's short visit came to an end, Lydia had persuaded Mr Morton to let her go to London.

As she travelled back to Bristol, Margaret knew that her own path was unlikely to be as smooth as Lydia's. Nevertheless, by the time she reached The Ivies her mind was completely made up. She was determined to become independent, and no one in the world was going to stop her.

2

Adult quarrels pass over the heads of small children. When Margaret returned to The Ivies after her visit to Bath, she went first of all to the nursery, knowing that Sophie's coldness would not have altered the warm affection she would be offered there. Matthew greeted her excitedly. He looked angelic with his golden curls falling to the lace collar of his Little Lord Fauntleroy suit, but his expression had been bored until he saw his aunt, for there was nothing he could do in case he spoiled the velvet. He shouted out his news at once.

'We're going to live in Grandpapa's house!'

If he hoped to surprise Margaret, he certainly succeeded. She did not discuss the matter further during the half hour which she spent playing with him and his little sister. But later that day, when once again she sought out William for a discussion, she opened the conversation with this subject.

'Matthew tells me you are moving to Brinsley House. Was it you, then, who bought the property while Papa was still alive?'

William smiled in satisfaction.

'Yes. Once the auction had failed, the Receiver was bound to accept even a low offer. If things had gone well, of course, I would have expected to inherit the house without payment. But even as it is, it did not cost me much.'

'Is it right that the creditors should get so little for an asset which I suppose belongs to them?'

William shrugged his shoulders.

'There was no one willing to pay more. This is not a time when many people can take on new commitments. I was fortunate that Lloyds paid the insurance claim on the *Georgiana* so promptly, so that I had a little money in my pocket, so to speak. The value of the house to myself is a sentimental one. And I was glad to relieve Father's anxieties. The thought of leaving his home caused him great distress. At least his last days were free from that fear.'

Margaret was forced to agree that this had been a great boon, although she still felt disturbed by the transaction. However, it was important that she should not antagonize her brother.

'William, I would like to discuss my future with you,' she said.

'Naturally, when we move to Brinsley House, your old room will still be at your disposal. Or if there is any other you would prefer – '

'You are kind, but I am not thinking of rooms,' said Margaret. 'I need an occupation. To spend the rest of my life doing needlework in your drawing room is not a prospect I can tolerate.'

'It had already occurred to me that you might feel like that,' said William. 'And I have noticed the affection which my children have for you. You might care to act as their governess. It would seem a most suitable solution to the problem.'

Margaret flushed slightly, but tried not to show that she was offended. The offer at least suggested that Sophie had spoken without consulting her husband for once, when she tried to persuade Margaret to leave.

'Have you asked Sophie for her opinion?' she said. 'I think you may find that she would prefer me not to be a member of her household. She has already suggested to me that I should look for a place as governess elsewhere.'

It was some comfort to Margaret to notice that her brother looked surprised; even annoyed.

'If she expressed such a thought, it was without my authority,' he said. 'Of course, if you prefer to live in another household, I cannot stop you. But you must not feel that there is any pressure on you to go. I can hardly hope to shoulder all Father's financial liabilities, but I regard myself as bound to take on his family responsibilities.'

'Neither of these courses commends itself to me,' said Margaret, taking care to keep her voice steady. 'I wish to become independent. Since I lack a fortune, I must acquire a qualification, and for that I must undergo a training.'

'Training? What training?' It was William's turn to be startled.

'I propose to become a doctor,' she said.

The first time she had spoken those words had been to a stranger, as though even at their first meeting she had guessed how important David Gregson's good opinion would become to her. The second time was to Lydia, only a few days earlier. On each occasion she had been listened to with respect, and this made it easier for her now to face the criticism which she knew would come.

William's first reaction was what she had expected.

'But it is not possible for a woman to become a doctor! Unless you propose to qualify in America. Or do you think yourself capable of going to Paris to take scientific examinations in French? I should think they would be too much for you even in English.'

Margaret ignored the sarcasm in his voice, for this at least she could answer.

'The position has changed since Mrs Garrett Anderson was forced to go to France in order to qualify,' she said. 'The University of London has agreed to examine women for degrees and this, in medicine, will allow them to be registered as doctors. The London School of Medicine for Women is already preparing students for this examination. I would like to enrol there, if they will have me.'

'To train as a doctor takes six or seven years,' protested William. 'I know you have always felt a desire to care for the sick. But you could become a nurse in a far shorter time. Since Miss Nightingale's reforms were introduced there can be no objection to a woman of good family adopting this profession. Indeed, I believe there is a demand for educated matrons.'

'When Ralph told you that he wished to be ordained, you did not suggest to him that he should instead become a verger.'

'The case is entirely different.'

'No,' said Margaret. 'It is not different at all. I have an ambition which is as precise and as clear as yours or Ralph's. Why should I be forced to accept a second best?'

'Because you are a woman. The work of a doctor is unsuitable and most unseemly for a lady. And the responsibilities would be too much for you.'

'That would be for my examiners and supervisors to decide,' said Margaret. 'My training would be the same as that of a man, and I would be expected to reach the same

225

standard. I would prefer to accept responsibility myself than to take instructions from someone I may not respect. As for its being unseemly, a great many women think it unseemly that they should be examined by a man. Children, too, are more at ease with a woman.' She paused, to remind herself that she had intended to avoid this aspect of the argument. 'I am not asking you, William, whether I *may* train as a doctor. I am telling you that I intend to try.'

'And how do you propose to pay the fees? Do you realize how expensive it will be to live in London?'

'Yes, I do,' said Margaret. 'If you should offer to be as generous to me as to Ralph, I would not be too proud to accept. But if you are determined not to approve, I shall manage somehow. My friend Lydia is resolved on the same course and she has a cousin in London who could spare us rooms. Mr Morton has most generously promised her an allowance during her training. It will keep me warm as well as her, and might stretch to feed me if it became necessary. As for the fees, I still own Lower Croft. A tenant might be found who would rent it. And one day the situation in Bristol must improve, so that it could be sold. It is possible, I believe, to borrow money on the security of a house. Now that I have determined what I will do, I am not prepared to admit of any obstacle.'

'Then why do you trouble to tell me of your plans? Why do you not simply pack your bags and leave?'

'Because I do not wish us to quarrel, William. I would like your approval. I should be sorry if you were reproached with abandoning your sister. And my situation in London will be easier if it is known that I have the support of my family. What is more, I have a favour to ask you.'

There was a long silence. William did not happily lose an argument. When at last he said 'Yes?' it was a recognition of the fact that his sister could not be stopped.

'We spoke earlier of Mrs Garrett Anderson,' said Margaret. 'I believe you are acquainted with her husband.'

'Skelton Anderson? Yes. His shipping company has just

226

become part of the new Orient Line. They are likely to become our greatest rivals.'

'Before the rivalry becomes too fierce, will you use your acquaintance to write me a letter of introduction so that I may meet his wife? My education has not qualified me very well to undertake a course of scientific study. If I am to be admitted to the School of Medicine I may need to have a sponsor.'

There was a second silence, which Margaret broke with her own laughter.

'William! Why not admit that you long to be quit of me? Sophie dislikes me. If I can say that, you need not deny it. Your offer to give me a home is a generous one, but we shall all be happiest if I come to it only for holidays, when we can enjoy each other's company without friction. If you help me to go, you will win praise for your liberality and sympathy for my headstrong behaviour. And you will not have to watch me growing older and older, more and more useless, more and more bad-tempered. Instead, when my training is finished I shall buy my own house and manage my own life, and instead of being ashamed of me you may pretend to be proud.'

She held out her hand to him impulsively to show that there was no need to quarrel. William, who never did anything on impulse, did not move to take it. But it seemed that she had appealed successfully to his head if not to his heart, for he gave the quick nod which increasingly he was copying from his father.

'I will write the letter to Anderson,' he said. 'And I will enquire about a tenant for Lower Croft. In the meantime, you had better estimate your annual costs. If they exceed the rent, I will lend you money as I am lending it to Ralph, and you may repay it when . . .' he paused, as though hardly even to conceive the thought, still less to say the words – 'when you begin to practise.'

'Thank you, William.' Margaret tried not to feel hurt by the ungracious manner in which her brother had agreed to her request. Their relationship had never been a warm one, and she had known even before she asked that William would disapprove of such an unusual suggestion. It was enough that he had agreed, however grudgingly. She stood up, breathing deeply with relief and happiness.

'I need to have a life of my own,' she said. 'Until now I have never been anything except my father's daughter. Rich and comfortable, but somehow not myself. I had hoped that with David . . .' She stopped, wishing she had not mentioned the name which abruptly checked her happiness. 'I had looked forward to making a life in my own home, with my own household. Now I must find another way.'

She took the first step towards it a few days later, travelling to London on the railway with the letter of introduction safe in her handbag. Dr Garrett Anderson proved helpful with advice, and arranged an appointment for her at the London School of Medicine for Women, but this was far from guaranteeing her admission. Even Lydia, who had attended a similar interview two days earlier, armed with recommendations from her schoolteachers, had obtained only provisional acceptance, and Margaret was conscious that the haphazard nature of her own studies was unlikely to impress the Dean.

After she had asked a series of searching questions, the Dean picked up a small notebook from her desk, and asked Margaret to look at it.

'We give each of our students one of these,' she said. 'It lists every disease she must study, every examination she must pass, every course of lectures she must attend, every period of practical hospital training. Not until each item in it has been dated and signed can she even submit herself for the final examination. Look inside, and tell me what you think.'

Margaret's heart sank as she turned the pages. Within the first year alone she would be expected to tackle chemistry, anatomy, physiology, botany, therapeutics, dissections, and something called materia medica. She had not the least idea what materia medica might be. Her chin jutted out in determination as she looked up again.

'I can hardly deny that I am ill-qualified to begin the course,' she said. 'But I have studied a little anatomy. If you would like to judge my understanding, I would be happy to answer questions on this subject.'

To her relief the Dean laughed.

'Your lecturers and examiners will find out soon enough whether you have the intelligence to be a doctor,' she said. 'And your supervisors in the hospitals will tell us whether you have the temperament. What I must assess is whether you have the determination to pursue a course of studies which lasts for many years and is certain at times to seem arduous. We invite any prospective student to undertake a short preliminary course, and nothing is lost if she then abandons it. But if a student leaves the school after two years or three, she has wasted our time as well as her own and she has nothing to show for it. We shall show ourselves unsympathetic towards young ladies, who decide, for example, to marry rather than to qualify.'

'I have no intention of marrying,' said Margaret firmly. 'I wish to have my own profession. And although I cannot praise my grasp of chemistry or dissections, I am prepared to give myself a reference in determination. It has not been easy even to get as far as this.'

The Dean nodded her understanding.

'You will find most of your fellow-students in the same situation,' she said. 'Their families have not succeeded in stopping them, but for the most part are far from approving. This is one reason why we shall expect your behaviour to be in all respects above reproach while you are a student. You will meet medical students of the other sex of whom the same cannot be said, but you will not follow their example.'

Margaret smiled with excitement as she noticed the Dean's change of emphasis.

'Then you are willing to enrol me?' she gasped.

'For the preliminary course only. You must pass its examination in September. If you are successful in that, you may apply for a place on the full course, which starts in October.'

Margaret emerged into Brunswick Square after her interview in a haze of happiness. For a little while she walked about without noticing where she was going. There were so many excitements to be considered at once. She was going to be a doctor. And she was going to live in London. This noisy, crowded, dirty city would be her home. As her head came out of the clouds and she looked around her, she noticed how many women there were of her own sort about on foot. In Bristol they would have sent a servant on their errands, or travelled in a carriage of some kind. But here they walked briskly about their own business, not always even waiting for the crossing sweeper to clear a way through the filth of the roads. But then, Margaret reminded herself, she must no longer think of anyone as being her own sort of woman any longer, whatever that had once been. She was going to be one of the new sort; one of the women who were jeered at in newspapers and mocked in cartoons. It was difficult to envisage the kind of life which lay ahead; but any touch of apprehension she felt was swiftly overwhelmed by excitement.

There was only one part of the interview which had caused her distress. She had promised that she would not marry. In her mind at that moment had been a silent reservation: 'unless David Gregson should return'. Now, with all the determination which she had more truthfully claimed to possess, she put the situation squarely to herself. David Gregson would not return. Or, even if he did, he would have no reason to seek out a woman who had sent him away in anger. Equally, he might not want to see her if she should ever manage to track him down to that part of the wide world in which he had taken refuge. The course to which she was committing herself would demand her whole concentration. She must not allow herself to be distracted by a possibility which did not really exist. She had told the Dean that she did not intend to marry, and the statement must be turned into truth.

Margaret stopped walking and felt in her handbag for the note which William had given her, listing the destinations of the Lorimer ships and the probable length of their voyages. For one last time, trying to control the anguish in her heart, she stared at the names of ships and ports: the *Rosa, Stella, Diana, Flora*: New York, Brisbane, Kingston, San Francisco. This was not her first attempt to convince herself that she would never see David again, but it must be the last. She loved him, she would always love him, but now she must try to forget him. She crumpled the paper into a ball and tossed it into the gutter.

3

Many houses have stronger personalities than the people who live in them, but an owner's character may be revealed by his choice of furnishings. Certainly this was true of William Lorimer. While Margaret was making a new life for herself in London, he was busily consolidating his position in Bristol. He began by returning to the Lorimer family house and altering it to reflect his own tastes.

When Samuel Lorimer built Brinsley House in 1785 he furnished and decorated it in the style of that year. He chose the best quality wood for his floors and set the choicest pieces of modern furniture on them. Doors and their frames were carved from rich red mahogany; but in order that the effect should not be too dark the walls were painted in the pale greens and blues which were then fashionable, with decorations of white stucco and gilt beading on panels and friezes.

Alexander, when he inherited the mansion, saw no

reason to change its style, although from time to time new coats of paint were applied. Alexander was a close man, loath to spend money on inessentials. John Junius, his son, was not mean in the same manner, but by the time he became master of the house in which he had grown up he was set in his ways. He paid little attention to his surroundings as long as they remained familiar, but was quick to complain of any change. So for almost a hundred years Brinsley House had retained its uncluttered Georgian elegance.

William changed all that. When his father's furniture was put up for auction he made no attempt to purchase more than a few pieces of sentimental value, such as Brinsley Lorimer's sea chest. At a time when his father and sister were too upset to notice what was happening, he had managed to smuggle some of the family table silver out of the house, to keep it from the Receiver's men, and this was now returned to its baize-lined drawers. But such small items were insignificant compared with what had gone and must now be replaced.

William ordered wood from the West Indies and the coast of Central America to be carried to Bristol on ships of the Lorimer Line. There was no problem in finding unemployed carpenters during the trading difficulties which followed the fall of Lorimer's Bank. While Sophie chose wallpapers and matched braids and tassels to the stuff of heavy curtains, William specified the sizes of tables and sideboards and display cabinets. A small man himself, he chose that everything around him should be large. His sister, when she came to spend her holidays with his family, might think the effect ponderous in comparison with the old furniture which he thought of as spindly but she had called elegant. He found the solidity of his new possessions reassuring.

Although it was easy to see that Margaret was puzzled by the degree of his affluence, he made no attempt to explain it to her. At the suggestion of John Junius he had borne in mind, when looking for a wife eight years earlier, the size of the marriage settlement likely to be offered. His choice of Sophie had proved wise in every respect. She had already provided him with two sons as well as a daughter. She was well-dressed and good-looking in public and submissive in private. Not only had she brought him a generous portion on the day of his marriage but she was the sole heiress of her father's property when he died a few months after John Junius Lorimer. William had good cause to be grateful for the impertinence of David Gregson and his own ill-tempered reaction to it. He had disposed of his shareholding in Lorimer's Bank just in time to avoid seeing his wife's money as well as his father's swept down the drain of the bankruptcy proceedings.

If he allowed Margaret to believe that his continuing wealth came only from the success of the shipping line, this was because he had almost come to think it himself: Sophie's money had become his on their wedding day. What he did remember was that his sister had despised arrangements of that sort, refusing an engagement which had appeared potentially profitable to all parties at the time it was first suggested. Since then, of course, there had been changes of fortune, and Margaret would have had good reason to complain if she had allowed herself to be tied to a family whose wealth had vanished as dramatically as her own. Mr Martin Crankshaw had been completely ruined by the collapse of the bank in which he was a director as well as a shareholder. He had seen the new dock development which had been the vision and hope of his whole working life sold over his head.

Privately, William thought him a fool. He should have borrowed money and bought his own business back for himself through a friend or nominee at a rock-bottom price, as William had done with Brinsley House. Then it could have been transferred unobtrusively to his son, Walter, and the Crankshaw family as a whole would have reaped the reward they deserved as the first docking berths opened.

William had given Martin Crankshaw time to think of all that for himself. Only when it became clear that his father's old friend was broken by the magnitude of the bank disaster and his own responsibilities and losses, retreating with quivering voice and hands into a premature old age – only then did William himself take advantage of the happy timing of his father-in-law's death to make a good investment.

The new docks were worth millions of pounds, so his interest was small as a percentage of the whole. But the shareholdings were fragmented and William had not found it difficult to arrange for his election to the board of directors. As John Junius had been well aware, the docks were very near to completion at the time when banking confidence finally collapsed – the first berthing fee had been paid even before John Junius fell to his death. Within three years they were not only showing a good profit but had enabled William to make long-term docking contracts of such advantage to the Lorimer Line that he had no hesitation in ordering replacements for the ill-fated *Georgiana*.

As for young Walter Crankshaw, it was clear that he had no financial sense at all. Any of his old friends in Bristol would have offered him the opportunity to profit from the city's resurgence, which was bound to come one day. But instead of asking for help he had left for London and was rumoured to have taken up some kind of salaried position. William heard the news with scorn. How could anyone who worked as an employee expect to make his fortune?

It was not money for its own sake which attracted William. In this he was typical of all the Lorimers from Brinsley onwards. Their pleasure lay in their work, but it was true that they needed to know that they were successful in it, and money was the measure of success. Every Lorimer son resolved to demonstrate his abilities in this way, and by the time he inherited the family responsibility himself, the habit was engrained. William's satisfaction came from the making of complicated plans and their development to fruition. He thought of his fortune and his reputation as inseparable and so was glad to see them rising together, but the steady increase in his income that now took place did not tempt him to ostentation. The years passed in quietly increasing prosperity, and by the time he was thirty-two he had forgotten the humiliations which followed the bank's collapse, and could think of himself as a solid man.

His family position seemed as secure as his business achievement. The three children were well-behaved in the half-hour a day which was all he saw of them. His wife gave him no cause for complaint. She did not excite him either, but that was not something he had ever expected of her. His younger brother had devoted himself to study at Oxford in a way which no one would ever have predicted of Clifton College's Captain of Cricket; and all reports suggested that Ralph's way of life was more sober and respectable than could be expected of any normal undergraduate.

As for his sister Margaret, William had never pretended to approve of the idea that a woman of respectable family should rudely force her way into the male profession of medicine. When he gave his permission, he had not expected her to survive the social problems and intellectual strains for more than a few months. But to his surprise she had done more than survive. Every visit made it clear that she was thriving on the difficulties of her training.

She was always tired when she arrived, and withdrawn, as though the horrors of what she saw in the hospital wards were too vivid to be dismissed from her mind in the course of the short journey from London to Bristol. But her first meeting with the children on each occasion was enough to dispel the strain. Within moments she was merry, laughing with a light-heartedness she had never displayed when she was living as the daughter of wealthy parents.

Her relationship with Matthew and Beatrice and Arthur was so close that William occasionally wondered whether their mother might become jealous. But Sophie only shrugged her shoulders. She did not wish to play in nurseries or schoolrooms herself, but had no objection to Margaret doing so as long as the discipline of the governess was not undermined. Sometimes William watched from a window as the children played on the lawn with their aunt. Margaret cuddled them in a way that no one else did and it was easy to see from the way they pressed up against her and fought to hold her hands how much they enjoyed the experience. Even Matthew, who was nine by now and far too old for nursery behaviour, clamoured for piggy-backs and wheel-barrow-walks with the others.

Once or twice William had been tempted to interfere, fearing that the boy would become soft. But although he was not a demonstrative man, he was sensitive enough to recognize that Margaret's feeling for Matthew was that of a mother rather than an aunt. She had loved him from babyhood, and her love seemed to have increased as it became more and more likely that she would never have a baby of her own.

This was something which William by now took for granted, though he could not guess whether Margaret herself still entertained any hopes. Even if she had not deliberately cut herself off from marriage by her choice of career, she had passed the age when she could expect to find a husband. William saw it as a kindness in himself to let her borrow Matthew, so to speak, as the target for all her family affection. John Junius had never encouraged his children to love him and had often caused them fear. William was anxious not to achieve the same effect with his own children. Unable to show any warmth to them himself, he was more liberal than many of his friends in allowing the nursery timetable to include a few moments of happiness.

Margaret had proved to be speaking the truth when she

236

claimed, before starting her training, that it would make family relationships easier and not more difficult. William had known even at that time that his sister would not have fitted comfortably into the household if she had been forced to live there as an unmarried woman without occupation. He could not have been as cool as Sophie about suggesting a paid post as governess elsewhere, for this would have reflected unfavourably on his ability to support his sister. As it was, she visited Bristol every Christmas and again for a month in the summer, bringing with her a brisk cheerfulness which made Brinsley House briefly a more lively place. Because she and William no longer had any common interests, there was nothing which could cause them to quarrel.

So, three and a half years after his father's death, it seemed that William's position as head of the Lorimer family was as successful as his business. The first sign of disturbance to its well-ordained routine came on Beatrice's fifth birthday. The day was a Saturday: Margaret had promised to travel by railway train from London to be present at the party, and to stay overnight. William had already sent his brougham to meet her at Temple Meads when he was surprised by the arrival of another member of the family.

Ralph had used Brinsley House as his home during the university vacations as a matter of course and now, after a holiday visit to a friend, came back to it without ceremony. Unlike Margaret he had little interest in children. He had forgotten that today was Beatrice's birthday, and did not even notice when his niece, already wearing her party frock, ran hopefully to the top of the stairs as he came through the door. As William stepped into the hall to greet his brother, he observed both Beatrice's silent disappointment and Ralph's frowning concentration on whatever it was that he had come to discuss.

They went together into the library. Since John Junius's death the tower room had been locked up. Sophie thought

237

it a dangerous temptation to the children, Margaret's last memory of it still filled her with horror and even William, who was not often sentimental, found its atmosphere forbidding. His ships no longer came up river to the old Bristol docks, so that the pride of watching them pass below had gone.

'Have you had your examination results yet?' he asked Ralph as they sat down.

His brother nodded.

'Yes. I have my degree, although not a good one. I only got a Third. But I was fortunate not to be plucked.'

It was all the same to William. By the time he was twenty-two – Ralph's age now – he had been an experienced businessman, and he set no very high value on a university education. He had sent Ralph to Oxford as a gesture to show that the Lorimers were not a family who surrendered to temporary setbacks and because the boy had set his heart on going. Shocked by the frivolity of most of the undergraduates, Ralph had worked hard. No one had expected him to do brilliantly and William did not propose to criticize, even though Ralph himself might be disappointed by the result of his Finals.

Whether or not Ralph's mind had improved, his physical development was striking. As part of the self-discipline with which he punished himself for his misbehaviour with Claudine he had abandoned cricket. Instead, needing some form of regular exercise, he had taken up rowing because he did not enjoy it. It strengthened his muscles and broadened his back and had helped to make him an outstandingly good-looking young man: his face had always been a handsome one. William – himself small and sharp-featured – looked appraisingly at his tall, blond brother.

'Now that you are down from Oxford you must allow Sophie to find you a wife,' he said jokingly. 'It is an activity very much to her taste, and you have everything to recommend you. She will guarantee you a fortune, and perhaps a pretty face as well.'

Ralph was not amused. His sense of humour had never been very keen – a failing which William himself shared – and on this occasion his expression showed the aversion he felt for the subject.

'I want to tell you my plans for the future,' he said, wasting no time. 'You already know of my determination to go as a missionary to the West Indies, to make what amends I can for what our family did there.'

'You told me your intention when you were younger,' William agreed. 'Has reflection not persuaded you that you have no personal responsibility? At least you must spend a little time in an English living to start with. You cannot hope to be noticed for preferment if you leave the country as soon as you take Holy Orders.'

'This is what I have to tell you,' said Ralph. 'I have considered the matter very carefully. I have decided to return to the Baptist faith.'

William did not attempt to conceal his angry astonishment. 'You have never been a Baptist! How can you return?'

'You understand me well enough. Our forefathers were Baptists: Brinsley and William and John.'

'Our forefathers were slave traders,' William said bluntly. 'If you are ashamed of that, why should you choose to associate yourself with any of their other attributes?'

'I have studied the situation in Jamaica as carefully as is possible at such a distance. From all I read it seems clear that the Church of England allied itself for so many years with the slave-owners – the planters and overseers and attorneys – that no minister of that denomination can even now hope to gain the confidence of the people descended from the slaves. It was the Baptists who fifty years ago helped the slaves in the years before and after emancipation, and who are trusted by their people still.'

'That is hardly a good enough reason to justify a change of faith,' said William.

Ralph pointed out that no change of faith was involved.

239

'Anglicans and Baptists are both Christians,' he said. 'The difference is one of authority. As a Baptist minister I shall enjoy more independence, both in my own thoughts and in matters of organization. I shall be able to minister to my congregation in the way that best suits them, not in a manner prescribed by an archbishop thousands of miles away. When our great-grandfather led his family into the Church of England, I suspect his motive was to identify himself with a certain class of society. That is my motive too in moving back again. I need to come as close as I can to the people of my new community and I see this as the best way to do it.'

'You are throwing away your life,' said William. He had observed the feelings of guilt and sin which had dominated Ralph since his schooldays, but had hoped that this would prove only a youthful phase, to be forgotten in the freedoms of adult life. Because his nature was a careful one, William himself had no extravagant vices, but he had never placed any kind of restraint on Ralph since John Junius's death. In fact, he would positively have welcomed some evidence that some of his brother's time at Oxford had revealed the kind of high spirits natural to his youth.

The Church would not have promised a fortune, but someone of Ralph's striking presence might have hoped to become at least a dean one day, if not a bishop, and the profession was a respectable one for a younger son. To bury himself as a Baptist minister in some steaming West Indian village for the few years in which a white man could hope to survive yellow fever was to bury at the same time not only ambition but talent. William made it his business to study character and beneath the self-criticism which he hoped was only a temporary ruler of Ralph's temperament he recognized qualities of application which could turn his brother into a good administrator or manager.

'You could be of value to me at Portishead,' he said abruptly. 'I stand in great need of someone down at the docks to calculate the most efficient uses of berthing and warehouse space. I will employ you tomorrow if you wish, and you will have every opportunity to advance yourself.'

'Do you not understand what vocation is?' asked Ralph. 'You are in a business exactly fitted to your tastes and talents, and no doubt you're happy in it. But what I feel is something far stronger than that. An absolute conviction that my destiny lies in one particular place, one special kind of work. A compulsion, you could say. As though it were out of my power to choose a different path. Margaret will understand that, because she has her own vocation.'

William fought successfully to control his annoyance. Unlike his father, he rarely made his displeasure obvious. One of his talents was the ability to recognize the occasions on which argument would be unprofitable. He was at this moment angry with Ralph on three separate counts. The sense of wasted talent combined with a social irritation which he did not formulate clearly even in his own mind – a consciousness that in moving from nonconformity to establishment three generations earlier the Lorimers had subtly increased their respectability, and that Ralph's move in the opposite direction was a threat to it. Added to these two thoughts was the even more prosaic one that all the money he had provided to complete Ralph's education had been wasted.

In spite of all this, Ralph was wrong if he thought that his elder brother did not understand the strength of his convictions. William was sensitive enough to accept the existence of a sense of vocation, although he had no sympathy for it. He muttered something non-committal, allowing Ralph to believe that his declaration had been accepted, without barring a return to the subject at some more promising time.

Ralph, having said what he had come to say, seized the chance to escape when the butler came in to announce that one of William's captains would like a word with him. William frowned to himself, thinking that an intrusion of

241

this kind could only mean bad news; but Captain Richards was apologetic. His ship had returned to Portishead the previous day from the Californian coast. He had already made his report to William and handed over the log and all the documents relating to the cargo. Now he confessed that he had forgotten at the same time to perform one more personal commission. He held out a letter, folded and sealed.

'Locked this in my box for safe keeping, sir,' he said. 'Went out of my mind till I was home last night. Gentleman in San Francisco asked me to do him the favour of setting it on its way.'

William looked at the inscription. The letter was addressed to Miss Margaret Lorimer.

'I'll see to it,' he said; and then added casually, 'What sort of a gentleman?'

'Difficult to say. Strange kind of clothes they wear in San Francisco. Run into someone looking like a tramp, and you find he owns a gold mine. See another fellow dressed fit to meet the Queen and you're warned that he lives on his card-playing. Not rich, not poor, this one, I'd say. Respectable tradesman, perhaps, neat and tidy. A good-looking young man, that I do remember. About your own age, I'd guess, Mr Lorimer.'

'Did he ask you any questions about Miss Lorimer? Whether she still lived in Bristol, for example?'

'That very question, yes. So I told him as she'd gone off to London and I didn't know where, but I would give this to you.'

'Thank you,' said William. He studied the inscription carefully for a moment and then tucked the letter into an inside pocket. None of his questions had really been necessary; nor was his identification of the handwriting. There were a good many people in San Franciso who might have reason to communicate with William Lorimer in the way of business. But there was only one man there who would address a letter to Margaret.

William bit his lower lip in annoyance as he considered
what to do. He had hoped that the Lorimers might have
heard the last of David Gregson.

4

A contented appearance is a dangerous disguise if it
conceals any secret longing for change. William observed
his sister closely from the moment she arrived at Brinsley
House, not long after Captain Richards had left. If Margaret had known what depended on her behaviour that day
she might have sighed and languished. But she did not
know, and so she arrived with a smile on her face and a
brisk eagerness to help with the party.

It was easy for William to avoid any mention of the
letter in his pocket until he had time to collect his thoughts
on the subject. Margaret could have no possible reason to
mention out of the blue a name which had not been spoken
in Brinsley House for three years. In any case, the birthday
excitement meant that she was in as much hurry to visit
Beatrice as Beatrice was to see her. The little girl's previous
disappointment at Ralph's empty-handed arrival was quite
forgotten in the pleasure of discovering a rosy-cheeked
Dutch doll inside the box which Margaret was carrying.

Already the other young guests and their nursemaids
were beginning to arrive. Their white flounced muslin
dresses and pale blue sashes fluttered over the lawns as
though a swarm of butterflies had suddenly descended. It
was a pretty sight – although William frowned to see that
Arthur, who was nearly four and should have known
better, had stained his satin suit with green by sliding
down one of the grassy banks. His over-excitement showed
itself in noise and naughtiness. He chased the girls, jumping
to tug at their hair ribbons, until Margaret calmed him
with the responsibility of forming the first bridge for a

game of Oranges and Lemons. Matthew, by contrast, stood aloof, knowing himself too old for a gathering of such little girls, and yet accepting some of the responsibilities of a host. He was quick to help anyone who tripped and fell, but between such duties returned to stand, straight-backed and solemn, at the head of the stone steps.

William noted his elder son's grave courtesy with a pride which expanded to take in the whole occasion. Who could have imagined, four years earlier, that the children of the best families in Bristol would ever play in the gardens of Brinsley House as his guests? The achievement was as satisfactory as it had been swift. He nodded to himself in self-approval as he stood at the library window. Then he returned his thoughts to the question of Margaret and the letter.

There was no opportunity to talk to her during the afternoon. When it was time for the party tea, she stood watchfully in the background to make sure that no shy guest found herself neglected and no spilt jelly led to tears. Afterwards, in the great drawing room, she sat beside Beatrice as the conjuror produced doves from his hat and yards of coloured silk handkerchiefs from his sleeve. It was not until later that evening, when the party was over and the Lorimer children had been taken upstairs, that William had the opportunity to test her attitude. The four adults were sitting together in the family drawing room as he asked her first about the progress of her training.

She smiled with pleasure at his show of interest.

'I have had more examinations to pass this summer,' she said. 'But they were not as important as last year's First M.B. Most important of all will be the Second M.B. If I feel myself to be sufficiently prepared, I shall sit for that in July next year.'

'What does the Second M.B. comprise?' asked Ralph, still near enough to a life of examinations to be interested in his sister's.

244

'Everything you can imagine. Pathology, surgery, midwifery, medicine and forensic medicine. Even toxicology. As well as the written papers, there is a *viva voce* on each, and practical sessions of dissection and analysis. I am frightened already by the thought of it all.' But she was smiling as she spoke, so that William, watching her closely, could detect her excitement at the challenge of the course.

'So for this coming year you will still be studying?' he checked.

'Yes, but in a different way from before. Although we must still attend lectures, most of our time now is spent in hospitals, seeing as wide a variety of cases as we can. My midwifery practical experience is already complete. Since June I have delivered sixty-five babies. My new work, starting next Monday, will be at the Hospital for Sick Children in East London, as clerk to the house-physician. I look forward to this very much. For three years I have been dissecting dead bodies. To care for patients who may be helped to recovery should be a most rewarding task.'

William found it difficult to conceal his distaste for the information she gave in such a casual manner. The cutting up of dead bodies could not in any circumstances be described as a suitable occupation for a woman. Yet he was a man who respected success in any field and he had made his own enquiries. He knew, for example, that the examinations which punctuated the studies of any medical student were stringent. To pass each of them at the first attempt, as Margaret had done so far, was an achievement not to be despised. In any case, he was not one to waste time regretting decisions which had been made and put into effect long ago. All that concerned him now was whether Margaret herself was happy in her work.

There could be no doubt about the answer. Her smile, at once confident and excited, might have softened the heart of a warmer man. In William's case it served only to confirm his opinion that since his sister appeared to have fashioned a life so congenial to herself, she should be allowed to continue in it without interruption. While he pondered the matter, Ralph took up the questioning.

'Do you intend to specialize after you qualify?' he asked.

'Either in paediatrics or obstetrics,' Margaret told him. 'I haven't yet decided which. Each has the advantage that at least amongst the patients there is little prejudice against women, and that would not be true if I went into general practice.'

'Do Miss Morton's interests lie in the same sphere as yours?' asked Ralph, with a casual air.

'No, Lydia has her own enthusiasms,' said Margaret. 'If her choice were free, I believe that she would go to India as a medical missionary. She has been influenced by some of our fellow-students who have returned from that part of the world especially in order to increase their usefulness by medical training. But Mr Morton is in poor health, and Mrs Morton becomes upset at the possibility of her daughter going so far away. So Lydia intends instead to specialize in public health. There is a great deal to be learned, and much that is already known has yet to be applied. Even in hospitals, the older doctors and nurses have been very slow to understand the need for sterilization or even cleanliness. I am appalled every day by what I see. We are all told to be tactful, for the sake of the other women who will follow us, but sometimes it is very hard to keep silent.'

The conversation continued for a little longer before Sophie showed her boredom with the subject by interrupting. William listened, and watched, and considered. After the others had retired for the night he sat for half an hour in the library, with the letter which had been on his mind all evening lying on the desk in front of him.

Margaret had not yet learned of Ralph's decision to become a Baptist missionary, and knew nothing of the interview which had taken place between the two brothers earlier in the day. She would have thought it monstrously unfair if she had discovered that because William resented the waste of money on his brother's Oxford education he was taking on himself the right to decide whether his sister's training should or should not go for nothing in the same way – or that, because he was sensitive to a fall in social status through Ralph, he could hardly bear the thought of his sister allying herself to a fugitive from the law who could be described as 'perhaps a respectable tradesman'.

William himself knew that it was unjust on his part to decide Margaret's future without allowing her to express her own opinion, but he did not intend to let her argue the matter with him. Like his father, he believed himself entitled to keep all family decisions in his own hands, even when they concerned others more than himself.

He stared down at the desk, his fingers tapping. Although he was now considering whether or not to destroy the letter, the thought of opening and reading it never occurred to him. Such an action would be dishonourable, whereas the course he was debating with himself might be all for the best.

Perhaps one reason why he was not tempted to read the contents was his certainty that he could guess them accurately. With a warrant still out for his arrest, David Gregson would not have taken the risk of revealing where he was merely in order to continue a disagreement. A letter to Margaret could have only one purpose – to end the quarrel with which they must have parted. William could not know the details, but his sister's distress at the time suggested that she had dismissed her lover in a way she later regretted.

It seemed safe to make the assumption that she was now being invited to travel to San Francisco, to marry a man who after so long would be almost a stranger. William knew well enough that young women found it difficult to reject any invitation of this kind, and felt it his responsibility to decide on Margaret's behalf what was best for her. Four years earlier, such a marriage might have brought her happiness. But today?

In speaking of his vocation Ralph had claimed that Margaret would understand it because her own sense of vocation was strong. Even if he had not sensed that already, the evening's conversation would have been enough to convince William of its truth. He would be doing his sister no kindness by unsettling her now. She had been happy in her training and she looked forward with satisfaction to a life which – whatever William himself might think – she believed would be of value both to herself and to society. At no time during the past four years had she shown any sign of regret for her broken engagement. Her present mood was, in a single word, serene.

How different it would be if she were suddenly to learn that a relationship which she had thought buried might still be revived. In the first place she would have all the emotional anxiety of deciding what her feelings were for a man she had not seen for so long. She herself had changed greatly during the past four years, and so certainly had David Gregson, but she would be expected to make a choice before seeing him again. In the second place, if she decided to go, she would feel guilt at the knowledge that she was wasting her training by abandoning it before the acquisition of the necessary practical experience. If, on the other hand, she resolved to stay, she would undoubtedly wonder from time to time whether she had made the right choice. The uncertainty could blight a life which otherwise would be contented.

There was one other point to be considered. If Margaret were to meet David Gregson again, the last months of Lorimer's Bank before its failure would necessarily be discussed between them. What she did not know, and need not know, was that their father's death had left a good many questions unanswered although the creditors had pressed as hard as they could. The plain fact was that John Junius's fortune had diminished in the year before his death, but no one had been able to discover where the missing funds had gone.

The mystery of Georgiana's rubies had never been adequately explained. During the course of the bankruptcy proceedings it was discovered that John Junius had quietly disposed of all the most valuable pieces of his collection of jade, replacing them with a few cheap carvings so that the gaps should not be conspicuous. He had claimed – or so Margaret reported at the time – that the most priceless carvings were stored for safe keeping in the vaults of Lorimer's, but they had never been found and there was no record of their deposit. William had assumed at first that John Junius had sold them to raise the price of the rubies, but the later discovery that the jewellery itself was only paste had introduced a new puzzle.

It was a puzzle which nobody had solved, and one to which William gave a good deal of thought. To him it seemed clear that his father had made an attempt to rescue a large sum of money from the crash he foresaw, and that he had done so in order that the family should not be ruined. The real disaster was that he died without revealing to his elder son where the reserve was concealed. William felt sure that one day he would be able to work out the answer to this problem and discover a hidden fortune; but until that day came it was not in his interest that anyone else should remember the discrepancy which had been the subject of so much agitation at the time but which had now ceased to be newsworthy. David Gregson and Margaret, together talking over the events which had parted them, might inadvertently revive a controversy which was best forgotten.

So many thousand miles away, what harm could they do? William forced himself to recognize that this last objection to the renewing of old ties was not in Margaret's true interest. The other arguments were a different matter. For some time longer he stared at the unopened letter in front of him. Then he made up his mind.

Margaret had made her own choice. She had been happy in her decision, and to be offered the same choice for a second time could only bring uncertainty. Whatever she decided to do, she would be unhappy about what she had to reject. To force her into such a situation would be unkind. The past, thought William to himself, is best left undisturbed.

His conscience did not disturb him at all. He had thought the matter through and was confident that the conclusion he reached as head of the family was in his sister's best interest. And no one would ever know. He lit a spill from the lamp on his desk and applied it to the letter from San Francisco, holding a corner until the flame burned his finger and thumb. Then he dropped the charred sheet into the fireplace and stirred it with a poker into ash.

PART II
Margaret and Charles

1

Forced to spend their working hours at close quarters with death, medical students in every age and country devote their leisure to the most robust manifestations of life. The young ladies who enrolled at the London School of Medicine for Women were no exception to this rule. True, they did not hurl themselves about the rugger field or propel unstable boats up and down the river or deprive policemen of their helmets in the course of inebriated evenings. But there was a light-hearted gaiety about them which Margaret at first found extraordinary, and then almost at once took for granted. There had been a time, in the bad year of 1878, when she had thought that she would never be happy again. Now, four years later, it seemed to her as she went exhausted to bed each night that she had never been happy before.

The group had its own private language. When an alphabetical list of new students was pinned up on the first day of the preliminary course, they noticed at once that each of the first fifteen letters of the alphabet was represented, and by one surname only. They christened themselves the Alpha Beta class, and addressed each other by their initial letters instead of names. They embroidered the letters on the white linen smocks which they wore in the hospital wards, so that patients and instructors alike found it simple to pick up the habit. Even Margaret and Lydia, who had been friends for so long, adapted their speech to the private language during the term, becoming Miss L and Miss M.

So Miss Lorimer and Miss Morton became holiday

people only. It was like dying and being born again, Margaret sometimes thought: she had become a new woman. She could hardly believe that the girl who had lived in Bristol, doing her conscientious best to find some useful occupation for at least an hour or two of the day, was the same person as herself.

Right from the beginning the work had been hard. There were moments during the preliminary course when Margaret was convinced that she would not be accepted for full training – or, if she were, would never be able to endure its more advanced stages. Later she discovered that those first few months were deliberately made taxing as a test of intelligence and staying power. When Ralph wrote anxious letters to her from Oxford during this period, hoping that she was managing to avoid the temptations and wickednesses of London life, she was able to assure him that she had not yet had time to find out what or where they were.

There had been plenty of time, though, to discover the poverty and dirt in which so many Londoners lived. Her midwifery had taken her, often in the middle of the night, into dark and foul-smelling courts round which dilapidated tenements insecurely clustered. She became familiar with drunkenness and foul language and – because so many babies chose to arrive at two or three o'clock in the morning – soon ceased to be frightened by the hurried footsteps of a thief surprised at his work or the glimpse of a body rolled up in newspaper, a dosser who might or might not wake up when morning came.

Even in the most sordid surroundings, she never felt in any danger. The messenger who came to call her, whether husband or child or neighbour of the woman in labour, always escorted her into the slums and out again, calling on the empty streets to let the doctor through, so that there should be no misunderstanding about her errand. Even as a girl she had never been nervous, and now she simply took it for granted that she should go where she was most useful.

It was as a result of this attitude and experience that she saw nothing extraordinary about the Sick Children's Hospital when she started to work there on the Monday following Beatrice's fifth birthday. The building had originally been a warehouse, and the change of use had not been accompanied by any conversion of its structure. A hundred iron bedsteads and twenty wooden cradles had been installed, but otherwise the accommodation provided for the children was little better than that enjoyed by the sacks of cloves or ginger whose aroma still lingered. The walls were of wood, pierced by openings from which the old hoist platforms still projected. Arriving in September, Margaret accepted that the ventilation thus provided must have been pleasantly cool in the summer, but wondered with misgiving whether the mists and fogs of autumn and the chill winds of winter would prove healthy for the young patients.

If coldness was still only in prospect, dampness was already in possession. The warehouse was supported half on land and half on piers sunk into the bed of the river. So near the autumn equinox, the tide was at its highest, lapping the floor of the overhanging section and splashing against its side almost into the windows. As a result, all the wood was damp and much of it was rotten.

The ground floor, with no windows to illuminate it, was not used by the children. A pair of oil lamps hung there to welcome new arrivals. Their other greeting came from Jamie, the porter, whose body was powerful but whose mind was dim. Too large ever to stand straight under the low wooden ceiling, he sent the oil lamps rocking with blows from his head even when he stooped. But he was kind and harmless, and lifted the sick children up the steep ladders which emerged through trapdoors on to the main floor; carrying them as though they were snowflakes, weightless and fragile.

Margaret's days in the hospital were busy ones. In the mornings she accompanied the house physician, Dr Ferguson, on his ward round, visiting every bed in the two long lines. It came as a relief on her first day to discover that his views on female doctors were tolerant. He believed that they should confine themselves to the care of children, but since the care of children was what he had agreed to teach her, there was no cause for disagreement between them. It seemed to Margaret, in fact, that he was especially meticulous in his supervision, as though by training her well he hoped to persuade her to choose this specialization. He made her conduct her own examinations and give her opinion before making his own pronouncement on the disease and its treatment. The hospital had no surgical unit. Even the charitable optimists who had looked at a derelict warehouse and seen a vision of care and healing had recognized that the facilities were not good enough for surgery.

After Margaret had made up her notes for the morning, it was time to help with the out-patients. Officially her task was to keep the records, but from the start she was expected to offer practical help. The area was one of the poorest in London, and its children appeared either to be particularly adventurous or particularly unlucky. They crashed through rotten floorboards, they were hit by cargoes swinging from cranes, they were hauled half-drowned out of docks, they were bitten in bed by rats. For Margaret's first day or two the responsibility frightened her, but there was too much work for time to be spent in wondering whether she was doing it in the right way. She advised on convulsions, set broken limbs in splints, and identified spots and rashes before sending their owners off to the isolation hospital. Each night she arrived home exhausted and could do no more than exchange a few experiences with Lydia over supper before falling into bed.

It was on the Wednesday of her sixth week that she arrived in the morning to find a strange difference in the atmosphere. It was not easy to discover what had caused it. Most of the babies in the wooden cradles seemed to be crying, and there was a smell of vomit in the air, but this was normal. The older children in the beds, irrepressible even in sickness, were engaged in throwing at each other whatever articles were in reach; and even some of those who lay flat, with only their white faces showing above the scarlet blankets, were able to shout a cheerful insult from time to time, although it might take them five minutes' panting to regain their breath.

All this was normal too, and so unfortunately was the fact that a few children lay with their eyes closed, too weak to contribute to the noise and bustle. One of these was in the bed beside the trapdoor through which Margaret had just appeared. She looked anxiously at his dead-white face and blue lips and put a hand to his wrist even before taking off her cloak. His neighbour, a cheerful boy with the mark of his father's drunken anger stitched in a livid scar across his forehead, leaned forward informatively.

''E's croaking, Miss.'

Margaret made no comment. She pushed aside the curtain which cut off Matron's tiny cubicle from the open ward and let it fall back behind her.

'Peter's gone,' she said.

Matron – an elderly woman, neat in a long blue dress with stiffly starched cuffs and cap – nodded gravely.

'Ten minutes ago,' she said. 'I'll have Jamie up from below to fetch him in a moment or two. But we've had an emergency here. Young Kelly's leg. Gangrene, I'm afraid. He's too ill to move. St Bartholomew's have sent a surgeon to amputate. I want to be free when he's finished, so I'm hoping none of them will notice Peter for a moment.'

The operation explained the atmosphere. All the children were terrified of being 'cut'. It happened here only in the gravest emergencies, but whenever a surgeon was seen to arrive, a tension grew like the feeling in a prison on execution day. The young patients themselves fought

255

against the anaesthetic as fiercely as they would have sought to evade the knife, and even the noisiest of the other children were silenced by the sound of the screaming. Jamie, too, who was called upon to hold the child down until the chloroform had taken effect, was upset by this duty. He loved children, and wished to be kind to them. His limited intelligence could not comprehend that a child must be restrained and hurt for his own good. Jamie did whatever he was told, but he was not happy about it.

As Margaret turned to hang up her cloak, the curtain was pulled aside again. The stranger who came in – a man of about thirty – was almost as tall as Jamie. He had thick fair hair and troubled blue eyes in a strong and handsome face.

The overwhelming impression of the young surgeon was one of bulk, for in addition to his height he was broad-shouldered and solidly built. Margaret stepped back as though only some such movement would enable them all to breathe in Matron's tiny cubicle. Even then they were so close that she could see the fresh blood which stained his frock coat: the sawdust which clung to his boots was coloured in the same manner.

'I've had to take the leg off above the knee, Matron,' he said. 'And even now . . .' He shrugged his shoulders compassionately. 'I don't give much for his chances, I'm afraid. You'd better get his mother here.'

'No family,' said Matron. 'He's been working as a crossing-sweeper and living rough. That's how he came to be walking round with a rusty nail stuck in his foot for the best part of eight days.'

'Mm. Well, keep him warm. Hot drinks as often as he can take them. If you've a drop of brandy to spare, that would be his best medicine. He won't feel the pain for a few hours. I'll come back this evening to see how he's getting on.'

'Thank you, Doctor,' said Matron. 'We're very much obliged to you, I'm sure.'

He stepped backwards, raising one hand above his head to move the blanket aside. As he did so, he glanced at Margaret for the first time. It seemed to her that what he saw disturbed him, for he frowned slightly to himself and stood for a moment without moving as though holding a pose for a photograph. Then, almost imperceptibly, he shook his head. Whatever was puzzling him was not worth the time he would need to unravel it. He ducked under the beam and within a second could be heard clattering down the ladder, with a thud as he jumped the last few feet.

Margaret stared at the place where he had stood. If he had gone straight out without pausing, it would never have occurred to her that she had seen him somewhere before. But his moment of puzzlement had proved infectious. His face was somehow familiar, but she could not remember any occasion on which they could have met. Clearly he had had the same difficulty. Perhaps his name would give a clue.

'Who was the surgeon?' she asked Matron.

'Come to think, he never gave me his name,' said Matron, unconcerned. 'When he arrived, he said that his Resident Surgeon had asked him to come, and where was the boy? I was too glad to see him to be bothered about introductions.'

A hysterical shout came from the other side of the partition.

''E's croaked. Matron, come 'ere. Peter's croaked.'

'This is going to be a bad day,' said Matron. 'When I saw young Kelly this morning I thought we were starting with the worst, but now I've got that feeling in my bones that there's more to come. A bad day.'

She hurried out of the cubicle. Margaret heard her voice – an artificial sharpness to it – ordering Mickey to get back in his bed and Johnny to stop making that terrible noise. Jamie was called for and came heavily up the ladder, still disturbed by the operation. From the other direction a young nurse came hurrying to help. Margaret watched the activity through a gap in the curtain, but thought it best to keep out of the way. Unlike Matron, she had no gloomy feelings about the day. Her brief exchange of glances with the surgeon had aroused her interest. His appearance was attractive. Whoever he was, she would like him to notice her.

It could easily be arranged, she thought. He had promised to return in the evening. If she were to stay a little later than usual, she could ask him to discuss the effects of the operation with her.

This plan was foiled, unintentionally, by Matron. The Sick Children's Hospital undertook no night casualty work; and because there was no lighting in the long ward except for the lamps carried by the nurses, the in-patients were settled to sleep as soon as darkness fell. On this particular evening that moment arrived early, for the first of the autumn's sea fogs came swirling up the river to be trapped beneath the pall of smoke which at this season thatched the roof of London's atmosphere. Margaret had written up her notes for the day slowly and painstakingly but by six o'clock it was clear that there was nothing more for her to do at the hospital. Dr Ferguson had left long before, and Matron frowned to herself as the thick yellow fog blanketed the building more closely.

'You should be on your way, Miss L.' Like everyone else, Matron used the initial as though it were Margaret's full name. 'In half an hour it won't be safe to walk through the streets. Jamie had better go with you to the station.'

'No, thank you, Matron. That won't be necessary.' Even at the best of times Jamie had always to be given a note in his pocket to state his destination, ready for the moment when he lost himself. He would never find his way back to the hospital in the fog. But Margaret realized the wisdom of Matron's advice. Besides, in such weather it was likely that the surgeon would cancel his journey, so that any further procrastination would be for nothing.

She clutched her cloak tightly about her while she

climbed down the ladder to the ground floor and called a cheerful goodnight to Jamie. He was stumbling about in the shadows, groaning to himself, and did not answer her as she stepped briskly out. The fog was not yet dense, but swirled up the street in tall columns, like ghosts walking. At one moment she could see the buildings across the way clearly: then they were gone, and with them went all sound. Even her own footsteps were muffled when she reluctantly began to move away.

Twice she thought she heard a horse approaching: twice she stopped to listen and told herself she was imagining the sound. On the second occasion the pause was longer, for it was necessary to deliver a short lecture to herself. What did she think she was doing, loitering like a shopgirl? Was she trying to force herself on the attention of a busy professional man who had no reason to give her a second glance? Margaret felt bewildered by her own behaviour. She was twenty-five years old and dedicated to the calling she had chosen. She had loved a man once and would never love another. Her life as a doctor lay clear ahead. How could she have allowed a brief glimpse of a stranger to complicate her feelings? She resolved to put him out of her mind at once.

With this settled, she took at least two brisk steps before finding another excuse to pause. The fog, settling more thickly, had trapped the black smoke which rose from a million chimneys and filled the lower air with grit. Margaret began to cough as the irritation, more smoky than she ever remembered it before, reached her throat. She untied her scarf and wound it round her mouth to act as a mask. While she was doing so, she heard the sound of a horse's hooves and the rattling of wheels.

This time there could be no mistake, but the perverse acoustics created by the fog made it impossible to tell the direction of the carriage. She turned to look back, and caught her breath in horror at what she saw. As the yellow fog eddied and briefly rose along the river bank, it revealed

259

glimpses of a bright orange flame through the doorway she had recently left. The children's hospital was on fire.

2

Fire! The word alone inspires fear, but even the fearful may see rescue as more necessary than escape. Appalled by the danger to the children in the hospital, there was a second in which Margaret was too shocked to move. Then, without even looking to see whether the road was clear, she picked up her skirts and began to run back as fast as she could. She had covered only a few yards when the shoulder of a horse sent her flying. So hard was the blow that it knocked her clear of the hooves. She heard the cabbie swearing as he pulled up, and heard too the footsteps of the passenger who jumped out of the cab and ran towards her.

It was the young surgeon. He helped her gently to her feet. While her swimming head was steadying itself she saw that he recognized her.

'You shouldn't be out on foot on a night like this,' he scolded. 'Wait for me in the cab. I shan't be long.'

Margaret shook her head. Either from shock or as a result of her fall she was too winded to speak. The hospital had become invisible again behind a curtain of fog, so without considering what he would think of her behaviour, she took hold of the surgeon's arm and pulled him towards it.

Only a few steps, and the reason for her urgency was all too apparent. Black smoke poured out of the ground-floor doorway as though it were a factory chimney. Margaret guessed that oil from the lamps must have caught fire. The dampness of the wood at that level might prevent the fire itself from spreading, but even smoke would be a danger to the sick children above. She pulled her scarf more tightly over her mouth and nose as she ran.

Jamie was lying on the ground just inside the door. His forehead was bleeding and it was easy enough to see that he must have hit one of the hanging lamps hard enough to dislodge it. He was too heavy for Margaret to move. She left her companion to drag him out to the open air while she herself ran with smarting eyes to where the ladder should be.

Unlike the wooden walls of the warehouse, the ladder was new and dry. Its feet were standing in a pool of burning oil and the lower rungs were already on fire. Margaret had only her head and shoulders through the trapdoor when she felt the support slipping away from her feet. She flung herself forward and managed to pull herself on to the floor of the ward.

Most of the children were coughing, and the babies were crying; but there was no movement in the long room, no feeling of panic. The two night nurses must have assumed that the thickening of the atmosphere was caused by the fog. They had hung a blanket across the opening in the wall which led to the hoist platform of the old warehouse, and were cheerfully chatting to Matron at the far end of the ward over a cup of tea.

As Margaret straightened herself she heard the cabhorse cantering away; she hoped desperately that the cabbie would summon a fire engine quickly. A shout came from below.

'Where are you?'

'The ladder's gone,' she shouted back. 'Go round beneath the hoist.'

Startled by the exchange, Matron came hurrying down the ward. She smelt the smoke as she approached and her eyes widened with alarm.

It was impossible to estimate how great the danger was. Dampness was a friend, but draught an enemy which might prove more powerful. The hospital was almost full, so that there were more than a hundred children at risk. With as few words as possible, the four women set to work to clear the ward. The least ill of the children were taken from their beds so that their mattresses could be thrown down to the ground. Then one of the nurses climbed up on to the hoist platform and lay flat, with Matron anxiously clutching her ankles. She lowered the other nurse until her feet almost touched the ground. The young surgeon, frustrated by his inability to reach the upper storey, was on hand to catch her. Now there was someone to care for the children as they joined her.

The young patients followed by the same route. Cradles were flung out first, and then the babies lowered in slings made from blankets. It was tempting to hurry, but dangerous. Matron, supervising the first few drops, made the nurse wait each time until the sling had ceased to swing, so that it would fall safely into the surgeon's arms. Margaret, meanwhile, was busy in the ward.

By now all the children who could walk were crowded below the opening high in the wall. They were too frightened to jostle, but all of them were coughing and most were crying. Margaret lifted each in turn up to Matron, hurrying away in between to carry one of the more helpless children nearer. She took a moment to throw a mattress over the open trapdoor in the hope of reducing the smoke. But the floorboards were badly fitting and full of knotholes. With every moment that passed the air became thicker and more choking. There was no piped water on this floor, so Margaret soaked her scarf in the nurses' kettle for a mask, and set the eldest children to tear up a sheet and dip the strips for the others to use as they waited.

It was a time for instant decisions. Chest cases must go quickly: broken bones were best left till last, in the hope that a ladder would arrive in time. Long after she had reached the point of exhaustion Margaret worked on, choosing and carrying and lifting, her eyes streaming and her head swimming. She could not see what was happening in the street, and she could hear nothing but the sounds of coughing and crying and the quick gasps – not yet quite screams – as the children began to panic. Not even the clanging of the fire brigade's great brass bell penetrated the fog outside and the confusion within: not even the crashing of ladders against the side of the platform. When the first two firemen appeared in the opening and jumped down into the ward, it came as a surprise as well as an overwhelming relief.

They were followed by the young surgeon. He stood for a moment on the platform, looking round, and then ran across to Margaret's side.

'Are you all right?'

Margaret nodded and allowed him to take from her arms the little girl she was holding. But she knew that it would be fatal to relax her efforts. One by one the wooden pillars which supported the floor were collapsing and the planks nearest to the trapdoor were already smouldering. It could only be a matter of moments before this drier wood began to blaze. Revitalized by companionship, she worked even faster than before.

Two ladders now were propped against the outside platform, so that while one fireman carried a young patient down one side, a second could be seen climbing up the other. Matron and the second nurse had been sent down to the street with armfuls of scarlet blankets snatched off the beds to protect the children already rescued against the weather. To them, safe from the fire, the rescue had become an excitement.

Inside the ward it was different. Margaret had been frightened on the children's behalf ever since the fire started, but on her own account had been conscious only of discomfort and tiredness. Now she became apprehensive for her own safety. She could hear the roaring of flames below one end of the ward, and the air was as hot as a baker's oven. Once she had to stop and stamp on the smouldering hem of her skirt before it flared up. To move away from the comparative safety of the opening towards one of the further beds required more courage each time. Yet the surgeon was not hesitating, nor were the firemen. Margaret forced herself to keep going.

At long last the ward was empty. One of the firemen pulled her on to the platform and steadied her as she staggered. The surgeon, just about to follow, suddenly stopped.

'The lad I operated on this morning. Is he out?'

Margaret caught her breath in horror. To minimize the disturbance to him, young Kelly had been left at the far end of the ward, in the cubicle which had served as an emergency operating theatre. She pointed, unable to speak, and the surgeon vanished into the smoke. He was gone only for a moment, but to Margaret it seemed a lifetime. She held her breath until he reappeared, and it was as though the world stood still. She could hear no sound, see no movement. All she could do was to lean against the wall, exhausted and wait.

When he returned he was walking more slowly, looking grimly down at the boy he carried in his arms. Margaret signed for him to go first down the ladder, since she herself felt unable to move. One of the firemen, realizing that she was at the point of collapse, lifted her over his shoulder and carried her down. She was too tired even to think how undignified this was.

Once on the pavement outside, she sat down regardless of the dirt, for her legs would not support her. Fog and smoke combined to make the rest of the world invisible, but there was a great deal of noise. She could hear water hissing from hoses, axes chopping at wood, flames crackling as they devoured the building, children crying, onlookers shouting. And, nearer at hand, the surgeon talking to Matron.

'Any casualties?'

'I'm afraid so,' said Matron. 'The weakest, as you would

expect. Three of the babies, one asthma case and one haemorrhage.'

'And the boy with gangrene, I'm sorry to say. Still, that might have happened in any case. Oh, and the big man I found below. It looked as though he'd knocked himself unconscious. He was badly burned before I got to him.'

'Poor Jamie!' sighed Matron. There was a moment's silence. 'I felt it was going to be a bad day. But not as bad as this.' She sighed again, and then spoke with a little of her old briskness. 'Well, I must find somewhere for these children to sleep. I've sent messages to their families. As many as possible will have to go home for the night. It won't be good for them, but what else can I do?'

'I told my cabbie to come back for me after he'd raised the firemen,' said the surgeon. 'I'll call in at Bart's on my way back and get them to send you some help. The Registrar's a friend of mine. If he hasn't got room for all the children himself, he'll send messengers and find out who can take them.' He paused. 'The young woman,' he said. 'She was here when I came this morning. Who is she?'

'Miss L? Medical student. Acting as clinical clerk to Dr Ferguson. I must find her and thank her. What we'd have done without her today, God only knows. Miss L! Miss L, where are you?'

Margaret tried to call in reply, but was too weak to utter a word. She was discovered only when Matron tripped over her.

'Miss L, are you all right? You saved their lives, you know. I shall tell Dr Ferguson. Are you hurt?'

Still sitting on the high kerb of the pavement, Margaret found to her shame that she was crying. She buried her head in her hands, for there was simply no strength left in her to lift it. She could see Matron's blue skirt, dirty and tattered now, close to her own feet – and a pair of boots which came to stand beside it.

'There's some shock here, I think,' said the surgeon. 'I'll get her home. Cabbie! Cabbie!'

The cab-driver had led his horse well away from the flames which would have terrified it, so several calls were necessary before an answering shout was heard. Matron took the opportunity to praise Margaret and thank her over and over again. Margaret did her best to respond, but was relieved to feel herself being helped into the cab.

'Where do you live?' asked the surgeon.

'Bart's first for you,' muttered Margaret. 'More important.'

'Are you sure?' His tone was solicitous, but she could tell from it that he agreed with her order of priority. 'St Bartholomew's Hospital,' he said to the cabbie. 'And quickly!'

'On a night like this, guv'nor?' The driver moved off at a pace which might be sensible in the thick fog, but which seemed unbearably slow to his passengers.

As the tension of mind and body relaxed, Margaret found herself trembling and shivering with cold. She was conscious of an arm round her waist, pulling her close against her companion's side: she felt her head topple sideways, like a broken puppet's, to rest on his shoulders. On the verge of fainting, she had ceased to be capable of any further effort or even thought.

As they neared St Bartholomew's the plodding steps of the cabhorse became even more hesitant. The hospital was next to the meat market at Smithfield, and already the cobbled streets around were rumbling with huge drays and wagons, bringing in from the country the carcasses which would be sold in the early hours of the morning. Margaret, her head steadier now, felt the surgeon fidgeting with impatience.

'I could make better speed on foot,' he muttered to himself.

'Then please don't delay on my account,' Margaret

urged. 'If you prefer to walk from here, the cab can take me home and return to the hospital for you.'

'Are you sure? Do you promise me you are not hurt at all? Will there be someone to look after you when you arrive?'

'I shall be treated like an invalid and put straight into a warm bed, although there is nothing wrong with me at all,' she assured him. 'Whom should the driver ask for when he returns to Bart's?'

'There is no reason for him to come back. I have no further use for him. Earlier in the evening I was in a hurry to call on my young patient on my way to a theatre, but by now I have missed my evening's entertainment. If you are quite sure, then . . .' He knocked on the glass to bring the cab to a halt. After dismounting, he leaned inside and held out his hand. His firm grip as she took it restored some of her spirits.

'You will allow me, I hope, to express my profound admiration for your efforts this evening,' he said. 'A great number of those children must owe their lives to you.'

'They are still in need of help,' Margaret reminded him. 'Should I come with you?'

'No, no,' he replied. 'I forbid it absolutely. You are in no state to do more.'

His expression was troubled, reflecting the responsibility which he still faced, but he smiled at her as he released her hand. Then the puzzled look that she had noticed once before returned briefly to his face. He drew in a breath as though to ask her something, but must have realized that his business at the hospital was more urgent. The question became the more necessary one of asking the address to which the cab should take her. He repeated it to the driver, and Margaret heard the chink of money changing hands. Then she was jolted off again over the slippery cobbles of the market area, the horse clattering and wheezing between the shafts.

Lydia hurried down from their first-floor apartments to

meet Margaret as soon as the cab came to a halt in front of the house. She had been so worried, she exclaimed, and then her eyes opened in astonishment at the sight of her friend's appearance. In the hallway, Margaret glanced at herself in the glass which hung at the end of the passage. She could not suppress a burst of hysterical laughter.

'What is it?' asked Lydia, more worried than ever. 'Are you all right? What has happened to you?'

Margaret stifled her laughter, but continued to stare for a moment at her torn and charred skirt, the untidy red hair which had long ago escaped from its tight bun to fall in smoky tresses over her shoulders, and her face, smeared with black where she had wiped away the sweat of the last hot, terrifying half hour inside the hospital and later the tears of relief.

'It has been a terrible evening,' she said. The very memory of it made her shudder again. 'It is curious, isn't it, that when something horrible occurs, one seems to grasp at even the most frivolous excuse for shutting the scene out of one's mind. I was thinking – today I met a gentleman whom I found interesting. I couldn't help hoping that he in turn might be interested in me. Now suddenly I see what a peculiarly unattractive appearance I presented to him. But really I feel more like crying than laughing.'

Lydia helped her upstairs to sit by the fire. Betty – who had willingly abandoned her training as a lady's maid after the bank crash to become instead a maid of all work for Lydia and Margaret – was sent bustling on a series of errands: to fill the copper warming pan for Margaret's bed, to ask in the kitchen that water should be heated for a bath, to bring up the meal which had been kept warm. Only then did Lydia allow Margaret to tell her what had happened.

In bed that night, Margaret was awakened more than once by a nightmare. She saw the young surgeon turn and hurry away from her. Sometimes he was walking down the long ward: sometimes it was an unfamiliar room that he was leaving. But always his errand was urgent, making him break into a run. Margaret knew that he was hurrying into danger, even when she could not tell what the danger was. She tried each time to call him back, but could not do it because she did not know his name.

That was always the moment when she woke up. Her mouth was open ready to warn him, but she had no word to shout. Once awake, she reminded herself each time that the danger was over, but the nightmare recurred as soon as she closed her eyes again. In the end, she had to force herself to stay awake for long enough to consider honestly what was troubling her. The fire, which had done so much harm, could do no more now. Could the uneasiness which disturbed her sleep be caused by the simple fact that a man she would like to meet again did not know her name, nor she his? What was so frightening about that? She knew where he worked. He knew where she lived. If he wanted to see her again he would have no trouble in finding her. He might not wish to do so, but that was another matter. If he felt any interest in her at all, he would come.

She remembered the way in which his arm had tightened round her waist, the look in his eyes as he said goodbye, and felt no real doubt in the matter. She would see him again. Little by little her tired body relaxed in the warm bed and she fell into a dreamless sleep.

3

Flowers may speak the language of love, but what use are their messages if they bear no signature? On the day after the fire, Margaret returned wearily to her lodgings in the evening. Her broken night had been followed by an exhausting series of visits to all the dispersed children, to see how much they had been harmed by their experience. The sight of the out-of-season roses which had arrived by messenger during the afternoon cheered her at once. She tore open the tiny envelope which accompanied them and studied the card inside with eagerness.

'Who is your admirer?' asked Lydia, who had finished her own duty earlier.

'I don't know.' Margaret began to laugh, and showed the card to her friend. '"To Miss Ell, in admiration. C. S." He must think that's my real name, and he takes it for granted that I know what his name is.'

'But you know who sent the flowers?'

'Oh yes. There are not so many possibilities from which to choose.' The first glance which the surgeon had given her might have been a puzzled one, but by the end of the day his attitude had changed to something quite different. Margaret could not describe it to Lydia without being immodest, so instead she puzzled over the initials.

'C.S.' she repeated. 'Christopher, do you think? Christopher would be a suitable name for someone who carried children to safety. Or Charles. He looks like a Charles.'

'What do Charleses look like?' asked Lydia, teasing.

'Oh; strong, and kind, and dependable.' Margaret remembered how he had kept his promise to return to the hospital in the slums even when he was looking forward to an evening at the theatre. 'Solid, somehow.'

'You had better see if you can arrange to do your surgical dressing training at St Bartholomew's. Then you may meet this solid Charles or Christopher again.'

As it happened, Margaret had called at the London School of Medicine on her way home that evening and had arranged to do precisely what Lydia suggested. She buried her face in the roses so that Lydia should not notice her blushes – but then looked up again, startled, as she heard the doorbell ring below. 'Has he come so soon? I am not fit to receive a call.'

'Do you believe you are the only person in this house likely to be called upon?'

Lydia might continue to tease, but Margaret hurried to

her bedroom to wash her face and tidy her hair. There was no time, she supposed, to change from her plain skirt and over-blouse into something more becoming. In fact, she was still struggling with hairpins when Betty knocked on the door.

'If you please, Miss, it's Mr Ralph Lorimer to see you.'

Margaret was severe with her quick flash of disappointment, but she abandoned the attempt to make herself look her best. Tidy hair was of no great importance in greeting a brother, and she hurried into the sitting room. Lydia and Ralph were talking together in an animated manner and for a moment, pausing in the doorway, Margaret looked at her brother as Lydia might be seeing him.

In the years which had passed since he left school, Ralph had grown steadily more good-looking. His expression had lost the sulky pout with which he had so often reacted to the reprimands of his father or the sermons of Clifton's overpowering headmaster, Dr Percival. Gone, too, was the guilty strain and anxiety which had shown on his face when Claudine's condition was revealed. It was as though he had managed to conquer his consciousness of personal guilt by changing it into a feeling of shame for the more general sins of his slave-trading ancestors. Now, having taken the decision to make what amends he could for these, he could once again face the world with a resolute and untroubled expression.

Lydia made no attempt to hide her admiration of his upright bearing and handsome face.

'You are to be a missionary, I hear, Mr Lorimer,' she said. 'When do you leave for Jamaica?'

'In two days' time. My visit here is to say goodbye. I shall not be in England again for three years. But to make the farewell a cheerful one, I have brought tickets for the new Savoy opera. Since it is only the second night, I felt reasonably sure that you would not have seen it. I hope that you have no other arrangements for the evening.'

271

Margaret had intended to go early to bed, but the invitation was irresistible.

'I shall be delighted,' she declared. Ralph turned to Lydia.

'And you also, Miss Morton, I hope.'

'You mean you have a ticket for me as well?' Margaret was interested to see that Lydia's sallow cheeks were flushing. Remembering her own blushes earlier that evening, she was careful to make no comment.

'I came early so that you might have time to prepare yourselves,' Ralph said. 'If the plan is an agreeable one, I will leave you now and come back in an hour's time.'

He left two excited young women behind him. Margaret had brought from Bristol some of the gowns which she had acquired during her father's period of generosity shortly before his death. Although styles had changed in the past four years, she had bought no new fashionable clothes during that period, so one of these would have to do. But the dresses had been thought smart at the time, and she chose one which would serve well enough.

Margaret and Lydia were delighted to discover that their evening's entertainment was to be *Iolanthe*, the new light opera by Mr Gilbert and Mr Sullivan. Their lives as medical students left them without either the energy or the money to arrange such diversions for themselves. They were pleased, in addition, to be escorted by such a handsome young man as Ralph. During the intervals they strolled up and down beneath the chandeliers, one on each side of him.

In the course of the last of these promenades, Margaret came to a sudden standstill. Her hand fell from Ralph's arm – but he, deep in conversation with Lydia, strolled on without noticing.

'Miss Ell.' The young surgeon bowed over her hand. 'We meet in very different circumstances.'

'This is surely an extraordinary coincidence, Dr ...' Margaret found that she was stammering in her surprise,

272

and had started a sentence she could not finish. 'I mean, not to have met before, and then twice within so short a time.'

'Perhaps we have been passing each other at intervals all through our lives, but only now noticing it.'

'I have to thank you for the flowers,' said Margaret. 'They gave me great pleasure. I should have written, of course, but I don't know your name.'

He laughed, and bowed for a second time.

'Charles Scott at your service. I would have called in person, but I expected you to be spending the day in bed, recovering from your exertions. Indeed, I think you *ought* to be resting.'

'I had intended to do so, at least this evening. But my brother is about to leave England for three years. When he arrived unexpectedly with the tickets for this performance, I could not refuse.' She was aware even as she spoke that Charles, who was so suitably Charles in reality as well as in imagination, did not need the details. It was she who was anxious to make it clear that her good-looking companion was a brother – and the point was noted, for Charles smiled again.

'Then I may hope to be received if I call?'

'Of course. Although you will be aware that I am not a lady of leisure, with nothing to do in the afternoons but wait for the doorbell to ring. It's only at weekends that I am likely to be found at home.' Margaret wondered whether she was being too forward in making it clear how much she would like to see him. She and Lydia had so much lost the habit of entertaining young gentlemen that she did not know what was encouraged or frowned upon by London rules of etiquette. But she could not bear to think of him coming when she was at a lecture or in a hospital, and perhaps not bothering to call again. It would have been best to invite him for a definite time, but before she could decide whether this would be proper, Ralph and Lydia returned to her side.

'Oh, Lydia, may I present Dr Charles Scott to you,' said Margaret. She did her best not to seem flustered and frowned slightly at the smile on her friend's lips. Lydia must have guessed at once who Charles was. 'Dr Scott, my friend Miss Morton. And my brother, Mr Ralph Lorimer.'

'Your servant.' There was a general shaking of hands, but Charles was frowning. He seemed to be not so much surprised as disconcerted.

'Lorimer, did you say? I thought Matron told me that your name was . . .'

'Miss L is only a nickname,' Margaret explained. 'Miss Morton is called Miss M in the same way by our fellow-students and the people we work with in the hospitals. Margaret Lorimer is my full name.'

He bowed yet again as their introduction was at last formally completed. The warning bells for the next act were ringing and it was time for them to part and return to their seats. Margaret smiled to herself as she turned away. Last night he had seen her dirty, shabby and tearful. Tonight she was dressed expensively and her face and hair were shining with cleanliness. She must surely have made a good impression; and he had asked if he might call! It could hardly have been better arranged if she had done it deliberately.

The parting from Ralph later that evening was an affecting one. He was excited by the adventure which lay ahead, and Margaret was careful to conceal her fears about the unhealthy climate in which he would be living. After he had gone she continued to worry for a while; but little by little the happiness of her evening broke through. She found herself humming the catchy tunes that Mr Sullivan had written for *Iolanthe*. But Lydia's silence was provoking.

'Well?' she demanded at last.

'Well what?' It took Lydia a moment to understand what she was being asked to say, but then the distracted expression left her face and she smiled mischievously.

274

'Oh yes, I congratulate you. He looks a most promising acquaintance. I could see how much he admires you.'

'Do you think so?' Margaret allowed herself to be elated by the observation. 'Do you think it very fickle of me to feel interest in another gentleman after being so sure that I could never love anyone but David?' she asked.

'Three years is a great time,' said Lydia. 'A man who is silent for so long cannot expect fidelity.'

'He could not have expected it in any case,' said Margaret. 'The engagement was broken before he left.'

'Then you have no reason to feel guilt. Once upon a time I felt as strongly as you that it would be faithless to love for a second time. Now I sometimes wonder whether the dead would wish for our loyalty. Do you think they would wish us to be lonely when we could be happy?'

Her voice was far from happy, and Margaret knew that Lydia was thinking of her dead lieutenant. They were both silent for a while but Margaret's emotions could not be repressed.

'He is very handsome, would you not agree?'

'Dr Scott?' It cost Lydia an effort of willpower to adjust her thoughts. 'Not handsome in the sense that your brother is handsome. But good-looking, yes. I think your own choice of adjective earlier was the right one. He looks dependable, in a sturdy way.'

'How odd that there should be two Doctor Scotts in my life!' Margaret exclaimed. Whether it was ladylike or not, she thought of her new acquaintance as Charles. Even so soon after learning his surname, she had almost forgotten it again until Lydia's reminder. 'One Doctor Scott brought me into the world.' She wondered whether this second one might prove to have an equal importance in her life. It was too soon to put such an idea into words, but Lydia seemed to guess what she was feeling.

'You have not yet had time to know this one well,' she warned. 'A good appearance is not everything.'

'I respect his profession,' Margaret pointed out. 'And I

have had the opportunity to observe his courage.' She had not intended to make comparisons, even in her own mind, but found them irresistible. 'A first impression may not be completely accurate, but it is surely a good guide. I remember my very first meeting with David. I was sure at once that he was clever, and ambitious, and that he was a man who would be successful in life. In spite of what happened, I still believe I was right. Those were virtues which I had been brought up to admire, and I loved him for them. Now events have taught me that other qualities may be more important.'

Lydia raised her eyebrows and Margaret did not evade the unspoken question.

'Kindness and loyalty,' she said. 'One needs, above all, a husband on whom one can depend.'

Was she revealing too much? And was she being tactless as well? For a second time Lydia's expression became grave, almost sad, and it occurred to Margaret that the cause of the sadness might be Ralph's departure. Had Lydia, she wondered, entertained any hopes in that direction? If so, it was clear enough that she had been disappointed. It was time to abandon the dangerous subject and go to bed.

By her own words Margaret had ruled out any possibility of seeing Charles before the weekend; but when Saturday arrived it became hard to conceal her excitement. She dressed that morning with particular care, choosing a plain dress so that Lydia would not notice that there was anything special about it, but one which emphasized her slimness. Although cold, the day was bright and sunny, and in the afternoon Lydia suggested that they should go to Hampstead and take a walk over the Heath. Margaret, however, was not prepared to leave the house. She excused herself on the grounds of an urgent need to complete her notes on the patients at the Sick Children's Hospital.

The excuse was not entirely an invention. As a result of the fire, the hospital had ceased to exist. During the week there had been plenty for Margaret to do, visiting the children in the various hospitals to which they had been transferred, noting how they had been affected by the disturbance, and passing on to the doctors now in charge of them some information about their past history. Meanwhile, the Dean had arranged for another supervisor to take charge of her studies in child health, and from Monday until Christmas Margaret would work at Great Ormond Street. So it was true that her notes required attention – but it was not the whole truth.

As soon as Lydia had left for her walk Margaret spread papers and reference books all over the table in the sitting room which the two of them shared. The effect was impressively studious, and from time to time Margaret did in fact do some work. But every time footsteps approached along the pavement she lifted her head to listen. A hundred small hopes were succeeded by a hundred small disappointments; and when at last some footsteps did approach the front door, they were only Lydia's.

He would come on Sunday then – and on Sunday it rained so hard that there was no question of either of them wishing to leave the warm fire in the sitting room. They wrote letters and toasted muffins, chatted a little and read a little. No one came to disturb their relaxation.

Margaret hid her feelings behind unspoken rationalizations. Perhaps Charles lived in the suburbs, or even in the country. If he had to travel to St Bartholomew's whenever he was on duty he might be reluctant to repeat the journey into London on one of his few free days. It would have been more prudent to consider that, when she so officiously tried to determine when he would come. On the other hand, he might be on duty this weekend and not free until the next. There were all sorts of possible reasons to explain why he had not called. Margaret did her best to believe all of them at once, until next Sunday should arrive.

Next Sunday arrived, and again Charles did not call: nor on any of the Sundays which followed. Margaret was too honest to pretend to herself that she was not hurt. Like Lydia, she had seen admiration in his eyes as they talked together at the theatre, and he had said that he would come: it was not something which she had merely imagined out of hope. So far from being dependable, he had let down the first expectation she had ever held of him. He had asked if he might call, had received permission, but had failed either to come or to explain his change of mind. It was not quite a broken promise, but fell little short of one.

As Christmas approached, a more complicated feeling unsettled her. In the new year she would be starting a six-month period as a surgical dresser at St Bartholomew's. In the first flush of her liking for Charles she had applied specially to be assigned to that hospital. Lydia would be there as well, encouraged by Margaret to make a similar application so that they could work together. Margaret's original hope, before their encounter in the theatre, had been that she could greet Charles in the hospital with real pleasure and feigned surprise, and that he would reciprocate the pleasure. But now he was more likely to be embarrassed – even angered – if he thought himself pursued by a young woman when for some reason he did not choose to renew a chance acquaintance.

When the first day of her new duty came, Margaret dressed neatly and severely and told herself that in no circumstances must she become upset. But she could not resist a moment of day dreaming. She would see Charles and he would smile and apologize. He had been ill, he had been away, he had forgotten her address. There must, after all, be an explanation.

When obligations conflict, a reputation for reliability in one sphere can be preserved only by causing disappointment in another. If Charles Scott had known that Margaret's impression of him was of a dependable man he would have been pleased, for this was a character he wished to deserve. But on this dependability others had first claim. It was because he would not betray those who already relied on him that he was forced to break what he too recognized to have been a near-promise. Nothing prevented him from making the call which had been arranged except his own decision to stay at home: but it was a decision that he had no power to change.

At their first encounter, on the morning of the fire, it had seemed to him that he had seen the young student somewhere before. Her red hair and freckled face were distinctive, but he could not put a name or occasion to the memory, and he was in too much of a hurry to pursue a matter of little importance. A great many students came to St Bartholomew's Hospital for a few weeks or months in the course of their training. It was true that not many of them were women, and Charles would certainly have remembered if he had had this one under his direct supervision; but it was likely enough that at some time they had passed in a ward or corridor.

Their second meeting was a different matter. After the discovery of the fire, Charles's first concern had been to drag Jamie out of danger. When that was accomplished, he was appalled to discover that the collapse of the burning ladder left him unable to follow Miss L up into the children's ward. The firemen came as quickly as could be expected in the fog, he supposed, but every moment of waiting was an agony to him. When at last he was able to scramble up to the hoist platform and found her not only safe but working calmly and speedily inside the ward to bring each child in turn within reach of rescue, his relief and admiration were as heartfelt as his previous anxiety. But it was afterwards, in the cab, that a new and more protective emotion was born. Margaret, who had been ashamed of her grimy skin and smoky clothes, and even more ashamed of her tears of nervous and physical exhaustion, would have been astonished to learn that this was the moment when Charles fell in love with her.

He was amazed himself by the suddenness of his reaction to her collapse, but this did not prevent him from instinctively making good use of the situation by slipping a supporting arm round her waist. Her slimness and the trusting way in which she allowed her tired body to relax against his side excited him. He made sure of her address before parting, he sent flowers on the next day, and he planned to visit her on the Saturday, assuming that she would need all the intervening time to recover from the shock of her experiences. Considering that their acquaintance was such a short one, it appeared to be developing at a gratifying speed.

The unexpected meeting at the theatre changed his intentions in the passage of a single sentence. When he caught sight of her from a distance at the end of the first act, there was a moment of jealousy: the blond gentleman – who, he hoped, might be attached to the plain young woman sitting beside him – turned to Miss L, whose smile indicated that their relationship was an affectionate one. But she herself was able to relieve his anxiety when they met later in the promenade, introducing the handsome companion as her brother. Then his happiness was cruelly shattered as she told him her full name.

Margaret Lorimer!

In his distress he walked all the way home from the theatre. At every step he tried to persuade himself that Lorimer, although not as common a name as Scott, was

280

yet by no means unusual. There must be thousands of Lorimers in England. Yes, but how many of them would be called Margaret, and how many of the Margaret Lorimers would have red hair, and how many red-haired Margaret Lorimers would have a brother called Ralph?

There was no need to torture himself in a private inquisition. As soon as he heard the name, he had remembered where he had seen Margaret Lorimer before. It was in Bristol, a good many years ago. Charles had spent little of his life there after the age of twelve. He had gone to boarding school then and came to London when he began his medical training at the age of eighteen. But holidays had been spent at home and although his father did not mix socially with his richer patients, Charles had once attended a concert at which the Lorimer family was pointed out to him.

Margaret would have been no more than fifteen years old at that time, but he had noticed even then the mature, determined expression which impressed him again now. It would be possible, he told himself, to write for confirmation to one of his boyhood friends who still lived in Bristol. It would be known there whether John Junius Lorimer's daughter had left the city to take a medical training. Yet the letter would not be worth the time devoted to writing it. The answer must be as certain as doomsday. He had fallen in love with the only woman in the world whom he could not possibly marry.

Charles himself was rational enough on the subject. When her father's bank collapsed, Margaret Lorimer had been only twenty-one. She could not conceivably bear any responsibility for what had happened. No one, as far as he knew, had even accused her of extravagance. There had certainly been gossip about the young man she proposed to marry, but the fact that the engagement had come to nothing was in her favour. If Charles had lived alone, responsible only for himself, he would have added to his earlier feelings an even deeper admiration for a young woman who had wasted no time in weeping over the riches she had lost. All credit to her for setting to work to make herself a useful member of society!

Charles, however, did not live alone. He shared his cramped suburban home with his parents. There had been no choice in the matter, for the Receiver who administered the affairs of Lorimer's Bank after its collapse had left his father and mother destitute. Their house, their furniture, and all their savings had been sucked into the almost bottomless pit of debt for which the bank's shareholders found themselves responsible. Charles had accepted his responsibilities as a dutiful son, assuring his parents that they could rely on him for support. So Margaret had been perfectly correct in her estimate of him as dependable, but it was this which must inevitably prevent him from ever meeting her again.

His mother wanted him to marry. Her abrupt change of fortune had shocked her into a state of querulous frailty. She was bewildered by the need to leave her comfortable home in Clifton and live in the narrow terrace house in Islington which was all that Charles could afford. To see her only son married, to hold the first grandchild in her arms, was her fondest hope. It would be a sign that her life was returning to normal again.

Her husband, though, would never return to normal. In years he was not an old man. There had been a time, immediately after the disaster, when Charles had reluctantly considered the possibility of leaving London and setting himself up as a general practitioner in the country. There, his father might share the practice and heal himself by a return to work.

The idea had never been more than a dream. Dr Scott senior was not likely to recover from the shock of his ruin, as his demented behaviour at Brinsley House had foreshadowed. Even to himself Charles did not use the word 'mad' but he had to accept that on this one subject his father's mind was unhinged. Not only that, but it was all too easy for almost everything that happened to be connected with the one subject, however carefully Charles fought to control every conversation. It would be out of the question to mention Margaret Lorimer, even as a stranger glimpsed at a casual meeting. To expect that she could ever be received as a daughter-in-law was to reach for the moon.

As he strode through the chilly streets of London on the way home from the theatre that evening, Charles tried desperately to find a way round the impasse. Suppose he never brought Margaret home, never mentioned her name. They could meet in her lodgings, in hospitals, in public places. Even as he imagined it, he knew that all this was impossible. His parents might live for another twenty years. They would never change their attitude. How could he possibly expect a young woman to accept such a situation with no prospect of its ending?

Only as he arrived at his own front door did he admit to himself in so many words what had happened. 'I have fallen in love with Margaret Lorimer,' he said aloud, and sighed. Well, that was his mistake and his misfortune. No one had asked him to do it, and he must stifle his feelings as best he might. But there had been precious little time for Margaret Lorimer to fall in love with him. She had liked him; he felt pretty sure of that – and she would have been as flattered as any other woman when his flowers arrived. She might even be looking forward to his call; and if he kept his word she would have good reason for wondering whether he was interested in her. It would be too late after that to apologize and withdraw. He must come to a standstill now, before her emotions were involved. It was the only kindness which he had in his power to offer. 'Margaret Lorimer must not be allowed to fall in love with me,' he said; and tried to make the second statement as certain as the first.

If Charles had been a philanderer, he would not have bothered himself about the feelings of someone whom he

283

could drop from his life as soon as she became troublesome. It was because he was both kind and honourable that he forced himself to spend the weekend on which he had intended to call doing an extra duty on behalf of one of the other surgeons. Both then and afterwards he was unhappy, but he supposed that the hurt in his heart would heal as time passed. Nothing, he told himself, could alter his determination never to see Margaret Lorimer again.

For this reason the meeting which took place on the first Monday of the new year was unwelcome and disturbing – all the worse because he had no warning of it. The supervision of students was a normal part of his duties as a surgeon in a teaching hospital: and because so many of the older surgeons in his own and other hospitals were still not reconciled to the introduction of women to their profession, Charles found himself allotted a larger proportion of the students from the London School of Medicine for Women than would have come his way had they been divided evenly between the teaching hospitals. So there was nothing to dismay him in his first glimpse of the two young women who awaited his arrival that morning, neatly dressed in clean white smocks and plain skirts and with their hair strained severely back into buns. It was a different matter when he came near enough to recognize them.

For a moment he was unable to speak. Then he gave a quick nod of recognition.

'Miss Lorimer. Miss Morton.'

His voice emerged coldly; it was because he could not think what else to say. His behaviour in turning away without a further word was brusque to the point of rudeness, he knew; it was because his thoughts were confused.

Margaret Lorimer was owed an apology: there could be no doubt of that. But if he made one – at least with enough sincerity to render it acceptable – he would be in danger of restoring the very situation which he had determined to avoid. It was impossible for him to make a friend of Margaret Lorimer. Therefore, it would be a kindness, surely, for this to be made clear from the first moments. If he had to work with her for the next six or eight weeks, that was something which would have to be endured; but he must start by making it clear that the relationship could only be one of teacher and pupil.

Another thought intruded. He had met Margaret Lorimer for the first time in her adult life by accident. Their second encounter, at the theatre, had been a coincidence, but one coincidence was not unusual in a relationship. A second coincidence, however, was less easy to accept. This third meeting, it was true, arose naturally out of their shared profession of medicine. Nevertheless, Margaret must have been aware that in coming to Bart's she was likely to see him again. She knew he worked there, and knew he was a surgeon. It seemed likely that she had actually asked to do her surgical work with him. In that case, she was pursuing him. If any embarrassment was to be felt at this unfortunate meeting, she – who had contrived it – should be the one to feel it.

She did feel it. His behaviour that day was unforgivable, and he could see that she was upset by it. He was abrupt and uninformative in assigning the work to be done by her. Whenever there was an unusual dressing to be removed and replaced, it was Miss Morton he called. Out of the corner of his eye he watched Margaret as she worked alone. He noted the firm but gentle neatness with which she applied the routine dressings, her sympathetic manner with the patients, the hopeful air with which she reported that she had done everything he had asked, the disappointment with which she heard that Miss Morton might accompany him into the operating theatre but that there was no room for both of them.

The silent struggle continued for five days. It was an unhappy period for Charles, for he was fighting his own considerate nature as well as his more particular feelings about Margaret. He was not surprised, although he pretended to be, when at the end of the week she asked whether she could speak to him.

'Of course.' Still maintaining his pretence of indifference, he waited to hear that she intended to move to another hospital.

'I would be glad if our conversation could be a little less public.' Margaret looked round at all the occupants of the surgical ward in which they were standing. Charles shrugged his shoulders and thought for a moment. There were few places in the hospital which could be called private, but it was possible that the library might be empty. He led the way there and opened the door for her to go inside. She turned to face him without sitting down.

'In July I shall be sitting for my diploma examination in Surgery,' she said. 'I am not likely to do well in it if the rest of my time here is spent as fruitlessly as this past week. No doubt I can find somewhere else to offer me more valuable experience. But I would be interested to know before I leave why you have gone to such pains to deny it to me here.'

He had thought that she would slip away from St Bartholomew's in silence, perhaps even in tears, and had certainly not expected to find himself accused. As a doctor, he had a good deal of experience of women who were sick, of helpless women like his mother, of frivolous women, and of earnest but still subservient women like the other female students he had supervised in the past. He was not at all accustomed to women who stood up for themselves.

'I am sorry if you have found me unhelpful,' he said weakly.

'You are not sorry at all,' Margaret replied. 'Your unhelpfulness has been so sustained that it must have a purpose, and I take the purpose to be my departure. You will discover soon, I hope, that you have succeeded. But I shall have to explain to the Dean my application to be transferred. What reason am I to give? I thought at first that you must be one of those who disapprove of women students, but you have been considerate to my friend. I have done something to anger you, and it seems that it

286

happened between our first meeting and this week. But you have given me no clue to what it might be. I think I deserve an explanation.'

'Yes,' he said. He longed to comfort her, for behind the bold words he could hear her voice trembling. She was not finding it easy to challenge him. 'I mean, yes, you deserve an explanation. But I cannot give it to you. When I said I was sorry, I meant it. My behaviour may have disappointed you earlier as well, and if you noticed it I apologize for that as well. But it is not a matter I can discuss. Your plan to move to another hospital is a wise one. I will send a note to your Dean to say that it is no longer possible for me to supervise two students at once.'

'After I have gone, you will never be troubled by me again,' said Margaret. 'So tell me now what this explanation is which cannot be given. Should I not in fairness be allowed to judge for myself what I have done to deserve your coldness?'

Charles turned away and paced up and down the library for a few moments. He had achieved the effect he intended. For her own sake, he had told himself, Margaret must not be allowed to like him, and her antagonism now was clear enough. It would be foolish to jeopardize this success just for the sake of letting her leave with a true picture of his motives. If he hesitated, it was because his respect for Margaret had been increased by her behaviour in the past few days and the past few minutes. Between what he longed to say and what he knew it would be sensible to say, there was a chasm impossible to bridge.

'Dr Scott,' Margaret began. Her tone rebuked him. Distraught, he turned back to face her.

'Have you never said those two words before?' he demanded. 'When you learned my name, did it not strike you as familiar?'

Before answering, Margaret paused long enough to show him that it was unnecessary to continue the conversation;

she had already guessed what he had at last made up his mind to tell her.

'Yes,' she said quietly. 'I remarked on it to Lydia. But Scott is a common enough name, and London is not Bristol. It seemed too unlikely a coincidence that we should prove to have been even so remotely connected in the past. You are telling me, then, that our family physician was . . .'

'My father,' he agreed. 'My father, whom the behaviour of *your* father has driven to the borders of sanity, and perhaps beyond.' It was the first time he had made such an admission. 'Because of a Lorimer, my parents are destitute, dependent entirely upon myself. Because of a Lorimer, my father is no longer able to face the world.'

'I am sorry, deeply sorry. But do you hold me to blame for that?'

'No,' he confessed. 'And if I had met you in normal circumstances; if I had been properly introduced, knowing your name before I had time to form any opinion on your character, if I had found you to be of no more interest to me than a casual acquaintance, I should have been as polite to you as to any other young lady. If I have been rude – well, I admit frankly that I have treated you inexcusably – it is because my real wish was to know you better, and I was angry that fate should have interposed this barrier between us. I feel as Romeo must have done when he learned who Juliet was. Yet my situation is worse even than Romeo's. I love my father and have no wish to evade my duty to him; nor can I be happy if I cause him pain. The impediment is in my own mind. If it were any other barrier, I could break it down: but not this one.'

'It would have been kinder of you to tell me this earlier,' suggested Margaret. She had become very pale and Charles feared that she might faint. He pulled out a chair from beneath one of the library tables and put out a hand to support her, but she moved just far enough away to avoid his touch as she sat down.

'You will understand that I was not aware of your full name until I learned it at the theatre, just as we were parting,' he said. 'After that I thought it wisest to make you angry. I could not trust myself to hold to my purpose if you were kind to me; and I did not believe that you could understand my responsibilities to my parents.' By now he was as upset as she was, though he struggled to conceal it.

'I loved my father as much as you love yours,' she told him. 'At the time when the bank collapsed I was engaged to be married – were you aware of that? The engagement proved to be incompatible with my affection for my father, so it was ended. I am perfectly able to understand your feelings.' There was a very long silence. Then she looked up at him and forced a smile. 'But that is not to say that I agree with the way you have chosen to express them.'

'How would you have had me behave? How would you have me behave now?'

'By all means think of yourself as Romeo if you wish,' she said. 'But it would be foolish of you to cast me as Juliet. I am not a fourteen-year-old girl pining for a husband. I am twenty-six years old, and in the middle of a professional training. When I am qualified I intend to practise as a doctor. In the course of my career I hope to make many friends amongst my colleagues. Male friends as well as female. You have the reputation, Dr Scott, of being able to accept the prospect of women working as doctors. Can you not also entertain the revolutionary notion of offering them friendship as though they were men?'

'That would make little difference to the difficulties within my family. I could never so much as mention your name at home.'

'You have friends, no doubt, on the staff of this hospital,' said Margaret. 'Do you take them all home and present them to your father, or amuse him in the evenings by reciting their names? I suspect not. But are they any less your friends for meeting you in one side of your life only? If you feel that it would be a deceit even to continue knowing me as a professional acquaintance, I cannot argue with that. But my own conscience is not at risk, and it is not necessarily just that you should sacrifice me to yours.'

'I did not see myself as sacrificing you,' said Charles, 'but as keeping you free from an acquaintanceship which could have nothing to offer and which might cause you distress. I cannot look into the future of my life as clearly as you evidently can into yours.'

'My view of the future is limited by examinations,' said Margaret. She stood up again, straight-backed and steady-eyed, smiling as cheerfully as though the conversation just ended had been about trivialities, and not one which might have altered the whole course of his life. 'You must remember from your own student days how implacably each examination follows the one before. At the moment I have only one concern, and that is to acquire as much knowledge and experience of surgery as possible. I hope very much that you are going to tell me now that I may return here next week and count on you to teach me everything you know.'

Charles looked down at her with an unhappiness he could not fathom. He had said far more than he ever intended, but all the agonizing justification for his previous silence and bad manners had been swept away by Margaret's understanding. He had pretended, even to himself, that his boorish behaviour had been entirely in her interest, not his own. Now he had to recognize that he had been protecting himself, and that his defences had been destroyed.

What he had explained to Margaret, and what she seemed to have accepted, was only half the probelm. She had heard him talk of Romeo and Juliet but had interpreted his words solely in terms of Montagues and Capulets, of feuds between fathers. Her solution absolved him of any anxieties on her account, but did not alter the fact that he loved her and yet would never be able to tell her so more openly than today. The friendship which she seemed to think would be enough for her might be a source of more pain than pleasure to him. This was his last chance to turn away. He could be rude once more, finally and unforgivably rude. He could watch her eyes cloud with hurt and disappointment. He could see her walk out of the room and be sure that this time she would never come back. All this was possible. He struggled to collect his courage.

No, it was not possible. She was smiling at him. Her freckled face was friendly, and trusting even though she had no grounds for trust. He could not bring himself to hurt her again. Instead, he smiled back.

'You had better come early on Monday,' he said. 'I intend to perform an ovariotomy. The operation is almost as dangerous as the condition it hopes to relieve. I undertake it only as a last resort for a patient who will certainly die if nothing is done. Many surgeons refuse to attempt it at all, because the high rate of failure does their reputations no good. You have probably not had the opportunity to observe the operation before. It will be useful to you in forming your opinion on its desirability. I shall look forward to seeing you then.'

Margaret's renewed smile was sufficient reward. She held out her hand as though the gesture sealed some kind of compact between them. Charles leaned a little forward as he took it: wanting to kiss her, wishing that she would kiss him. It was impossible, of course. He restrained himself, and she presumably had no such feelings to restrain. Margaret went smiling from the room, leaving him to come to terms as best he could with the bitter-sweetness of a love which was neither rejected nor acknowledged.

5

Every actress longs for the applause of the crowd – the craving is an inherent part of her nature. Even criticism is better than silence. Margaret's performance, however, had been of an unusual kind. Charles had been her only audience and, since the purpose of her performance was to deceive him, she could not allow him even to guess that she was acting, much less to praise her ability.

The need for appreciation may have been the reason why Margaret took the first opportunity after her return from St Bartholomew's to tell Lydia what had happened, although to herself she made other excuses. Because she had confided in her friend after the fire and again after her encounter with Charles at the theatre, the young surgeon's behaviour at the hospital had come as a shock to Lydia, and his pronounced favouritism towards her had made her uncomfortable. Margaret did not care to be pitied, so it was with a brisk satisfaction that she was able to announce the reason for Charles's cold attitude, and the agreement they had reached for the future.

At first Lydia's reactions were all that could be desired. She was shocked to hear about the elder Dr Scott's condition and his relationship to Charles: she sympathized with the younger man's difficulties and understood his reaction to them. But when it came to the solution which Margaret had produced, Lydia's response was not praise but a frown.

'Do you think this is wise?' she asked. 'It seems to me that in the circumstances Charles Scott's decision was a good one, although his means of implementing it was harsh. If it is true that his father's view of your family cannot be changed, it would surely be best to make the break a complete one?'

'Are you not prepared to believe that a man and a woman can have an ordinary affectionate friendship?' demanded Margaret, piqued by the implied criticism.

'An older woman and an older man, perhaps.'

'How old does one need to be? I am hardly a girl any longer.'

'Age is not really important,' said Lydia. 'What matters is that you are in love with him. You are talking about friendship, but you are hoping for something more. Something which you can never have.'

'"Never" is a very long time,' protested Margaret. 'Dr Scott – the father, I mean – cannot live for ever.'

'He may live for a good many years, all the same, and it can hardly be a Christian way of life to pass one's time hoping for the death of another. And suppose, Margaret, that your Charles believes that what you have asked for is all you sincerely want. He may give you friendship, but he could still honourably regard himself as free to look for marriage with someone else. You could waste many years in waiting, and be disappointed at the end.'

'If I am to be disappointed in five years' time, let us say, it could be no worse than my disappointment if we were to part for ever now, and I shall have been happy for those five years. You speak as though I were sacrificing some other lover in favour of an impossible relationship, but all I propose to do is to add a little warmth to a life which otherwise consists only of work. Once in my life already I have had to say goodbye to a man I loved, and only because I am a Lorimer. No one, surely, could expect me to do the same thing again. I must confess that I had expected more sympathy from you, Lydia.'

'I sympathize, indeed I do. My only anxiety is that you shall not make yourself unhappy. It seems to me that the man you love is an honourable man. Because of that he will not change his mind, and because of that it will not occur to him that what you tell him and what you feel for him may not be exactly the same.'

Margaret was silent, unable to argue with the truth. By now the elated mood in which she returned from the hospital had evaporated.

'You are quite right, of course,' she said. 'But the plain fact is, Lydia, that I have no choice. I cannot bring myself to say now that I will never see him again, and yet he would not let me continue his acquaintance in any way other than the one I have proposed. I may be made unhappy in the future if we have to part; but I shall certainly be unhappy if we part now. And I do sincerely believe that we can be friends.'

'Let us hope you are right.' The warmth of Lydia's nature made her anxious to support her friend, and the conversation ended with an embrace. However, it provided a warning which Margaret took to heart. During the whole period of her attendance at St Bartholomew's she was careful to behave only as an attentive student. She was not acting when she showed herself to be a helpful and reliable assistant, and her professional attitude must have dissolved any doubts which Charles still felt. He treated her as though she were a man; and this, Margaret supposed, was what she wanted.

Summer brought with it the end of her practical training and the beginning of her final M.B. examinations. On her last day at Bart's Margaret waited until Lydia had left before she said goodbye to Charles.

'I wish you the best of luck,' he said. 'If all your subjects are as good as your Surgery, you will have no cause for anxiety. What are your plans when you have qualified?'

Until the day of the fire it had been Margaret's intention to return to Bristol as soon as she could. Charles, without knowing it, had changed all that.

'I hope for an appointment in a London hospital which will enable me to continue studying for my M.D.,' she said. 'Lydia will be staying on to take a special qualification in Public Health, and the arrangement by which we share lodgings suits us both very well. I would like to specialize

294

in obstetrics and I expect to find a greater variety of experience in London, as well as the best supervision.'

'Then I hope I may call on you when you have finished your examinations,' said Charles.

Margaret tried hard not to show how important it had been to her that he should suggest a future meeting, now that their working relationship had reached its end.

'Last time you said that, your hopes were not fulfilled,' she teasingly commented. It was a measure of the friendship which had developed between them that they were both able to smile at the memory.

He must have made a special point of seeing the results of the examinations, for as soon as they were posted he came to call, carrying bouquets of congratulation for both Margaret and Lydia. He brought a friend with him. Henry Mason was another doctor, and before leaving he invited the two young women to spend the next Saturday at his parents' house in Kew.

'I must give you warning of the entertainment we propose,' Henry said. 'My sister and I have acquired bicycles and intend to learn how to ride them. You will understand that we need to have skilled medical help at hand to mend our broken bones. Charles and I will supply the same attentions to you if you are prepared to attempt the new art.'

Margaret's heart jumped with pleasure at the realization that Charles, because he could not invite her to his own house, must have arranged this instead. She accepted quickly, without giving Lydia time to express any doubts. But Lydia, in a carefree mood following four and a half years of hard study and a month of important examinations, expressed equal pleasure at the prospect.

Saturday, when it came, was devoted to laughter and easy conversation. Margaret was relieved to find that the two bicycles were not penny-farthings, but the much lower safety models. Henry's sister had already mastered the technique and gave a wobbly demonstration round and, round the family's large garden before falling off at the end of the ride. It was agreed that stopping was the most difficult part of bicycling. Two at a time they embarked on their first trial trips, with a good deal of mock alarm, while Mr and Mrs Mason watched in amusement from the drawing-room window.

When it came to Margaret's turn, it was Charles who brought the machine to her. He held it while she mounted, with one hand beneath the saddle and the other on the handlebars; but once she started to pedal, forcing him to run beside her, one of his hands moved up to her waist in order to steady her. Margaret found herself overwhelmed by his closeness. She could hardly bear her own happiness and pedalled faster and faster in her excitement. Unable to stop, she tried to turn as they approached the end of the lawn, but found herself leaning sideways. Charles's other hand moved along the handlebar to cover her own hand and grip the brake, but it was too late to stop her falling. They toppled to the ground together, with the bicycle on top of them. Their friends were beside themselves with laughter in the distance, but for Margaret the world seemed to have gone suddenly quiet. She lay on the grass, not daring to look at Charles, and for a moment neither of them moved. Then he pushed the bicycle away with his foot and picked himself up before holding out his hands to raise her.

'Not hurt?' he asked.

Too much in love with him to speak, Margaret shook her head. She staggered a little as he pulled her gently to her feet, and for a second he stood very close as he steadied her.

'Oh, my dear!' he said, and then shook his head, sighing in distress. Margaret had already hoped that he loved her as much as she loved him: now she knew that she was right. She realized at the same time that he must be aware of her own feelings. They were both very quiet as they wheeled the bicycle back towards the house.

After this there was little incentive for Margaret to improve her performance. She claimed that her balance was poor and continued to demand support. It came each time from Charles. The recklessness with which they tacitly admitted their feelings to each other was eloquent to their friends as well. Lydia may have disapproved, but she made no attempt to interfere. After lunch, when they all chose to avoid further bruising and take a walk along the bank of the river, none of the other three appeared to notice as Margaret and Charles fell further and further behind.

For a long time they still did not dare to speak to each other. It was Margaret in the end who broke both the silence and the resolve which she had made six months earlier.

'Would it not be possible,' she asked without preamble, 'to persuade your father that I have suffered almost as much as he from the collapse of my father's business? If he could see us as victims together, he might be less disposed to blame me for my father's faults.'

'I think you have profited by the collapse rather than suffered,' said Charles. 'Your present way of life would never have been open to you while your parents lived.'

'But so far as money is concerned I have nothing.'

'It would be difficult to persuade my father of that.'

'Would he not believe my word?'

'Were you present when your father died?' asked Charles. It seemed an abrupt change of subject, and Margaret looked at him in surprise.

'Yes. That is to say, at the actual moment of his death I was a little way away from him, hurrying to fetch help.'

'Then you did not hear his last words?'

'I was not aware that he had spoken any.'

'You will remember that my father had been called to attend him. He was bending over Mr Lorimer and heard him call out in his last agony.'

'What did my father say?' Margaret prompted, when Charles seemed unable to continue.

'"Who will care for my treasure?" He said it twice, and then he died. "Who will care for my treasure?" My father has never forgotten the words. He dreams of finding the treasure. In the middle of the night he goes out into my small garden and digs it up, because he is so sure that somewhere in the earth John Junius Lorimer hid his fortune away from his creditors.'

'There is no fortune,' Margaret assured him, troubled.

'How can I persuade him of that? His belief has become irrational, but it must have some fact as its basis. I believe that your father did speak those words. He may have been irrational himself at the moment of death – he may have believed that he was still rich and must now by dying abandon his riches. I can explain the possibilities to myself, but not to my father. The obsession goes too deep. And even if you tried to explain your own position, he would point to that of your brother.'

'Ralph?'

'No. Your elder brother. He lives in Brinsley House, I understand, as your father did before him. His shipping company has survived the misfortunes from which almost every other business in Bristol suffered. He does not live in the style of a man who has been ruined.'

'My sister-in-law had money of her own,' said Margaret. 'It came to her on her father's death, after the crash, and was not affected by the legal proceedings.' She spoke as confidently as she could in her anxiety to persuade Charles, but an uneasiness stirred in her mind. She knew that William had been saved from the distresses of the other shareholders in Lorimer's Bank by the accident of selling his own holding shortly before the collapse. She knew also that the insurance money paid for the *Georgiana* had enabled him to buy the family home at a distress price. But she too had been surprised at the speed with which he had managed to re-establish the name of Lorimer amongst that part of the Bristol community which respected a man according to the degree of his wealth and trading power.

298

They had been walking only slowly, but now Charles came to a complete halt and looked earnestly down at her.

'You must understand that I am not speaking on my own account,' he said. 'To me, you are yourself and I – I value you only as yourself. You cannot have been to blame in any way for the past. I am answering your question only because you asked it, trying to make you realize what my father thinks, not what I think myself. He was upset when he lost all his money, as any man might be. It was when he heard those dying words of your father's that he became deranged. I came to Bristol at that time, to comfort my mother and to do what I could to calm him. I know that what fed his madness was the business of the rubies.'

'The rubies?' Margaret was genuinely puzzled.

'The rubies which your mother wore to a ball in Bristol shortly before her death. They were thought to be worth a fortune, but after your father died were found to be worthless. It was not possible for me or for anyone else to persuade my father that the Lorimers had no secret fortune when it seemed – to others beside himself – that not everything had been satisfactorily explained. This makes no difference to my own feelings for you, but it will come between my father and any member of your family as long as he lives. There is no chance at all that I can persuade him to change his view. I even think it would be better if you and I did not discuss the past.'

Margaret still hesitated for a moment, but Charles's opinion was so definite that she did not feel able to argue: nor did she wish to spoil a day which had been full of happiness. That evening, however, she wrote to William.

Charles had mentioned the rubies in particular, and Margaret remembered now that she too had been puzzled at the time by the discovery that the jewels deposited in the bank were imitations. There was that other matter, as well, which she had not mentioned to Charles. She had asked her father on one occasion what had happened to the jade animals which she so much liked, and which were

299

reputed to be of great value, and he had answered that these too were held by the bank for safe keeping. It occurred to her now that no one had made any mention of the jade collection when the value of John Junius's assets were under public scrutiny. She asked William about both these mysteries and waited anxiously for an answer.

His letter, when it came, did little to reassure her. He wrote with unusual frankness, telling her that their father had sold the most valuable pieces of jade in a manner which could only be described as surreptitious; the replacements which he had purchased to fill the gaps in his cabinets were of little value.

'My own view,' William continued, 'is that the money raised from the sale of the jade was used to purchase the stones – the genuine stones – for the present of jewellery which he gave to our mother. I then think – although it can only be a guess on my part – that after he had ordered Parker to set the real stones, he had a copy made at some establishment outside Bristol where he was not well known. We know that the copy was deposited in the bank. Perhaps we shall never learn what happened to the real jewels. My personal opinion is that they must exist, but have been hidden and are unlikely to be recovered, unless by chance. I need hardly tell you that this surmise is for your own eyes only. It would be most unwise to discuss the matter with anyone else at all. You should destroy this letter.'

Margaret stared at it unhappily. She found it a terrible thing that William should be accusing their father of what seemed to be a deliberate deception. If his theory was a true one, it would add substance to the ravings of Charles's father: certainly, it could not be used to challenge his suspicions. She sighed to herself once more as she tore the letter up. It seemed that she had no choice but to accept Charles's opinion. The subject was indeed one which should not be discussed between them again. Her friendship with Charles must remain one which forgot the past and did not allow any hope for the future.

6

News of a stranger's death can be curiously cheering to those who survive, but not when it is the wrong stranger. It was Charles Scott's mother, not his father, who broke her hip in a fall shortly before Christmas in 1885: she died of pneumonia three weeks later. By that time Margaret was twenty-eight years old: a professional woman. She had passed her M.D. examination with honour and now had a good appointment as resident obstetrician at the Lying-In Hospital for Women. The hospital supplied her with accommodation, but she still contributed to the rent of Lydia's apartments and used them when she was off duty.

Deliberately she organized her work so that there should not be much time to think about her private life, although her friendship with Charles had deepened as the years passed. They were both members of a committee whose purpose was to improve the health of London school-children. It pressed for regular medical inspections in the schools and raised money to send poor children from the city slums to the country or seaside for a week's holiday. Margaret was whole-heartedly in sympathy with the committee's aims, but valued its meetings additionally for the assurance they gave her that she would see Charles at least once a month.

Mrs Scott's accident, however, interrupted the pattern of the time they spent together. Charles wrote often to Margaret – first during his mother's illness and then at her death. Later there were letters of a different kind, apologizing for the fact that he could not leave his father for more than the hours of hospital duty. Margaret studied the words anxiously, wondering whether he was preparing her for the news that he would not be able to see her again.

This three-month period during which they did not meet

seemed more like three years to Margaret. Her loneliness reminded her how much she relied for happiness on the hope of catching at least a glimpse of him. When at last a letter arrived to propose a meeting, her relief and excitement were tinged with fear.

His invitation was for an evening together. It was tacitly agreed between them that when Charles visited her in the apartments which she shared with Lydia, her friend should always be present. But in the freer atmosphere of the capital city there seemed no objection – now that Margaret was no longer a young girl – to theatre visits and even dinners in public restaurants without a chaperone. It was an invitation of this sort which Charles now offered in February of 1886.

She was unprepared for the change in his appearance since their last meeting. His eyes were black with tiredness, as though he had not slept for nights, and his forehead was lined with strain. Assuming that all his obvious unhappiness was caused by the death of his mother, she repeated the condolences which she had already written. This must have revealed to Charles that he was not appearing as the most stimulating of companions, for he made an attempt at cheerfulness, although his gaiety was forced. Margaret responded to it, accepting his suggestion that after dinner they should go to a music hall instead of a play.

The atmosphere inside the music hall made cheerfulness compulsory. The vulgarity of the comedians and the earthy energy of the dancers did not allow for half measures: the audience was forced willy-nilly into disapproval or delight. Margaret became aware that her companion was gradually relaxing in her company. Whatever had been troubling him seemed for the moment to be forgotten. He clapped as vigorously as she at the jugglers. With just as much amusement he laughed at the clowning of the gentleman whose baggy trousers threatened to engulf him as he balanced a bowler hat by its brim on his forehead, his nose, or his toe.

As this act ended the accompanying band changed the style of its music from a brisk brassiness to a plaintive whisper of strings. The chattering audience was hushed into silence by the appearance of the next performer – a little girl, only eight or nine years old. She was dressed in rags, in imitation of an adult style; but the beauty of her face and the shine of the strawberry blonde hair which contrasted so astonishingly with the drab grey of her long skirt and shawl, robbed the whole theatre of its breath. There was no sound from the audience as she began to sing, as though it were assumed that her voice would be as small as her body. But her sweet, pure tones projected to the back of the theatre as professionally as those of her predecessors on the stage.

Her song was sentimental, even maudlin. 'I have to be a mother to my father,' she carolled, acting out the words of each verse in a childish way which contrasted strongly with the maturity of her voice. Margaret found her own attention gripped more closely than the act itself could justify. The child's face was familiar, although she could not remember where she had seen it before. The recognition carried with it an association of unhappiness. Margaret puzzled over this without being able to take her eyes off the agile, graceful figure.

'I have to be a mother to my father,' sang the child for the last time, ''cos my mother went to heaven long ago.' She curtsied and smiled and ran off to the heaviest applause of the evening. Margaret opened her programme and looked inside.

The name told her all she needed to know. 'Alexa, child of song.' Margaret remembered the imperceptible cough from a baby's cradle. 'Her name is Alexandra, but I call her Alexa,' Luisa had said. And on the day before John Junius Lorimer fell to his death, Margaret had seen that baby again, a little older, sucking her thumb shyly in a corner, but already beautiful. Luisa was a teacher of music and would certainly have trained her own child. There could be no doubt that this was the very same girl.

Margaret sat through the last comedy act of the show and the final chorus without giving them any of her attention. She wanted to ask Charles whether he would take her backstage to find Alexa and her mother, who must surely be caring for the child. But first she would need to explain how she had come to recognize Alexa. That meant referring to her life in Bristol, which by mutual agreement had become a subject not to be discussed.

The rule would have to be broken. Alexa, after all, had nothing to do with the Lorimer family. It would be possible to speak of her without referring to any of the forbidden subjects. They rose to their feet, still clapping the exuberant last chorus.

'I recognized one of the performers as someone I know,' Margaret said. 'I would very much like to speak to her. Will you escort me?'

He hesitated, and she realized with a shock that he was going to refuse. Perhaps that was because he did not consider music-hall performers to be proper companions for her. About to reveal to him the age of her acquaintance, she was checked by the expression which clouded his face. Whatever had troubled him when they first met that evening had returned to make him even more unhappy than before.

'Not now, if you will excuse me,' he said. 'I hardly feel fit company for comedians. There is something I have to say to you, and I have postponed saying it long enough. It cannot wait any longer.'

He offered her his arm and she took it doubtfully. The programme at the music hall changed each week. By the time she could return, Alexa might have moved on. Margaret was reluctant to miss the opportunity; but she could feel the intensity of Charles's concentration on whatever it was he wanted to say. Suppose that should prove to be what she most hoped to hear. His mother's death must have changed his circumstances. Perhaps he was going to tell her that his father's condition now necessitated treatment in some kind of private asylum, setting Charles himself free to live his own life. Because of his unhappy look, she had not allowed herself to consider such a possibility before but now she found it difficult to control a surge of hope.

'Are you cold?' he asked.

'No,' she said, although the night was chilly. If they went back to her rooms, Lydia would be there; and whatever the subject of this conversation might prove to be, Margaret assumed it would be private.

They walked in silence until they reached the river. Then at last, leaning over the parapet of the embankment wall, he turned to face her.

'My father has been much affected by my mother's death,' he said. 'She was his companion throughout the day, while I was working at the hospital. It was not merely that she acted as our housekeeper: she allowed him to talk to her, to rave about his grievances. I find now that he cannot be left alone for very long. Yet I cannot find a servant patient enough to bear with his rages.'

'Ought he perhaps to receive hospital care?' asked Margaret.

'He is lucid enough for part of the time to understand what his condition is. He has lost everything in life except the support of his only son. I cannot rob him of that as well.'

Margaret felt her body chilling with something sharper than the frost in the air.

'So what do you intend to do?' she asked quietly.

Charles gave a single deep sigh. Then he spoke in a businesslike manner.

'My father has a widowed sister who lives in the country,' he said. 'She came to London for my mother's funeral and was shocked at the change in her brother's condition. She has written to tell me that the doctor in her village is about to retire. I have decided to buy his practice and settle down to country life with my father.'

'But you are a surgeon!' exclaimed Margaret, using the professional objection to express all the disappointment she felt.

Charles shrugged his shoulders.

'I have become a very bad surgeon in these past weeks. My life at home has not been good for my concentration at work. I am as well fitted as any other medical man for general practice, and I may do as much good there as in a hospital. My aunt has already found a village woman who will act as our housekeeper. She is a simple soul, I am told, but kind. My father's situation has been explained to her and she will indulge his outbursts without becoming upset or indignant herself. My aunt is willing for him to walk each day to visit her. The walk will occupy a little time, providing exercise and fresh air, and she will give him tea and company before he walks back again. It all represents an offer which I cannot bring myself to refuse.'

'I see that the arrangement is a convenient one for your father,' Margaret said quietly. 'You can hardly expect it to seem equally welcome to me.'

'No,' agreed Charles. He stared down into the water as though he could not face her. 'We have always known, haven't we, that this moment might come? It need not be the end of our friendship. We can correspond. It would help to reconcile me to my quieter life if I could share it with you at least in letters.'

Margaret slowly shook her head.

'I don't think I could bear to go on in such a way.'

'But it was you who first said with such assurance that we could be friends.'

'That was three years ago.' As she spoke, Margaret wondered whether it had been true even then. Certainly it was not enough for her now. Only hope had enabled her to endure it for so long. She looked into his eyes. 'In that time I have grown to love you. I cannot any longer bear the strain of longing for something I may not have. But there has never been any way for me to conquer my longing unless you should send me away. The first time you tried I would not allow it. Lydia told me then that I was unwise, and perhaps she was right. Now that it is happening again, I must try to accept it.'

'I am not sending you away,' said Charles. 'I have to go away myself, but that is a different matter.'

'The effect is the same.'

'But I love you too!' he exclaimed. He flung his arms over the parapet, groaning to himself. 'Oh, if only you were any other woman! Any other woman in the whole world! If the obstacle were your name alone, I would marry you and present you to my father as Mrs Scott and we would invent a whole past life with which to answer his questions. But he knows your face. I cannot let him see you.'

'Then there is nothing more to say, is there?' Margaret bit her lip, determined not to weep.

'I cannot endure that you should be angry with me.'

'I am not angry. I admire your loyalty to your father. It is my misfortune that I cannot deserve the same loyalty myself. But I am well aware that the sins of the fathers must be paid for by their daughters.'

I have paid twice, she thought to herself, but she was ashamed that at this moment the memory of David Gregson should intrude into her mind. Instead she looked steadily at Charles, trying to memorize for ever his strong features, his kind eyes, his thick, fair hair, his sturdy shoulders and firm hands.

'You have no choice,' she continued. 'Perhaps it is unkind of me not to continue as you would like. But if I were to consent, I am afraid that I would quickly come to wish for your father's death; the very thought makes me feel wicked. Now it is time for me to plan a career for myself. I had always intended to return to Bristol. It was only because you were in London that I stayed on, taking

307

whatever appointment I could find in the hope that it in fact need only be temporary. It is time for me to be selfish in considering my own future.'

She lacked the strength to face the sadness in his eyes and instead looked down into the river, as he had done earlier. The water was dark, moving imperceptibly to break the reflections of the gas lamps into darts and splinters of yellow light. A mass of floating brushwood was trapped just below, borne down towards the sea by the current of the river and then pressed back again by the tide surging up from the estuary. She had been like that herself for the past three years – floating in a backwater, waiting for some stronger current to carry her away. It was not a way of life of which she could be proud. She might see herself now as striking out into midstream, but the current could only carry her out to sea, further and further away from any prospect of the home and family life which she had been brought up to believe provided the natural, the most contented existence for a woman.

From herself she could not conceal her yearning for such a life – but she could conceal it from Charles, who had nothing of the kind to offer and must not be allowed to feel guilty. She smiled at him again with as much cheerfulness as she could summon.

'You have been honest with me from the moment you discovered who I was,' she said. 'I am grateful to you for that. It is not your fault or mine that the obstacle between us is insurmountable. I very much regret that my father's misfortunes should prove to have such disastrous effects on my own relationships. But the time has come, has it not, to accept the situation? Will you take me home now?'

Once before he had held her in his arms, and Margaret still remembered the happiness which had overwhelmed her then. Now, as he stepped forward and pressed her close to his body, they were both equally unhappy. Neither of them spoke, for there was nothing more to say.

The silence lasted until a cab carried them away from

the river. The horse's hooves struck the road with a clear sharp sound, as if each step were hammering a nail into the coffin of Margaret's love. Charles escorted her up the steps to her door, but still they could not speak. Margaret left him standing there as she ran up the stairs to the sitting room where Lydia was waiting for her.

'There is a letter for you, from your brother in Jamaica,' Lydia told her. Her cheeks were flushed as she held it out. It was ridiculous that such a small thing could break Margaret's control, but if she had not hurried straight into her own bedroom she would have burst into tears at once.

'Tomorrow,' she mumbled. 'I'm too tired now.'

When she began to cry, with the door locked and her head pressed down into the pillow, there was anger in her distress. Why should life go on for everyone else as though nothing had happened, when her own life was ruined? Why should everyone else be free to follow their own inclinations when she and Charles were imprisoned by history? The unfairness of it all overwhelmed her and she was still resentful when she sobbed herself to sleep.

Next morning, forcing herself to be calm and cool, she apologized to Lydia for her brusqueness on the previous evening. Lydia was hesitant about making any comment until the cause of her friend's unhappiness was revealed, and Margaret could not bring herself to say in so many words that she had parted from Charles for ever.

'I have decided to return to Bristol, Lydia,' she said. 'I shall look for an appointment there as soon as possible.'

'And Dr Scott?' Lydia asked.

'Will be moving to a country practice with his father.' There was an awkward pause. 'You told me a long time ago that I was unwise to continue such a friendship. I am taking your advice at last.'

Lydia looked at her with eyes full of sympathy, but Margaret hurried to change the subject.

'You said there was a letter from Ralph?'

'Yes,' Lydia went to fetch it. 'He has been in Jamaica

for three years. He must surely be planning to return to England soon for a holiday.'

The eagerness in her voice could not be disguised. It was clear that she was in love with Ralph, and there was no reason why she should not be fortunate in her love. For a second all Margaret's indignation returned. That she and she alone should be prevented from finding happiness by events which were none of her making seemed very hard. Then she managed to smile at her friend as she opened the letter and looked first of all at its ending.

'Yes,' she said. 'You are right. He is coming home.' She frowned a little to herself at the last sentence of all.

'And I trust that I may see you as soon as I arrive back,' he wrote. 'I am in a considerable difficulty – all of my own making – and badly need advice.'

Margaret forgot both her own unhappiness and the pleasure which Lydia was trying vainly to conceal. Her memory darted back to an incident she had almost forgotten. She remembered Claudine shivering in the hall of Brinsley House; and Ralph, white-faced, on his knees beside his bed. But he had been only a boy when he succumbed to the temptation offered by the French girl. Now he was a man, a man of God. It was unthinkable that his predicament on this occasion could be of the same kind.

Unthinkable – yet often, during the next few weeks, as she waited to see him again, Margaret's mind returned to the question. What could have happened in Jamaica to cause Ralph such anxiety?

PART III

Ralph and Margaret

1

It is common for a missionary who has never before left his home country to make unconsciously two contradictory assumptions: that tropical islands are hot, humid and frequently filthy; but that mission stations function with clean, neat and bustling efficiency. When Ralph arrived in Jamaica to take up his pastorate as a Baptist minister he was prepared for the island's high temperature and steamy atmosphere and not surpised to find the streets of Kingston thick with refuse in which pigs and goats foraged for their suppers. But he had expected the mission itself to be hygienic and well-ordered.

Hope Valley was neither. He reached it after nightfall and was welcomed at once to the simple two-roomed house which for the past thirteen years had been the home of Pastor Conway and would now become his own. Early the next morning he was taken on a tour of inspection, and was not impressed by what he saw.

The village stood on both sides of a stream which fell sharply from the mountains further inland towards the sea. It was a collection of ramshackle wooden huts, each perched untidily on a pile of rocks to raise it from the ground. The walls of the huts were made of any material which had come to hand: splintered planks or sections of old packing cases for the most part, the gaps between them patched with sacking and split bamboo cane. To prevent the roofs from blowing off they had been piled with heavy objects for which no immediate use could be found. Each hut was surrounded by its own small patch of land. In it a wood fire burned, pigs and hens scratched around, and an undisciplined variety of plants flourished luxuriantly. In the walled garden of Brinsley House vegetables had been grown in cleanly-weeded straight lines. Ralph viewed the haphazard system of cultivation here with disapproval.

The sun was shining now with a heat which made him uncomfortable in his black suit, but there had been rain in the night and the mud paths which led steeply from one shack to another had become slippery streams. Steam rose from the ground like mist, carrying with it a smell which made him wonder about the villagers' sanitary arrangements. But he had enough tact to conceal his thoughts.

'Hope was one of the first Free Valleys,' Pastor Conway explained. 'When the slaves were emancipated, the planters in this area refused to allow them to stay on the plots of land which they'd previously cultivated for their own support. The men had to find new homes, and our mission was given this valley to form a new village.'

He looked proudly around, as though unconscious of any shortcomings in his surroundings. Ralph looked with him. There seemed to be a great many people within a small area. Young men sat on the ground with their backs against the trunks of trees, doing nothing; plump women moved ponderously around their plots, and more children than seemed reasonable tumbled about the area, shouting and running. In Kingston Ralph had noticed all shades of colour, but here the people were very black, their white teeth continually flashing in happy smiles. They looked as poor as could be imagined, but contented.

'Can the community support itself from the land?' Ralph asked.

'Not any longer, alas! Many of the plantations nearby have been allowed to run down. Their owners live in England and take no interest, except in their revenue; they are selfish men who do not recognize obligations. Their overseers tell them that sugar is no longer an economic crop, with the cost of labour here and high duties at home, and they are not prepared to expend either thought or money in restocking the estates. So some of our older men have become unemployed, and many of the younger ones have never worked at all. A great many difficulties are caused by lack of money and enforced idleness.' Pastor Conway hesitated. 'You will discover very quickly, I fear, that the morals of these poor people leave much to be desired. Centuries of slavery in which they were forbidden to marry have left their mark. They seem to feel that marriage and settled family life are matters of no importance. You will find that the women become mothers very frequently, but are much slower to become wives.'

By now they had reached the chapel, constructed out of wood, but a larger building than the rest. It stood on a platform of rock, high in the settled part of the valley, like an acropolis. Ralph stood for a moment, enjoying the breeze and looking down at the huddle of shacks on either side of the stream. They came to an end along what was clearly a demarcation line, but it was difficult to see why, since the flatter ground below was an uncultivated jungle.

'Is all the land which was given to the mission under cultivation?' he asked.

'The fields below, stretching from the line you can see right to the coast, were all sugar-cane fields when the grant was first made and were not included in it. The stream at that point is a boundary between two estates; Larchmont on the left and Bristow on the right. We have no claim to either, although in both cases their owners appear to have abandoned all responsibility. The higher ground is ours, but you will see the difficulties.'

Pastor Conway led Ralph to the other side of the chapel so that they could look up to the head of the valley. It seemed to Ralph that he had never in his life seen such intense greenness, unrelieved by any other colour. The hills on either side of the stream rose so steeply here that they almost formed a gorge. But although its sides were like cliffs, they were entirely covered by trees, each with so

313

little space that half the roots dangled downwards, searching for earth. The need for light had drawn all the trees up, so that coconut palms rose above the feathery branches of casuarinas but were overshadowed by mango trees, and these in turn were made to look small by cottonwoods. As if each foot of earth were not sufficiently occupied, creepers and vines entwined the trunks of the trees with their huge golden-veined leaves before sending tendrils dropping from the top to root again.

'There is food to be found there,' said Pastor Conway. 'In the right seasons the children can pick ackees or mangoes or coconuts or breadfruit. And these people are very generous. Whatever food there is will be shared. But you will see that this upper land is far too steep for houses, and the layer of earth above the stone is too thin for cultivation. We must be content, I fear, with what we have.'

There was one more sight which he wished to show. They scrambled up the side of the stream until they could go no higher, for the water fell sheer over rocks at the head of the valley. It came down with a clatter and a dazzle of spray and was then absorbed into a deep round hole, darkened by the trees above it.

'The people call it the Baptist Hole,' Pastor Conway explained. 'They told me when I came that baptisms had always taken place here, and so I kept up the practice. But I have sometimes wondered whether it may have had a significance to them long before the mission came here. If you want to change the custom, your first weeks here might be the right time.'

Ralph thought it better to wait until he had formed his own impression, but he accepted Pastor Conway's other recommendation – that Sister Martha, a stiff-backed grandmother, should continue as housekeeper. It did not take him long to learn that she was accustomed to lay down the law in the pastor's name – even, if necessary, to the pastor himself. It was Sister Martha who informed Ralph when and what he would eat, what duties he should perform, and which families must be summoned for reprimand.

Ralph obeyed her instructions at first, choosing to start his ministry cautiously. From the very beginning he found difficulty in adapting his own temperament to that of his congregation. As a boy in his father's house, and a schoolboy at Clifton College under the regime of Dr Percival, he had been subject to harsh discipline, and as Captain of Cricket had applied the same strictness to his team. But the people of Hope Valley appeared to recognize no rules. If he asked them to do something they cheerfully agreed, and as cheerfully forgot about it. The guilt which had oppressed Ralph in relation to Claudine was directly related to the high moral standard which had been instilled into him. He accepted its absolutes and recognized himself as a sinner. But what he had done only once, his people here did regularly, and without any sense of sin whatsoever. Most startling of all was the fact that they did not appear to be sorry for themselves. Ralph had come to Jamaica out of shame that his ancestors should have done so much wrong, to their own great profit. But nobody he met appeared to bear any grudge or to recognize that any penance was necessary.

The confusion of values troubled his mind but did not distract him from his duties. He visited each family, discussing their problems. He started a Sunday School for the children and struggled to distinguish them from each other and to remember their names. He prepared sermons with care and tried to introduce a Bible-reading scheme amongst the women. When he discovered that they were illiterate, he began to formulate a plan for teaching children to read and encouraging them at the same time to teach their own mothers. The study of the Bible he saw as the greatest benefit he could bring to his community.

At the same time, however, the physical conditions in which the people of Hope Valley lived disturbed him quite as much as the state of their souls and he was determined, with God's help, to make some improvements. Although he had been careful not to reveal too much interest, it seemed to him a sign from Above that on his very first morning he had heard mention of Bristow.

Little enough had ever been said at home about the plantation which his great-great-uncle Matthew had established in 1790, but what Ralph did know was that it had been given the old name of the city of Bristol. To find that it was so close to Hope Valley whetted his curiosity. After some weeks, when he was settled in and familiar with the affairs of his own community, he put on his wide-brimmed straw hat and set off to explore. The afternoon was hot under a blazing sun and even the butterflies seemed to be sleeping. No one took any notice of his departure.

His donkey carried him along winding tracks, barely distinguishable from the overgrown land around. Only a chimney, built of good English brick, showed where the sugar factory had once stood: only the foundations of a few stone walls marked the site of the slave hospital. Bristow Great House itself – built on a high point to catch the breeze – was damp and dilapidated, the windows gaping and the floors covered with bird droppings.

Ralph hitched the donkey to a palm tree which must once have formed part of an impressive avenue, and went up the stone steps which led to the main floor. He walked precariously over the rotten floorboards of the lower verandah and into the large central drawing room, whose proportions gave it dignity even in its present state. The louvred jalousies which should have covered the windows had fallen away from rusted hinges, so that Ralph was able to look straight out. His eyes widened in surprise as he crossed to take a closer look. Someone had made a garden at the back.

In order to protect it from hurricanes, the great house had not been built quite at the top of the hill. The land which continued to rise behind the house had been landscaped as a pleasure garden in the English style, with terraces retained by banks of local stone and specimen trees set in lawns of broad-bladed crab grass. The plants in the garden were untidy and over-luxuriant: climbing white lilies had entwined themselves round the branches of the trees, and what might once have been neat hedges of hibiscus now threatened to engulf the bright red tips of the poinsettias which they encircled. Although a newcomer, Ralph had been in Jamaica long enough to know that an area like this would have returned to jungle within a year if left untended. The estate might have been deserted many years ago, but someone was caring for the garden still. Would it be a Jamaican? The people seemed lazy enough even when it was a question of looking after the crops essential to their own living: it seemed inconceivable that any of them should spend what energy they had on something as unproductive as a flower garden, the neglected decoration to an uninhabited house.

While he stood puzzling over the problem, the sound of a footstep startled him. He swung round quickly, ready to defend himself if necessary. But the man who stood there, although he carried the cutlass which was the all-purpose agricultural tool of these parts, showed no sign of hostility. He was a thick-set man in his middle years. In England Ralph would have thought of him simply as a Negro, but already his eye had become able to interpret the variations in colour and feature which had resulted from the liaisons between masters and slaves. This man he recognized as a mulatto. His skin was lighter than that of most families in the Hope Valley community: his nose was longer and his lips thinner. But his most extraordinary feature was his hair. Not as tightly curled as that of a full Negro, the ends of its thick waves were a bright orange colour. He had dyed it, Ralph supposed, although it seemed a curious thing to do.

'I was admiring the garden,' Ralph said, since something seemed to be expected. 'Who keeps it so well?'

'That crazy ol' man.' The mulatto came across to the

317

window and gave a nod in the direction of the upper terrace. Ralph looked where he was directed and saw a coloured man with white hair slowly hoeing round the roots of a croton bush.

'Why does he do it?'

''Cause he's crazy, why else? One day when him little boy, Massa Matty tol' him, "Keep the garden just so till yo' white cousin come." An' he keep it an' he keep it an' white cousin won't never come. I tell him; he don't heed me.'

'Is he your father?'

'That's right, master. That crazy ol' man.'

An uneasy suspicion froze Ralph's heart. No one in the Lorimer family had spoken much about his great-great-uncle Matthew. That he had bought slaves and worked them Ralph knew, and that he had bequeathed them to his nephew. But the phrase 'white cousin' – even if it were a joke – suggested that he might on occasion have demanded a relationship closer than that of master and slave. Was there, Ralph asked himself, looking at those bright orange locks – could there possibly be – such a thing as a red-headed Negro?

'What's the old man's name?' he asked, trying to keep the tremor from his voice.

'Rascal Mattison, master.' The words rolled out with a sonority which added to Ralph's dismay. Rascal, son of Matthew: it was like a bad joke.

'Was he the only one?' Ralph asked, still avoiding the direct question. The younger Mattison seemed to know well enough what he meant.

'Massa Matty done father ten little childer here on Bristow, master. But after he done die, then the bad days come. And the overseer, he done the childer wrong. All but the one, 'cause his own daughter fancied him. That crazy ol' man's the last one living, talking all the time about that white cousin. When white cousin don't come, he say house all his own, land all his own.'

318

'Crazy, as you say,' said Ralph, and was relieved that the son did not disagree. They moved away from the window.

'What's your name?'

'Red Mattison, master.'

Ralph nodded.

'I came to see the old house,' he said. 'It's sad when something like this rots away.'

He returned to his donkey, his mind busy with questions. That orange-haired stranger must be a cousin of a sort. Ralph's conscience told him that he ought to acknowledge the relationship but there was more to make him hesitate than a natural distaste. He had been in Hope Valley long enough to realize that the name of Lorimer meant nothing to the families he served. Perhaps it had not been widely used even while Matthew was alive. Certainly it seemed that almost seventy years had been enough to obliterate it. Ralph had no wish to be linked in any way in the minds of his congregation with the memory of their former oppressors. For that reason it was tempting to keep away from the Lorimer estate altogether. Yet the land was more tempting still; and Ralph knew better than anyone else how unlikely it was that anyone would ever claim it.

What he had in mind troubled his conscience more than the unwelcome discovery and rejection of a distant cousin. As he urged the donkey through the thick, tangled land of the lower plantation, he was mentally clearing and replanting. Later that evening, as the rain thundered down on his roof, his brain was busy first on the legal, and only then on the ethical aspect of his discovery.

Matthew Lorimer had left the estate to his nephew Alexander; Ralph was certain of that. He was not sure how he knew, but it was part of the family history that Lorimer's Bank had been founded with the compensation paid for the slaves after they were given their freedom. It was possible that Alexander had sold the land as soon as emancipation made the running of a sugar plantation

319

uneconomic. Ralph assumed that he could discover that from the land office in Spanish Town. If it was not sold, Alexander would have left it to John Junius, his only son. And if John Junius had not sold it either, it ought to have been put on the market by the Receiver at the time of the bank crash. In no circumstances could William have been entitled to inherit it, for John Junius had nothing legally left to bequeath at the time of his death.

So there was one fixed point: that William had no rights. Then there was the unknown factor: a possible purchase of the plantation by an outsider. That could be checked. If both those potential claimants were eliminated, the land might be said to be in limbo. The bank's debts had been wound up, and no good could come from revealing the existence of a new asset which had been overlooked. It might stir up old troubles and old hatreds but would bring advantage to no one, for it was likely that the estate had little or no cash value. Yet to the members of his congregation it could represent a Promised Land into which Ralph himself, like Moses, could lead his people; out of poverty and towards a new life.

Suppose the land were indeed in limbo, what then was the moral position? Ralph assured himself that John Junius would have wished him to have it. It had never been the old man's intention that his younger son should have no inheritance. He would have made a settlement, as he had done in William's case, as soon as Ralph had reached the age of twenty-one. Accident alone had prevented him. This gave Ralph a moral right, surely, to use for the advantage of others what lay so conveniently to hand. Perhaps even a duty, for who but the Almighty had guided him to Bristow? What he had in mind would be for the good of the people and would bring no personal advantage. As the night wore on, Ralph became more and more convinced that he would be justified in carrying out his plans.

It is humiliating for a man of God to discover after telling
a lie that he would have achieved more by telling the
truth. When, a few weeks after his exploration of Bristow,
Ralph had an opportunity to make the journey into Spanish
Town, he went first of all to the shabby shingled office
which housed the land records. It took him only a short
time to discover that the Bristow estate was last registered
as being the property of Alexander Lorimer of Bristol.
Ralph asked to see the most senior person in the office.

'So you have inherited Bristow, have you, Mr Lorimer?'
said that gentleman, after Ralph had put forward his claim
with as much confidence as he could muster. 'Well, you've
come only just in time.'

'Why is that?'

'There's new legislation in force to deal with some of the
land problems on the island. I don't know whether you've
been here long enough to see the position for yourself.
Good land lying uncultivated; and willing workers fretting
for the chance of a plot of their own. Under the new
regulations, any land that hasn't been worked for fifty
years is liable for reallocation unless the owner appears
with an undertaking to cultivate it again himself.'

'What do you mean by reallocation?'

'It will be divided into smallholdings and made available
to deserving families. The head of the household has to be
sponsored by someone in a responsible position – someone
such as yourself. We give him a seven-year lease to begin
with. At the end of that period, if he's looked after the land
and no legal owner has come forward to claim it, we shall
grant a freehold right. Bristow was eligible for reallocation.
But it's a different matter now if there's an owner on the

spot. Have you brought any documents with you, sir, to support your claim?'

'They all lie in Bristol,' said Ralph untruthfully. 'They can be sent for when I know what you need to see. But let me consider for a moment.'

He was angry with himself for not having made a more thorough study of the present situation before deciding on his approach. The reallocation scheme which had just been described was precisely what the people of Hope Valley would want. However, Ralph was not prepared to admit that he had lied, and there was no other way of withdrawing his claim to ownership.

'I am the pastor of Hope Valley,' he said. 'I would not have troubled to claim Bristow on my own account. I am content with a life of poverty and have no wish to be a property-owner. My intention in coming to you was to divide the land amongst the people of my community.'

'There's nothing to stop you doing that, sir. Once the estate is registered in your name, you can do what you like with it.'

'But it seems to me now that the reallocation scheme you have described would be a more suitable way of achieving this end. As pastor, I could provide the recommendations you need. You could issue the seven-year leases – and the land would be under cultivation more quickly than if we have to wait while letters are sent to Bristol and documents searched out.'

Ralph had taken the risk of putting in his claim on the basis of his observation that in such a hot climate no one wished to be rigid about regulations. A white man who spoke with confidence automatically carried a certain authority. Assurances were likely to be accepted, based on promises which need never be kept. He waited now, while the land officer wiped the sweat from his forehead, to see whether he had judged correctly.

'Well now, sir, let's consider. There's plenty of land to come under the scheme. The first to be allocated ought to be the estates where we don't expect any owner to appear. You can see for yourself, it will cause discontent if a man clears his patch and digs it for seven years and then sees it go back to a stranger. That may have to happen in some cases, but we must avoid it if we can.'

'But since in any case I intend the people of Hope Valley to have the estate . . .'

'Well, you say that now, sir, but you could change your mind. Or, more to the point, you could die, and your heirs might feel differently.' He considered the matter in silence for a moment. 'How about this for an answer, Mr Lorimer? I give you a seven-year lease on the whole of Bristow estate under the reallocation scheme. That way we don't need to wait for your documents. At the end of the seven years, the freehold right comes to you automatically because if you're the owner in any case, no other owner will have turned up with a claim. If you want to give the land to your congregation after that, it's no business of ours.'

It was as easy as that. He would have to make another journey to Spanish Town in order to sign the documents which would specify the Bristow boundaries, but the matter was settled.

At the beginning of the day Ralph had been sincere in his intention to divide the Bristow land amongst the people of Hope Valley: only because of this could he justify to himself his false claim. But as he travelled back that evening, he was assailed by another temptation. The documents which would transfer the land to his care were legal, involving no untruthful statements. All the rights would be in his own name. Would he not be wise to retain control, in the best interests of the community? Divided into small plots, the Bristow estate would soon become the same kind of agricultural slum as Hope Valley. The heads of some families would prove neglectful, and there would be no sanctions by which they could be made to support their families. Ralph believed in discipline. As the owner of the land he could reward hard work and penalize laziness. He could plan a proper balance of crops and ensure co-operation on such matters as drainage and irrigation. He would transform Bristow into a model plantation. Yet again, he told himself, the hand of God had led him by devious paths to discover at last what was for the best.

Until his plans were complete, Ralph kept his own counsel. Then one Sunday morning he addressed his congregation more directly than usual. The next day, he told them, he would preach at six in the morning at the Baptist Hole. The words he spoke then would change their lives, and every adult member of the community who was not in paid employment must be there. He did not ask but ordered them, using the tone of voice which he had so often heard from his father. It was the first time he had spoken in such a way, and he was conscious of his hearers' approval. They had not understood his reasoned sermons, so carefully prepared, but now he was going to tell them in simple terms what they ought to do, and they would obey. The idlest of the unemployed men had not come to the chapel, but he could trust their women to see that they kept the morning rendezvous.

They were all there before him, waiting at the foot of the waterfall as dawn broke. As he climbed to the ledge of rock from which he could see them all, even the children were silent. He began to address them, and it was as though he had been visited with the gift of tongues. All the reticence and hesitations of his upbringing fell away from him as he reminded his people of the oppression under which their fathers had suffered, the poverty in which they themselves lived. His audience groaned in sympathy for themselves as they listened: they began to rock and moan. Then, as his mood changed, so did theirs. 'Hallelujah!' they cried out, and 'Amen!' as he called to them that the Lord spoke through him, promising His people a land of milk and honey. It was not through the long journey-ings of the children of Israel that they would come at last to the Promised Land, but by many days of labouring in the vineyard. He was here to lead them to their new future: they would start the work at once.

He had prepared a hymn with which to encourage them, but was given no chance to introduce it. As though she had known in advance the words with which he would come to an end, Sister Martha emitted a sound which was something between a wail and a trumpet call, and within seconds the whole congregation was singing. As they sang, they formed themselves into a procession and began to march: not like soldiers, but swinging their hips and shoulders and clapping their hands. 'Hear ye the word of the Lord,' they chanted, over and over again: the words were appropriate but the rhythm was disturbing.

Ralph, however, did not allow himself to be disturbed. He placed himself at the head of the procession and led it towards the Bristow land. As they went, the men dropped away to collect their cutlasses and rejoined the line at its end. By seven o'clock every adult member of the community who was fit to work and had no paid employment was slashing at the undergrowth, while the children and the older women pulled the cut vegetation out of the way, separating it into wood which could be burned when it was old, foliage which would make fodder for the animals, and debris which was fit for nothing but a bonfire.

It was not to be expected that the first frenzy would last for more than a day. Ralph reminded himself of his duty to see that the children were schooled. The women must spend part of their day about their domestic duties, and the land already under cultivation in the valley must not be neglected. But the unemployed were expected to put in a full day's work, and the others to come whenever they could.

In the months which followed there were many difficulties. Those whose homes were cramped expected that they could build new ones on the newly cleared land. Those who owned no ground looked for their own farms. Ralph's own ideas were at variance with these hopes. If the new project was to be self-supporting the land must be used to raise two or three crops in a quantity which could be profitably sold. He recognized the need in the first year to plant annual crops, such as corn and melons, partly in order that a quick harvest might provide encouragement for the future and partly to raise funds for the purchase of banana plants and cattle. But even this could be better done in large fields worked by all the villagers than in a patchwork of individual plots.

He was not a sensitive man, and was so sure of his own rightness that it took him some time to comprehend the depth of the feeling which opposed him. Of the members of his congregation only the three oldest had been slaves; but what the others had learned from their fathers and grandfathers had affected their whole thinking. It was part of their freedom that they should work their own land.

Once he had understood, Ralph saw that he must compromise. He redrew his plans, allocating plots of un-cleared land on annual tenancies, and fixing rents for them not in money but in man-hours of work on the common area. His assumption of authority was more acceptable to the congregation than the most democratic attitude with which he had begun his ministry, and he himself found it congenial. He did not realize that, however faithfully he might perform his Sunday duties, he was every day becoming less of a pastor and more of a planter.

But something else was happening which he could not disguise from himself so easily. An instinct which he did not attempt to rationalize had made him leave the land immediately around Bristow Great House out of his plans. He told himself that there was quite enough work to be done elsewhere, that it would be a pity to disturb old Rascal while he still lived. More truthfully he did not wish to associate himself with his slave-owning great-great-uncle by visiting the house too often: nor did he want to be disturbed by meeting the Mattisons. But it became his habit on every evening except Sunday, just before sunset, to walk round the boundaries of the cleared land as they gradually extended. It was on one of these walks that he first caught sight of Chelsea Mattison.

At that time he did not know her name, of course. All he knew was what he could see, that she was the most beautiful creature in Jamaica. She was washing clothes in the Bristow river when he first caught sight of her, and he stood still at once, so that she should not know that she was observed. Her skin was a creamy brown and her nose was long and straight. She sang as she beat the clothes, and her brown eyes flashed as brightly as her dazzling white teeth. She was a tall girl, with a neat, small head on a long neck. Her shoulders were square and her hips slim and she held herself with a straightness which Ralph had never seen in England. His sister Margaret had suffered many hours strapped to a backboard as a child, and her good posture showed it, but this girl's taut slenderness was something outside Ralph's experience. Had he been nearer, he could hardly have restrained himself from touching her. As it was, his eyes studied her body, trying to memorize it.

She was wearing a bright cotton cloth, twisted round her body beneath her arms and revealing most of her long legs. When she had finished her work she stepped into the stream and splashed herself all over for coolness. The wet cloth clung tightly to her skin. She was full-breasted, Ralph saw, in spite of her youth and slenderness. He groaned silently to himself and turned away, unable to bear the sight any longer. But every evening after that his walk took him in the same direction.

Nothing in Jamaica remained a secret for long. It could not have been a coincidence that a few months after his first glimpse of her the girl was brought to his house by Red Mattison, who introduced himself as her father. It was on this occasion that Ralph first learned her name, as Red offered the pastor his daughter's services in the house.

'No, thank you,' said Ralph, his voice hoarse. 'I am well looked after already.'

327

'Sister Martha ol' woman,' Red pointed out. 'Chelsea fourteen year old. You teach her what you like; she do it. Good strong girl.'

There was no need for him to put into words what he had in mind: it was clear to both men. In just such a way must Matthew have acquired his various housekeepers; who accounted it an honour, perhaps, to bear children of a colour lighter than themselves. Chelsea, although so young, almost certainly had the same idea. Ralph had preached so many sermons on the evils of promiscuity, and had seen his warnings so universally disregarded, that he knew marriage would not be expected either by the girl or by her father. Kindness and acknowledgement of her position would be enough. He was being offered a gift. There was nothing he would rather accept; and nothing which in his position was more impossible. He forced himself to speak angrily as he turned the girl away, and that night rocked himself to sleep in an agony of frustration.

At least from that time onwards he was able to acknowledge his sinfulness to himself. In the half-dreaming moments between waking and sleeping he indulged his lust: in his prayers and self-reproaches he reviled himself for it. The situation extended itself to become part of his life: an obsession which he could not evade without even greater unhappiness.

Towards the end of his third rainy season in Jamaica, he became ill. The time of his first furlough was approaching, and in his anxiety to see that the farm was left in good condition when he went, he paid even less attention than usual to the heavy downpours of rain which made Jamaica so fertile. Two or three times in a day he became soaked to the skin and then within an hour was steamed dry again by the blazing sun. This was a process which by now he took as much for granted as did the people of the village; nevertheless, when he woke in the middle of one night to find himself shivering with a coldness which no weight of blankets would alleviate, he at first assumed it to be only a chill. It was Sister Martha, arriving next morning to prepare his breakfast, who recognized that he was suffering from malaria.

He needed to be nursed day and night, and for the first few days was not aware who was caring for him. But as the fever abated he discovered that Sister Martha had found someone to share the task. Chelsea Mattison was sixteen by now, an adult by Jamaican standards. It was she who sat by his bed, patiently cooling his forehead and covering him with blankets again after each bout of tossing. At first he thought he must be dreaming, and later he pretended that he was, lying very still with his eyes closed and listening as she sang under her breath, almost too softly to be heard.

Later, as he recovered his health, the pretence could not be maintained. It was possible – for he had been sweating freely – that she had given him a bed bath earlier in his illness; if so, he had not known about it. Now, when he was almost too weak to move, but perfectly conscious of his surroundings, she brought hot water to his bedside again. As she washed and dried his face and shoulders and chest, smiling directly into his eyes as she did so, he felt an ecstasy which was heightened by his helplessness. She reached his waist, and prepared to roll the blanket down. Ralph gripped her wrist to prevent it. It was the first time he had allowed himself to touch her, although he had suffered himself to be touched; and its effects terrified him. He sent her away, saying that he had no more need of nursing. Then he washed and dressed himself, although his legs would hardly support him.

Chelsea Mattison was only just sixteen, but her judgement was as mature as her body. Eight days later she returned to the pastor's house in the darkness of a tropical evening, and stood silently in front of him. Equally tongue-tied, Ralph discovered that he was too weak to send her away, but not too weak to turn his fantasies into facts. It was on the morning after this, in an agony of self-disgust, that he wrote his letter to Margaret.

3

Unhappiness is a good traveller, as anyone discovers who tries to solve a problem with a change of scenery. In the weeks which followed her parting from Charles, Margaret had kept herself busy packing up everything she owned in London and taking it back to Bristol. She needed all the strength of character she possessed to banish her resentment at the unfairness of fate and to summon the determination to make a useful life for herself. In this preoccupation with her own unhappiness, she had allowed the anxiety which Ralph had expressed in his last letter from Jamaica to go out of her mind.

Because of this, her welcome to him on his arrival at Brinsley House for his first furlough was one of pleasure and affection only. She noticed that he was reticent about his own affairs, preferring to talk about her career. But this, she assumed, was because he had not expected to find her in Bristol and was sensitive to the friction which had arisen between her and William over her decision to work in her home city. She shrugged off his worried comments on the strain which showed in her face, explaining it with references to the long years of examinations and the responsibilities of her work since she qualified: she was not prepared to describe the true cause of her unhappiness.

In her own defence she pressed Ralph for details of his life in Jamaica and felt him gradually relax in the warmth of their old affectionate relationship. Leaning on the parapet of the upper terrace and staring down at the river, he described his congregation and the work he had provided for them.

'So I can flatter myself that my first pastorate goes well,'

330

he concluded. Then he looked at her with despair in his eyes. 'But oh, Margaret, what am I going to do about women?'

For a moment Margaret was too much taken aback to answer. But although startled by her brother's outburst, she was not shocked. Her medical training had taught her a good deal about life. Almost twenty-nine now, she no longer had much in common with that young girl who ten years earlier had been disgusted at the thought of marrying an habitué of the Joy Street area. Yet it took her a long time to probe to the root of Ralph's problem. He was a Baptist minister, after all, not a Catholic priest vowed to celibacy.

His own reluctance to elucidate caused a good deal of confusion as she tried to understand his difficulty. At first Margaret thought he was saying that there were no eligible white women in Jamaica – or that, even if there were, they were of the rich planter class who would not expect to live in poverty and who would be rejected by the Hope Valley community. When it transpired that the immediate problem was caused by a brown girl rather than a white one, Margaret began to feel out of her depth. How could she be expected to know what taboos might operate in a country she had never visited, what might or might not be expected of a pastor?

But was even this the real problem? Ralph appeared to appreciate for himself that such a girl would be completely unsuitable as a wife, and it was a wife he wanted.

Margaret thought immediately of Lydia, but had more tact than to be specific. 'I will introduce you to some of my friends,' she said gaily. 'The medical students of my year have all been so earnestly determined to pursue their careers that none of them has succumbed to matrimony. Within a week, if you say the word, I can surround you with intelligent and useful young women who will be swept off their feet by your handsome face!' she stopped as she saw that her brother was in no mood for joking. 'What is it, Ralph? Is there something I don't know?'

He nodded miserably, ready at last to confess. 'You remember Claudine?'

'Yes. Do you still worry about her? I'm sure that by now she is happily settled back in her village. With the dowry that Papa gave her she can have had no trouble finding a husband. Anyone who meets you now and loves you should certainly be able to forgive something that happened while you were still a schoolboy. You might not even find it necessary to speak of Claudine at all.'

'I married her,' said Ralph.

Margaret stared at him, unable to believe her ears. 'What did you say?'

'I married her early in the morning before she went back to France. How could I let a young girl like that carry the shame of motherhood in such circumstances? To allow her to return to France as a married woman was the only honourable thing to do.'

Margaret could produce no quick response to such a revelation. Impulsively she squeezed his hand in sympathy. How characteristic of Ralph to make honourable amends for being seduced! His high-minded headmaster, Dr Percival, would have approved.

'You were not twenty-one at that time,' she said at last. 'I take it that Papa knew nothing of the matter. Would such a marriage be legal without his consent?'

'Certainly I didn't tell him. I didn't dare. As for whether or not the marriage was legal, Claudine believed it was, so I have a moral obligation . . .'

'Tell me one thing first, Ralph,' interrupted Margaret. 'Do you want Claudine to live with you as your wife?'

Ralph shook his head. 'I had no feeling for her even at that time. To say that she tempted me is to betray a weakness, but I was too young then to understand how quickly I could be roused. The wife I need now is of a very particular sort. A woman I can love, but also a woman

332

who can be of use in Hope Valley, and who is capable of providing intellectual companionship. Claudine would be of little help in that respect. Nor did she have any more interest in me, I'm sure, than I did in her.'

'Oh, my poor brother! I cannot think what to suggest. Why not speak to William? He would give you better advice than I in such a matter.'

'I am ashamed to tell him.'

'He already knows about the baby; and although the marriage may be inconvenient now, it is to your credit.'

Ralph was too depressed to answer and Margaret respected his feelings.

'At least allow me to discuss it with him,' she begged. 'I do not always find William sympathetic, but he is a man of affairs. He will judge what can or cannot be done.'

Ralph gave his permission reluctantly, announcing at the same time that he intended to visit one of his university friends for the next two weeks. It was clear to Margaret that he would rather not be in the house while his problems were under discussion. She mentioned this sensitivity, amongst other things, when she told the whole story to William.

'Even if the marriage could be annulled on the grounds of Ralph's age at the time, he would be frightened of the publicity from the proceedings,' she pointed out.

William frowned in thought and then said abruptly, 'Would you consider making a visit to France?'

'To see Claudine, you mean?'

William nodded. 'You would find it easier than I to investigate her way of life. I can hardly believe that a girl like that will have lived like a celibate all these years on account of such a marriage. You should be able to judge, without having to ask her in so many words, whether there is any danger of her making a nuisance of herself in the future. I will add a second suggestion to the first. If you are willing to make the journey, would you take Matthew with you? Now that he is eleven, he knows enough French to make a visit to France a useful part of his education. I would pay your expenses, of course.'

Margaret needed little persuasion to take a free trip abroad. Her departure from London had been impulsive and she had not yet succeeded in obtaining employment in Bristol. Although William made it clear that he did not expect her to contribute to the expenses of Brinsley House, she disliked the feeling of living as a dependant. Already she was approaching the point when her visit would seem to be more than a mere holiday. It was true that this offer replaced one form of hospitality with another, but she could regard it as being more to Ralph's advantage than her own, which made it easier to accept. Matthew and she were great friends and she knew that they would both enjoy the holiday.

It was decided that Matthew's tutor should accompany them, to make the most of every educational opportunity and to provide the protection of a male escort. This meant that Betty had to be taken too, to act as a chaperone as well as attending to her mistress's wants.

'We are all looking after each other!' exclaimed Margaret laughingly as they stood in a wind-whipped row at the rail of the cross-channel steamer, straining their eyes for the first glimpse of France.

Matthew looked up at her. 'Who do I look after?'

'Whom,' corrected Mr Renfrew, but Margaret answered without bothering about grammar.

'Why, Betty, of course. She doesn't speak a word of French. Whenever she needs to ask a question or to buy anything for me in a shop, you must go with her and speak for her. And tell her what the answer means, as well.'

'You needn't worry, Betty,' Matthew said reassuringly, accepting his responsibilities. 'I'll see you're all right.'

'Thank you, Master Matthew.' Margaret and Mr Renfrew were both finding it difficult to keep a straight face, but Betty's relief sounded genuine: already the sound of French voices on the steamer had made her uneasy.

The itinerary had been planned by William ostensibly to improve Matthew's education. Claudine had presumably returned to her father's farm in the valley of the Dordogne. In order to break the journey, Margaret and her companions were to spend some days in Paris on the way, lingering to admire its works of art.

To Margaret's great surprise, Matthew – who had probably never been inside an art gallery before – did not need to be bribed or bullied into fulfilling his father's requirements. The crowded galleries of the Palais du Louvre reduced him to an awed silence. He showed little interest in landscape painting, and none at all in still life, but any representation of the human face seemed to fascinate him. Mr Renfrew, improving the occasion as was his duty, embarked upon a lecture on Renaissance art, but Margaret shook her head to silence him. The gesture was unnecessary, for Matthew was not listening. All his concentration was on the pictures in front of him. It was an unexpected enthusiasm for an eleven-year-old boy. Watching him, Margaret was reminded of her father. In just this way had John Junius Lorimer been able to cut himself off from the outside world as he cradled a jade carving in his hand and stroked it with a thick finger.

The excuse for making the long journey south had been that Matthew should be shown the prehistoric cave paintings at Sarlat and Les Eyzies. When the plan was made, William had merely been looking for the most acceptable cultural destination in the neighbourhood of Claudine's village. He had had no reason to expect that his son would have the slightest interest in the paintings. Yet it seemed possible to Margaret that Matthew might after all turn the excuse into a worthwhile experience. Already he had asked to be given a sketchpad. The pencils which came with it dissatisfied him, for he had noticed already that the painters he now admired used light and shade, not hard lines, to achieve their effects. Margaret hoped that he would find the prehistoric outlines of mammoths and reindeer more satisfactory to copy.

They arrived at Sarlat late in the evening, tired after so much travelling, and were driven straight to their hotel. From the window of her room there, Margaret looked out at the narrow street. Old houses, solidly built in stone and surmounted by pepperpot roofs of grey slate, crowded together on either side of its steep cobbled inclines. Everything within sight appeared to be at least two hundred years old, including the huge four-poster bed in which she was to sleep. In fact she did not sleep well, worried about the interview with Claudine the next day.

In spite of Mr Renfrew's anxiety she went alone, hiring for transport something between a cart and a carriage, drawn by a single horse. The driver was a silent man, who brushed aside the name of the farm she mentioned – asking instead which family lived in it – and then did not speak again. It gave Margaret the opportunity to collect her thoughts and practise in silence the questions she would need to ask.

Her mission was delicate and demanded some subtlety. It would have been difficult even in English, but in French! Like Matthew, she had learned the language from books, and although she had been an apt pupil in the schoolroom, twelve years had passed since then. Claudine had understood little English, so not much help could be expected from that quarter. In every situation which she had so far encountered in France, Margaret had been able to formulate a simple, direct question or statement. But this was going to be neither simple nor direct.

The driver clicked with his tongue, and the horse came to a standstill. The man who appeared at the boundary of his small vineyard at the sound of strangers looked at Margaret in a curious way, but answered her questions civilly enough. Claudine was his sister, he told her. She was married and lived on another farm not far away. With one of her questions already answered, Margaret waited while the new destination was communicated to the driver, who spat to one side in a gesture of acknowledgement.

Instead of turning back to the road they continued along the same rough track, jolting downwards between wooded cliffs. The sheer sides were pierced with the openings of caves, and Margaret allowed herself to wonder whether Matthew was at this moment enjoying his own expedition with Mr Renfrew to an underground cavern. Then the driver spat again, and she successfully translated this as meaning that they had arrived.

Jumping down to the ground, she looked at the solid stone farmhouse which lay in a hollow in front of her. Its living quarters occupied a single storey, but this was raised from the ground to allow animals to shelter underneath. Cowsheds and a barn stood at right angles to the farmhouse, so that the yard was enclosed on three sides.

The approach was not a welcoming one. Cow dung lay thick in the yard, and its sharp smell carried a long way on such a hot day. A group of mud-caked pigs nosed amongst it, slurping down the kitchen waste which must have been recently flung out of the nearest door. Flies circled by the hundred, but their buzzing was drowned by the barking of dogs. The noisiest and the most vicious in appearance of these was on a long chain which slid up and down a wire, enabling him to guard a considerable area, but his two companions, unconfined, seemed equally unfriendly. Margaret stood still for a moment, hoping that the hubbub would bring a member of the family out to her.

Her hope was quickly realized. A new noise was added to the general confusion, as a dozen or more grey geese came running out of the barn, protesting angrily at their eviction. Behind them – the cause of their haste – a young boy banged with a stick on an old tin bucket and shouted shrill directions about the way they should go.

Margaret stared at the boy. Even in the slums of London she had rarely seen any filthier urchin. His legs rivalled the pigs for muddiness: he seemed not to notice the muck in which he trod. He had grown too tall for his trousers, which were torn as high as his knees. Margaret noted all this, but immediately ignored it, for her eyes were riveted on his head.

At first sight it seemed that he had been in some ludicrous manner thatched with straw. Certainly there was plenty of straw mixed with his hair, as though he had recently been burrowing in the barn. But the hair itself was straw-coloured. Many small boys had fair hair, Margaret knew – although not so many in this part of France. But she could think of only one grown man who had preserved precisely this shade of yellowness.

Another of her questions had been answered before it was asked. She had found Ralph's son.

4

Seekers after truth can be divided into two categories: those who hope to find proof of what they already believe, and those who would prefer to discover that no such proof exists. The sight of the Lorimer features, dirty but still distinctive in the unlikely setting of a French farmyard, ought not to have surprised Margaret. Had she not been expecting to find just such a boy? Yet subconsciously she must have been hoping that Claudine had deceived the family, had earned herself a dowry by a lie. Nothing else would explain why the expected meeting came as such an unwelcome surprise.

The boy had seen her now. He gave one last clang with his stick and the geese scurried away with an attempt at high-headed dignity. Then he stood in front of the visitor, waiting for her to speak.

Ralph's long nose and face were recognizable, as well as the hair, but the cheekbones were higher and wider, narrowing his eyes. In her careful French, Margaret asked him his name.

'Jean-Claude, Madame.'

'Is your mother here, Jean-Claude?'

He shouted for her. The dogs, which had reduced their welcome to an occasional menacing growl, began to bark again. A woman came out of the kitchen door and stood at the top of the stone steps, wiping her hands on the apron tied round her waist.

Claudine had grown fat, and was not very much cleaner than her son, but her smile as she recognized Margaret was as warm as ever. During her brief reign as nursery governess she had never behaved like a servant and now, mistress of her own house, she greeted her visitor without deference. Jean-Claude was chivvied away with a series of shrill instructions to remember his duties with the geese. Then she turned again to Margaret.

'You will understand, Mademoiselle,' she said, speaking her native language more slowly for the benefit of a foreigner, 'that he believes himself to be the son of my husband.'

The words were a caution. A surprise as well. But one which was likely to suit the Lorimer plans. Margaret assured Claudine that she had no intention of saying anything which would disturb the life of the family, and was at once rewarded by an invitation into the kitchen.

Three other children playing on the floor there were shooed away, swept out by a flapping of their mother's skirts as though they were geese or pigs which had strayed into the wrong part of the farm.

'So!' Claudine poured two cups of coffee from a pan which stood on the hob and motioned Margaret to sit on one of the wooden chairs. 'It is a great pleasure to see you again, Mam'selle. I hope that all your family are in good health. Your father, for example. He was very generous to me. I remember him in my prayers every day.'

'My father is dead,' said Margaret.

'I am sorry,' said Claudine. 'Is that the reason for your visit?'

She lowered her voice out of respect as she spoke, but Margaret noticed that her eyes had brightened at the news. What they expressed was not precisely greed; rather a natural acceptance of the possibility that a rich man would wish to remember all his grandsons in his will.

'Before he died, my father lost all his money,' Margaret told her. 'The bank . . .' she searched for the right word and failed to find it. 'All his business was in ruins. There was nothing left.' Noticing that her appearance was under scrutiny, she added – almost as though she needed to excuse herself – 'I have to work for my living now.'

Claudine shrugged her shoulders, not allowing herself to be depressed by disappointment in a possibility which had occurred to her only a few seconds earlier. 'You have my sympathy, Mam'selle,' she murmured.

'Tell me your own news, Claudine,' said Margaret. 'How long have you been married?'

'As soon as I returned to my family. It was necessary for me to find a husband at once so that my baby should be born in wedlock.' The word she used was unfamiliar but its sense was clear enough, and startling.

'But – I understood . . .' Margaret stopped to consider. Had Claudine not realized that the ceremony which Ralph had arranged was one of marriage? If that were the case, was it wise to speak of it now? Claudine, cheerful again, was shrewd enough to follow her visitor's train of thought.

'Your brother told you, perhaps, that he had married me,' she said. 'I was very happy when that happened; because I could say to my father that my child would not be a bastard. But the priest spoke to my mother and told her that in the eyes of Holy Church what had happened was no marriage at all.'

Margaret found it difficult not to laugh. Ralph, a schoolboy at the time, could be excused for not realizing that Claudine must be Roman Catholic. It was more surprising

340

that the point had not occurred to William. His own smug Anglicanism must have blinded him to the implications.

'The priest said I should send for Monsieur Ralph so that a second ceremony could be performed,' Claudine continued. 'But how could I ask such a thing? It was brave of him to escape from his father for the first time. He would not be allowed to come to France, and I had promised that I would never return to England. Besides . . .' she looked down at her apron, laughing to herself, 'if he had come and the priest had married us, I should have been tied for the rest of my life to a man I could never see again. In England, I was frightened. But here at home I decided that was not the way a woman should live.'

Margaret said nothing, but sipped the bitter coffee.

'It was easier to look for a husband in my own village,' Claudine continued. 'In the country it is not the same as in Bristol. Here, a man does not marry a girl until he is sure that she will bear children. True, he prefers his sons to be his own, but your father's dowry was generous. With it, Guillaume was able to buy this farm. We breed Périgord geese – to make the pâté de foie gras, you understand – and we enjoy a good living. I am content.'

'So you don't think of Monsieur Ralph as your husband?'

'He is not my husband,' said Claudine emphatically. 'The priest explained to me most carefully that the words in England meant nothing. And from the moment Jean-Claude was born, Guillaume has been his father. If your brother has sent you here as a messenger, because he wants his son, the answer is that he has no son. Will you tell him that? I ask for your promise.'

To Margaret, translating the French word by word in her head, the request came as a demand. It was reasonable, she supposed. If Claudine had suffered at the hands of the Lorimer family once, it would hardly come as a recompense now to split up her own family and challenge the validity of her marriage. Margaret's first reaction to her discovery had been that Jean-Claude should be rescued from poverty and offered whatever comforts the Lorimers were still able to afford. But Claudine's anxious expression showed her how selfish such a thought had been. Here in France the boy was part of a loving family, a secure community. The Lorimers had nothing comparable to offer.

And there was no real choice. Jean-Claude's mother had taken a decision, and it must be respected. Margaret looked into Claudine's eyes and Claudine stared steadily back. Margaret nodded her head slightly. It was the nod with which John Junius had been accustomed to signify his acceptance of a situation as the prelude to dismissing it from his thoughts. The two women shook hands, both happy that the matter was settled. As she left, Margaret paused to take a last look at the urchin chasing geese. For a Lorimer, he did not seem very successful in his profession.

For the rest of the stay in Sarlat, she joined Matthew on his expeditions to the paintings and carvings which had been made in the prehistoric days when this area, it seemed, was the cultural centre of Europe. She had intended, once she had investigated the situation at her first meeting with Claudine, to take Matthew to the farm for a reunion with his one-time governess. But now she realized that if she was to keep her promise, her two young nephews must not be allowed to meet. Matthew's introduction to the art of portraiture in the Paris galleries had led him in the following days to scrutinize faces and study features. It was by no means inconceivable that he might notice the resemblance between the boy on the farm and his uncle Ralph. Fortunately, no one had ever mentioned to Matthew the true reason for the journey to France.

Back in England Margaret reported her discovery to William, who rubbed his hands in satisfaction.

'Then we need worry no more about it,' he said. 'Ralph can be told that he is a free man.'

'That is not exactly the case. The marriage may not have been a valid one for Claudine, but surely Ralph is bound by it.'

'Nonsense,' said William briskly. 'Ralph was too young. Without his father's consent, whatever ceremony he went through was merely a form of words.'

'If that was the case, it was hardly necessary for me to go to France, was it?' It did not occur to Margaret to doubt her brother's word, but she was annoyed by the implication that her journey had been for nothing.

'We have to think of Ralph's moral position, not merely his legal one,' William pointed out. 'Without the news you have discovered, we could never have persuaded him that he could honourably abandon Claudine. He was married in his own eyes and in the eyes of *his* Church, if not of Claudine's, and we know that his religious feelings are strong. A man of less firm principles would have forgotten the whole affair long ago. I will tell him to forget it now. The interests of all three of them lie together. Claudine and her son wish to hear no more of Ralph, and Ralph wishes to hear no more of Claudine. Leave it to me to speak to him. For your part, if you have an unmarried friend whom he might find pleasant company, please feel at liberty to invite her to visit you at Brinsley House. Sophie too will put her mind to the subject. Ralph's furlough is not a long one, and he has made his wishes clear enough.'

Margaret realized, as she accepted her congé, that there was a good deal to be said for decisive action in such a situation. Even so she was unprepared for William's method of handling it. Less than an hour after their conversation, Ralph came striding across the upper lawn to join her as she leant against the parapet on her favourite part of the terrace.

'William tells me that your travels in France took you near to the place where Claudine's parents lived,' he said. 'I was grieved to hear of her death last year.'

Margaret stared at him without trusting herself to speak. She was horrified that William should have put such a lie

343

into her mouth – but now that it had been told and believed, would it be wise to contradict the falsehood?

'And did William also tell you about the child?' she asked.

'That there never was a baby. Yes. It was foolish of me to believe the story. William has been trying to console me with the assurance that many young men are deceived in such a way, and I suppose it is true.' He had shown a genuine grief when speaking of Claudine's death, but now he smiled shyly. When he spoke again, it might have seemed to anyone but Margaret that he was changing the subject. 'We have wasted too much time talking about my foolishness. Tell me more about your own plans. Now that you are coming to live in Bristol, what does Miss Morton intend to do? Will she stay on in the lodgings which you shared in London?'

'That was her intention when I left, but I suspect that she will soon be driven out of London by her own high standards. She has specialized in questions of public health and hygiene, and the capital is intractably large and dirty. While I was there we had a pleasant way of life together. But I think she will now be looking for a post in some smaller place, where projects can be set afoot not just for the running of a hospital but for the improved health of a whole community. Since she has a few days' holiday due, I am about to invite her to visit me here for a week. Perhaps she will find something in Bristol, suited to her talents. You will be able to talk to her yourself about her ideas.'

'I shall look forward to meeting her again,' said Ralph. His intentions were transparent, and Margaret's wish to be truthful about Claudine was overruled by the thought of the obstacles she would be placing between her friend and her brother merely for the sake of her own conscience. She had suffered so much herself from an ill-fated love that she could not inflict the same unhappiness on two people for whom she felt such affection. Her silence in Ralph's presence did not, however, prevent her from expressing her anger when she was next alone with William.

'You are too squeamish,' said her brother, amused rather than disturbed by her indignation. 'And too selfish as well. Look at it from Ralph's point of view, which is all that matters now. What I told him has made no change in the actual situation. Claudine is dead to him by her own request, and you reported to me her own words that Ralph has no son by her. All I have done is to change a metaphor into a fact in order that there can be no possible feeling of guilt or regret.'

'At the sacrifice of truth,' Margaret pointed out.

'To be honest at the expense of others is a self-indulgence. You may discover for yourself one day that it can be kinder to express the spirit of a situation rather than its bleaker facts. Ralph feels himself free to marry. He would have been free in any case, but now he is not restrained even by doubts. I have done him a good turn.'

The lie had been such a definite one that it could not bear amendment, only acceptance or outright challenge. For a moment longer Margaret hesitated. She was by nature truthful, and knew that she would never be able to live easily with a deception of this kind. But on the other hand, she had made a promise to Claudine, who had the right to expect that it would be kept. If Ralph were to learn the truth, conscience might drive him to see his son, even if he made no greater attempt than that to interfere in Claudine's life. Two forms of integrity – the truth and the promise – struggled for precedence in Margaret's mind. Truth was the loser, as William no doubt had always taken for granted it would be. The lie he had told would keep five people happy – the boy himself, Claudine and her husband, Ralph and, probably, Lydia. The truth would benefit only Margaret's conscience, so that to insist on it would be mere selfishness. Still angry, she confined herself to one last attack.

'I trust, William, that you will never take it upon yourself to decide where *my* best interests lie without referring the matter to me first.'

He made no answer and Margaret – although she had expected none – felt a second's uneasiness at his silence. But when she looked at him suspiciously, he merely smiled.

'And you will write to one of your friends?' he urged, pressing her into complicity.

She nodded and went straight to the morning room; but stopped to think before she took up her writing materials. This was no ordinary invitation. It was almost certain that if Lydia came to Brinsley House, Ralph would make her an offer of marriage. If Lydia accepted it, she would be committing herself to a life of poverty on an unhealthy island far from all her friends. If she refused, Ralph would be made unhappy again. Would it be best to consider . . .? Margaret checked her own thoughts with the same impatience she had shown to William. She was making the same mistake that she had just criticized in her elder brother. People had the right to make their own decisions.

As the invitation was written and dispatched, she felt little doubt what the decision would be. When they first started their training, Lydia had been as emphatic as herself that marriage would never tempt her away from her work and the memory of her dead love. But Margaret knew that in her own case she had not been able to subdue her nature: she still longed for a family life, with a husband and children. If Charles were suddenly to find himself free . . . She shook the dream out of her head. But there the impediment was personal to Charles and herself. Lydia must often have felt the same longings and in her case there was no reason why she should not be grateful for this chance. Ralph had admired her in the past, and Lydia in return had welcomed the interest he showed in her. If she came to Brinsley House, Ralph would propose and Lydia would accept him.

Her prophecy proved to be correct. Ralph and Lydia were married that summer and sailed for Jamaica a few days after the ceremony. Margaret said goodbye to her friend with a heavy heart. She was uneasy about the hazards of a tropical life and, for her own part, knew how much she would miss her companion and confidante. Lydia's departure marked the end of that happy period in which they had lived together as fellow students and fellow doctors, and it brought a finality to the remnants of Margaret's relationship with Charles. She had already had time to accept that her friendship with him was over and that her love could never be expressed, but now she had lost the one person with whom it was possible to discuss her feelings.

Even had Margaret been tempted to uncover her thoughts, however, they would have been overwhelmed by the happiness which shone in the eyes of both bride and bridegroom. They had both thought themselves condemned to solitary lives, and both were overjoyed by their good fortune in finding each other. There was no reason to doubt that the marriage would be successful. They would be happy, and Claudine was happy already. William's lies had done nothing but good, it seemed – but they could not alter the facts.

As Margaret stood on the quayside at Portishead and waved her friend and her brother goodbye at the start of their voyage, she reflected on the most important fact which could not be changed: that in a Dordogne farmhouse lived a boy with straw-coloured hair who was the grandson of John Junius Lorimer. He was never likely to visit England, would never speak a word of English, would never meet his father – but he was, all the same, part of the Lorimer line.

PART IV

Margaret, Alexa and Charles

1

Water was the life-blood of Bristol. It brought prosperity to the port, but at the same time it sapped the strength of those who lived there. The dampness of the city, with its high rainfall and the frequent flooding of the low-lying areas around its two rivers – the areas in which the poorer families lived – provided fertile ground for such diseases as pneumonia, bronchitis and consumption. As an untrained charitable visitor, Margaret had once visited such suffering families with palliatives but without cures. Now she visited as a doctor – and all too often found herself almost as ineffectual as before.

Her efforts to obtain a hospital appointment in Bristol had proved unsuccessful. The growing number of female medical students in the capital was gradually breaking down resistance to their employment there, but this enlightened attitude had not yet reached the provinces. Margaret had to be content with the opportunity to act as locum for a doctor who had caught consumption himself. More fortunate than his patients, he was able to prescribe himself a year in a Swiss mountain sanatorium. In finding someone as well qualified as Dr Lorimer to look after his practice, he was too grateful to hold her sex against her.

As well as the practice, Dr Miller's house in Portland Square was at Margaret's disposal, so that she could live near to her patients. When she first returned to Bristol, she had considered the possibility of making her home in Lower Croft, the house which John Junius had given her. But it was too large, and too expensive to run for a woman alone. Instead, she had taken William's advice and sold it to the convalescent home in whose grounds it stood. She used some of the proceeds to pay William himself the balance of the money with which he had financed her studies, and allowed him to invest the remainder in a way which brought her in a small income every quarter.

William had made no secret of the reason for his advice. He wished her to live at Brinsley House. If his sister insisted on working in Bristol, it was necessary to his pride as head of the Lorimer family that she should be seen to be under his protection. As politely as she could, Margaret rejected the invitation. Dr Miller's house was dark and damp, with the neglected air of a widower's establishment, but she was glad to escape from Sophie's undisguised disapproval and be independent.

She was conscientious in her visits, although the neighbourhood was a poor one and the patients could pay little for the time she spent with them. Late one afternoon she was just ending the last of her day's calls, on a consumptive fourteen-year-old, when the girl's mother stopped her at the door.

'There's another one upstairs, doctor.'

'Another what?'

'Another one sick, like my Kathleen. Sinking fast, she is. Too proud to ask for help when she'd no money to pay. But she told me this morning that her little girl had earned a penny or two. She couldn't give you much, but she asked me to say that she'd be glad to see a doctor, if one would come.'

'I'll go up straight away. And don't forget what I said about Kathleen. If your sister could find room for her in the country, the air would be far better than any medicine I can prescribe.'

Tired though she was, Margaret climbed the bare wooden stairs and knocked at the door of the attic room. It was opened by a nine-year-old girl whose golden hair was tinged with red. She knew at a glance that this was Alexa.

Without that clue it would not have been possible to

recognize her old music teacher. Luisa lay on the bed beneath the tiny window like a bundle of bones and rags. She was not only ill but starving. Lacking the deceptive rosy-cheeked appearance of most of Margaret's consumptive patients, she was emaciated and gaunt.

'My dear Luisa! How have you allowed yourself to come to such a state? Why did you not let your friends know that you needed help?'

'Ill and couldn't work,' murmured Luisa through swollen lips. 'No work, no money. No money, no way to get well.'

'I have some money,' said Alexa, coming to stand beside her mother's bedside. 'I want to buy medicine to make Mama well again.'

Margaret put an arm round the child's shoulders. Her own distress was so great that for a moment she could not speak, for it was plain to her practised eye that Luisa had sunk too low to be saved.

'What your mother needs first of all is some food,' she said. 'Can you carry a message for me?' She scribbled a note to Betty and gave it to Alexa, with instructions how to reach Dr Miller's house. 'When you get there, give Betty this note. First she will find you something to eat, and then she will bring a bowl of broth for your mother. You can show her the way.'

The child nodded solemnly and ran off. Margaret looked round the room. She was about to ask what had brought Luisa to such a condition when her attention was distracted. Except for the bed, the room contained barely any furniture, but hanging on the wall was the portrait of John Junius Lorimer which had once taken pride of place in the line of Margaret's ancestors at Brinsley House.

'How does my father's portrait come to be here?' she asked.

'Because a picture of John Junius Lorimer has no value even to a pawnbroker. If it had, it would have gone like everything else.' Luisa attempted a laugh, but it turned into a cough.

'But I mean, how did it come to be here in the first place?'

'I bought it,' said Luisa. Her voice seemed to strengthen as she remembered a time when she had been better off. 'In an auction at Brinsley House. I had a little money then. Your father gave me what he could. And no one wanted his portrait. It was very cheap. A bargain.'

'I don't see why you should have wanted it.' But even as she spoke, Margaret began to understand. 'Are you telling me . . .?' she began.

Again Luisa began to laugh; again the laughter turned into a cough. She held a handkerchief to her mouth as the coughing went on and on. When she lay back again, exhausted, Margaret could see the blood which stained it.

'Your father was good to me, as long as he was able,' Luisa whispered when she was strong enough to speak. 'I was fond of him. Sorry for him as well. He had little kindness from your mother, I think. But now I have upset you.'

Margaret felt herself blushing. If it was difficult, looking at the gaunt figure on the bed, to remember how voluptuously beautiful Luisa had once been, it was even more difficult to believe that her own father, in his seventies, should have had a secret life of such a kind. Both women were silent for a long time, one from weakness and the other from shock. Then Margaret forced herself to remember that there was a more urgent problem to be considered.

'We must build up your strength, Luisa,' she said briskly. 'It was foolish of you to starve yourself in such a way. If you were too proud to come to your friends, there are charities which would have helped you. And Alexa has been singing for money. You knew that, I suppose?'

Luisa nodded weakly.

'I asked a friend who works the music halls to look after her,' she said. 'I knew that she ought not to stay here and sleep in this room with me. It was hard to send her away, but for her own good. The little she earned hardly paid for

351

her own food and lodging. But she saved what she could, the dear child, and insisted on bringing it home. She has been away for six months, and returned today. I have been forcing myself to stay alive just long enough to see her again.'

'You would have been more certain of succeeding had you provided yourself with a better diet.'

'I had no money.' Luisa gave a deep sigh. 'Everything that could be sold or pawned had already gone. One cannot eat rubies.'

'Rubies?' queried Margaret. It took her a moment or two to collect her thoughts, and yet even as she asked the question she suspected what the answer was going to be.

Luisa lifted a thin hand from the grimy blanket which covered her and began to grope feebly beneath the bed.

'You cannot imagine how glad I am that you are here,' she said. 'Ever since I knew that I was dying, I have wondered who to tell about the rubies. It has been my great anxiety, not knowing who I could trust to look after them for Alexa. I did not know that you had returned to Bristol, otherwise I would have sent a message asking for your help. You were always a good friend to me.' Her hand dropped in exhaustion after the small and unsuccessful effort. 'The box is under the bed. I cannot reach.'

Margaret stooped down and felt along the floor until she found a black leather box with a metal lock. The key was on a chain round Luisa's neck. Margaret held the box close so that the sick woman could unlock it.

She had seen its contents before – though in another age, it seemed. Even in this hovel the jewels sparkled with light and fire on their cushions of black velvet. Margaret drew out the three separate shelves of the box and stared at them. The mystery which had puzzled not only William and herself, but the whole of Bristol, was solved.

Her father must have had an exact copy made, presumably somewhere where he was not known. That much had been widely supposed already, although Margaret in her loyalty had found the theory difficult to accept. Mr Parker of Bristol had made the genuine pieces, and Georgiana had worn them in front of the Prince of Wales at the ball; but it must have been the copies which were deposited in the bank the next morning. At a time when his ship of fortune was already leaking and would soon be wrecked, John Junius had chosen this method of providing for a mistress whose existence could not be openly acknowledged.

The moment was a bitter one for Margaret, reminding her of all she had suffered because of her faith that her father had been an honest man and intended to defraud no one. She had defended him against David's accusation that her engagement had been tolerated – even engineered – for discreditable reasons: but there could be no honest explanation of this gift to Luisa. Everything about it, from the surreptitious sale of the jade to meet the cost of the jewels to the equally furtive commissioning of the imitations, could only have been planned by a man deliberately intending to deceive and defraud his creditors. Margaret recalled her own struggles of conscience about the ownership of Lower Croft, how she had tried to think what her father, as an upright man, would have wanted her to do. Now she had his answer. He had been intentionally providing for his daughter without regard to his debts, as he had been providing for his mistress at the same time.

It was far too late for anger. When Margaret sighed, it was with sadness at the shattering of an illusion. Then she returned her attention to the problems of the moment.

'How foolish of you to deny yourself so much when you had ample means of purchasing food and comfort at hand!' she exclaimed.

'Some gifts are over-generous,' Luisa whispered. 'What do you think would have happened if I had tried to sell the jewels? I should have been accused of stealing them. Who would have believed that a poor woman like me could have come by them honestly? And if I told truthfully how I was given them, they would have been taken from me to pay your father's debts. Even if I gave no explanation, anyone in Bristol would have known that the jewels should have been part of his estate. Don't you remember all the letters written to the newspapers about this jewellery? I would not have been allowed to keep it, nor its value.' She was silent again, as though so much talking had drained her of all energy. But then she roused herself with some of her old passion. 'Besides, the jewels are not mine to sell. They were given to Alexa. One day she will be the most beautiful woman in England, and she must be able to dress like a queen.'

She made a weak sign with her hand that Margaret should close the box.

'Alexa has never seen them,' she murmured. 'I could not risk her speaking of them. But they are hers. Will you keep them for her? And the portrait, as well.'

'Yes,' said Margaret. Neither of them wasted any time in pretending that Luisa had a chance of recovery.

Margaret's distress at her friend's condition did not prevent her from feeling unhappy on her own account. 'Who will care for my treasure?' John Junius had asked as he died, and the question had built an irremoveable obstacle between his daughter and the man she later came to love. It was the question which had brought on Dr Scott's obsession and sent him mad. But he had been right. There had been a treasure all the time – in fact, not merely in his imagination. In a second moment of bitterness, Margaret could not refrain from telling Luisa part of this.

'My father spoke of the jewellery as he was dying,' she said. '"Who will care for my treasure?" he asked. Yet he must have had confidence that you would cherish the jewels.'

Luisa shook her head. 'You are wrong,' she said. 'His treasure was Alexa. It was what he always called her. Never Alexandra or Alexa, but "my treasure".'

Margaret stared down at Luisa.

'You mean she is his daughter?'

354

'Of course. He loved her, even more than he loved me. She was so beautiful, you see. From the moment of her birth, so perfect. Your father had a great love of beautiful things.'

'Yes, I know.' Margaret was still trying to steady her swimming head. She reproached herself for naïvety. It had not been easy to accept the fact that her father had kept a mistress, but once that was known, the deduction that he had also fathered Luisa's child should have been obvious. It meant, of course, that the liaison must have started much earlier than Margaret had assumed; that he had lied to his daughter as well as deceiving his wife. She remembered how secure and happy she had imagined her family life to be throughout the years when she was growing up. Yet all the time it had been as rotten as the affairs of the bank.

She put the leather box inside her doctor's bag as the door opened and Betty came in, carrying a can of broth in a hay jar to keep it hot. Behind her was Alexa, who ran breathlessly to her mother and embraced her, kneeling on the floor beside the bed. Luisa looked at Margaret with tears in her eyes.

'I have waited so impatiently for her return,' she said. 'But I think she should not sleep with me here.'

Margaret nodded her agreement. 'I will find you a nurse,' she said. 'Then Alexa can come home with me for the night.'

'No!' The little girl scrambled to her feet and stared defiantly at each of them in turn. 'I must stay with Mama. I am going to make her well again.'

'You will do that best by letting her sleep quietly,' said Margaret sympathetically. 'If you come with me Betty will let you go down to the kitchen with her again, and you can help her prepare some dishes to tempt your mother's appetite. Tomorrow morning we will come back together to see her.'

Alexa was still rebellious, but her mother murmured

something to her in Italian. When she had finished, the girl frowned and stared doubtfully at Margaret.

'Help your mother to enjoy her broth,' said Margaret as cheerfully as she could. 'She will need one person to support her and another to hold the spoon. By the time I return with a nurse, I expect the bowl to be empty.'

Alexa's defiance faded at the suggestion of something helpful to do, and by the time Margaret returned half an hour later Luisa was either asleep or pretending to be. Still doubtful, the little girl accepted Margaret's hand and allowed herself to be led away.

The next morning they returned together, and the nurse greeted them with the news which Margaret had expected. Happy to have seen her daughter just once more, Luisa had abandoned her struggle for life. She lay as peacefully on the bed as though she were still sleeping, but at some moment during the night her heart had ceased to beat.

Alexa's reaction was violent. At first she was alarmed, then unbelieving. Before the nurse could restrain her, she tugged at her mother's shoulders, trying to shake life back into her. Then her tears and anger erupted together. She stamped and shouted and screamed, her voice rising hysterically in rage and grief and a refusal to accept what had happened. Margaret allowed her to express her feelings without interruption until the moment when her shouts became sobs. Then she stepped forward.

'Sing something for your mother,' she said.

Wild-eyed, Alexa looked at her. 'Sing what?' she demanded.

'What was your mother's favourite song?' Margaret asked. 'Was there something that she loved to hear? You could give her the sound as a farewell present.'

Alexa had to breathe deeply several times before she could begin, and the effect steadied her emotions as well as her body. When she was ready she knelt beside her mother's bed.

The purity of her voice in the silent room was eerie. She

356

sang in Italian, so that neither of her hearers understood the words, but the sweet sadness of the song was so poignant that even the unsentimental nurse was forced to sniff away a tear. As for Margaret, she found herself completely overcome. Since there was no furniture in the room, she sat down on the bare floorboards and buried her head in her hands, sobbing with almost as much grief as Alexa had expressed a few moments earlier.

It was not only the death of a friend which so much upset her professional poise. Alexa's song turned a key in her heart, from which all the unhappiness of the past years could escape. She was weeping for the betrayals of the past and the loneliness of the future. At any other time she would have reminded herself that she was a well-trained woman with a useful role to play in society. But for just as long as the sad song continued she allowed herself the luxury of misery.

Alexa came to the end and pressed her head for a moment on her mother's body. Then she stood up and looked around uncertainly. The hysterical mourner and the mature singer had both disappeared. She was a little girl alone in the world.

She looked towards Margaret – and Margaret held out her arms. Alexa ran into her half-sister's embrace.

2

The helplessness of a bereaved child arouses sympathy even in those who bear no responsibility. It was not sentimentality, however, which led Margaret to undertake Alexa's support. The child was a Lorimer, and the Lorimers must look after her. As soon as her mother had been buried, it was necessary to consider the problem of her future.

Margaret had already decided to say nothing about the

rubies. Whatever she might feel about the morality of her father's actions, the settlement he had made would best be left undisturbed. The affairs of Lorimer's Bank had been wound up long ago. The process had continued over three years, and during that time the Portishead docks had opened at last, proving to be just as profitable as John Junius had always anticipated. The payments which flowed from them into the hands of the bank's administrator came too late to save the shareholders, but in time to pay off a high proportion of the creditors' claims. From the moment when David Gregson's flight was discovered, public opinion had begun to move back towards it previous respect for John Junius Lorimer, and, strange though it might seem, this process had been helped by the sight of his son living as a rich business man in his old home. Every year saw the scandal sinking further into oblivion. Margaret herself might be disillusioned about her father's character, but she retained sufficient family pride to conceal what she had learned from the outside world.

Not even to William did she mention the box of jewels. Although confident that he would not consider transferring their value to the bank's creditors, she believed him capable of arguing that the genuine rubies had been a gift to his mother and should therefore have been inherited by himself, not appropriated by an outsider. Margaret did not propose to allow him that opportunity. She believed that Luisa had told her the truth and that by keeping the jewellery for Alexa she was carrying out her father's last wishes.

The question of Alexa herself, however, was not one which could be left undiscussed. When Margaret next visited Brinsley House she took the nine-year-old girl with her, neatly dressed in new clothes. As was her custom, she went first of all to the schoolroom where she introduced Alexa as her ward and asked the governess if the little girl could stay there with the other children for an hour. Then she sought an interview with William.

He was horrified enough to learn that John Junius had fathered an illegitimate child in the last years of his life, but what Margaret went on to propose was so much more appalling that for a moment he was robbed of speech.

'You are seriously suggesting that I should bring up such a child in my own household, with my own children?'

'She comes between Matthew and Beatrice in age. There would be no need to make separate provision for her. She could share Beatrice's lessons and amusements. Your establishment is a large one. You would hardly need to know that she was here.'

'The suggestion is ridiculous. I have no responsibility for the girl.'

'She is your sister,' Margaret reminded him.

'An illegitimate half-sister. That hardly constitutes a recognizable relationship.'

'She is your father's daughter,' said Margaret more firmly. 'What are the alternatives, William? She is an orphan. If we – her family – abandon her, what is to become of her? You can hardly condemn her to the workhouse.'

'If you feel so strongly on the matter, why do you not bring her up yourself?'

'I shall do that, certainly, if you reject my suggestion. Since I shall probably never have children of my own, it would give me pleasure. But I have little to offer her. There would be no other children for company. I cannot afford to employ a governess and in order to earn a living at all I must be out of the house for a great part of the day. Alexa would have no family life. However, if you will not help her, I shall do what I can.'

'You would naturally not acknowledge any relationship with her.'

'If she is to live with me, I shall do what I like, William.' Margaret was exasperated by her brother's assumption that he could avoid any responsibility himself and yet order the manner in which she should shoulder it. She did in fact recognize that for the sake of her father's reputation it would be wise to conceal Alexa's parentage, but to admit this at once would be throwing away a bargaining point in her debate with William. Certainly her declaration made him think again.

'Where is the child now?' he asked.

'Matthew and Beatrice and Arthur are looking after her while I speak to you. Naturally, they know nothing about her.'

William's forehead creased in annoyance, but he merely said, in the curtest of tones, that he would like to see her. They went together to the schoolroom and opened the door.

William's three children were sitting in a row in their wooden chairs. In front of them, on the table, Alexa was dancing. She was singing as well to provide herself with a musical accompaniment. The audience, with its back to the door, did not notice the arrival of the adults, but the effect on Alexa was to stimulate her into even more energetic movements, culminating in a high kick which revealed her undergarments. William stepped backwards out of the room and slammed the door behind him.

'A guttersnipe!' he exclaimed. 'Straight out of the slums! And you consider her fit company for three well-brought-up children? You must be out of your mind, Margaret. I cannot possibly consider a proposition of that sort.'

Margaret's heart had sunk at the sight of Alexa's ill-timed exhibition, and her brother's reaction was what she expected. But for Alexa's sake she could not abandon her request.

'The girl has had little education, William. She has been brought up in poverty. When her circumstances are altered, her behaviour will alter as well. She is the daughter of a gentleman and has natural good manners. All that is required is discipline and an ordered programme of learning – and at nine years old she is not too old to be amenable. At the moment she possesses only one talent, although it is a considerable one. It is natural that she should wish to display it.'

The sound of clapping could be heard through the door. William opened it for a second time, and on this occasion they both went inside. Matthew was helping Alexa down from the table with great care, while his young brother still jumped up and down with excitement at the impromptu concert. Only Beatrice stood a little aloof, looking at the visitor with prim disapproval.

Poor Beatrice, thought Margaret suddenly. She had inherited her father's sharp features instead of Sophie's calm good looks, and she was old enough now to realize that she was ill-favoured. The arrival of such a beautiful rival for the affections of her adored elder brother was clearly a source of grievance.

'This is Alexa, Father,' said Matthew, presenting her in a proprietorial manner.

'Yes,' said William. There was no warmth in his voice, but at least he was not rude.

Unaware that she had made a bad impression, Alexa smiled shyly. How could William fail to be affected by her beauty? Margaret wondered. On the stage of the music hall, and again as she danced on the table a few moments earlier, Alexa's face had been vivacious, extravagantly mobile as it expressed pathos or mischief or vulgarity. In repose it changed character completely, its oval shape and perfectly proportioned features becoming peaceful, almost placid; a Venus from a Renaissance painting. The new garments which Margaret had bought for her – a high-necked smocked blouse, plain skirt and black stockings and boots – were demure and unostentatious, and a wide hair ribbon held back the strawberry blonde hair which was her most striking feature; but no degree of restraint in her clothing could dim her beauty.

Matthew made a fit partner for her as they stood side by side. He had recently started to grow taller at a great rate, but at twelve years old his face retained an almost feminine

361

attractiveness, with its soft complexion and long dark eyelashes. He made no secret of the effect Alexa had had on him. Margaret remembered his unexpected reaction to the treasures of the Paris museums. Like his grandfather, Matthew was an admirer of beautiful things.

'Will you bring Alexa with you again when you come here, Aunt Margaret?' he asked.

Margaret waited for a second before she answered, in the hope that William would make some gesture. When he remained silent, she could only say, 'I'll see,' and stretch out her hand to take Alexa away.

'I'll write to you,' said William abruptly. 'I need time to consider. You will not speak of this to anyone, I imagine, nor rush into any arrangement which you may later regret.'

Margaret acknowledged the concession with a bow of her head. It suggested that her brother might after all accept his responsibility as head of the Lorimer family. As she took Alexa back to Dr Miller's home, so cramped and dark compared to Brinsley House, Margaret wondered whether she truly wanted him to.

She had spoken the truth when she told him that she would take pleasure in bringing up Alexa herself. But the prospect was frightening as well as exciting. Nothing in Margaret's own upbringing had prepared her for the strains and complications of living as an unsupported woman. From the day of her birth it had been assumed by everyone she knew – and for a long time also by herself – that she would pass from the protection of a father to that of a husband. If she was not lucky enough to find a husband, one of her two brothers would have the obligation of caring for her.

To break away from all these assumptions and embark on a medical training had required a good deal of courage, but she had not been without the support which came from companionship at that time. Other women facing the same problems had provided reassurance and their Dean was helpful with advice. The very difficulty of the syllabus, with its frequent tests and written examinations and the movement from one form of practical training to another, had provided a framework which left little time for doubts. Afterwards, when she took employment in London, the routines of hospital life gave her the same kind of support.

That time was over. Now she had to plan for a future which was the rest of her life and not simply the period before the next examination. To accept the responsibility for a child's life when she hardly knew whether she could manage her own was not something lightly to be undertaken.

William had promised to write, but instead he came to call on her, looking with distaste around Dr Miller's gloomy sitting room.

'How long do you propose to remain here?' he asked.

'The arrangement is temporary,' Margaret told him. 'I hope to find a permanent appointment in a hospital for women or children. Once I have secure employment, I shall decide what kind of home I want and can afford.'

'I have a suggestion to make,' said William stiffly. 'Where is the child?'

'Asleep.'

'Good,' he said. 'Now then, the post of physician at the Ashley Down orphanage is vacant. Would work of that sort interest you? You probably know that Father was very generous to the orphanage when it was founded. I have succeeded him as one of the trustees. Assuming that you can offer satisfactory references, I could make sure that the trustees do not allow your sex to prejudice them. The salary is lower than might be offered by an ordinary hospital, so there may not be many applicants.'

'I cannot live on less than anyone else,' said Margaret.

'Please let me finish,' said William. 'I have not yet come to the end of my suggestions. You asked me to take responsibility for our father's – for Alexa. With reluctance – with *great* reluctance – I accept that something will have to be done for her. I am agreeable to educating her with

363

my own children as you ask, for a trial period of four years. That would also be the term of your initial appointment at Ashley Down. But it would have to be clearly understood that in no circumstances am I prepared to acknowledge any relationship. If she should ever try to claim one, I would consider that fair grounds for her instant removal.'

'She doesn't know . . .' Margaret began, but her brother interrupted her curtly.

'Quite. And she must not know. The arrangement I propose is this. What the world in general may be told is that she was the daughter of a patient of yours who died; that you were sorry for her orphaned state and decided to bring her up as your own child. So much is true. Alexa herself will know in addition that the patient concerned was an acquaintance of yours, but that detail need not be broadcast. She may be called Alexa Lorimer by virtue of your guardianship. You know that I have never approved of your decision to return to Bristol and be seen working for money as though I were too poor or mean to provide for you. But if you are adamant on the subject I would regard charitable work of the kind offered by the orphanage as more suitable to your station in life. To recompense you for the lower salary I invite you and Alexa to live at Brinsley House. Society will consider it entirely proper that you yourself should live with me while you are in Bristol, and Alexa's presence under my roof will be all the easier to explain if you have already assumed responsibility for her.'

There was a calculated coldness in William's voice which tempted Margaret to reject his proposals and resolve her affairs for herself. But prudence prompted her to consider his offer seriously. The medical care of a large number of orphaned children would be a satisfying field of employment, for she would be able to look after their health all the time, practising preventative medicine. William's promise to use his influence did not disturb her conscience – she knew from her experience in London how few appointments were free from considerations of this kind.

Ashley Down was woman's work and she was well qualified for it. Whatever reservations she might have about living with William and Sophie, the arrangement would be the best possible one for Alexa. Even while she was asking her brother to allow her a day for consideration, she had already made up her mind.

After William had left, she went into the bedroom where Alexa was sleeping. Except for the jewel box, which Margaret kept in her own care, all the child's possessions, such as they were, had been brought into this room. The portrait of John Junius Lorimer was propped up against the wall. Margaret stared at it for a long time. Alexa did not know who the subject was. Margaret, who had loved her father, wondered how much even she had known him.

She laughed silently – but without merriment – at the unexpectedness of life. After the collapse of her father's empire she had thought that the doors of Brinsley House were closed to her for ever. But now, after seven years of independence, it was to be her home once more. Even more strange was the fact that the portrait of John Junius Lorimer, sold in shame, bought with furtiveness and housed in squalor, would also be returning to its ancestral home.

3

Good news becomes bad news when the wrong man brings it. Seven years after her parting with Charles, Margaret still secretly hoped that he might one day come to tell her that he was free of responsibility for his father. But it was William who said at breakfast one morning, 'I hear that Dr Scott is dead.'

For a moment Margaret's heart stood still. 'You mean our old physician?' she asked, controlling her voice with difficulty.

'Who else?' William's face expressed surprise at the

365

question. 'I understand that for many years he has been out of his mind. His death must have come as a merciful release.'

'How did you learn the news?'

'His son is in Bristol and has informed several of his father's old patients.' William returned to his kedgeree and *The Times*, indicating that he would be grateful for silence in which to study Mr Gladstone's latest proposals for Irish Home Rule.

Margaret willingly obliged, hoping that the agitation in her mind would not betray itself on her face. If Charles was telling others and not herself the news of his release from his claims of duty, what grounds had she for hope? She had told him to forget her, and this was evidence that he had succeeded in doing so. Quietly she left the table before her misery could be detected.

It was part of her arrangement with William that she would take sole charge of Alexa on Saturdays and Sundays. On these days she was not required to attend at the orphanage except in the event of some medical emergency. But today was a special occasion, an Open Day when those benefactors who contributed to the cost of caring for the children, or who might be persuaded to do so, were invited to inspect the building and its inmates, which they did rather in the manner of visitors to Clifton Zoo. Margaret, as a member of the staff, was expected to act as one of the hosts or keepers.

She went to see whether Alexa was ready to leave, and found her ward still untying the rags from her hair. Alexa turned every public appearance into a performance. In her own room she was untidy, but before leaving the house for any purpose at all she would spend hours making sure that every pleat was in place, every ribbon precisely tied, every hair of her head brushed and shining. Margaret chivvied her affectionately and they set off together to Ashley Down.

In the long dining room examples of the girls' needlework and the boys' woodwork were on display, ready to be admired and, if possible, sold. The children themselves, brushed and scrubbed and uniformly dressed in blue smocks, stood in demure lines along the walls, their hands clasped in front of them.

The sight was enough to make Alexa show off, tossing her head in a disdainful manner as though she were one of the rich ladies who were already beginning to perambulate through the hall. She disliked the orphanage, possibly because she guessed how near she had come to entering it herself. She was concerned to make it clear to everyone who saw her that she was not one of its residents, but the demonstration was hardly necessary. The shimmering waves of reddish-gold hair which framed her face were in striking contrast to the tight plaits strained off the foreheads of the less fortunate girls present.

As the visitors began to arrive, Margaret forced herself to do her duty. She was reassuring to trustees and encouraging to anyone who might be persuaded to be generous to the orphanage. It was necessary to tread a delicate path, making it clear at one and the same time that the children were well fed and cared for while every possible economy was practised. But although she said and did everything that could be expected of her, beneath the professional mask her feelings were in turmoil. Where was Charles at this moment? Did he know that she was in Bristol? Would he come to see her? If he did not, was there any way in which she could without impropriety visit him? Did she even care about propriety? The questions churned and jostled in her mind even while she was defending to one of the trustees the cost of heating water for washing the hair of the orphans.

The first of her questions was answered almost at once. She was still talking to the trustee when Charles Scott came into the hall. In mid-sentence she abandoned what she was saying and stared wordlessly across the room. Although she had known he was in Bristol – although she was at that very second hoping to see him – his sudden

367

appearance came as such a shock that her heart seemed to stop beating: for a moment she was even unable to breathe.

Charles was escorting two ladies: Mrs Braithwaite, a widow who was one of the patrons of the orphanage, and her unmarried daughter. The daughter was pretty, and Margaret had to control a second reaction, of jealousy and apprehension. Suppose it was not herself but someone else who had drawn him back to Bristol. Margaret had set him free to form other attachments, but she could not bear to think that he might have done so.

Charles's attention was not wholly on his companions. He was looking round the hall, studying each face in turn. Suddenly his eyes alighted on Margaret and he stood stock still, bringing the two ladies to an unexpected halt beside him.

As he stared at Margaret, so she gazed steadily back at him across the room, wondering whether she could bear it if he were to speak to her and knowing that she could not bear it if he were to turn away. She saw him bend and say something to Mrs Braithwaite, who looked round just as he himself had done a moment earlier. The trustee who had been talking to Margaret, sensing her distraction, moved politely away. To conceal her confusion, Margaret began to speak to Alexa, chattering any sort of nonsense that came into her head.

It was Alexa who drew her attention to the trio approaching them.

'How are you, Mrs Braithwaite?' Margaret addressed the plump widow, but she could not take her eyes off Charles.

'Not as well as I would wish, Dr Lorimer, but it is kind of you to enquire. May I present Dr Charles Scott to you?'

Margaret swallowed the lump in her throat and held out her hand. 'We are already acquainted,' she murmured, hardly conscious of what she was saying. Charles was gripping her fingers so tightly that for a moment she thought she would faint.

Mrs Braithwaite showed signs of annoyance. 'Already acquainted? Then why did you insist on being presented, Dr Scott?'

'So many years have passed since our last meeting that I could hardly expect Dr Lorimer to recognize me,' he said. He was still holding her hand.

The superintendent of the orphanage, recognizing Mrs Braithwaite as a valuable benefactor, came up to greet her unctuously and to bear her and her daughter away for an inspection of the samplers embroidered by the girls. Alexa attached herself to them, and Margaret and Charles stood alone in the crowded room.

'I suppose that after all this time you could not be sure that you recognized me,' said Margaret, although in truth she felt that she had changed little. Her eyes might sparkle less than in the battling days of her youth, but the bright redness of her hair, she knew, showed no signs of fading – and unlike her married friends who had become stout with childbearing, she had retained her trim figure.

'Of course I recognized you,' said Charles softly. 'But I was too much of a coward to ask a busybody directly whether you were still Dr Lorimer or whether you had become Mrs Smith or Mrs Jones. Margaret! My dear Margaret! Do you find the atmosphere here oppressive, I wonder? Perhaps we might inspect the gardens.'

She left the hall on his arm, feeling as though she were walking a foot above the ground. She was well aware that their departure would set malicious tongues wagging, but she was reckless with the excitement of being close to him again. Her whole body was tingling with exhilaration and relief at the magical transition from despair to hope.

Neither of them made any pretence of admiring the gardens. Instead, Charles led her to a wooden seat beneath a cedar tree. They did not speak at once. The tension which had built up in Margaret's mind during the morning of unhappiness and the shock of actually seeing Charles again had slipped away with the touch of his hand. She could afford to take things slowly now. Whatever words they might use would be irrelevant: their true communication was through their fingertips. It was as though their hearts were beating in unison. To prolong the preliminaries with superficial conversation would almost be a pleasure, so sure was she that they would arrive together at a happy conclusion.

Perhaps Charles shared the same feeling, for – without relaxing his grip on her hand – he allowed himself to be apparently distracted by the sight of Alexa. She appeared in the doorway just as Charles and Margaret had sat down; but when she saw the two of them together she stood still for a moment as though posing, and then returned inside.

'I noticed you were talking earlier to that beautiful young girl,' said Charles. 'I was curious, in fact. She reminded me of yourself in a way I could not quite define.'

'The appearance of a beautiful young girl has little in common with mine,' laughed Margaret.

'Nonsense. Your eyes very much resemble each other's, for one thing. And although the child's hair is so much fairer than your own, it is tinged with red, is it not, and has the same texture.'

'She is my ward,' Alexa,' said Margaret. 'Her parents both died before she was ten years old, and she has lived with me ever since.'

'That is a very generous act on your part.'

'Her mother was a patient of mine. When she died, Alexa was quite alone in the world. As you have remarked, she is very beautiful. It was unthinkable to condemn her to the drab life of an orphanage, even such a happy one as this. I have always enjoyed young company. To have a child in my care has given me great pleasure.'

The explanation for Alexa's situation was one which Margaret had repeated many times, and in her happiness and excitement she did not pause to wonder now whether Charles deserved a more accurate version. For the time being she was not concerned with Alexa's circumstances; only with her own.

'I was sorry to hear of your father's death,' she said.

'You have learned of that already?' He was startled.

'It was my impression that I was one of the last to hear.'

'I had quite forgotten the speed at which gossip travels in Bristol,' he confessed. 'This was a piece of news which I particularly wished to give you myself. I arrived here only yesterday, and used the politeness of announcing the information to my father's old patients as my excuse.'

'Did you need an excuse?'

'I came to find out about you,' he said simply. 'To discover whether you were working, whether you were married, whether you were happy.'

'And what have you learnt, Charles?'

'The answers to my first two questions. The third I must ask more directly.' His eyes searched hers. 'Are you happy, Margaret?' he asked.

She did not answer at once. So often in the past she had invented this meeting in waking dreams. Now that it had happened in reality, she still hardly dared to believe it. She forced herself to meet his look, as she had done earlier in the hall. Less intensely than in those first few seconds, she studied his appearance.

In seven years he had ceased to be a young man. She knew his age. He was forty now, and looked older. His clothes were creased and shabby. The soft features of his face were lined with years of worry. His fair hair had faded into a paleness which was not yet quite grey. He was still a big man, and strong; but he was tired, and crumpled like his clothes – a man in need of care and comfort. She had thought that she could never love him more than she did on the night of their parting, all those years ago, but the depth of her feelings now proved her wrong.

'I am happy to see you again,' she said. 'Very, very happy.'

Charles gripped both her hands with his own. 'I had no

right to expect anything – anything at all,' he said, his face glowing. 'I sacrificed my own happiness – and yours as well, I know – for the sake of an old man who for years had not even been able to recognize me as his son.'

'You deserve respect for being so dutiful,' Margaret told him. Now that the time of waiting was over, she could even forgive the demands which had been made on him.

'I am ashamed to admit that I had hoped also for his gratitude. But of course he could not know what I had sacrificed for his sake. He expected more and more, thinking of it as his by right. Well, now that is over. I bring you an invitation to visit my aunt.'

'I have never met your aunt. Why should she wish to see me?' Margaret's voice was teasing. She would do anything that Charles suggested.

'She lives near me and invites you at my request. She is very old and will hardly be able to offer much entertainment. But I am anxious for you to see at first hand the village in which I have made my home, to experience the slow pace of its life.'

'You went there for your father's sake, did you not? Do you intend to remain there?'

Charles nodded. 'What skill I had as a surgeon is gone. I am too old to work up a new practice for nothing, and too poor to buy one, but in a village where I know everyone I can be of use. I must recognize, though, that such a community would not have much in the way of excitement or employment to offer my wife.' He looked into her eyes again. 'The only question I truly want to ask you is whether you will marry me,' he said. 'But I cannot ask it until you know what the answer would involve. My way of life may prove to be too dull for you.'

Margaret could truthfully have assured him that she asked nothing better than to live with him wherever he chose. But the pleasure of postponing for as long as possible the moment when everything between them would be settled made her tease him for a second time.

372

'It's rash of you to move so fast with a woman you have not seen for seven years,' she said.

'I have respect for my own good judgement,' he replied. The loving happiness of his smile suggested that he had seen in her eyes the answer to the question which he had not directly asked. 'I decided long ago that I should never want to marry anyone but you, and I feel confident that the qualities I admired are still there. You never doubted, surely, that I would come to find you again as soon as I could.'

'I needed to do more than doubt it,' Margaret said. 'I had to try to convince myself that I would never see you again. I could not have endured to spend so many years in a day-to-day hope that might never be fulfilled. Although sometimes, I must admit – ' She flushed at the memory of the day-dreams in which she had so often indulged, and did not complete the confession. 'As time passed, it seemed more likely that I was telling myself the truth. I thought that when you were free to make your own life you would want a complete family of your own – you would choose a younger woman for your wife. After so many years of being a loyal son, you deserve to be a beloved father.'

'It's true that I would like to have children; but I want them to be yours.'

'I am thirty-five,' she reminded him.

'That is not too old, if one has courage, as you have. When I came into that hall half an hour ago and saw you standing there with Alexa, I thought to myself that if you were to have a daughter that is exactly what she would look like.'

Margaret felt a sudden stab of alarm. 'I hope you didn't think . . .'

'Oh no, no. Of course not. It is just that your children would be beautiful in the same way.'

'I am responsible for Alexa,' Margaret said – apprehensive even as she spoke lest this should prove at the last moment to be a stumbling block.

'So much the better, for we shall then have a ready-made family.' Charles could not have expected such an imposition when he set out for Bristol, but he accepted it without hesitation. 'She will be company for you when I am away from home, and I shall learn to love her because you love her and I love you.'

Reassured for herself, it nevertheless occurred to Margaret to wonder whether an arrangement which promised so much fulfilment to her would be equally welcomed by a town child who was on the verge of becoming a young woman and whose pleasure lay in displaying her clothes and talents before as varied an audience as possible. But the prospect of happiness had slipped through Margaret's fingers too often already. This time she was determined to hold it fast. She smiled into Charles's eyes, and his fingers tightened round hers as he smiled back. She was conscious of him leaning forward towards her.

'The whole of Bristol is watching us,' she reminded him.

'Good. Then if I kiss you now, we shall each equally have compromised each other. Society will practically force us to marry. You will have no escape.'

'I am not looking for an escape,' said Margaret softly. But she allowed him, nevertheless, to lead her through the garden to a less public place. And as he kissed her at last, she felt that she was indeed escaping: from strain and loneliness into a prospect of perfect happiness.

4

A bachelor who takes pride in making his home fit for a new wife is often disconcerted by the energy which she displays in altering it. Charles Scott did not make that mistake. The house to which he brought Margaret after their marriage in the August of 1893 was a substantial stone building, separated from the cluster of village cottages by an avenue of ancient elms which bordered the manorial park. But over the past seven years Charles's housekeeper had been fully occupied in caring for the elder Dr Scott, and careless in supervising the maids. The house had become shabby, even dirty in places, losing much of the dignity which its fine proportions deserved.

The arrival of a new mistress and her maid changed the atmosphere overnight and the house within a few weeks. While Betty scrubbed and swept, Margaret set to work with her needle, sewing chintzes and cottons for curtains and covers. Charles watched her with affectionate pride. He had married a professional woman, used to earning her own living, and one who had been brought up to depend entirely on servants to run the house. He was amused as well as admiring to see how quickly marriage converted her into a home-maker, proud of her achievements as one room after another fell beneath her attack and became clean and bright.

When all of them were ready except for the bedrooms which would not be needed until guests arrived, William's wedding present was delivered: a grand piano. Charles knew that William had been surprised by his sister's engagement, but not disapproving. Fifteen years earlier a match with the son of the family physician would not have aroused any pleasure at all within the Lorimer family. William, however, had clearly given up hope that his sister would ever marry and was glad to be proved wrong. Better even a doctor's wife than a spinster! He had not liked to see her working for money, especially near his own door-step, and Charles suspected – though no one had ever said so – that he had no great affection for Alexa and was glad to be rid of her.

At any rate, William had accepted the announcement with as much show of enthusiasm as he ever permitted himself on any subject. Margaret had been married from Brinsley House, and William had shown himself eager to donate the most generous of wedding gifts. Charles was impressed with the elegance which the piano imparted to the drawing room, a large room which still lacked sufficient furniture. Margaret was happy to remember and play the simple pieces which she had not practised since her father's death. But it was Alexa – Alexa who in the beginning had been at a loss to know how to occupy herself in the unfamiliar country surroundings – whose life was changed by its arrival. She spent hours each day at the keyboard. Sometimes she played for the sake of playing, but more often she accompanied herself as she sang.

Charles remarked on her talent to Margaret.

'Her mother was a music teacher,' Margaret told him. 'Alexa must have sat through many lessons while she was a child, and I paid for her to have her own at Brinsley House. She will have to earn her living when she is older, and I imagine that to be a music teacher herself would be a congenial occupation.'

'I think Alexa's face may prove to be fortune enough for her,' said Charles. 'But certainly she should not neglect her gift.'

He was delighted that everything had fallen so smoothly into place. He had accepted Alexa into his home because the woman he loved could not desert her, but there had certainly been moments before the wedding when he had doubts on this score. In the event, however, the girl had proved less frivolous than her liking for pretty dresses and elaborate hair arrangements suggested. Her nature was affectionate, and she helped Margaret without complaint in whatever had to be done. Only at visiting aged and poorly villagers did she draw the line, wrinkling her nose fastidiously at the smell and dirt.

Charles was equally delighted at Margaret's whole-hearted acceptance of domestic life. One thing alone was needed to make his happiness perfect, and he did not have long to wait for that. Almost before he had dared to start hoping, Margaret was able to announce that at the end of May the next year he could expect to become a father.

At first he tried to cosset her, insisting that she should rest for part of each day. But just as the contentment of her marriage had made her look young again, so her pregnancy brought with it a surge of new energy. Hunting had become Charles's recreation since he moved to the country. Margaret had never been taught to ride, and he would certainly not allow her to learn at such a time, but she walked with him to every meet for the sake of the exercise, and followed the hounds for part of the way on foot. He rejoiced in her good health, which showed itself in the springiness of her step and cheerfulness in every occupation: he noted with satisfaction that the lines of responsibility and strain which the orphanage work had etched on her forehead were being smoothed away by serenity.

As the old year ended and the new one began, Charles remembered how his life had been on the last New Year's Eve – in a bleak house, with only a lunatic for company, and Margaret seemingly lost to him for ever. His heart filled with thankfulness for his good fortune. How different 1894 would prove to be!

The year had a cold beginning, but by the end of February the last of the snow had melted. March was wet and blustery. The wind tossed the trees like sailing ships and whipped the rain against the windows. Prevented from taking her daily walk, Margaret helped Betty prepare a nursery for the baby. Charles recognized his wife's need to do something constructive at a time when she seemed to have more rather than less energy than usual. When the nursery was ready, he suggested that he would be requiring a bedroom of his own during the period of her confinement.

'Which will you choose out of this great mansion of ours?' she asked. They were talking after dinner in the evening, sitting in front of a crackling log fire with no other light than its flames. Alexa had gone up to her own room, leaving them to a cosy, intimate half hour, the time of day which Charles most enjoyed. The shutters were closed against the rain, the curtains drawn across, even the dog cured of his restlessness by the drowsy warmth of the fire. Later they would light the gas and Charles would read aloud to his wife as she rested on the chaise longue with her feet up. But for the moment he was happy with their murmured conversation and thought himself the luckiest of men.

'There is a small room next to Alexa's,' he suggested: 'I need nothing but a bed. There would be no point in preparing one of the grander rooms for such a short period.'

'Let us look at it together now,' she said. 'You can tell me how you would like it and I will set to work tomorrow morning.'

He was reluctant to move from the warm room, but already Margaret was on her feet, holding out a hand to tug him towards the door. Laughing, he allowed himself to be bullied into lighting a candle and following her upstairs.

The room had a musty smell, suggesting that many years had passed since the sash windows were last opened. Margaret tugged at them to let in a little fresh air, and the force of the gale outside extinguished the candle at once, and slammed the door. The laughed together in the darkness, teasing each other with ghostly howls like a pair of children until Charles had succeeded in closing the window and relighting the candle.

By its flickering light they examined the room. It was certainly small, but would serve well enough. At the moment it was cluttered with pieces of unwanted furniture – a pair of cane-seated chairs, a roll of carpet, a marble-topped wash-stand.

'You are not to move any of these things yourself,' said Charles severely. 'If Betty needs help, she must apply to me.'

'Yes, sir. Of course, sir.' Margaret dipped a mock curtsey and Charles put his arm around her waist and hugged her gently. Then he looked curiously at a large picture in a heavy black frame which stood propped on the floor with its face to the wall.

'What is that?' He turned the picture round as he spoke and recognized the subject at once, although twenty years had passed since his last sight of John Junius Lorimer. Margaret did not say anything as he steadied it and stepped a little back for a better view.

'It was tactful of you not to ask that it should hang in this house,' he said. For a moment he wondered whether he could make the gesture of offering the portrait a place downstairs. The man was, after all, Margaret's father. She never spoke of him, but it was reasonable to imagine that just as Charles himself had struggled to retain his affection for a father who was deranged, so Margaret might have continued to love the memory of a father who was no better than a criminal. Much as he wanted to make her happy in every possible way, when it came to the point this was a way which stuck in his throat. His father's frenzied hatred of John Junius Lorimer, however irrational, had instilled in Charles himself an instinctive antipathy to the same man – not so much because of his family's financial ruin, but as the cause of his father's mental disintegration.

'Would it not be more appropriate,' he asked, trying not to make the question sound critical, 'if you were to make William a present of this? In Brinsley House it would have its proper setting.'

A moment ago Margaret had been laughing like a child. Now he was conscious of a sudden chill in the atmosphere. Not because she was angry – he was sensitive to her moods and could distinguish delicately between them – but because there was something that she was trying both to say and to suppress at the same moment. The battle was won by speech.

'The portrait is not my property,' she said. 'If it were, I would have given it to William long ago, as you suggest.'

'Then how did it come here?'

'It belongs to Alexa. Her mother left few possessions behind her when she died, but this was one. I have always felt that a child who is orphaned needs some tangible object, however valueless, to remind her that she was once the beloved daughter of her natural parents. Rightly or wrongly, it seemed to me that I had no right to dispose of this, when she had so little else.'

'But ...' Charles was confused – 'how did Alexa's mother come to own it? I am not mistaken, am I? This is surely a portrait of your father?'

Again the silence, again the chill. Margaret gave an almost imperceptible sigh.

'Yes,' she said. 'It is my father. And Alexa's.'

She faced him steadily as he struggled to understand. There was no sort of defiance in her look. A hint of relief mingled with her evident determination not to be ashamed.

'Why did you not tell me this before?' he asked.

'At least I told you no lies. Her father died when she was little more than a baby: that was true. Her mother was a patient of mine: that also was true.'

'But hardly the whole truth.'

'No,' she agreed. 'When you came so unexpectedly to Bristol, when you first enquired about Alexa, I told you what I had promised William I would tell everyone. The girl does not even know herself, you see. I had no right to give her secret away, particularly to someone I had not seen for so long, who might be gone again the next day. Then afterwards, when you showed so quickly that you wished to marry, I lacked the courage to change the story. I was frightened already that you might retreat from your proposal when you discovered that I had made myself responsible for Alexa. If you had learned at the same moment that she was my father's daughter, you might have walked away from me, or forced me to part from her. But I was committed to care for her. And I loved you so much, Charles. How could I risk losing you?'

'You did not have to bring Alexa under my roof. She could have stayed with William.'

Margaret shook her head.

'He gave her shelter most unwillingly and only so that I might be persuaded to stay in Brinsley House. It offended his family pride that I should live and work independently. He has never liked Alexa. But she has found herself alone in the world once already. How could I suddenly snatch away from her the little security she enjoys now? It is not her fault that she is my father's daughter. She could not choose her parentage. There are really no illegitimate children, are there, Charles: only illegitimate parents.'

Charles forced himself to be calm, reminding himself how unhappy he would have been if Margaret had placed any obstacle in the way of their marriage. He recognized that his reaction to the news now had been unreasonable. If he loved one daughter of John Junius Lorimer, there was no reason why he should dislike the other. He held both hands out towards his wife.

'I ought not to have suggested that you lied to me,' he said. 'I am sorry, Margaret.' He turned the face of the portrait back to the wall and began to return downstairs with her. 'Tell me about her mother?'

'She was a friend of mine. My old music teacher. A patient, too, as I told you, although I was called too late to save her.'

'So she left her daughter nothing but a portrait?'

For the third time that evening he felt a barrier rising between them. Margaret's hand tightened on his arm and she stood still, half way down the stairs. There was a long pause before she answered, and when she did her voice was husky with anxiety.

'I did not lie to you before and I will not now,' she said. 'You asked the question, so I will answer it. Yes, there was something else besides the portrait.'

'I would like to see it,' he said.

He recognized the alarm in her eyes and was even aware of the almost imperceptible shake of the head with which she seemed to beseech him not to press the request. It was enough to tell him that he was acting unwisely. But if he retreated now he would always wonder what had been concealed from him and the barrier would remain. He stared in puzzlement into Margaret's eyes, desperately trying to solve the enigma.

She did not flinch, but after a moment or two bowed to his determination with a shrug of resignation.

'I will bring it downstairs to show you,' she said quietly. Taking the candle from him, she turned back towards their bedroom. There was still time for Charles to stop her. It had been Margaret's fear which first chilled him: now it was his own. Irresolute, he slid his hand down the polished banisters to guide him as he felt his way slowly down the stairs.

The fire was low. He threw on more logs. They spat and crackled before resigning themselves to the flames. The dog, disturbed, growled in his sleep but did not wake. Charles stood with his back to the fire, warming himself as he waited for Margaret to come down.

When she rejoined him, she was carrying a black leather box. Unlocking this, she drew out its inner shelves one by one. Then she moved her sewing from a low table and set out the contents of the box, like a priest reluctantly unveiling his holy relics.

The jewels glowed in the firelight like the heart of a furnace. Earrings, a necklace, a tiara whose tremblers revealed that Margaret's hands were shaking as she set it out.

'This is Alexa's inheritance,' she said quietly.

Charles stared for a moment without speaking and then turned away to light the gas mantles on either side of the fireplace. The blood had rushed to his head at the sight of the jewellery, flooding him with anger – although he could not yet be certain that anger was justified. He struggled to control himself, knowing that the wrong words might wreck his happiness; yet it was impossible to remain silent.

In the gaslight the jewels looked different. The diamonds,

if they were diamonds, were yellower: the rubies, if they were rubies, flat and lifeless.

'Are they real?' he asked, his voice carefully soft and even.

'I believe so. I have never shown them to anyone who could value them, but yes, I think so.'

'A gift from your father?'

'To Alexa, yes.'

'Stolen from his estate.'

'No,' said Margaret. Her voice seemed to plead for his understanding. 'They were given before his death – before the collapse of the bank.'

'The Lorimer rubies! Don't think that I haven't read what has been written about them,' Charles said. 'My father kept cuttings from the newspapers in a scrapbook. The jewels could not have been given to Alexa until after the ball at which your mother wore them. By that time your father already knew that his fortune was doomed.'

'Whether he knew or not, that was not the reason for the gift. It is true that he was forced to act surreptitiously – but only because he would not have wanted to hurt my mother and the rest of the family by allowing us to learn of his indiscretions. It was affection for his love-child which prompted his generosity.'

'How do you know?' asked Charles. 'What do you know about your father? What have you ever known? I have never blamed you, Margaret, for anything that happened to the bank, or for any of the consequences of its collapse: how could I? But you must have realized, as soon as you saw all this wealth, that your father had no moral right to dispose of his money at such a time and in such a way.'

'I learned of the jewellery's existence only eight years ago. By that time the bank's affairs were long settled. It was surely too late to reopen the whole matter. In any case, that aspect didn't occur to me then. What concerned me was that the jewels belonged to Alexa, a gift from a man who wished to make what provision he could for his baby. He was old, and must have known that he would not be able to support her mother for much longer. And Alexa has nothing else by which she may remember her parents when she is grown. How could I possibly have broken my promise to Luisa, and deprived the child of her only possessions?'

Her lips trembled as she spoke, and she turned her face unhappily towards him. Charles could see that she was on the verge of tears, but his anger could not be contained.

'It was a promise you had no right to make!' he cried. 'Eight years ago my father was still alive. Eight years ago he had not yet reached the state of frenzy in which he died. He was demented, certainly. Oh yes: everyone recognized that! He had a fixed idea that somewhere in the world John Junius Lorimer had concealed a treasure. Everyone who suffered under his obsession thought him mad, and so he became mad. And all the time – all the time – '

His voice choked on sympathy for his father's ravings. He pushed away Margaret's attempts to calm or comfort him, and was still further angered by the sound of a knock on the door.

It was Betty. 'If you please, sir, it's John Taylor from the cottages. His wife's time has come and she's in great trouble.'

'I can't come out now,' said Charles, irritated by the interruption. 'Tell him that Mother Barrett can deal with it as well as I could. He doesn't need a doctor for a simple birth.'

'Yes, sir.' Betty withdrew in silent disapproval; but she returned a moment later.

'If you please sir. John Taylor says to tell you that Mother Barrett's been there for six hours already and it's she who says that she can't do without a doctor. And he asks to remind you respectfully that he's paid into the club without missing a week.'

'You must go,' said Margaret quietly. 'Think if it were our baby and no one would come to help.'

384

'Yes,' said Charles. 'I must go. John Taylor has paid his weekly penny, and for pennies I must go out into the storm and deliver a baby into a stinking cottage. And all the time there has been a fortune concealed. A treasure. Who will care for my treasure? your father asked. Now we know the answer. *You* have cared for his treasure. So my mother's health was broken, my father's mind unhinged, my own career ruined, all in order that your father's by-blow could wear a fortune round her neck. Tell Taylor to saddle my horse, Betty. I will go to deliver his brat, and when I come back John Junius Lorimer's bastard can leave my house and take her inheritance with her.'

Margaret was crouched on the floor by the low table. She was weeping and he was tempted to take her in his arms. It was rare for him to lose his temper, but the provocation had been great and the relief of expressing the full depth of his anger was great as well.

Before the echo of the door slamming behind him had died away, he recognized that he was being unfair. Margaret had made a wrong decision, an error of judgement, but the real crime had been committed many years earlier, and she had been in no way to blame for that. When he returned he would tell her so, comforting her and himself at the same time. But at the moment he could not trust himself to be kind or even coherent. He needed something on which to vent his rage. Since it was too late to take a stick to John Junius Lorimer, his mare must bear the brunt of it.

He leapt into the saddle without speaking to the anxious father-to-be, and shortened the reins with a sharpness which caused the mare to rear, whinnying, as she turned. With an equally uncharacteristic viciousness he dug in his heels and galloped away down his own drive and along the great elm avenue which led to the centre of the village. He was conscious of John Taylor shouting something after him, but the wind whipped away the words and he was in no mood to turn back. Down the dark avenue he rode at full stretch, as though he were chasing the devil. The driving wind and rain beat against his face. It was because he kept his head down against them that he did not see the huge trunk of an elm which had fallen across the road. His mare, a gallant hunter, might have cleared the obstacle if left to herself, but Charles was startled by the change of pace as she gathered herself for the leap, and pulled up her head so that she checked in mid-air. Her forelegs hit the further side of the trunk and buckled under her, sending Charles over her head. As they fell together, he could not tell whether it was the stony road or his mare's flailing hoof which split open his head. Whichever it was, it made no difference.

5

The shock of bereavement freezes the emotions and paralyses the will. How much stronger is the effect when it is tinged with guilt! Margaret had loved Charles for so long, and enjoyed his company as a husband for so short a time, that his loss would have been enough in itself to make her despair. But to her natural unhappiness was added a burden of responsibility made heavier by the fact that she dared not tell anyone what had happened. Her marriage had ended with a quarrel: the first quarrel – the only quarrel – they had ever had; and it had been all her fault. She had made Charles angry. He had died with his mind turned against her, and she could not doubt that his anger had contributed to his death. There was no one to whom she could confess her guilt, because the story would be incomplete unless the rubies were mentioned.

The rubies had caused enough trouble already. Margaret believed now that she had been wrong to accept responsibility for keeping them secretly until Alexa came of age. But having made that one wrong decision, she had been right when she decided never to tell anyone of their existence – not even Alexa herself until her twenty-first birthday. The tragedy had occurred because she broke her resolve, and she did not intend to make the same mistake again. The need for secrecy combined with her misery to make her withdraw from the world into a depression which no one at first could penetrate.

Alexa did her best. She tried to soothe her guardian by playing and singing to her; but the music, whether bright or sad, caused Margaret's tears to flow. Nor could any comfort be provided by embraces or assurances of undying love: if Margaret could not hear Charles's voice, she would not listen to any other. But Alexa must have taken one other step, for within two days William arrived at Elm Lodge.

His sympathy displayed itself in practical help. He arranged the funeral and visited Charles's lawyer and banker to discuss Margaret's financial position on her behalf. The needs of his own business meant, however, that he could not stay too long away from Bristol. Margaret was still in the throes of her first grief when he tried, before leaving, to make her consider plans for her future.

'As soon as I arrive at Brinsley House I shall arrange for a suite of rooms to be prepared for you,' he said. 'You must make your home with us again, of course, and you would be wise, for the sake of your child, to come as soon as possible. The business of closing up Elm Lodge and deciding whether it should be sold or let can be postponed until after your confinement. After the shock you have had to endure, I feel sure you ought to rest and be calm.'

It was impossible for Margaret to be calm, but even more impossible for her to agree without thought to what he took for granted. There was nothing unexpected about her brother's suggestion. Since his father's death William had accepted without hesitation his responsibilities as head of the Lorimer family. All the hesitations now were on Margaret's side. She had not given any thought to the future – indeed, she had hardly yet come to terms with the fact that it must be a future without Charles. But the independent streak in her nature forced itself through the listlessness of bereavement, making her reluctant to return to a way of life which she had already rejected once.

'You are very generous, William,' she said. 'But I no longer have any employment in Bristol.'

'If you come to Bristol, you will not *need* employment. You can devote yourself to your child. You will owe it to him to do so. And I must tell you frankly, your income is not enough to maintain you here.'

The need to think clearly and express arguments acted as a first step to lift Margaret out of her apathy.

'Country life is less demanding than Bristol society, and has more to offer,' she pointed out. 'The investment you made for me when Lower Croft was sold will keep us clothed. We grow all the vegetables we need. There is fruit to come, the pigs are fattening and the hens are laying well. A good many families have to exist on a smallholding no larger than the grounds of Elm Lodge. And I am learning how to live as a farmer's wife. Already I can bottle fruit and preserve eggs and smoke hams like a countrywoman born.'

William's expression showed what he thought of this state of affairs, but Margaret refused to be ashamed. Her practical nature had taken pride in the speed with which she had acquired new skills at the beginning of her married life. 'Besides,' she added, 'if I stay here I can increase my income by taking over the practice.'

'That is a ridiculous idea. You would never be accepted as a doctor here.'

'I am as well qualified as Charles was.'

'That has nothing to do with it. Do you seriously imagine that a farm labourer would allow himself to be examined by a woman, even if it were proper for you to make such an examination?'

'He has no objection to his wife being examined by a

388

man,' she retorted. Then she controlled her tongue. Her arguments with William too often developed into quarrels, but she did not wish to offend him now. Even if his invitation were prompted more by a sense of duty than by affection, it was a kind one. It would be ungrateful of her to tell him how stifling she found Sophie's cold company. During her last stay at Brinsley House she had at least been able to escape to her work at the orphanage. If she were to return now, she would be expected to stay at home and devote herself entirely to her baby, in spite of the fact that all the actual work of bringing him up would be performed by servants. The prospect was a suffocating one – and yet William might prove to be right when he claimed that she had no alternative.

'It is too soon for me to make decisions of this sort, William,' she said. 'Please believe that I am grateful to you for your generous invitation. Whether I accept it or not, I do most sincerely appreciate the knowledge that I can rely on your support and turn to you in an emergency. But the whole pattern of my future life will be affected by this choice, and I must think about it carefully.'

'You have no choice,' said William bluntly. 'For the child's sake, you must come to Brinsley House. But I can see that I have spoken too soon. You are not yet able to think clearly enough to come to any sensible conclusion. My invitation will remain open until you are ready to accept it. You may write to me at any time.'

After he had left, Margaret paced up and down her drawing room, trying to resolve her own uncertainties. She knew that a good deal of what William had said was true. The birth of the baby would increase the regular expenses of the household right from the beginning – for before Margaret could undertake to work, she must employ a nursemaid – whereas her income would always be irregular.

It was also true that the villagers would not easily accept a female doctor. And yet, thought Margaret, they would have no choice. The area was too poor to support two doctors. If she announced that she was continuing Charles's practice, it would not seem worthwhile for any other practitioner to put up his plate in the area. Nor would Charles's patients want to see their years of club payments wasted. They would be forced to come to Margaret as long as they were in credit; and if she did her work well, they would surely be prepared to continue the payments.

It might be possible, she thought, and allowed herself to contrast in her mind the stiff formality of life at Brinsley House with a softer picture of Alexa singing to a baby as she rocked its cradle, while Margaret herself sewed peacefully by the fire. With economy and hard work, it could be done.

But what if she were to fall ill? Suppose – with Alexa and a baby both dependent solely on herself – something should happen to make her unable to support them. Was it fair to expose a child to the risk of insecurity when he had been offered the sort of comfortable upbringing that she herself had enjoyed?

But then, even her own childhood security had collapsed. Nothing in life could be relied upon to last for ever. The speed of her pacing increased as she put to herself first one side of each argument and then the other. Only two hours earlier she had been listless and tearful. William had at least succeeded in jolting her out of that state and into a consideration of her new position. But now she found herself driven to distraction in a new way. To return to Brinsley House would be cowardly: to refuse the invitation would be rash. The two conclusions were instinctive, not logical, and she was unable to reconcile them. A single course of action could be regarded as either sensible or weak, depending only on the viewpoint. Looking from each side in turn, Margaret found herself reduced once again to tears, although this time their cause was not loss but mental strain.

From this stress she was rescued by the arrival of Ralph and Lydia and the two children, Kate and Brinsley, who had been born in Jamaica. Margaret had known that they would be arriving in England for a three-month home furlough at about this time, but was expecting a visit only after they had rested for some days in Bristol. Instead they came at once, without warning, explaining after the first embraces and cries of surprise and sympathy were over that they had been anxious not to put Margaret to the trouble of preparing for them. Charles's death had occurred while they were still at sea, on their way home from Jamaica, but Sophie had told them the news as soon as they arrived at Bristol.

'You will hardly find me a cheerful hostess,' said Margaret, aware that Ralph was looking anxiously at her swollen eyes, reddened with weeping. Indeed, he turned almost at once to his wife to suggest that they ought not to inflict themselves for more than an hour on a household in mourning, but Lydia brushed the suggestion aside.

'With Betty's help, I shall do everything that is needed,' she declared. 'I make no apologies, Margaret, for bursting into your home in such a way. My years in Jamaica have taught me that it is a waste of time there to make tactful suggestions or ask permission to take liberties. I have become a managing busy-body, and I cannot shake off the habit so soon after leaving the mission. I hope you are a good enough friend to forgive me.'

Margaret was far too pleased to see Lydia and Ralph to make any objection. She stood up, intending to accompany her friend upstairs, but at once was forced to sit down again.

'How useless I am!' she exclaimed, angry at her own weakness. 'Just within these last few days I seem to have become so heavy. And without energy to do anything at all.'

'Are you eating properly?' asked Lydia.

'I have no appetite.'

'And sleeping?'

'How can I sleep when I am so unhappy?' Margaret

found herself yet again on the brink of tears. She saw Lydia signal to Ralph, who without hesitation picked up his sister and carried her up to her bedroom. Lydia followed, shooing him out of the room as soon as he had laid Margaret down on her bed.

'How far are you?' she asked.

'Seven months.'

'Then you are being very foolish,' said Lydia. She spoke sternly, but held Margaret's hand as she did so. 'You know the risk to a baby at precisely this time. I've no doubt all your friends have advised you to rest, and you have brushed aside their advice. But I am speaking as your doctor, and I am *ordering* you to rest. You are to stay in bed for the next two weeks and you are to eat whatever I send up. For the sake of the baby's health, if you have no regard for your own. Who is looking after the practice?'

'No one,' said Margaret.

'Then who is going to deliver your child?'

'I don't know. I don't care.'

'You deserve to have your face slapped for speaking in such a way,' said Lydia briskly. 'Well, it doesn't matter. For the next three months I am the village doctor. And yours.'

'You can't spend your holiday working.'

'I'm only happy when I'm working,' said Lydia. 'Ralph may travel round and visit his bachelor friends if he wishes. I shall be content to stay here, and no place could be healthier for the children. May I ask Betty to find me a girl from the village who will care for them?'

'Of course.' Margaret managed to smile, in spite of her swimming head. 'You are very good to me, Lydia.'

Lydia kissed her affectionately. 'I know you would do the same for me,' she said. 'I am going to produce the most beautiful baby for you, and I shall be so proud of him that you will hardly be allowed to remember that you are his mother. I shall expect you to obey my orders. There is nothing I can do to console you in your distress at Charles's death, I know, but you have made yourself ill, and your body must be restored to strength before you can hope to regain your full courage.'

Courage. It was a curious word for Lydia to choose, Margaret thought as, later that evening, warmed by a fire in her bedroom and a drink of hot milk, she began at last to drift towards sleep. Perhaps her friend had been referring only to the pains of childbirth. But it was equally true that courage was needed simply to accept the prospect of a future in which Charles could play no part, to take charge of her own life. The choice which William had presented to her earlier that day would have to be made sooner or later, but for the moment she was content to relax in her friend's care. Earlier, she had been frightened by the feeling that her distracted mind was causing the collapse of her body. It came as a wonderful relief to be told that it was the weakness of the body which was more probably causing the confusion of her mind. She pushed away the decisions which must soon be made, and slept.

The days and weeks passed gently, uneventfully. As soon as Lydia allowed her to come down from her bed to a sofa, Margaret found herself able to enjoy Alexa's playing and singing without any of the anguish it had caused her earlier. Lydia's reports of her reception in the village were amusing; but could not all be regarded as a joke. Margaret pressed for more details as time passed, and gradually came to satisfy herself that Lydia's brisk efficiency was having an effect. By the time Margaret herself was ready to take over, the first shock of seeing a woman doctor would have faded; it might not yet seem a normal thing to the villagers, but at least it could no longer be regarded as an impossibility.

In the early hours of the first day of June Margaret was awakened by the sudden onset of her labour pains. She lay for a little while without moving, knowing from her experience as a doctor that there was plenty of time. But between the contractions she felt the need to move about, changing her position; and soon, restless, she got out of bed and wrapped herself warmly. Lydia would not mind being awakened too soon, and the time would pass more easily if they could talk.

On the way, she paused to open each door in turn, illuminating the rooms briefly with her candle. Alexa was asleep in the first room, her beautiful hair covering the white pillow with reddish gold. Behind the next door, the nursery was waiting for its future occupant. What sort of life would he have, this new person who was now demanding to be born?

As she asked herself the question, she knew that she was ready to find the answer. The very violence of the pains that jerked her into rigidity at steady intervals carried a curious reassurance. They told her that her body had recovered, and so her mind could once again be expected to perform rationally. In a few hours she would no doubt be tired again, needing to rest and recover for a second time. This was the moment when she should consider again the choice which William had put to her.

Her instincts had not changed. To return to Brinsley House would be an act of cowardice. But was the alternative realistic? Would she be able, alone, to launch Alexa into the world and bring up a child from babyhood?

Any father must sometimes ask himself the same question, she supposed, although with less choice in the answer. Were men ever frightened at the thought of the responsibilities to which they were committed? The question reminded her of her own father. She closed the door of the nursery which would not be empty for very much longer, and went into the little room where the quarrel with Charles had begun.

The portrait of John Junius Lorimer was still propped with its face to the wall. She bent down to lift and turn it, but it was heavier than she had expected. As she strained at the weight, her body was gripped by a pain so much greater than any which had come before that for a moment

394

she could not move. When at last her muscles relaxed, allowing her to straighten herself, she knew that there was no more time to be wasted. 'Lydia!' she called. 'Lydia!'

Four hours later, Margaret looked at her son for the first time and wept. She wept for the baby who would never have a father; and for Charles, who would have loved this little boy. Lydia, understanding, made no attempt either to tease or console her, but took the newly-born child away again to be washed and wrapped. By the time she came back with the tiny white bundle, Margaret had sobbed her grief under control and was waiting, exhausted but calm, to take the baby into her arms.

He was a Lorimer, not a Scott. Though he would be christened Robert Charles Scott, there was no sign of Charles's grave solidity in the mobile face and the tiny, threshing fists which seemed already to be exploring the new world in which he found himself. He was a small baby, as Margaret had been, and his downy hair was bright red.

Margaret lay for a little while without moving, happy in her exhaustion. Beside her, Robert whimpered, and his lips sucked at the air. As she put him to her breast for the first time, she was amazed at the sudden flood of love which filled her heart. Although her body was so tired that she hardly had the strength to lift an arm, she felt strong and protective – and, at the same time, serious. She was responsible for Robert, and it was time to make the decision which would determine the course of his life. She asked Lydia if the portrait of John Junius could be brought into the room, and within a few moments it had been propped up on a chair so that she could see it without lifting her head. She stared across the room at her father's face as the baby sucked for a little while and then fell asleep with his head pillowed on her breast.

As though it were yesterday, she remembered when she had first seen the portrait, because it was the day on which she first met David Gregson – a day which had seemed to bring her happiness but which had proved to be the start of a chapter of disasters. How much of what was to happen had John Junius anticipated? she wondered. His greenish eyes seemed to pierce their way out of the portrait from beneath an untroubled brow: his mouth was firm with confidence. If his anxieties had already begun at the time of the sittings, he had taken care to give the artist no hint of them.

His memory offered no guidance to his daughter, who had loved him so deeply while he lived and had suffered so much from his actions since he died. As far as women were concerned, he had been a man of his time. Women, in his eyes, were intended by nature to be dependent creatures. He cherished his wife as a possession even when he no longer cared for her in any other way; and he would have taken it for granted that his daughter should stay at home until she married – for the whole of her life if no husband could be found. There could be no doubt that he would wholly have approved the way in which William assumed that a widowed sister should return to Brinsley House.

It seemed that there was no help to be found there – and yet, as she gazed at the likeness, Margaret felt her blood stir: it was, after all, Lorimer blood. Brinsley Lorimer had set sail across the ocean with no fear of the storms he would face when he was far from land. John Junius Lorimer had faced the even stormier seas of finance and industry with an equal courage. He had been defeated in the end, but the earlier years of his career had been full of risk and resolution. All the Lorimers had been adventurers at heart, and Margaret herself had shown the same spirit of adventure fifteen years earlier when she broke away from the conventions of her society and resolved to make herself independent. What was independence worth if she could relinquish it whenever a difficulty arose? Of what value was a burst of initiative if it faded at the first setback? If Brinsley Lorimer's first ship had sunk beneath him he would have built himself another, and she could do the same. All that she needed was courage.

'Have I enough?' she asked aloud, still staring at the portrait, and found her answer in the solid, autocratic face of a man who had always claimed the right to control his own life, even to choosing the moment of his death. He had brought her up in the prosperous and comfortable style which he thought that a Lorimer deserved, and that style had been snatched away from her even before his death. He had left her a legacy of deceit and confusion, robbing her in turn of the only two men she had ever loved and bringing this part of her life to as final a conclusion as the other. One thing remained, something which could never be taken away. She was a Lorimer, and from this man she had inherited the Lorimer spirit, a compound of intelligence and application and flair with, above all, the willingness to take a risk. Yes, she had enough courage.

Newly awake, Alexa appeared in the doorway, still wearing her white nightgown. Her long hair, a more golden shade of red than the baby's, streamed unbrushed over her shoulders; her eyes were bright with excitement.

'May I hold him?'

'Of course.'

They made a pretty picture: the beautiful young girl looking down at the sleeping child. In a gesture copied from John Junius himself, Margaret gave a quick nod towards the portrait. It signified that a decision had been taken, the matter under consideration was settled. William had given her the strength that came from opposition, and Lydia the strength of example; but from Robert she took the even greater strength of love. In the past she had accepted support from a father, brother, husband. That period was over. This was not the first time in her life that she had resolved to be independent, but it was the most important, because there were more lives than her own at stake. Exhausted though she was, she felt her body flooding with joy and excitement. By her own efforts she would

397

provide support for Alexa and baby Robert, the daughter and grandson of John Junius Lorimer. As her eyes at last closed in weariness, she made herself a promise. She would not fail them.

Outstanding women's fiction in Panther Books

Mary E Pearce

Apple Tree Lean Down	85p ☐
Jack Mercybright	85p ☐
The Land Endures	£1.50 ☐
Apple Tree Saga	£2.50 ☐
Polsinney Harbour	£1.95 ☐

Kathleen Winsor

Wanderers Eastward, Wanderers West (omnibus)	£3.95 ☐

Margaret Thomson Davis

The Breadmakers Saga	£2.95 ☐
The Breadmakers	£1.50 ☐
A Baby Might Be Crying	£1.50 ☐
A Sort of Peace	£1.50 ☐

Helena Leigh

The Vintage Years 1: The Grapes of Paradise	£1.95 ☐
The Vintage Years 2: Wild Vines	£2.50 ☐
The Vintage Years 3: Kingdoms of the Vine	£1.95 ☐

Rebecca Brandewyne

Love, Cherish Me	£2.50 ☐
Rose of Rapture	£2.50 ☐

Pamela Jekel

Sea Star	£2.50 ☐

Henry Denker

The Healers	£2.50 ☐

Chloe Gartner

Still Falls the Rain	£2.50 ☐

Nora Roberts

Promise Me Tomorrow	£1.95 ☐

To order direct from the publisher just tick the titles you want
and fill in the order form.

All these books are available at your local bookshop or newsagent, or can be ordered direct from the publisher..

To order direct from the publisher just tick the titles you want and fill in the form below.

Name_____

Address _____

_____

Send to:
Panther Cash Sales
PO Box 11, Falmouth, Cornwall TR10 9EN.

Please enclose remittance to the value of the cover price plus:

UK 45p for the first book, 20p for the second book plus 14p per copy for each additional book ordered to a maximum charge of £1.63.

BFPO and Eire 45p for the first book, 20p for the second book plus 14p per copy for the next 7 books, thereafter 8p per book.

Overseas 75p for the first book and 21p for each additional book.

Panther Books reserve the right to show new retail prices on covers, which may differ from those previously advertised in the text or elsewhere.

Anne Melville, daughter of the author and lecturer Bernard Newman, was born and brought up in Harrow, Middlesex. She read Modern History at Oxford as a Scholar of St Hugh's College, and after graduating she taught and travelled in the Middle East. On returning to England, she edited a children's magazine for a few years, but now devotes all her working time to writing. She and her husband live in Oxford.

By the same author

The Lorimer Legacy
Lorimers in Love
Lorimers at War
Last of the Lorimers
The Lorimer Loyalties